Donald Seaman was a report[illegible]
for twenty-five years with the *Daily Express*. He is married
with three children and he lives in Cornwall.

Also by Donald Seaman

THE BOMB THAT COULD LIP-READ

Donald Seaman

The Defector

Futura Publications Limited
A Futura Book

A Futura Book

First published in Great Britain 1975
by Hamish Hamilton Ltd.

First Futura Publications edition 1977

ISBN 0 8600 75109 9
Printed in Great Britain by
Hazell Watson & Viney Ltd
Aylesbury, Bucks

Futura Publications Limited
110 Warner Road
Camberwell, London SE5

For Irene and Patrick

FOREWORD

This is a work of fiction, and the characters portrayed in it are all imaginary.

The reader may like to know that I spent the best part of twenty-five years as a roving reporter, meeting some fascinating characters on the way. I have drawn something from a number of such chance meetings to invent all the people and some of the incidents in this book.

I once met a famous judge, now dead, who was irreverently known in my trade as 'the hanging judge'. I took a plane once in very bad weather and was forced to make an unscheduled stopover, where I met a foreign scientist who told me, after many drinks to celebrate our safe landing, that he was engaged on secret research which could make 'nuclear energy seem as outdated as the first steam engine'. Some of the claims he made have been used as background in this novel. I have also met men on both sides of the fence who were real-life secret agents. In this case I claim nothing but journalistic licence. I have been assured, on good authority, that British intelligence agents do not execute their enemies in peace-time, but I have always kept an open mind on that.

My thanks for considerable help given in my own fields of research are due to a fine barrister, to Con Coughlin of the *Daily Telegraph* and chairman of the Central Criminal Court Journalists' Association, to John King, reporter, Ted Brisland, librarian, both of the *Daily Express*, and to Bernard Hall who was once a reporter on the same newspaper.

1

THE INTRUDER

The coal strike was at its height, and because of the ensuing energy crisis every lamp in the long, tree-lined avenue was unlit on government orders: but even allowing for that, the darkness was overwhelming, claustrophobic, and all who ventured out in it knew how it must feel to be blind. To add to the man-made gloom, dense cloud blotted out moon and star-light as completely as the lid on a coffin. The only way that the intruder could make progress was from memory, following the compass of his mind, but even that meant a snail-like journey in which every bush, root and briar snagged at his legs while hanging branches whipped his face, and brought tears to his eyes.

Away to his right a dog heard him, and barked a warning. At once other dogs roused from their half-sleep and began to echo the alarm, none of them knowing quite where the man was, but all acknowledging the unseen threat out there in the night. As the clamour grew the man halted for a while, and bent on one knee, silently cursing the dogs and willing them to be quiet.

After a while it began to rain, softly at first and then harder and harder until there was a continual drumming on the ground, on branches and leaves and stones, windows and roofs, chimney pots and doors, merging into a vast Niagara of sound that cloaked his clumsy approach and appeased the dogs.

It's an ill wind, thought the intruder, welcoming the rain that coursed down his neck and on to his sweating body: at least it keeps those bastards quiet.

He got up again and started to push on in the direction of

the house, more confidently now, for his hands had told him he had reached the lawn.

The night was still too dark for him to make out the brick outline of the house, although he reckoned himself to be no more than fifty yards off. Suddenly he missed his footing, and fell forward, biting into his lower lip to cut off a cry of alarm as he landed on all fours in eighteen inches of water, jarred and shaken: Jesus-Christ-all-bloody-mighty, he had forgotten the ornamental fish pond! Once more he sent up a silent vote of thanks for the storm that raged about him, for the hiss of rain and rumble of distant thunder that allowed his clumsiness to pass unnoticed. No light shone from any window, no challenge came from the house, and after pausing briefly to collect his wits, the man waded out of the pond and stepped back on to the grass. He knew precisely where he was now, and reached out until he found the first of a line of paving stones that led to the patio.

The rest of the way he walked upright, sure that he could not blunder again, and minutes later he came to some tall french windows. The luminous hands of his watch told him it was 1.30 in the morning.

He fitted exactly into the mood of the night, for he was dressed in black from head to toe. A nylon monkey-jacket zipped tight from his throat to his hips. Nylon leggings hugged his thin calves, to fasten under boots of finest leather—like those a boxer wears in the ring—while his fingers were hidden in gloves so fine they could have been fashioned from human skin. A leather holdall was slung across his back by a thin leather belt. All of him except his face was black as coal, and this he proceeded to amend accordingly. He tugged the holdall round to his belly, groped inside for a torch, and shielded the beam until he found a stocking, also of black nylon.

He now drew this over his head, adjusting the cloth on his damp face with some difficulty until he found its two eye-slits. At last he was ready. Now that he was up to the house and below bedroom observation-level, he used the torch more freely. He shone it into the holdall to select a thin strip of steel set in a variety of cuts and grooves, slid it into the window lock and let himself into the house. It was the simplest of entries by any standards and he refused to credit his good luck. He quickly pulled the door to, to shut out the noise of the teeming rain and remained motionless for some time in the heavily curtained room, fearing a hidden alarm system and ready to run back the way he had come. He turned his masked head this way and that as he listened to the sleeping house, making no attempt to move on until satisfied he had entered unnoticed. A smell of dead cigar smoke clung to the room. A crumpled newspaper lay at his feet. All looked helpless and defenceless: whatever he sought there seemed to be his for the taking.

While he stood by the door he let his torch prowl round the room in case there was something that took his eye. The ceiling was lower than he had expected, the room itself smaller and now he could see that it was no more than an extension, a study or sun-room perhaps overlooking the long garden he had just crossed. A roll-top desk stood against the wall to his left, offering an untidy heap of papers and scribbled notes for inspection: he ignored them. Ahead of him a handsome wickerwork table stood on a rug, with matching wicker chairs pulled round. Behind that was a long teak sideboard, and over it hung a framed enlargement of an old photograph, showing a timbered house set among trees that were powdered with snow. No silverware, jewellery, or ornament of any value. Now he crossed to the desk, opened each drawer with great care and searched inside, but found nothing worth taking.

He padded over the rug and came to a heavy sliding door secured by another lock. This proved much more difficult to force. Finally it gave, with a faint crack! He waited a few more moments, lifted the holdall over his head and entered the main part of the house to settle down to serious work.

The house was numbered 28, and had been chosen with great care to suit the exact requirements of its present owners. Its rooms were spacious enough and tastefully furnished, but in no way grand. It was set in ample grounds, about one and a half acres, and was situated in what the citizens of south-east England are pleased to call the 'stockbroker belt'.

Clearly, their first consideration here had been privacy: privacy, that is, as distinct from isolation, a desire to avoid too close inspection yet still blend with surroundings, a wish to stand alone but not be too lonely and therefore vulnerable. Number 28 was the sort of house a casual passer-by might envy but would have little cause to remember. It was merely a pleasant house in a delightful road that boasted a hundred equally pleasant houses, all handsome properties set down in a district where reserve, standoffishness if you like, certainly a marked reticence to mingle too closely with one's neighbours, was looked upon as a right rather than rudeness. It was solidly middle class, and it knew its place: it stood in a road where a family—if it chose—could live for years without reaching first-name terms with other families known by sight, and passed in the street with a wave or friendly greeting while never called upon to become too closely involved.

It lay some forty yards back from the road. A gravel drive led into a garage built against one wall, so that (if he wished) a caller could enter the house via the side-door without being seen by passers-by. A hedge of laurel ran in a curve more than fifteen feet high across its front like a living green curtain. Its present occupants, Mr and Mrs John Stevens, had lived there for almost a year now, and remained an unknown quantity to all but their immediate neighbours. Tradesmen were paid by cheque, and promptly: none were encouraged to gossip on the doorstep. The Stevens usually went out by car and were rarely seen in local shops. They did not go to church, and the local vicar—one of the very few to call unannounced—had not come again, for his reception had been distinctly cool if polite. Occasionally, a small group of men would drive up to number 28 but clearly by appointment, for they entered the house by the door inside the garage and left the same way, and so quietly that not even Mrs Wright, the wealthy widow who lived with her daughter opposite in number 31 and who spent much time at her windows, could have recognised one had she passed him later in the street.

Every house in the road had landscaped gardens, back lawns dotted with laburnum, silver birch and weeping willow, all encased with hedges of blackthorn so thick and spiky that accidental intrusion on privacy was impossible. At the far end of number 28, a copse of oak and ash marked the boundary line, all of it fenced with chestnut palings for good measure. Beyond the fence lay a private park, jointly owned by all residents, and safeguarded from development (and possible intrusion) by a long-standing deed trust. It held two hard courts, Residents Association only, maintained by a gardener paid out of association funds. A new gardener had taken the job quite soon after the Stevens moved in, a retired policeman who welcomed the extra money as an addition to his small pension. The park was unused by the Stevens, who kept no dog and who—as far as was known—never played tennis or strolled beyond the limits of their own garden.

Much of the year its two acres were strictly for the birds, magpies, jays, blackbirds, thrushes and woodpigeons, and an attendant army of grey squirrels. If you wanted to enter any garden in the road unseen, or just to creep up and spy on a particular house, this was the way to approach, when the gardener was not about. It was the way chosen more than a week ago by the man in black to spy out the land, and the same way he had picked to come in tonight.

The storm had all but blown itself out when a late gust of wind seized a rain squall and flung it spitefully against the windows of number 28, rat-a-tat-tatting on every pane, demanding attention, invading dreams. Mrs Stevens, who had been restless for some time, was startled into wakefulness. She sat upright in bed, clutching the warm clothes to her throat: for one fleeting second she was confused, wondering where on earth she could be, and felt her heart pound in rare alarm. Then, as the other sounds of the night filtered through, wind scampering through fallen leaves, the steady pattern of her husband's breathing, the faint drone of a distant 'plane, she remembered, and settled back into fitful sleep.

How long she lay there drowsing, what passing faint sound it was that roused her again, she could not say: but something, some inner alarm bell rang in her ears, and told her immediately and for certain that what had disturbed her this time was an alien sound and one that had come from within the house.

It was the sound of something made to move, the overquick release of a doorhandle that had snapped back in protest perhaps, or the forcing of a lock: whatever it was it woke her, and she identified it as a man-made noise in the stillness of a house asleep. She sat up in bed once more, and listened intently. Her nerves were badly frayed, but she knew that she had not been mistaken. Bump! bump! bump! went her heart as she sat bolt upright, listening. After a minute or two she heard another sound, this time a crack, come and gone in an instant—like the forcing of a drawer—too slight to have wakened a sleeping person maybe, but not her, with her senses so acutely tuned. This time she did not hesitate.

She reached out and pressed the switch on her bedside lamp. No light came on. She tried again, and still it would not light up. Thoroughly alarmed now she slipped out of bed and tried the switch on the bedroom wall, but the room remained in total darkness. She reached out a hand and gently shook her husband. As he roused she placed her hand on his lips in warning.

'Sssshhh,' she said. 'Someone in the house! Listen.'

For a long time he lay still, listening with her, but heard nothing.

'Put the light on,' he whispered.

'I can't,' she said helplessly. 'They won't work.'

He sat up cautiously and groped for his torch. He switched it on and swung noiselessly out of bed, moving as though to a long-practised drill. Without a word he padded across the carpet and by the light of the torch he slipped two thin nickel bolts into position, at the top and bottom of the bedroom door. He pushed them very slowly, careful not to make a sound. He gave her the torch to hold and felt in his bedroom locker for some matches. He struck one and lit the two candles that had been placed for emergency use on their chest-of-drawers. As they flickered into life they threw wavering shadows on the walls and ceiling. Husband and wife were both trembling with fear.

'I'll call the number,' he said.

'Yes. Quickly!'

He sat on the edge of his bed, and picked up the telephone. He dialled a code without hesitation: as his fingers selected each digit and released the dial, the whirr of the return spring sounded hideously loud in the silence of their room. They listened impatiently as the call rang out at the other end of the line, burr! burr! burr! burr! There was no answer. John Stevens rang off, and tried again. Still no response. He looked at his wife, and there was real fear in both their eyes now.

'No one there,' he whispered harshly. 'So much for Sydenham's promises!'

They sat close together in wretched silence, tense as two mice aware of a cat poised to spring, straining their ears to catch some further identifying sound. Seconds that seemed like whole days dragged by in this way. The woman's eyes were wide with fright, one hand stayed pressed to her mouth as if to stifle a scream. The man's face was deathly pale. Dark hair tumbled over his high forehead, his eyebrows pinched together in a scowl, even, white teeth chewed incessantly on his lower lip.

'It's them,' she said, mouthing the words. 'They've found us.'

'I don't know,' he replied, shaking his head, 'I don't know.'

'What can we do?' she begged him.

He was a big man: his hands looked strong and capable. His face was smooth and unlined, his jaw square and clean-cut. Yet for all his outward appearance of strength he seemed desperately nervous and uncertain: she could see a film of sweat on his forehead. He twitched, and wrung his hands, washing his fingers with invisible soap. Finally he reached a decision and seemed to brace himself. He leaned across the bed so that their faces were almost touching.

'I'll have to go down,' he whispered. 'We can't sit here like this. Don't you leave this room whatever happens, you hear?'

'They'll kill you!'

'I'll take the gun. At least it gives us a chance.'

He slid open the drawer of his bedside table and took out a revolver, fitted with a barrel no longer than a man's thumb. He had no need to check to see if it was loaded. He pulled on a dressing gown, though he could not say why and pushed the gun into his pocket.

'Bolt the door behind me and stay inside till I get back. Keep trying that number all the time.'

She put out a hand and touched his face in a caress. Then she crept behind him to the door, waiting while he slid the bolts once more. For a moment the light of the candles picked out the banisters, and head of the stairs: then it was dark again as she shut the door behind him, bolting herself in. He switched on his torch and began to inch his way downstairs.

As her husband crept down, Mrs Stevens picked up the phone and once more dialled the number they both knew by heart. Halfway through the code her finger slipped, forcing her to cut off the call and begin again. She was very close to tears. Her hands shook violently as she dialled once more, saying to herself over and over again, answer, please answer this time, please, they're here inside the house, damn you....

She felt in her bones no one would reply: there was no logic to her thinking, only despair, but it helped her make up her mind what to do now. She rang off and dialled 999.

This time a man's voice spoke to her at once, a cool and competent man who prompted her—what service did the caller want, police, fire brigade or ambulance?

'Police.' She still spoke in a whisper.

'I can't hear you, caller. Speak up, please. What service do you want, police, fire brigade or—'

Suddenly the dam burst.

'POLICE!' shouted Mrs Stevens at the top of her voice, 'POLICE!' She was crying aloud now, not caring who heard her.

'POLICE! EMERGENCY!'

John Stevens heard her shout as he reached the hallway at the foot of the stairs. Panic in his wife's voice sparked off his own, stripped off any remaining pretext of self-control and forced him into positive action. He threw open the door to the lounge and ran in, torch in one hand, gun in the other. By sheer chance both pointed at the human target inside the room.

Householder and intruder found themselves no more than eight feet apart. Neither said a word. In the instant of confrontation, each man's brain took, developed and printed a mental picture that was grossly distorted by fear and dismay, and they reacted accordingly. In the bright glare of his torch Stevens saw an apparition, a grotesque thing from the shadows of the night itself, a man-spider, with thin black limbs poking out from a shimmering black trunk, and with eyes that glittered from slits in a silken black hood. In his wildest dreams he had never imagined anything quite like this. Everything he saw he exaggerated: the torch that was grasped in a black-gloved hand turned into a weapon, an iron bar perhaps, ready to batter down on his skull. He felt his legs melt with fright, and he found it strangely difficult to breathe.

The man in black saw only the glare of the torch at first. Then he made out the tall figure of a man, and then—very clearly—he saw the gun. Its barrel seemed to point straight at his head and in turn, he panicked too: in his mind's eye he could see a finger curled round the trigger and he imagined death to be no more than the touch of a hair-spring away. He could not make out the face of the man behind the gun: it showed only as a white and menacing blur. Every nerve in the intruder's body signalled urgently, do something, quick, before the bloody fool kills you!

Both men saw the same, exaggerated picture in the same moment of time, and both their reactions were as illogical and, in retrospect, provocative. Stevens began to shout in a language the burglar had never heard before and could not begin to understand. What he was shouting was angry and almost defiant: the gun held in his hand demanded instant obedience, but obedience to what command? The intruder's mind went numb with terror. He became incapable of acting calmly or sensibly. He wanted to cry out 'Please don't shoot, I can't understand a bloody word you're saying' but his mouth, his vocal chords, seized up.

Instead, some curious mental somersault prompted him to shout back—not calmly, not sensibly, not even in English, his native tongue—but in the one foreign language he had ever spoken, and that badly, many years before.

With a desperate effort of memory, he began to babble a few words to try to stop this madman firing the gun.

'*Nicht schiessen, bitte,*' he cried, '*nicht schiessen, nicht schiessen.*'

He did not live long enough to explain to anyone why he had begged for his life in German: while the words brought him momentary reprieve, they also contributed directly to his death.

Stevens was never entirely sure, in the days and weeks that followed, just what he had expected the man in black to say and do: as it was the unlikely response baffled him, threw him off guard, so that he hesitated and lowered the gun. The movement of dropping the gun to his side could be clearly seen in the light of the torch. The intruder thought he saw his opportunity to escape from danger. He jumped forward and swung his own torch like a cosh, trying to knock the revolver out of the other man's hand. If the chance was there, he fumbled it. His aim was wild, his arm too slow, the move fatal. Up came the gun again, instinctively, and this time it was fired, with blind panic on the trigger.

Bang! went the snub-nosed revolver, bang! bang! bang! again and again, until the room was a nightmare of explosions, acrid smoke, shouts and screams.

Upstairs in her bedroom, behind the bolted door and not knowing who was shooting whom, Mrs Stevens screamed into the telephone and was heard three miles away—in the local police station, where a Sergeant Evans was taking her 999 call.

'Help!' she shrieked. 'Help, they're killing my husband!'

Down in the lounge, John Stevens levelled the torch and fired away, unaware that he shouted aloud each time he pulled the trigger, uttering great roars of rage and fright like a bull that turns on the matador, cries that released the flood-gates of months of terror and anxiety. The din that he made was heard by his wife and set her crying and shouting in turn.

The man in black shouted and screamed too, first as a bullet thudded into his rib-cage, and again as one entered his stomach via the wall of his groin: he screamed loudest of all as he wriggled on the floor, unable to crawl away, and felt another shatter his spinal cord, bringing paralysis after unbelievable pain. He kept on screaming, less loudly but continually, for some time afterwards, until he whimpered and choked and coughed and bled into merciful oblivion, and death.

Some of this could be heard by the sergeant at his desk and his hackles rose.

'Hey, Johnson!' he bawled at the top of his voice. 'Johnson! Get that bloody Panda of yours round here quick, you hear me? Johnson! Move your bloody self, lad!'

Two startled faces peered round his door. The whole of the force available, two young police constables roused for the first real emergency in months of night-duty at Saddlers Hill station, tried to grasp what was happening.

'What's up, Sarge?'

He seized his truncheon and hurried towards them.

'A shooting match,' he said tersely, and repeated the address that Mrs Stevens had just given him over the telephone. 'I don't know how many dead but by Christ, it sounds bad. Johnson, get that Panda round to the front, you and me are going down to take a dekko. Quick now, don't waste any more time.'

He spoke to the second P.C. as he ran through the door.

'You, Norman,' he said, 'get on the blower to County and get the Murder Squad over here, fast.'

Impatiently, he repeated the address.

'Tell the Super there's been shooting, armed robbery by the sound of it. We want a doctor and an ambulance, too. Move yourself, boy, Johnson and me might want some help.'

2

THE GUARDIAN

His wristwatch told Sydenham that it was nearly five in the morning, and he sighed as he thought of the warm and spacious bed that awaited him in the next room At the same time, the mirror on the bathroom wall cried shame on a man who normally prided himself on both toilet and outward appearance: he looked like a tramp after a street brawl.

His clothes were muddied and wet. One shoulder of his well-cut suit was ripped open, his trousers were dirty and bedraggled, his shirt stank of damp and sweat. His fingernails were filthy, his shoes a disgrace, while his feet were so swollen and blistered that he limped like a man in calipers as he hobbled to the mirror to assess the full extent of the damage to his face.

A bright red welt showed on the top of his skull, its soreness enhanced by the total absence of hair: it positively glowed as he touched it, tenderly. There was a cut under his right eye, with the surrounding flesh markedly bruised. The pudgy pink cheek on that side of his face was badly grazed and inflamed. He patted it with fingers that were covered in grime, and sighed: this was no time to crawl into bed. Like Wesley, he rated cleanliness next to godliness, for like all fat men he took especial pains with his personal appearance to try to moderate the cruelty of Nature's malformation of his body.

He turned on the bath taps, and as the hot water gushed out, dabbed at his wounds with paper tissues dipped in healing antiseptic, like an actor back in his dressing room after the final curtain call. He let the bath fill and waddled into the living room to pour himself a bumper glass of Scotch, and slumped in an armchair to reflect on the indignities of the night.

Even without his injuries, Sydenham was no Adonis. Men and women who met him for the first time were wont to thank God for their own good fortune, for he was a parody of the body beautiful so much admired today by the human race. Bald head and fat, round shoulders joined in a single curving outline that seemed to dispense with the need for any supporting neck. He was hairless, with not even a monk's fringe of relief above his small, flat ears: nostrils and ear-holes were likewise devoid of any hirsute growth, and only a redness, a deepening of skin colour, showed where his eyebrows ought to have been. Strict dieting had failed to bring his weight below seventeen stones, so that his stomach bulged over enormous thighs, to give him a kind of Toby Jug squatness. His back was broad, and spoke of considerable strength, but this was challenged by the smallness of his hands.

There were some points in his favour, and worth noting. His eyes, set very deep, were pale blue, shrewd and knowing: immensely steady, and resolute. His mouth was full and generous, set in a permanent smile that was calculated to disarm the sharpest critic of the gross frame below. It was an asset he used shamelessly on friend and foe alike, to get his way, and he was a very determined and resourceful man.

He swallowed the whisky in a gulp and poured another to take with him into the bathroom. As he threw his shirt into the linen basket and stepped into the tub, the telephone rang.

'Sydenham.'

The cradle of the phone was set into the bathroom wall. He lay back and allowed the hot water to ease his aches and pains. His voice was deep and melodious, his manner naturally polite.

'Mrs Stevens.' At five in the morning, his concern was real enough. 'What's happened?'

He listened to her carefully. More than two years of patient planning and plotting, all of it at risk of human life and international incident—not to mention considerable expense to the unwitting British taxpayer—had preceded the arrival of Mr and Mrs Stevens at number 28, and to Sydenham the news of the shooting came as a real calamity.

'You say you are speaking from the police station now? From the superintendent's office? I see. Now then, I will be with you very soon: in the meantime, you are to say nothing more to anyone, is that understood? Excellent, excellent, you were absolutely right not to do so, my dear. Time is very important to all of us, Mrs Stevens, so I will ask you to wait there as patiently as you can until I arrive. In the meantime, let me speak to the police superintendent, if you please.'

He sank deeper into the bath, concentrating furiously as the steam rose about him.

'Good morning, superintendent. My name is Sydenham. Home Office.' He gave a telephone number to the police chief, and urged him to lose no time in calling the night duty operator at his office in Whitehall for confirmation of his appointment and status.

'Now, sir. There is very little I can say over the telephone, but I have to impress upon you that the incident which you have investigated involves matters of high security. The very highest, in fact. I must ask you to warn all your officers there must be no premature release of information concerning their investigation, in particular to the Press.'

The detective superintendent interrupted him.

'I think you ought to know your man's already been charged. Yes, manslaughter. No way round it, and touch and go as a matter of fact whether I made it murder. That charge will stand, no matter what.'

Sydenham was out of the bath and drying himself with one hand as he spoke into the mouthpiece.

'I fully understand, superintendent, and assure you there is no question whatever of trying to interfere with the due processes of the law: good heavens, none whatever. At the same time, I desperately need your help. Can I count on that? Thank you indeed. Look, I can be with you before six this morning. Can you set the wheels turning to arrange a special court, so that we can get the hearing over before any word gets out?'

He listened to the reply.

'Good. I'll see that your Chief Constable gets to hear about your very fine spirit of cooperation. He's a personal friend of mine,' said Sydenham, knowing that the claim was unlikely to be checked at this hour of the morning.

'Meantime, can you let Mrs Stevens join her husband, lay on a cup of tea, something like that? Right, then. I'll leave it in your capable hands, and be with you inside the hour. Thank you again, superintendent.'

Before he dressed, Sydenham made two more telephone calls. The first was to wake up a Scotland Yard commander responsible for all traffic in and through the metropolis.

'Colin,' he said. 'It's Sydenham! Sorry to wake you at this unearthly hour: top level emergency, I'm afraid. Can you have a car standing by to escort me from the Chiswick flyover through London, south to Saddlers Hill—no holds barred—in fifteen minutes from now? Marvellous. Tell your men I will be driving my red Jaguar, the official car's had it, in a bit of a pile-up last night. Thanks, Colin. Tell you all about it later. Fifteen minutes, then, and sharp's the word.'

The second call was to his immediate superior.

'Sydenham here, sir,' he said formally. This time he made no attempt to apologise for the hour of day. 'Stevens is in serious trouble. Shot a burglar, as far as I can make out, somewhere around two this morning. Yes, sir. Dead as a dodo, with our man charged with manslaughter.'

He lit a cigarette and leaned back, with his eyes shut, as the voice at the end of the telephone fired off a stream of angry questions.

'Very disappointing, I agree, sir—but *not* negligence. I was in that house myself until a couple of hours before the incident, on a routine check. I was also night duty cover, but a tree trunk fell on my car on the way home, in that storm. I came to in a ditch and had to walk miles to get to a 'phone. No. I'm all right, a few aches and pains: the car's a write-off, though. Look, sir, I have to get mobile, we're laying on a special court to hear the charge, but I need some fast spade work done while I'm on the way to Saddlers Hill. Well, sir, specifically I want that superintendent instructed not to oppose bail: trouble is, that's a Home

Counties force, not the Yard, I don't know anyone these days. You do? Good. The magistrates also need to play ball, and that means a word in their Clerk's ear by the police before the hearing. We can't afford to have anything more go wrong at this stage, I want Stevens released into my personal care by that court this morning. We can't stop him going for trial, of course. It's just that I don't want any words or pictures in the papers at this stage.'

He looked anxiously at his watch as the voice on the 'phone made several more comments

'A trial means a judge,' Sydenham pointed out, 'and I agree that raises a more serious problem. But let's cross that bridge when we reach it. The Attorney-General and the D.P.P. between them ought to be able to advise us on that when the time comes. Meantime, I really have to move, and fast. Of course. A full report, as soon as the hearing's over and I've got Stevens safely tucked away.'

Sydenham's car was cutting through rain and early traffic at more than 80 m.p.h. as it approached the flyover. The police car sounded its siren, a white Jaguar overtook Sydenham's red one and led the way to Saddlers Hill in a cloud of spray, ignoring lights and speed limit signs en route. He climbed out of his driving seat, inside the station yard at Saddlers Hill, at nine minutes to six. It had been a nerve-wracking journey.

'Fast enough for you, sir?' asked the young police driver.

'Fast enough,' Sydenham admitted, 'to frighten the hell out of me! I'll recommend your Commander to enter you at Le Mans, young man: you're wasted in that job.'

He trotted up the steps of the tiny police station with a wave of his hand.

The fruits of his last telephone call were made apparent as soon as he stepped inside. A station sergeant waved aside the proffered identity card, and took him straight into a small room marked C.I.D. It reeked of wet clothes, tobacco smoke, and cheap linoleum, and not for the first time Sydenham wondered why the great British public, which by and large professes to admire its policemen, so often condemns them to work in quarters so bleak and shabby and out-dated they would give grounds for instant strike action in any self-respecting factory in the land. The room was crammed with men, the full Murder Squad team from county headquarters as well as a handful of local detectives hurriedly called in.

They gazed thoughtfully at the fat man who appeared before them, dressed in clean clothes now, but still with a cluster of cuts and bruises showing on his head and face. One of them found Sydenham a chair, another silently placed a mug of steaming tea on the desk in front of him.

The superintendent stood up to shake hands, and addressed him as 'sir'.

'You made very good time, sir,' he said. 'Must have stepped on it coming through London.'

Sydenham sipped the tea gratefully, and purred his thanks, like a tom cat at the milk bowl.

'Broke the speed limit enough times to get jail for life,' he said shamelessly. 'My god, this tea's welcome, thank you, gentlemen.'

His pale blue eyes counted the number of policemen in the crowded room, and signalled an urgent, unspoken request to the superintendent.

The C.I.D. chief took the hint. He was a chunky, hard-looking man with tired eyes, and an air of authority. In that small room, filled with big men, he stood out like a bull elephant from the herd.

'All right, you chaps,' he said. 'You've all got your orders. Make sure all statements are signed before you leave, then go home and get some sleep. Sergeant Evans, I want two men on duty at that house, day and night, till this gentleman says otherwise, got that? No need for anyone here to be present at the special court hearing. All of you remember, I don't want tonight's events discussed with anyone, inside or outside the station. That's all.'

After they had gone, the superintendent sat down and filled his briar, rubbing each damp curly-cut flake between thumb and forefinger before he tamped them down in the bowl. He kept his eyes on Sydenham as he struck a match, and puffed out clouds of smoke, waiting for his visitor to speak first.

'Both in the cells?' asked Sydenham.

'Yes, sir.' Puff, puff. 'Quiet as mice. I think Mrs Stevens is in a fair old state of shock, by the look of her when she came in here. Had the doc give her a sedative after you telephoned, as a matter of fact. No charge against her, of course. We'll need her as a witness, later.'

'Naturally.' Sydenham produced his own heavy silver case and lit up, to add to the fug. 'I'd like you to tell me what's happened so far. From the beginning, please. Don't miss out a thing.'

The superintendent looked through his notes, and began.

The Stevens' house lay in the Home counties of south-east England, close to London but outside the jurisdiction of Scotland Yard, and the local police station responsible for dealing with every misdemeanour in the area was named Saddlers Hill, after the rise it stood on.

Serious crime was rare, even in these permissive times. Bank robberies, mugging, smash-and-grab, knife-fights and drug addiction were offences that most residents read about in their daily papers: murder was unknown. House-breaking was on the increase, as it was everywhere in Britain, but, until this night, no case had been accompanied by violence for more than seven years. There were no known juvenile offenders. There was no colour problem, because Saddlers Hill was an all-white district. It was essentially a two-car, high-income residential area with all that that implied. Occasionally, a car was reported stolen but this was usually found to be an outside job. The daily round of the policemen who served there ranged from the prevention of crime to the niggling ridiculous, from Panda patrol of quiet, well-maintained streets to the recovery of missing dogs, cats and even budgerigars. It was a doddle, from the police point of view.

None the less, the force at Saddlers Hill was considerably below strength, and its resources stretched to the limit, to maintain the status quo. Sydenham, of course, knew all this: he had delved into local incident statistics with great thoroughness before buying number 28—with public funds—eleven months earlier. He therefore listened with considerable interest as the superintendent told him in detail what his two officers had found when they reached the house after taking the 999 call four hours earlier.

It had ceased raining when they arrived, but it still blew a gale: the wind tugged at their coats, flapped at their knees, it scattered dead leaves in abandon, and howled through the tree tops like an express rushing through a tunnel. They had no difficulty in locating the house. Lights blazed from a number of windows now that the power cut had ended, to shine on the laurel hedge and the path, and beckon them in. No neighbours seemed to have heard the shooting. No other lights were visible, and no group of sympathetic figures stood at the door of number 28 to offer help or sympathy.

P.C. Johnson looked about him in disgust as he hammered the door knocker.

'Must have been enough ruddy noise here to wake the dead,' he remarked to his sergeant, 'but where are the neighbours, eh? Too scared to come and find out what happened—or too stuck-up?'

He remembered that they were unarmed, and clutched the truncheon in his hand.

'Doubt if anyone heard much,' said the sergeant, more reasonably. 'Not in this weather.' He, too, swung his truncheon and looked carefully round the garden as they waited.

The door swung open, and he stared at a woman framed against the light in the hall. He put her age at about twenty-five or thirty. Hair the colour of wheat tumbled over her shoulders, rippling and straying in the wind. She was very pale. He saw that her skin was clear and smooth. Her house coat was open. Beneath it he could glimpse a blue nightdress. Her feet were bare. She had been weeping, and her eyes were puffy and swollen. She stood aside without a word to let them in.

Sergeant Evans cleared his throat.

'Police, mum,' he said unnecessarily, and felt distinctly foolish with the truncheon swinging in his hand.

'What's been going on?'

She pointed into the house. She began to sway: the sergeant thought her to be badly shocked, and motioned to his aide.

'Look after her, Johnson,' he ordered, 'while I take a look round inside. Keep her out of harm's way 'till I call you.'

He left them in the hall, and stepped through an open door. At once he smelled the bitter, gunsmoke smell and gripped his truncheon nervously, not knowing what awaited him. He looked round the room, and saw a man with long hair, slumped on the settee, holding his head in his hands, obviously alive and seemingly unhurt: beyond him, something black and bloodied and oddly still lay sprawled on the carpet.

The sergeant advanced further into the room.

'What happened?' he demanded of the man on the settee. The man did not look up.

'I asked you what happened,' he said loudly. 'Police sergeant Evans. From Saddlers Hill. I took the 999 call.'

With that, the man got up—he was as tall as the sergeant—felt in his dressing gown pocket, and held out a revolver. Evans hesitated for a moment, wondering what to do. Then he took a handkerchief from his own pocket, feeling oddly pleased to find it clean and unused, gripped the weapon firmly in the white linen square, and promptly set it down again on a nearby table. He waved the man back to the settee, and walked over to the shape on the carpet.

It seemed pointless to examine the body: he had no need to pronounce the man dead, for it lay in that curious posture, one of emptiness, almost, that always marks the flight of the spirit from the flesh. Whoever it was lay face down, and had bled copiously, from many wounds. What intrigued the sergeant was his attire, stocking mask, jacket, leggings, boots, gloves—all as black as the night outside. He knelt down and lifted the head, peeling away the stocking to gaze at the face beneath. I don't know you, chummy, he said to himself, but I'll lay odds you're on record in the C.R.O. files. He dropped the head, bump! back on the carpet and felt the pulse, as a formality. Odd how warm the wrist still was, he thought. A black holdall lay open nearby, and he cast an eye on the silver it contained, and the tools of the burglar's trade. He saw a torch on the floor. He looked about him for signs of another weapon, but found none.

'Want to tell me about it, sir?'

He kept his voice low and even, but stationed himself between the man on the settee, and the gun that lay in his handkerchief on the table. Just as casually, he took out a notebook, and began to write.

'Look, sir,' said the sergeant after a while, 'you're going to have to tell someone, sooner or later. Now, then, how did it happen?'

The man in the dressing gown took his hands from his face. He looked to be in his late thirties: like those of his wife, his features were curiously smooth and unlined.

'He came at me,' he said, as if that were sufficient explanation. 'I thought he was going to kill me.'

'Is this your gun, sir?'

'Yes.'

'And you shot him with it when he came for you?'

'Yes.'

The sergeant wrote furiously in his notebook.

'Could I see your permit for this gun, sir?'

'No. Well, I don't have one. Not officially, I mean,' he sounded very confused—'it was given to me for my own protection, in case there was any attempt to kill me. Or my wife.'

The sergeant wrote it all down. 'Who gave it to you?'

No reply.

'What made you think someone was trying to kill you?'

No answer.

'Have you seen this man before? Did he threaten you?'

Silence.

'Look, sir, you're in serious trouble, you'd better answer me. He's got a bag full of loot there, it's easy enough to see why he was here—but what made you shoot him? When he came at you, did he have a gun or a weapon of any kind?'

The man in the dressing gown shook his head, but refused to answer. As the sergeant tried again, he heard a hammering on the door. P.C. Johnson opened it to admit the Murder Squad.

'That's where I came into the picture,' said the superintendent to Sydenham. 'It looked like an open-and-shut case. I knew chummy on the carpet, right away, by the way he was dressed. Man called Williams, known as The Country Boy: got a record as long as my arm! Used to specialise in country mansions after the war, that's how he got his name, come down in the world quite a bit now. Bloody fool, always dresses up like that: it was his gimmick in the old days, and he never had the sense to realise no one needed any better identification after a job.'

'A dangerous type?' Sydenham asked him.

'That's just it. Never known to offer violence, never known to carry any kind of weapon. It looked to me like a case of someone crossing their lines, but Stevens and his wife acted very strangely: it quite obviously wasn't all due to shock. They refused to say a word, except to insist that one of them should speak to you. I had half a mind to book him for murder.'

'He was only following instructions,' Sydenham pointed out.

'But put yourself in my shoes, sir. Three o'clock in the morning, damn near, he admits firing the gun that killed Williams and he refuses to say another word. There are only two courses open to any officer in circumstances like that. One is to lock him in a cell and submit a report to the Director of Public Prosecutions, which is tantamount to admitting you're inefficient, or book him on anything you like, from possession of firearms upwards to murder, and hold him for a while to "assist us in our inquiries". There was something phoney about this whole set-up.

'In the end I rang my chief superintendent, and it was decided I should book Stevens for manslaughter. I cautioned him then and there, in his house, "That you unlawfully killed ..." and so on, you know the drill as well as I do. Then I brought him along here, and had another go at him. While I questioned him, my inspector had a go at Mrs Stevens. Neither of them would say a bloody word. It was clear they had no intention of calling a lawyer. We tried your number several times without getting a reply. In the end, she got you herself on a call from my office.'

'Nothing else you could have done,' Sydenham agreed. 'The thing is, superintendent, these two are very special people: not what you think. I want them back in my personal care, and fast.'

'The thing that beats me,' said the C.I.D. man, 'is why there was no burglar alarm. I know now why you weren't around. But there must have been provision for that. Why no alarm?'

'There was one,' Sydenham told him. 'Very sophisticated job, working on the volume metric system, you know, re-action to a difference in pressure. Any intruder in that room should have been picked up by the infra-red sensitisors, with the body heat raising the room temperature and setting off our alarm. The trouble obviously came with the power-cuts. The fail-safe mechanism operates on standby batteries, but they have to be re-charged after 48 hours. I slipped up there.'

'A costly miss, sir.'

'Yes.' Sydenham was in no mood for self-recrimination. 'Are the magistrates on their way?'

'Yes, two coming over now.'

'They'll grant bail?'

'Yes. We won't oppose the application. I've had a word with the Clerk. He'll speak to the magistrates before they sit. No need for any lawyer to be present. Stevens will be handed back to you before you can say Jack Robinson.'

'There will have to be a further lower court hearing,' Sydenham replied. 'What about that?'

'Reporting restrictions will not be lifted, your lawyers will see to that. So what's left? Householder on a manslaughter charge, after defending his property during a break-in. Not much there to rouse any excitement: paragraph or two in the local papers, but no more.'

They heard a car pull up in the courtyard. The superintendent looked out of his window, and saw the magistrates approach.

'Here they are,' he said. 'Let's go down and get it over with.'

The special court sat at 6.45 a.m. Everything that took place was strictly within the law, for there are no restrictions whatever as to the time a court may sit (except on a Sunday), nor is there any set procedure laid down as to place, or presence. Even so, all was carefully stage-managed to help Sydenham and his friend, householder John Stevens.

The only persons present at that hour were Stevens and his

wife, the police, the two presiding magistrates, their Clerk, and Sydenham. It was all over in a matter of minutes, rather like a puppet show. There was no lawyer present—apart from the magistrates clerk, who was also a local solicitor—no newspaper reporter, no relative of the dead man, no member of the general public bar Sydenham himself.

One of the magistrates said: 'Yes?'

The superintendent rose and addressed the Bench.

'Your worships,' he said blandly, 'early this morning the police were called to number 28'—here he named the road, and postal district—'in answer to an emergency 999 call, and found the body of a man. I have since made certain inquiries into this case. The accused, John Stevens, householder, is charged with shooting a burglar, the circumstances being that he was in fear of his life. The charge is manslaughter. We are not going to oppose bail in the circumstances, as the accused is known otherwise to be a man of excellent character.'

The magistrates heard him, and whispered together for all of thirty seconds.

'Very well,' said one of them. Now he addressed Stevens, for the first time.

'Would you like legal aid?'

'No.' Sydenham stood up, and answered for him. No one asked him who he was or why he was there.

'Very well.' Another whispered exchange, this time with the Clerk of the court.

Stevens was remanded to appear again in fourteen days time, on surety of £100 in his own recognisance. That was all. The two magistrates rose, and the court dispersed. Sydenham told Stevens and his wife to remain seated, and walked across to the superintendent. His blue eyes shone with genuine admiration.

'Thank you,' he said. 'Most professionally done! I shall not forget this good office. Now, superintendent, we will trouble you no longer. You have my number. I will be back to see you tomorrow, so that we can iron out all the wrinkles. My thanks again.'

John Stevens was pale and silent as he followed Sydenham to

the car. His wife clung to his arm. There was no one to watch them as Sydenham opened the doors, and handed them a rug: he fussed around them like an old hen until he was sure they were comfortable, and then climbed into his driving seat. He moved off carefully into the line of traffic that was forming up for the Gadarene rush to London.

'Mr Sydenham,' said Mrs Stevens as he drove along, 'I want to go back to the house for a moment. I need some clothes. So does my husband.'

He caught her eye in the mirror.

'I don't think that's a very good idea just now,' he told her. 'We might get the Press, or the neighbours, coming round at any time. I'm going to take you somewhere out of the way until the trial is over. I'll make arrangements to have all your things brought from the house. Don't worry now, it's going to be all right, I promise you.'

John Stevens said nothing, and the three of them travelled in complete silence for the rest of the journey.

There is a tall building near Whitehall which houses various sections of Britain's intelligence services. Thousands of people, locals and tourists, pass by it every day without an upward glance, for there is no outward way of distinguishing it from any one of a hundred similar office buildings in the area. As soon as he had handed the Stevens over to suitable guard, and medical care, at a 'safe' house close to Richmond, in Surrey, Sydenham issued urgent instructions concerning the contents of number 28, and then drove at speed to the mini-skyscraper in Whitehall to report to his superiors.

The Director's office was known to the staff simply as 'The Board Room'. His desk, a superb creation in pale Japanese oak. stood against the street wall under a tall Georgian window that gave him a panoramic view of his governmental parish. On a corner of the desk there was a photograph of the Director's only son, a captain in the S.A.S. (the Special Air Service Regiment) who had died on active service among the mountain peaks of the Yemen years earlier. In the centre was a calendar, with separate pages for each day of each month, with the date lettered in red, and bearing a Biblical quotation below.

Today's date, Thursday the 15th, bore an ominous text from St Matthew:—

> 'It must needs be that offences come: but woe
> to that man by whom the offence cometh.'

The desk was uncluttered by official papers or files. It held a single square of virgin white blotting paper in a leather folder, a fountain pen, a graceful Waterford ashtray, and a wooden cigarette box, in front of the calendar. Behind it, were four telephones. They were RED LINE, direct to the Prime Minister in the Cabinet Room: WHITE LINE, Chequers, GREEN LINE, personal to the C.G.S., and BLUE LINE, for all other calls.

It was a spacious room, and took its unofficial title of 'Board Room' from the long dark table flanked by eight chairs—the ninth, his own, backed on to an open fireplace—that filled most of the central and lower part of the office.

It was a room that had witnessed some rare scenes in its time. More than one erring Minister of State had walked in here, to be confronted with a selection of photographs, or excerpts from secret tape-recordings, and then walked out to resign on grounds of 'ill-health'. A line of filing cabinets with contents worth a king's ransom stood in the far corner, guarded by a coded electronic device against prying eyes and unauthorised hands. If it was essentially a room of secrets, it was also a room that had known many a triumph, albeit unsung and unhonoured. A series of Russian spy-rings had been broken on orders master-minded from that polished table-top: unceasing campaigns plotted at that oaken desk, all of them sly, laborious, devious, patient struggles waged against the countless enemies of the state, spies, saboteurs, terrorists conspirators, double-agents and traitors.

It was a room which had known some truly first-rate Directors, and some poor ones, but all of them possessing one binding link, patriotism: all men whose sole purpose was to serve their country to the exclusion of all personal considerations and interests. Its present occupant, now impatiently waiting to hear from Sydenham, was a new man. He had not risen from the ranks and his staff knew little about him. His own background was Army intelligence, and before that, colonial service: his name was unknown to the British public he served, by 'D' notice instruction to newspapers, radio and TV networks, although ridiculously enough it frequently appeared in the foreign Press, who were hampered by no such regulations.

His job was to direct internal national security, an enormous task. His powers were vast, his discretion complete, many of his duties distasteful. He had been picked on reputation, and already his zeal and peculiarities were a byword in the department. A passion for the Old Testament had right away won him the nickname of 'Holy Joe'. The calendar stood on his desk by design, and was in constant use.

His deputy button-holed Sydenham as soon as he entered the building.

'Holy Joe's pretty steamed up,' he told him. 'Wants a report drafted for the P.M. before the day's out. I've already had my balls chewed off because Stevens was left unguarded. Your story had better be good.'

He looked at Sydenham's head. 'You all right?' he asked.

'I'll survive,' said Sydenham. 'Have you had a word with the D.P.P. yet? Good, come on then, let's get it over with,' and he outlined his ideas as they walked along the corridor.

A secretary led them at once into the Board Room. The Director sat in his chair by the fireplace, and waved the two officers to either side after a brief word of greeting. He addressed himself directly to the middle-aged woman secretary.

'I don't want to be disturbed,' he said, 'by *anyone*. No 'phone calls, no visitors, no interruptions of any kind whatever. Is that clear?'

'Quite clear, sir,' she replied equably. She had seen a covey of Directors come and go: Sydenham was a favourite of hers, and she had noticed his bruises right away.

'Would you gentlemen like coffee?'

'No.' said the Director, answering for them all.

He was a man in his mid-fifties, as tall and spare as Sydenham was gross and round. He carried the stamp of the old soldier with him still, clipped moustache, straight shiny hair cut very short back and sides, straight back, square shoulders, square jaw, eyes that looked at you as though straight down a gun-barrel. His skin was dry, leathered and yellowed by the years spent in Africa. He was dressed in hairy tweeds, a woollen shirt, and a hand-made Donegal tie: his brogues were boned to a glassy brilliance, and a dark green handkerchief stood to attention in his breast pocket. His hands were big and capable. Everything about him looked hard, and capable.

He ran his eye over the fat man at his side, and noted the lumps and bruises.

'Hurt yourself?' he asked in a voice that implied he might not find the possibility too painful to bear.

Sydenham's pale blue eyes regarded him steadily enough.

'Tree fell on my car last night,' he said evenly. 'As I made my way home after leaving the Stevens' house.'

'Ah yes, the Stevens.' The Director let the name hang in the air for a moment. 'Bad business, that. Can we retrieve the situation, Sydenham?'

'I think so, sir.'

Sydenham took him through the events of the night, from the time he had left the house until he had driven the Stevens away from the magistrates court.

'I've got them tucked away in Richmond, under guard and medical treatment for shock. Neither of them will set foot outside the house until we say so this time.'

'Well, that's something to be thankful for. What's the legal position?'

'Difficult, sir, but by no means impossible. One more lower court hearing, but with reporting restrictions enforced. Then an Old Bailey trial in two or three months' time.'

'What's going to happen there?'

'Nothing we can do about the jury, sir. Everything will depend on the trial judge, from our point of view.'

'Obviously. Who was this man he shot?'

'Fellow called Williams. Professional house-breaker with a string of convictions. The last was for six years, so there's no chance of any misplaced sympathy from the court, sir. I haven't had time to make very extensive inquiries so far, as you will appreciate. However, I'm advised that a plea of Not Guilty could well stand up in a court of law. If not, a suspended sentence would do us just as well. The essential thing is to make sure no one can report his true identity. We have to have that trial held in closed court.'

'What in God's name possessed this man Stevens to lose his head and shoot an unarmed man?'

'You've said it in one, sir: he lost his head. He has this very real fear that the opposition will find him and murder him: and I don't doubt for a minute they would, given the chance. That's why we gave him the gun in the first place.'

'And that,' said the Director bluntly, 'was an error of judgment, as subsequent events have shown. I hope for your sake we don't live to regret it.'

Sydenham made no attempt to answer that.

'Not the only error, and not even the worst one. This department was wrong in allowing this man to move into a private house without adequate, permanent guard. Armed guard.'

At that, Sydenham bridled.

'Not our pigeon, sir. We were under top-level pressure to get him back to work. I reported that both husband and wife were heading for a breakdown after being cooped up under guard for over a year. The psychiatrist advised us to take the course we did, and in the end the minister made it an order. An order which we carried out.'

'To hell with the minister,' said the Director. 'If this thing blows up in our faces, it will be this department that carries the can, not the minister. Well, it won't happen a second time, not while I'm in the chair.'

'As for the gun,' Sydenham went on doggedly, 'there was no way round that decision. Stevens insisted and refused point blank to work unless we met him in all his demands. I thought it a reasonable decision: that's why I sanctioned it, sir. If we had to put guards on everyone who sought asylum and feared possible assassination, we'd have no one left for intelligence duties at all. No one could have foreseen a burglar breaking in, dressed the way that man was, at the one time on the one night I was knocked out by a falling tree.'

He refrained from mentioning that he and his men had spent sixteen hours and more each day, seven days every week, watching over the Stevens from the moment they first moved in to number 28.

'That's as may be.' The Director was adamant. 'I repeat, it will not be allowed to happen again while I hold office.'

He turned to his deputy.

'What are the options open to us now?'

'Very few, I'm afraid, sir. We're holding the Stevens. We could —theoretically—persuade them to jump bail, and help them disappear a second time. But I don't advise it: too messy, too many ends to tie up: there would have to be a warrant out and it would leave us wide open to public comment. And, of course, he'd have to work for someone else, the Americans or the French: much good that would do us. No, he's got to stand his trial, and then start again with a clean sheet. That means we need an understanding judge, and a merciful sentence in the event of a guilty verdict. There's no other way, sir.'

Holy Joe lit a cigarette, and pushed the box around the table, signalling a rise in temperature if not actual forgiveness.

'I agree,' he said regretfully. 'There'd be hell to pay if Mister Stevens disappeared. Especially after Littlejohn! Numbers 23, gentlemen, be sure your sin will find you out.'

He managed a taut smile at his own joke.

'But tell me,' he said, 'where does one find this, ah, reliable judge. Sydenham?'

'Yes, sir.' Sydenham's white teeth showed in his first smile of the day, knowing and conspiratorial. 'The drill is as follows. The superintendent of police at Saddlers Hill has to submit his papers to the Director of Public Prosecutions, and we of course, have to be fully consulted. In turn, we approach the Attorney General, quite legitimately, on the grounds that high security is involved. We then need the Crown—legally, it has to be the Crown in such matters—to seek a hearing with the trial judge before the case opens to make an application for the case to be heard *in camera.*'

'Can we rely on that being granted?'

'Well, sir, such a decision is the sole prerogative of the trial judge. The trick is to select the judge. That would need help from the Attorney-General. He would have to speak to the Lord Chief Justice and explain our side of the coin, give our reasons for wanting to keep Stevens' true identity secret—and of course, emphasise the vital need for a merciful sentence, if sentence it has to be. I imagine it would be too much to ask the Lord Chief to take the case himself, after such an approach.'

Sydenham sounded genuinely concerned. 'But surely he could be persuaded to find the right man to dispense justice in his stead.'

The Director nodded.

'First class thinking, Sydenham. You'd better speak to the Attorney-General immediately.'

Sydenham's eyes were on the cigarette in his fingers.

'I'll try, sir.'

The deputy moved swiftly to his aid, as they had agreed in the corridor twenty minutes earlier.

'With respect, sir. Such an approach has to carry the maximum weight this department can bring to bear: after all, he's the government's senior legal adviser.' Now it was his turn to let the words hang in the air.

'There must be no possibility of any misunderstanding, sir. The A.G.'s a new man, he'll want to feel his way very carefully among the law lords at this stage of his career. We may have to pressure him, using the P.M. if need be. There is no way of by-passing the Attorney-General in this case. As the senior law officer he is the one person who can go to the Lord Chief Justice on such a delicate matter. One false step, and our goose is cooked.'

'I see.'

'There must be no suggestion of seeking improper privilege for our department. The request has to be made solely in the interests of state security.'

'Yes, I suppose so.'

'I don't think in those circumstances it would be fair to place the onus on Sydenham, sir. It has to be me. Or you.'

It was neatly done.

'Very well, I'll speak to the Attorney-General and see what can be done.'

Too late, he realised that the odium of hidden persuasion had been passed to him, skilfully and deliberately: but he was not done with them yet.

'If we get our man off the hook as a direct result, I want it clearly understood that there will be no more private lives, in an unguarded private house, for him or his wife. From the moment they step out of that courtroom, I will require a senior member of this department to stay with them at all times, breathing down their necks day and night.'

The invisible gun-barrel came round until it was aimed straight at Sydenham's eyes.

'And that man will be you, Sydenham.'

The scrape of his chair on the floor declared the meeting closed.

3

THE JUDGE

The Attorney-General puffed at his cigar, and waited for the screws to be turned: the spy-boys had done him very well, he had to concede that.

Since the chosen rendezvous was reputed to be run by one of their own men, he had allowed himself to be persuaded into accepting its set lunch, and a memorable experience it had proved to be. Danish schnapps, flavoured by a fragment of orange peel, had titillated the palate in an oddly satisfying way as each man, host and guest, had congratulated the other on his new appointment. Then came a Cornish crab pâté, tangy and salted as a sea breeze—now there was a rare choice on a day of London fumes and drizzle. Clever of them, too, to anticipate his weakness for the pink flesh of Loch Leven trout, while the Montrachet that accompanied the dish was regal: no other description could possibly do it justice. This was followed by an Angus steak, rare, red, and thick as a rich man's wallet, washed down by a Burgundy straight from the cellars of Bacchus himself.

A good meal, if plain: he felt in no wise cheated that favours were to be sought of him in return.

He had had a rapid rise to the eminence of his present position. Not so many years back he had been no more than a zealous young barrister with a nose for politics. Then he had married well, and from that moment on his star had risen into the skies of personal ambition. Her family guided him on to the short list for a safe Parliamentary seat, they saw to it that he emerged as unanimous choice for candidate, father-in-law pulled strings within the Party again to ensure fast and early promotion. He in turn made the most of his chances, conquering each political peak as surely as a Bonington in the Himalayas, rising to Solicitor-General the last time they were in power and Attorney-General this time, and still only in his forties. He was a good-looking man, tall and handsome, with a fine high forehead, and his striking appearance plus great skill in oratory were no mean assets for any man in politics or—for that matter—at the Bar. He was a natural wheeler-dealer, shrewd, calculating, and able. From his earliest days he had displayed a remarkable ability to run with the hare and hunt with the hounds: at school he had been christened 'Soapy' Benson.

The Director, who had studied his file that morning with great care, told him as much as he felt was right about John Stevens. Then he asked, casually, had his guest found time to look at the papers in the case?

'I have indeed,' said the Attorney-General. He had examined them before the meal in intimate session with the Director of Public Prosecutions. 'A sad business.'

'You don't know the half of it,' the Director told him. 'It took another Department more than a year—a difficult and dangerous time for all concerned—to arrange to have Stevens smuggled over here to work for us. His value to this country cannot be exaggerated. The man's a phenomenon. Unfortunately, there have been errors of judgment in handling him since his arrival. I myself would never have allowed him to live as he did in the last months, alone with his wife and largely unguarded. Be that as it may. On a single night everything went awry, Stevens shot this burglar and got himself arrested and charged in the process. Now I am under the most intense pressure from many quarters—the very highest—to do whatever can legally be done to have him set free, so that he can continue his work at the earliest possible moment.'

He looked at the A.G. with hooded eyes. 'How do we stand?'

The Attorney-General played for time in framing his answer.

'The legal procedure,' he said, 'is laid down, although your man did well in getting him released on bail so swiftly. Committal proceedings have still to be held in the magistrates' court once the fourteen days have elapsed, as you know. What happens there is routine. The Director of Public Prosecutions will send a barrister from his own department to present the case against your man Stevens, and I am quite sure you will take the necessary steps to make certain he is aware of your acute concern in the matter. All his barrister will do, basically, will be to hand over certain bundles of unsworn statements to the Bench. They will be from the police officers who first went to the house, the superintendent who interviewed and charged Stevens, the pathologist who examined the dead man, and the firearms expert who matched bullets taken from the body with your man's gun. You are naturally concerned about publicity, are you not? Well, there will be no need for any of those statements to be read aloud at that stage, nor will the accused be asked to plead. He will of course be represented by a solicitor supplied by you, and he will undoubtedly be committed for trial at the Central Criminal Court. Where are we now, February? Then the trial will be held in May, I imagine. You must ensure that reporting restrictions are not lifted at the committal hearing, so that there will be as little publicity as possible before that High Court trial. As far as the outside world is concerned, they will know only that a man with the very ordinary British name of Stevens has been committed to appear before judge and jury on a manslaughter charge. Nothing very shattering there.'

It was no answer at all.

'I know all that,' said the Director unhappily. 'It's what may happen inside the Old Bailey that worries us. We are desperately concerned lest Stevens' true identity should be revealed. His own people would be on to it at once. Anything could happen, then. They might try to kill him—I wouldn't rule that out in view of his importance—or, more likely, try to woo him back. You see the position. If he's faced with a jail sentence, no matter if it's deserved or not, he might well be tempted to return. Either way it would represent a setback of the first magnitude for this country.'

'No doubt it would.' The Attorney-General frowned. 'What is it you seek from me?'

'I want that trial heard *in camera.*'

'That doesn't rest with me, it's a decision for the trial judge, and no other. He's the one and only person empowered to grant such an application, and dammit all, your man hasn't even been committed for trial yet: there *is* no such judge at this moment in time.'

'Which is exactly what I'm driving at,' the Director told him bluntly. His eyes never left the face across the table. 'I want you to go to the Lord Chief Justice, now, while there's time, and er, appraise him of the situation facing us.'

'I see.' The younger man cupped his hands round his glass. 'You make it sound incredibly straightforward. Alas, one simply does not go around telling any judge how he would like a case conducted, least of all the Lord Chief.'

'Of course not.' The Director's tone was bland. 'But you're a lawyer, the government's senior legal adviser, you know how these things can best be done. I told you I'm under pressure from the very highest quarters to get something done. The P.M. himself is aware of our problem: we want everything possible—correction, everything *legally* possible—done to smooth the path for Stevens. My people tell me that you are the only man in authority who could correctly make such an approach on our behalf.'

'I imagine that's so,' said the new Attorney-General, somewhat mollified.

'No question whatever,' said the Director, 'of anyone seeking improper privilege.'

'I could not lend myself to such a course in any event.'

'Absolutely not! Your reputation speaks for itself. Clearly there has to be an unprejudiced trial, and our man must answer for what he has done. But allow me to take it a step further. Members of my department have already sought counsel's opinion on Stevens' chances in a court of law. It was immensely reassuring. We are advised that he has every chance of outright acquittal.'

'In which case you won't need help from anyone.'

'Well,' said the Director, beckoning to the waiter for more brandy, 'there's the jury, the unknown factor. Suppose my advice is wrong and they return a verdict of guilty? In view of Stevens' unique value to the country, one likes to think that in such a case, the judge might be inclined to be, well, merciful.'

There was a long silence at the table as the drinks were poured.

'It would be dangerously wrong,' warned the Attorney-General, 'of your departmental aides to believe that given certain circumstances, a trial judge can be nobbled, so to speak, like a horse in a prize race. I have been a barrister for a good many years, and do assure you, nothing could be further from the truth.'

The Director stood his ground.

'But you don't deny,' he asked, 'that in certain circumstances there has sometimes been a selection of cases? Horses for courses, to use your analogy?'

The lawyer countered with a question of his own.

'Leave that aside for a moment. Are you aware that trials held in the Central Criminal Court come before two different kinds of judge?'

'I don't know the niceties of the law,' admitted the Director, slowly. 'How would that affect our own case?'

'In this way. There are a great many courts in the new building, with a judge to sit in each. But there are only a few, two or three perhaps, known as High Court judges. Each one is titled the Honourable Mr Justice So-and-So: he has a knighthood, and is known in private life as Sir John, or Sir William So-and-So. He is what we call a Red Judge.

'The remainder are called Circuit judges. These are lesser mortals and known as His Honour Judge Bloggs, or whatever the case may be. The essential difference between the two is this: with rare exceptions, certain charges, such as murder or manslaughter—the offence with which your man Stevens is charged—may be heard only by a Red Judge. I do not for one moment suggest that one judge is more circumspect than any other. I mention this merely to demonstrate that even if your supposition is correct, namely, that there can be a selection of cases, it will still follow that the choice of a particular judge to take the Stevens case would be very limited. Are you with me?'

'Yes,' said the Director, thoughtfully.

'It's vital that you are.' The Attorney-General drew on his cigar. 'Come what may, John Stevens will appear before one of a very small group of judges, each of great seniority, all jealously and intensely aware of a long tradition of impartiality and incorruptibility, each one answerable—in the last resort—to the Queen herself, the Queen's Justice in fact as well as name. No one in government, no minister, no member of the Cabinet, not the Prime Minister even, can put pressure on or influence such a man: not even Parliament itself has the power to remove him from the bench. I know that your concern here is a patriotic one. Well, Red Judges are patriots too, but you will find that in their courts of law such men are less interested in patriotism than in the administration of justice, however unpalatable that may seem to you as a head of an intelligence department. I will do what I can, but, my friend, we need to tread very warily indeed. I cannot promise you a thing. I sincerely hope you have not held out a promise of automatic freedom to this unfortunate man, Stevens.'

For the first time the Director fully appreciated Sydenham's wisdom in handing over responsibility for these negotiations to him. Aloud he said:

'No, nothing has been promised.'

'That is as well. Juries are notoriously unpredictable. Suppose Stevens is found guilty: a very grave responsibility would then fall upon the judge, for even if the trial were heard *in camera*, sentence would still have to be passed in open court.'

The Director looked glum.

'I spent a great many years in colonial service,' he said. 'Things were somewhat easier there when the national interests were at stake.'

He signalled for more brandy and sought reassurance in the words of St Matthew, ask and it shall be given you: seek and ye shall find: knock, and it shall be opened unto you, and he returned to the attack.

'Britain has everything to lose here,' he insisted. 'That's why I have to look for a merciful and understanding judge. If Stevens is found guilty, then we want a suspended sentence—at worst.'

'You would have done better, I feel,' said the Attorney-General not unkindly, 'to have tried to persuade the police to drop all charges at the outset, and hand over the body to your men for disposal.'

'It was in our mind, in a gentle sort of way. But my man arrived too late to try.'

'I fear we are both in the same boat now.' The Attorney-General wiped his mouth with his napkin, and smiled. 'Of the same mind, but a little late. Thank you for a splendid lunch, my dear fellow. I will see what can be done, but remember, we have met unofficially and I promise nothing.'

They shook hands.

'I'll keep my fingers crossed,' said the Director. 'Thank you, and good luck.'

He sent the lawyer off in his own car, and marched back to the office in Whitehall. The sky was dark and overcast, and try as he might, he could not shake off a premonition of disaster.

Attorney-General and Lord Chief Justice met soon afterwards. The judge received his caller one evening in his apartment in King's Bench Walk, and as they stood at the window gazing down on the lamplit Thames, congratulated him warmly on his promotion.

'You've done well, Benson,' said the old man generously. 'Exceedingly well. Glass of sherry?'

'Thank you, my Lord, that is most kind.'

He sipped his drink as the Lord Chief moved in front of the coal fire to toast his thin quarters. He had appeared before him often enough in court, both as Silk and junior, and was as deferential now in his manner as he had been on his first day in wig and gown. Whatever the pleasantries, however improved his own status, and admitting his own considerable power, he was as wary of the great man as a fox of the huntsman. For a time the two men spoke in generalities and it was the judge who dictated every move. After a decent interval, the Lord Chief spoke of others he had known hold office as Attorney-General, and recalled some of the problems they had faced from time to time.

'I have no doubt, Benson,' he said gently, 'you will also find many an occasion when the lawyer in you finds himself at odds with the politician. Should such a situation arise, I trust you will feel yourself free to seek whatever advice I may be able to offer.'

Judges have their own intelligence network, and the Attorney-General suddenly realised this one already knew why he was there.

'Thank you, my Lord. Two months in office and indeed, I am confronted with such a situation.'

'Tell me about it.'

They discussed the ramifications of the Stevens case, not in the language of the courtroom, but as man to man.

'Naturally,' said Benson, 'they hope for an acquittal and expect their case to prove strong enough in law to secure one. If that should be so, well and good. But failing an acquittal, they look for the most lenient sentence the law can allow.'

He added quickly, 'The only commitment that I have entered into, is in coming to see your Lordship at all. None the less, I do see their dilemma: this is a matter of high state security, when all is said and done, and one feels sympathy with the view that in the event of harsh punishment, the nation may lose far more than the accused.'

The Lord Chief Justice regarded him steadily.

'I take the point,' he said at length. 'Since we have met privately we can speak frankly. Have you yourself studied every aspect of this case with the greatest care *as a lawyer*, and do you yourself feel, in all honesty, that the interests of the state should over-ride all others?'

'No, my Lord, not over-ride. But I feel they should be given due consideration, provided that justice is done.'

'You do not imagine, Benson, you are the first person holding that office to express such views when the state is involved? Clearly not, although I will not go into that now. The trouble sometimes is that these people, these honourable faceless persons charged with guarding the interests of the state, are apt to find the law a positive inconvenience, an obstacle in their path. That is why approaches such as this have to be made. They see where their duty lies and regard the law as an ass. And the unfortunate truth is that they tend to confuse the powers of my office with those of English kings in the days of old: dammit, man, none of us can say like Henry IV "the laws of England are my commandment." Granted that these are men of honour, granted that they seek nothing for themselves, granted that their one guiding star is patriotism—none the less we must guard against abuse of their special position, lest their role and influence should become a kind of necessary evil. Do I make myself clear?'

'Quite clear, my Lord.'

'They intend, you say, to ask that the trial be held *in camera*?'

'Yes.'

'I can only say that if such an application were put to me as trial judge in this case, I would in all the circumstances consider it favourably. It seems to me to meet reasonable security requirements without prejudice to the outcome of the hearing. That view I can, and will, make known in the appropriate quarter if the opportunity arises.'

'Thank you, my Lord.'

'Of course the accused will still have to take his chance with the jury. If the verdict is guilty, what do they hope for then?'

'A suspended sentence, my Lord.'

'I cannot prejudge any issue and would never presume to speak for my brother judges. However, on the facts that you have set out before me tonight, had the case come before me, I myself might have been persuaded to deal mercifully with the accused.'

The fire was scorching the seat of his striped trousers, and he edged forward.

'I won't take it, of course. It's likely to be set down for May, did you say, Benson? In that event'—he looked up at the ceiling—'there will only be two names available. Richards or Fisher. Not much room for selection there, eh, Benson?'

'Indeed no, my Lord.'

Still the Attorney-General did not know which way the wind would blow. He had every reason to hope that the case would be heard *in camera* as a result of his call, and that was a sizeable crumb from the table of justice. But the selection of judge was crucial, in spite of the shortness of the list. The Honourable Mr Justice Morston Richards would be a calamitous choice, from his point of view. His outspoken comments in recent months on the spread of violent crime, his repeated threat of dire punishment for all found guilty of such offence, had won him a variety of nicknames from the public, critics and admirers alike. The new Jeffreys, Bloody Morston, they called him: lawyers all knew him as Tyrannosaurus Rex. It would be a brave man who tried to influence any case that came before him. On the other hand the Honourable Mr Justice Rodney Roy Fisher—while no weakling, or the darling of the reformers—was by contrast a human marsh-mallow.

'Richards is the senior,' said the Lord Chief.

The Attorney-General's heart sank into his boots.

'On the other hand,' said the old judge with a smile, 'there is so much for them both to do. I am sure Richards will have enough on his plate as it is. It will have to be Fisher. You may take it, unofficially, it *will* be Fisher. I'll have a word with him.'

Now, that was generous indeed of the old man. Benson felt his spirits rise, but before he could comment the Lord Chief reminded him: 'I have done nothing,' he said carefully, 'except tell you privately the name of the only judge available to take this case.'

'Precisely, my Lord.'

'I have made no promises, nor would I. Make quite sure that those who approached you are aware of that.'

'I will, my Lord. In fact I made that clear from the outset.'

'Quite right. More sherry, Benson?'

'Thank you, my Lord. That is most kind.'

Sir Harry Morston Richards was eighty-five and the oldest Red Judge anyone could recall, but he steadfastly declined to give any indication when he might retire. And, since he had been appointed to the bench long before the introduction of the Judicial Pensions Act—which sets seventy-five as the normal age of retirement—he himself was bound by no statutory age limit. If he was physically frail, his mind was still lucid and alert, and he took fierce pride in the newspaper reports which acclaimed him as Britain's oldest full-time worker.

'*Tyrannosaurus Rex*' had been much in the headlines of late for his tough comments on the rise of violent crime in the country:

the sentences he handed down to the line of hoodlums who paraded before him were harsh and his strictures unyielding. Tonight he was guest of honour at the annual dinner given by the Central Criminal Court Journalists' Association, that distinguished corps of crime reporters who also work full-time at the Old Bailey, and he ended his speech of thanks in typical fashion.

'You gentlemen have written many words in recent years reflecting the sharp rise in violent crime in this country. To many minds, it has lately reached an intolerable level: I have had much to say about that, and you have wasted no opportunity to pass on to your readers my passionate feelings on the subject. At the same time, your reports have never failed to emphasise my advanced years.'

This was as close as Morston Richards would ever sail to humour, and his words were met by a dutiful round of laughter.

'Well, I have news for you, gentlemen. My health remains good—in spite of those years—and my will to remain in office and fight the good fight is wholly undiminished. In these increasingly lawless days, decent men and women everywhere look to the judges, and ask themselves, can they give us the protection we need or must the law of the jungle prevail? One hears on every hand growing demands for the setting-up of private armies to enforce the law of the land. I want none of that! I see the judiciary as the only rock, standing firm against the tide of violence: solid, immovable, incorruptible, unchanging. I am indeed an old man. But age has nothing to do with my views on crime and punishment. Be assured the clearest and dearest memory I cherish is of the day when I was first appointed judge. I regarded it then, and do still, as the very peak of my calling, believing sincerely that no greater honour can be conferred on any man.

'It is my proud boast that the ideals which guided me through my first day in office have in no wise diminished, changed or lessened over the years, as standards in all other walks of life have become slowly eroded. My old friend Birkett once said that the first quality in an advocate, above all others, was that he must be a man of character, honour and uprightness. Whatever else may be needed should the advocate be appointed judge, that first quality will play a large part in shaping his every judgment. Once his strength of character fails and falters, so his court will become a mockery of all that it stands for in our society.

'The law must apply, and be seen to apply, to all in the land, good and bad, high or low, to men of influence as well as the most humble, for it is the common law: and it remains both my delight and my duty to administer that common law when called upon to do so, without let or hindrance, without fear or favour.'

He held himself very straight and looked proudly round the room.

'Certainly I am an old man. I have far exceeded the allotted span of three score years and ten. But I am resolved to carry on, in the Queen's name, and do my duty. God knows much remains to be done, as all who have eyes must see.'

As the white-haired judge sat down, his hosts rose as one to applaud his speech. The hand-clapping went on and on, a remarkable scene, until their chairman led them into the words of Harry Lauder's song: 'Keep right on, to the end of the road, keep right on to the end'. They roared out the chorus as Morston Richards stared straight ahead, a rare tribute from a group of professional men who spend their lives in recording human frailty to another, chosen to pass judgment on that frailty and punish it accordingly.

Those closest to the guest of honour swore later they had seen his one good eye bright with tears.

Harry Richards was an only child. His mother died when he was one week old, carried off by the scarlet fever that visited so many English homes that year, and inadvertently condemned her son to spend his formative years in a preponderantly male world where adults honestly believed that to spare the rod was to spoil the child. Punishment for misdeeds real or imagined played a very big part in young Harry's life, and he grew to manhood accepting it as naturally as sunshine or rain.

His father was a City merchant whose warehouses were filled with goods shipped from the East, mainly silks and tea: in his loneliness he ran his private life much as he did his business, by command rather than affection, and without overmuch charity or compassion. If he loved the boy he was incapable of unbending, he could never find words to tell of the loneliness in his heart or the coldness of his marital bed, and he sought refuge from explanation behind the shield of discipline. Discipline was drilled in to the infant Harry first by a housekeeper who walked in dread of her master, and hammered in to the growing boy at a boarding school which prided itself on bullying, and corporal punishment. At home as in school, meals left unfinished owed nothing to poor cooking or to illness, or taste but became food wasted—food that had cost his father hard-earned money: and out would come the cane. Untidiness, dirty shoes, soiled clothing, torn breeches, grubby fingernails, any attempt to analyse (far less challenge) the ruling of an adult, the mildest display of temper or obstinacy, failure to be thought to be working hard, all these things and much more brought instant punishment in their wake.

'You horrid boy, your clothes are filthy. I am going to punish you.'

'Richards, your work this term has been less than satisfactory. I am going to punish you to teach you the error of your ways. Bend over, sir.'

'Master Harry, you have wasted your food again. Don't lie to me, you're not ill. You will be punished twice—for wasting food, *and* for lying. Come here.'

When Harry came home for his holidays, he saw his father as authority, God, to whom instant obedience was due. It mattered very little that he recited 'amo, amas, amat' countless times at school, for love played a very minor part in his life at any time. That father and son should find any common ground at all was a near miracle: but they did, and the influence of the man on the child was real, and far-reaching. Not to do wrong was the rule they worshipped above all others. Sundays at home were the best days for them both: he and his father went for long walks after church, through the green fields of Highgate. They would walk side by side, and sometimes even hold hands. He would be asked about his schooling—Harry learned to phrase his answers very carefully—and mostly he would be lectured, but at least they were communicating, an occasion of great importance to them both. It was such a Sunday morning walk that set the pattern for Harry's adult life and career.

'You are fourteen years of age,' his father began. 'It is time, I think, for you to take an interest in the affairs of the company which you may one day have to run. I am faced with a matter of grave concern there.'

The books for Morston Richards & Son, merchants, were kept by a senior clerk named Greaves. Profits in a good year were considerable, and Greaves held a position of trust, calling for long hours, and much responsibility. Harry had met him once or twice, a thin and sad middle-aged man whose voice sounded as arid and dull as the lading sheets he toiled over. He was aghast to hear that Greaves was in trouble: he could picture him now, perched on his high stool, scratching away industriously in a room full of equally sad, middle-aged men, and the idea of working in such an office filled him with dread.

'What has he done, father?'

'He's robbed us, Harry. And over a period of years, the scoundrel.'

It seemed that Greaves had been sending part of each consignment to rival wharves and enriching himself in the process. Now he was in Newgate gaol awaiting trial.

'I intend to see that he goes to prison for a very long time. And I shall take you to court to see how the law deals with evil men.'

The hours he spent in that dark and foul-smelling courtroom made an impression on the youth that stayed with him all his life. He saw the judge, not as an old man sniffing a nosegay and handing out punishment to a weak and erring Greaves, but as a kind of deity: the enormous deference paid to that bewigged figure on the bench was like nothing else he had seen in all his fourteen years, save the obedience paid to his own father at work and home. He saw it, not as a trial so much as a setting for inevitable punishment, inexorable and majestic, a parade of knights on white chargers thundering down on the forces of evil. It was as though he had waited to open a book at a special page to tell him what he must do in the years ahead.

Greaves was sentenced to twenty years hard labour. He knew it meant he would die in a prison cell, but his cry of anguish went unheard by the youth sitting in the high gallery. He had eyes and ears only for the judge: he could tell you his every word, seventy years later.

'Ronan Greaves, you have been rightly found guilty of one of the most despicable of crimes, the betrayal of a high position of trust. By your greed and dishonesty you have forfeited any hope of forgiveness from your employer, or mercy from this court. You deliberately embarked on a course of wicked deceit of a good man who had shown you much kindness, and but for prompt action on the part of the authorities you might have brought about the ruin of an honourable man who has long earned a reputation for fair trading and honest practice. Learned counsel has said on your behalf that you have a wife and four children, and that these unfortunates will be the worst to suffer for your misdeeds. I say to you you gave no thought to them when you decided to enrich yourself at the expense of an employer who took you in as a young man, and gave you advancement upon advancement until you were one of the most senior men in his company. Property has to be safeguarded. Not long ago you could have hanged for far less a crime than the one of which you have been convicted this day. Lawlessness is growing in this country, and some may think because of the lack of proper deterrent. The law-abiding look to the judiciary increasingly as violence, and dishonesty grow and ask for our protection: and I for one shall not fail them. You will go to prison for not less than twenty years, with hard labour.'

Father and son left the court and travelled home by hansom cab. It was a beautiful sunny day: rich men, poor men, beggar-men and thieves thronged the streets.

'You see what Greaves has lost,' said Mr Richards with a wave of his hand, 'as a result of his wicked behaviour. I doubt if he will ever walk in a street again.'

Greaves had been paid £200 a year, with the gift of a Christmas goose, for running a company with an annual turnover of tens of thousands of pounds. All Harry could think of was the scene he had witnessed of a court in session, and the awful majesty of the law unfolding, the unarguable logic of an eye-for-an-eye in crime and punishment. He still marvelled at the absolute power wielded by the old man in the scarlet robe, his complete sureness of purpose when punishing evil. Greatly daring, he decided to strike while the iron was hot.

'Father,' he said hesitantly, 'may I ask you something?'

Mr Richards was feeling enormously better for revenge gained. 'You may,' he said. 'What is it, boy?'

'Would you allow me to study for advocate, father?' Harry's voice was low and urgent as he struggled for words that would not offend. 'You said that one day I might be called upon to run your business, but ... it is not what I would choose for myself, I know that now. It was as if another voice was speaking to me in that courtroom along with the judge, and the advocates: I knew right away, that was what I wanted to do, to study law, and one day, perhaps, become a judge. Those men were defending you, father, just as surely as if they were soldiers in an army. It was a wonderful thing to see. I would like to become one of them, if you will permit me.'

His father approved of the request.

'It's a noble calling,' he agreed, thinking the boy could do worse in life than punish scoundrels like Greaves. 'You would have to work hard, Harry, much harder than you have so far done at school. Are you prepared for that?'

'Yes, father.'

'Very well then. I'll talk to my solicitors and see what they advise.'

In his second year as barrister, Harry Richards was in chambers in the Midlands, in Birmingham. The early crusading fire still burned as strong as ever, although he might have been dismayed to learn that for all his zeal and application, he was looked upon as a plodder by his seniors. Not that it would have mattered overmuch, except to his pride: his father was dead, and he was a man of some means, one who could afford to wait for the briefs which so far had been few and ill-paid.

Gas-lamps burned in the city centre as he walked home through deserted streets after dining at Albany with some friends: a walk of some three miles to his lodgings seemed pleasantly acceptable after so much wine, and so heavy a meal. He hummed a tune as he strode along, jingling the sovereigns in his pocket. Even when the line of lamps came to a halt, his way was still well lit, for there was a full moon. Harry Morston Richards was tall and thin, and his silk hat gleamed in the moonlight. He was more offended than afraid when two figures came slyly from the shadows and stood in his path.

'Get out of my way,' he ordered. He used the tone of voice normally reserved for the dog.

'Show us the colour of your money,' said a voice, 'and you won't get hurt.'

Footpads—they call them muggers today—were almost as common as rats in every city in those days. Harry Richards may have been physically incapable of fighting and beating two men, but he was likewise incapable of surrendering tamely to any threat of violence. His reaction was predictable: you are breaking the law, and you won't get away with it. He lashed out with his cane at the man nearest to him, and felt the silver tip crack home on flesh and bone. Then he turned on the other assailant, when prudence dictated he should take to his heels and run back into the safety of the flaring gaslights. A cudgel swished through the air to send his top hat sailing into the gutter. It came down a second time, on his skull.

'I'll see you two jailed,' he shouted, 'if it's the last thing I do! Help!'

They beat him up savagely as he began to call for help. Blows rained down on his head, his arms and legs. He felt hands grabbing and tearing at his clothes, taking the wallet first and then the watch and chain. Not once did he catch a glimpse of their faces: all he saw was one shadowy figure, and then another, wielding sticks that caused him terrible pain. It was all over in a few minutes. He lay motionless in the gutter for more than an hour until the police foot patrol found him, and took him by hand cart to the infirmary.

When they wiped the blood from his face, the doctors saw the full extent of the injury to his right eye. Something, a stick or a stone, had been used with tremendous force, and the damage to the optic nerve was severe. Eye surgery was in its infancy, while the emergency ward of any infirmary on any Saturday night was no place for the squeamish: and between them, the footpads and the tipsy doctors left Harry Richards totally blind in the right eye.

He was unable to practise for over a year, although there were those who said later, and cynically, that the loss of an eye played a bigger part in his eventual promotion to the bench than did professional ability. Certainly it prevented him from enlisting in two world wars, and unquestionably eased the way to his late appointment, at a time of shortage of manpower in all the legal ranks. He was never an outstanding advocate, and had none of the magnetism of men such as Birkett and Hastings: but at least he had a dogged tenacity in the courtroom, he was a tireless prosecutor motivated by a consuming love of his chosen profession, and the inevitable rewards came until he was at last appointed High Court judge.

Sir Harry had no wife or family living, and few really close friends, but some who knew him well enough privately believed he took his revenge for the Birmingham attack time and again over the years. He had worn the Black Cap often enough, while the terms of imprisonment handed out to the violent men unlucky enough to come before him now totalled some thousands of years. He would deal out sentences harsh enough to make the most hardened offender blink: woe betide the violent lout who stood before him in the dock, awaiting punishment. He used all his influence in private committee, and the lobbies, for the retention of the death sentence and when that was removed, inflicted sentences that were tougher than ever as a deterrent to violent crime. There is much that can be conveyed to a jury, simply by inflection of voice, or overlong pause, that may never show in the printed version of the summing-up, but none the less will leave that jury in no doubt as to the judge's own feelings: and Morston Richards was well known for his pregnant pauses, and sardonic tone. He was prone to interrupt counsel, and take over the questioning himself at times, so that the jury should miss nothing of the point being made: after a while he was freely referred to by a number of people as 'the hanging judge', and worse. He never once wavered or flinched in the face of sly comment or public criticism—there were even attacks by abolitionists in the Commons on one pretext or another—but continued to sit in his carved wooden chair like a Cyclops in scarlet, and to punish the evil doer as hard as the law allowed.

It was small wonder the Attorney-General had breathed a sigh of relief when he learned Fisher was to take *Rex. v. Stevens*, notwithstanding his own protestations that a selection of judges could make no difference to a man's chances in any court of law.

But the best laid plans can go wrong. Four days before the trial, the Honourable Mr Justice Fisher had a slight sore throat: he went to bed with a hot toddy of whisky and lemon juice, but felt no better next morning. He impressed on his doctor his need to get well and was stuffed with drugs and medicines. On the night before the trial was due to begin, he was told he had influenza and ordered back to bed.

'Damn the Lord Chief Justice,' said his doctor irreverently, 'this Asian 'flu is a killer for men of your age. You'll stay there until I return a verdict that you're well enough to get up!'

As he lay there with high temperature and aching limbs, Fisher dictated a message to the Lord Chief and had it sent by hand at once to the apartment in King's Bench. Within half an hour, Morston Richards was asked to take the case: there was no option but to call on him.

'Very well,' he said to the Lord Chief Justice. He was twenty years his senior, and regarded him as an upstart and an interloper: none the less, he was what he was and must needs be paid formal respect. 'Pity that Fisher failed to give us some prior indication that he was indisposed,' he added, wholly unaware of the desperate medical efforts that had been made to get m'Lud Fisher fit to go into court on the morrow. 'I'll talk to my Clerk and have him get on with it, first thing.'

His tone carried an unspoken suggestion that further conversation was unnecessary, if only because of the lateness of the hour. The Lord Chief Justice ignored it.

'There's one thing, Richards, this case coming before you is one that involved high state security. Fisher was telling me that he expected an application to be made—'

Morston Richards felt he was able to interrupt him now.

'In that case,' he said, 'I'll hear the application and give counsel my ruling tomorrow morning.' There was unmistakable emphasis on the words 'my ruling'.

'Very well.' The Lord Chief was equally terse now. 'Goodnight.'

'Goodnight to you.'

Sydenham was unaware of the change in judges as he drove to Richmond to collect his two charges next morning. Nor did he have any idea that his car was followed every inch of the way, as it had been for some days.

4

THE ASSASSINS

Any car can be followed easily enough in London's slow traffic without the driver being aware of pursuit, especially when it is trailed by a link system of two or three vehicles operated by experienced men. To avoid any unnecessary comment Sydenham chose deliberately not to request the Yard for an escort car on any journey to Richmond from the time of Stevens' arrest to the eve of the trial, and was therefore as vulnerable as any other driver.

As he made one such journey, two men sat chatting over a drink in a flat on Highgate West Hill, where the Russian 'trade delegation' to Britain houses its staff and standing—by coincidence —only a mile from the spot where Morston Richards spent his boyhood.

It was an exceptionally cold night for May, with flurries of light snow painting London white in the last flourish of a wintry spring, just sufficient to provide a home-from-home touch for the two Russians. The drink in their hands was whisky, a liquor they much preferred to their native vodka, as they did Virginia cigarettes to the garbage they normally inhaled through cardboard tubes. The two of them were completely relaxed, and talked easily as various points came to mind. Both were members of the K.G.B., the Russian secret service, and newly arrived in London on special assignment. Both were highly skilled in their specialist ways, both possessed a quite remarkable command of languages, and both were blessed with endless self-discipline and stolidity of mind. They were expert in the arts of assassination, and tonight awaited the man who was to name their target.

The flat where they relaxed was no ordinary apartment. It had been specially constructed, for instance, to combat 'bugging' or eavesdropping by devices planted by M.I.5, who have few rivals in that field for technique and imaginative cunning. This room where they drank was really an inner skin set inside the bricks and mortar laid by British workmen many years earlier and was guaranteed to thwart an electronic ear wherever placed, however operated. Not only was the room sound proofed, it was also physically guarded by a Soviet plain-clothes man at all times, someone armed with a gun who watched the entrance as long as the apartment was in use: consequently, there was no way by which any word uttered inside that room could be overheard, or taped and recorded on apparatus whirring round in some secret cellar, or conveniently parked van. Its security was total, and all who sat there were, quite literally, in a world of their own. As well as giving security against intrusion, the apartment held equipment that could send and decode messages to and from Moscow by microdot signal without risk of interference, jamming or interception. Every rich country has such a room in its important embassy quarters abroad.

'The colonel's late,' said one of the Russians. 'What could have kept him?'

'This terrible weather,' replied his companion, laughing. 'The television said tonight traffic in London was almost paralysed by the late snowfall. What would they do if they felt a real Russian blizzard, eh?' He looked out of the window. 'Call this snow? My wife puts more powder on her arse than that!'

Both men spoke the whole time in English. They had no identifiable accent, theirs were the classless voices of the well-drilled language school: and from time to time each would inject a catchphrase into his sentences that only an Englishman should have known.

'Amazing lot,' agreed the first speaker, whose name was Josef. 'Not only backward, but downright idle with it, too. Did you read that newspaper story about the car factory where the workers spend their time playing cards? Imagine our people trying that kind of nonsense in the Moscovitch plant at home, why, they'd be shot out of hand.'

'I know.' This was Andrei. 'They don't seem to care what the outside world thinks of them. Listen to them on television, they all seem to delight in running down their own institutions, yet they talk about communism as if it's some kind of disease, like rabies or V.D. Mind you, there are worse places. Think of Damascus or Guatemala. Bloody awful.'

The pair of them looked ordinary enough. Josef was the younger, a pale, slim man in his early thirties. His clothes were neat but inferior in cut and cloth, reach-me-downs sold by G.U.M. and a score of leading Eastern-bloc multiple stores in their tens of thousands in every month of each fashionless year. His shoes were strong and brushed clean but they lacked style, while his shirt and tie were nondescript. He boasted a fine head of hair, a black mop, curving in to a widow's peak that emphasised the thinness of his face and its pallor, and gave him the little-boy look so many women want to mother. He looked poor but presentable, an honest tryer, the clerk who would never quite make it to the highest stool. His bearing matched his clothes: ordinary. You could be fooled into thinking here was a man who would never say boo to a goose, and you would be instantly, fatally, wrong.

He was highly resourceful, not only a talented bomb-maker but an expert in the use of personal weapons ranging from knife to Derringer, knuckleduster, thong and cosh: but one of his greatest values to the organisation he served lay in a sixth sense, an instinctive 'feel' for the wrong-'un and an extraordinary nose for the hunt. Show Josef a photograph, hand him the dossier on a wanted man's mannerisms and habits, peculiarities of speech or walk or gesture, and it was like handing a shoe to a bloodhound. Slip his lead, and Josef could pick up the oldest, coldest trail to smell out a fugitive with uncanny accuracy. For all that he was a professional, not a hooligan: a selective executioner rather than a blind killer, a man who scorned to waste his talents, a servant of the state trained to remove enemies of that state, but no more.

Andrei, the other half of the team, was among other things a marksman, a crack shot who could pick off a target given just a fraction of time and opportunity. He was ten years older than

Josef but still reliably sharp in reaction to crisis. He stood nearly six feet in height, and had begun to run to fat: it showed already on the back of the neck, at the waist, and round the buttocks. In another three or four years' time, perhaps, his usefulness might be seriously impaired but not yet: he could call on experience and a cool head in an emergency to see him through. He was better dressed than his companion, and looked like a well-to-do businessman in his heavy woollen suit, well-filled waistcoat and white shirt. A plain gold ring showed on one finger of his right hand. He was pink-faced and clean-shaven and he had a thatch of soft, fluffy white hair that was as smooth as the down of an eider duck.

He looked bluff and hearty, a more solid character altogether, the office manager to Josef's clerk. His eyes were brown, laughter lines showed at the corners of his mouth and eyes, his manner was easy and avuncular. There was absolutely nothing about him to suggest the steel that lurked below.

If his white hair made him look older than his years, it was belied by his vitality, the extraordinary firmness of his grip. Like Josef, he excelled in close-quarter combat, and like him was also a karate expert: but he had lived longer than Josef and was by instinct more cautious and careful. Like Josef, he saw his job as one of service, long service in a war waged against the enemies of his country, nothing more and nothing less. He was incapable of killing indiscriminately, like a fox in a chicken run: he worked always, and only, to orders. He was a strong and fearless operative.

No conscience plagued him after an assignment. He did not look upon himself as a criminal, nor did he regard any of his colleagues in the squad in that light. He could be relied upon to do what had to be done regardless of personal risk or hardship. He did it without fuss, and he did it right, and he did it first time. Like Josef, he was an exceedingly dangerous man.

Drinks were poured again, and the television switched on, so that both men could watch film of the latest bombings in Ulster with a keen, professional eye. Suddenly, a light began to flash on the wall above the door, on, off, on, off.

'That will be the colonel,' said Andrei. He put down his glass, switched off the television and put out his cigarette, hastily, like a servant surprised in his master's study.

'Let him in, Josef.' Casual conversation had passed into an order, with seniority defined, in the four words.

The Russian who joined them now was aged about thirty. He was tailored by Savile Row, and would have passed as a successful young executive in any company, which indeed, he was. He was slimly built, of medium height: his skin glowed with good health, and his eyes were clear and bright, like those of an athlete in training. His step was springy and confident. The beautifully cut suit hung without crease or wrinkle. A hint of gold showed at the cuffs, and his fine leather shoes glistened like stars in the night sky. The colonel wore his hair short, but allowed it to curl in boyish abandon. He was a dandy, a most handsome young man, but he carried with him that indefinable air always worn by the right man in charge. In the present company he stood out like a peacock among the pigeons in Trafalgar Square.

'Sorry I'm late.' His lips smiled, but there was no apology in his voice. He spoke in the same class-less, accent-less English as the others. 'We'll get down to business in a moment. First, I may as well join you in a drink.'

His eyes noted the glasses hurriedly put down, with a hint of disapproval, as though his subordinates might have waited for permission. He remained standing while Josef served him, and then waved both men back to their chairs.

'Just right.' A tiny sip. 'Thank you. Now let's get on with it.' A gold lighter appeared in his hand to light a cigarette that came from nowhere, a double conjuring trick: he inhaled luxuriously and settled down.

Young as he was, Colonel Zabotin was reckoned a formidable opponent by every western counter-spy service, not least by his adversaries in London.

Unlike Josef and Andrei, who were members of the K.G.B. execution squad, based on Sverdlovsk, he was officially a diplomat and held the title of military attaché in London, as he had done earlier in Washington and before that, Pekin. He was in fact intelligence, a backroom boy specially selected to help rebuild the Russian London-based spy network that had been left in ruin after the debacle of 1971, when 105 diplomats and officials had been deported.

He had been drafted into K.G.B. service direct from university at Leningrad, and knew no other way of life. He had won his spurs in Washington, by penetration of the 'Minuteman' missile system, and now the London appointment was his reward. The colonel saw himself as an honourable man, an ambitious one, and a good Russian. He was a man of considerable personal charm and ingenuity, a genuine patriot and most zealous communist, and if he was privately critical of some of the outdated Old Guard men and ways of the Kremlin, he was none the less a true believer in the Cause which he honestly felt must one day—and hopefully in his own time—control the destiny of both the earth and space worlds. He was fluent in eight languages. He could fly a light aircraft. He was a squash player of international standard. He adored women, but made sure they could not become a personal weakness. His tastes were far from plebeian: he liked the best food and champagne—none of that champagnskaya rubbish for him!—while the very sight of Josef's drabness offended him. The C.I.A. had kept close if unavailing watch on his activities and had sent a long and detailed report ahead of him to London.

Zabotin was gently contemptuous of the British, as are so many young Russians. At an early private dinner in his embassy in London, he described his host country as the only Banana Republic with a Royal Family. He despised its backward industrial techniques, its rocketless technology, its pigmy navy that clung to memories of Nelson, its unending strikes and hooligan football fans: he regarded them all as symptoms of the same mortal illness, decadence, a kind of hardening of the national arteries after years of over-indulgence.

Not that he permitted any of this to colour his approach to the duties of under-cover agent. He was a realist. He never tired of reminding his staff that the days of Mata Hari were dead and gone, that seduction and subtlety had been replaced by plain cash and carry. There were no set rules: you improvised, he said, you probed tirelessly for flaws in the character, and twists in the mind. He felt that his own job was to eavesdrop and pry, to tunnel and ferret, coerce and bribe and tarnish, from behind the total security of his diplomatic shield. He was a very good organiser, and a patient one, but also a man ready to take daring chances when the prize was big enough. He believed his strength lay in the siting of reliable men in strategic centres, to serve as his long-distance eyes and ears.

He himself had little stomach for violence, which he considered as crude, last-ditch stuff but was willing to accept that there were times when nothing else would serve. When such an occasion should arise, he saw to it that the deed was done quickly, and as efficiently as possible, but always by hands less clean than his own. In those areas where he worked he left responsibility for killing—if killing it had to be—to Moscow, and had it carried out by 'The Goons', members of the Execution Squad like Josef and Andrei, and in such an operation he made quite sure he remained no more and no less than the middleman.

Zabotin infinitely preferred the sly intrigue, the delicate unlocking of secret doors in a man's mind that left him ripe for subtle pressure, to brute force.

Since he considered himself a man of honour, an unquestioned patriot, he loathed the occasional traitor who served him for greed or ideological beliefs, and it was in character that while he despised them, he held a most healthy respect—admiration, even—for men such as Sydenham who fought him with his own weapons, by stealth and counter-slyness, and who in his turn used all the corrupt and shameful practices of their joint calling.

He regarded the two men before him, and began to brief them, step by step.

'Before I tell you *who*, let's go back for a moment to 1971. That was a bad year for the Russian secret service. You've only just arrived, you can't begin to appreciate the full story of what happened here in London, how close we sailed to the complete breakdown of the whole intelligence machine. A lot of good men were expelled, there were some shocking defections, and even today a lot of our informants have gone to ground so damned scared they still won't come up for air. For a long time after 1971 we were in a bad way, operationally speaking.

'That's why I was sent in, to do a repair job. It soon became clear to me that we had to break new ground, and move right away from the old, traditional hunting grounds for sources of information. I will deal with only one such new area—one that directly concerns you. I took a leaf out of the book used so well, and so often, by British intelligence, and made contact with the London underworld. You both read the British newspapers, you know as well as anyone that crime in this country is big business today. But I wonder if you appreciate just how big, how widespread, and how efficient a business it has become.'

His audience listened in dutiful silence.

'We have nothing like it at home in Russia—I'm happy to say—not because our own people are any more honest, or trustworthy, but purely because of lack of opportunity offered by the regime. Not only do the British not have a secret police force, they don't even have a single State police force of any kind, so that criminals here find it much easier to operate. They cannot be shot, or hanged, no matter what they do: and it's woe betide any policeman caught manhandling a prisoner. There just is no real deterrent to serious crime. As a result of the decline in national discipline, some criminals in Britain have managed to become very powerful, and very rich: fortunately for us, also very greedy. Pay the right price to the right man, and you can buy anything. I don't mean material things, I am referring to information.

'It took me a long time to get this service organised, and I have not been over-ambitious: I don't want M.I.5 breathing down my neck any harder than they already are. But I am getting a number of interesting returns. For instance, by paying the asking price for professional services—and it comes high because they know we can never complain—I have found there are very few buildings here that can't be broken into. In the main, I have concentrated on industrial espionage, and it has been producing some excellent results in many fields. I have had offices entered, documents photographed, the negatives handed over AND the original papers replaced, all in the same night: and all this at no risk to our own people. I have also had private houses broken into, for a variety of reasons, information, blackmail, and so on. I have had cars followed, and individuals who interest me, watched. It's all beginning to work very smoothly. And it led directly to my call to Moscow that brought you two over here.'

Zabotin smiled, and was clearly enjoying himself with the recital.

'Christians have a saying in their Bible which goes something like this: "Cast thy bread upon the waters, for thou shalt find it after many days", and believe me, it could have been written for anyone in my line of business! I deal only with a handful of these British criminals, and always indirectly: obviously the rank and file they employ on my behalf are scum, burglars, safe breakers, blackmailers, the usual riff-raff. Now, not so long ago I sent one of my section to an agreed rendezvous to make payment for services rendered. The time and place selected was at the funeral of a burglar who had been killed breaking into someone's house. It seemed to me to be the very last place where there was any risk of my man being spotted, and recognised by British security agents or anyone else. But to his amazement, *he* saw and recognised an M.I.5 operative at the ceremony, a fat man named Sydenham, someone very well known to us at the embassy. You can imagine the panic stations!

'At first sight, it looked as if Sydenham was on to us, as if someone must have talked out of turn: and my man very wisely left the church at once and reported back to me. But I had to *know*. I just held on to the money, and sat back. Before I paid up I asked my contacts to make certain discreet inquiries, and it transpired that Mr Sydenham paid five thousand pounds, in cash, to the burglar's widow. Paid her, mark you, just to help her dry her tears, on a promise that she would make no fuss, and talk to no newspapers "after the trial".

'Interesting, was it not? Whose trial? Why was a senior British intelligence agent so interested in suppressing a possible newspaper report that he was able to hand out thousands of pounds to a burglar's widow?'

Colonel Zabotin raised his glass, as if he were toasting his own brilliance.

'You don't turn your back on a lucky break like that. I then persuaded my friends to follow Mr Sydenham as and when they could, to change from poacher to gamekeeper, so to speak. They certainly earned their money. We found that the burglar was shot trying to break into a house in a district called Saddlers Hill, look it's here,' and he pointed to the map.

'You needn't concern yourselves too much with that, it's of no importance now. But Sydenham paid many visits to the house after the attempted burglary, and so I had it broken into. You'll be interested to know that there wasn't so much as a matchstick on the floor, no furniture, no rug or carpet, not a scrap of paper in any drawer, nothing that could be traced to a source of supply so that we could find the buyer. Even the dustbins had been scoured and cleaned. There was nothing in that house but air.

'I got these people to make further inquiries: they could hardly go to the police, and they avoided neighbours, but they found local tradesmen, the vicar and one or two others who could help. They learned that a Mr and Mrs Stevens lived in the house, left the district the day after the shooting of the burglar, whereabouts unknown but with every outstanding bill settled by a very kind, very fat man. Sydenham, of course.'

Zabotin chuckled.

'He had personally supervised the cleaning of that house, and paid the bills. I wanted to know a little more about Mr and Mrs Stevens. Now then, here in Britain—unlike Russia—a man cannot be shot and killed, not even a criminal, without some action being taken by the local police, and there has to be a public record of their subsequent inquiry and prosecution, if any. We searched and found the answer, at least part of the answer, in the local newspaper that serves that particular district. Here it is.'

He took a newspaper from his briefcase and laid it out on the table. 'Look at that.'

Police reticence and neighbourly indifference notwithstanding, the editor of that little paper had still managed to demonstrate that he could not be gagged completely.

LOCAL MAN ON MANSLAUGHTER CHARGE, it said in a bold headline right across the front page. TO STAND TRIAL FOR KILLING BURGLAR, it proclaimed below. Beneath the headlines was a photograph of Number 28, a dead and lifeless picture that had won a place of honour on the same page as a further V sign to the uninformative police at Saddlers Hill.

'Don't bother to read below the photograph,' said the colonel, 'because you will learn even less than I can tell you. That is because the English operate a legal system that can prevent anything except bare details, such as names and charges, being reported from such a lowly court. It is a system supposed to protect the accused person from prejudice at his trial in a high court. In this case you can be sure it was enforced by the man Sydenham to protect his particular interests. You don't know the man's age, his occupation, or what he looks like. There is, however, one vital piece of information contained there and it concerns you two. It tells you that this man Stevens has been committed to stand trial at the Central Criminal Court, or the Old Bailey as it's known in this country, on Wednesday, May 11. It doesn't give you a lot of time to prepare for whatever may have to be done.'

Both men were watching the colonel intently now.

'I told you I've had Sydenham followed by my friends, and they've done well. They followed him from Saddlers Hill to a building in Whitehall, they picked him up again the same night and followed him again, this time to a house in Richmond. Richmond is *here*.

'That particular house is known to us at the embassy. It is a so-called "safe house" often used by the British intelligence services, for obvious purposes. My informants couldn't get inside but they could watch it, and they did. Sydenham has been seen going into, and coming out of, that house ever since. I believe he has the mysterious Mr and Mrs Stevens tucked up in there, safely hidden from sight until the time of the trial. The question we have to ask ourselves, is hidden from whom? From the newspapers? Possibly, but persistent though they are here in the west, it would hardly warrant the use of a "safe house" to keep them at bay.

'I think there has to be another explanation. And I think Sydenham has got them there, first, for total protection, and second, as a precaution against any further mistakes like shooting burglars and landing in trouble with the local police. And I mean *total* protection, which includes protection from people like us: people who might show more than curiosity if the real identity of Mr and Mrs Stevens should be revealed in some official way, such as their appearance in a court case.'

Zabotin held out his glass for Josef to refill.

'Let's add up the knowledge, and the guesswork, and see what can be made of it all. For some reason we don't yet know Mr Stevens found himself unprotected on the night of the burglary, and shot the man who broke in to his house. Although he was arrested, intelligence chief Sydenham intervened as soon as he heard about it, paid his bills, emptied his house of every piece of furniture and scrap of paper that could lead to his possible identification before the trial, rigged the lower court hearing so that there was no publicity at the time, got his man out on bail, and hid the pair of them in a "safe house" straight away. Whoever this man Stevens may really be, he has committed an offence for which he must answer under British law: and not even their secret service, with all its influence, can get him off without standing trial.

'Even if Stevens is as British as he sounds, and I stress "if", then protection under any circumstances for a specially favoured person would be given by the police themselves, not by one of the intelligence services, and that's something we must not ignore. This man, Stevens, is being looked after personally by our Mr Sydenham, an officer who holds higher rank than I myself do'—the colonel's eyes gleamed for a moment—'so I think it is safe to assume quite a number of things from that.

'Stevens is not what he appears to be, a simple householder up for trial. He is a V.I.P. of some sort. What's more, he's very likely a V.I.P. *foreigner*, and who springs to your mind to fit such a bill? A foreign potentate? Some rich foreign eccentric? I don't think so. But what about a defector? Now *that* would explain Sydenham's personal interest in his well-being, the secrecy before the trial, the bare boards and scoured dustbins in number 28. Above all, that would most certainly explain the urgent need for the use of a "safe house". And it was on that assumption that I contacted Moscow, and why you two were sent here to London.'

'But even if you are right,' said Andrei slowly, 'the word defector covers a very big area. Is there anything to suggest he might be one of ours? Or her?'

'Not a smell,' Zabotin admitted. 'Friend Sydenham has bolted tight every door on inquiry.'

'Have we got any idea what they look like?' Andrei persisted.

'Yes,' said Zabotin, 'but it doesn't help overmuch, take my word for it. You two were brought in as my insurance cover, nothing more, at this stage.'

He handed them a sketch pad. It contained a number of crude drawings, in coloured inks.

'I offered my friends cash for any likeness they could produce of the Stevens,' he told them. 'I told you the sort of person they had to speak to. Well, this is what they came up with.'

As far as anyone could judge. Stevens appeared to be a man of middle age, with dark hair, wide forehead, and firm jaw. His nose was a trifle long, no colour was offered as to his eyes: he could have been almost anyone. But even allowing for the inexperience of the artist, it was a face that hinted in some way at intelligence, and character. The woman seemed to be about half his age, and was fair haired. Otherwise there was nothing that left any real impression, except perhaps ordinariness.

'Not much to go on there,' Josef agreed. 'Bad drawings! If asked, I'd say they were European features rather than Slavonic. German, maybe.'

'You can do most things today with plastic surgery,' Zabotin pointed out. 'Don't let those drawings throw you: you wouldn't expect the British intelligence service to allow any defector to wander about unguarded unless he had been made unrecognisable, now, would you? Look, I had those faces copied and sent to Moscow in the bag. Not even the "Art Gallery" at Lubyanka could come up with more than wild guesses. That's all that any of us can do at this stage, guess and hope we're right.

'But it will be a very different matter when they go into court. You will see both of them there, in the flesh, over a period of some days, I hope. She will have to be called as a witness—wife, girl friend, sister, whoever she is—simply because she was in the house on the night of the shooting, and they'll need her evidence to get him off.

'Take your time over it. Have a long hard look at this interesting couple, and tell us what you think then.'

'I'll do that,' Josef promised him.

'There's one more point I have to mention,' said Zabotin, 'and it's a highly important one to my mind. This is Britain, not America. They don't allow the police here to carry guns in the normal way, never mind private citizens. Yet friend Stevens must have had a gun in that house to shoot the burglar, and it's obvious where it came from: Mr Sydenham, the man who paid his bills and emptied his dustbins, who else? The same man who is protecting them now. I tell you, Stevens has to be someone damned important.'

Andrei asked him: 'What do you want us to do with them?'

'There's no firm decision yet,' said Zabotin. 'First find out who they really are. You won't get any orders unless and until there is positive identification. If we don't know who they are, or if they're not ours, you just pack your bags and go home again. You're an insurance policy, like I said: nothing more. Now your first job will be to get into the Old Bailey on the day the trial begins, and you'll do that by queueing for places in the public gallery. That's perfectly normal behaviour in this strange country. If they turn out to be two of ours and on the wanted list, I want you there—on the spot.'

'Very well.'

'Don't attempt to take anything into court on the first day other than documents which I shall personally give you. Cameras are forbidden in every British courtroom, so don't try to smuggle in a Minox. Above all, no weapons. You will be searched if my hunch is right, and this Mr Sydenham has his way. Don't try any clever stuff, you hear me?'

'Of course, comrade-colonel.'

'I'll brief you on the Old Bailey security in a little while. Meantime, you have a week or so in hand. Familiarise yourselves with the side streets round the court, watch out for empty buildings, scaffolding, boarding, any hiding place overlooking the approach roads, in case you are ordered to set an ambush later. Don't make yourselves obvious, don't get into any trouble, and don't be seen together too early.'

'Understood.'

'Assume for a moment these two turn out to be who I think they are, and you need to make a hit. Security will be maximum, you can bank on that. Don't waste time with any ideas of an attack on the "safe house"—it's bound to be too heavily guarded.'

'Right.'

'Now, the roads from the house to the Old Bailey: I don't hold out much hope of a hit there, either. They are bound to be escorted at all times, and in any case, there is a wide choice of routes available. Your best chance has to lie in those final approach roads, but that's up to you, you're the experts.'

'We'll take a good look round, don't worry.'

'Let's look at the actual court security measures. First of all, the police on duty. I have exact figures on that. They keep an inspector, three sergeants, and twenty-three policemen on permanent duty in the court, and they are seasoned, reliable men. They know the building inside out, and they know everyone who works there. They're intelligent men who know exactly what they have to do to keep unwanted visitors away, and they won't stand on any ceremony. I don't know if they're armed or not: probably not, but my informants can't tell me if they have guns on call.

'As well as these regular police officers, there are a further eighty men on duty, known as attendants, but they're much more than that, they are all former police officers themselves trained in security measures, and they're placed inside the court-rooms, in all the public galleries, the corridors and so on: they form part of an overall security screen. The regular policemen are drawn from the City of London police, which is a quite separate force to Scotland Yard, but both organisations will supply as many extra men as may be needed if any special security risk is involved.

'I reckon that on the day Sydenham will have anything from one to two hundred men around, all with radio contact to one headquarters, and some with dogs. That's if Mr Stevens turns out to be the V.I.P. defector I believe him to be.'

Andrei looked extremely thoughtful.

'There is only one entry into the building from the street,' Zabotin went on, 'through a single revolving door. The first of the police guards are stationed immediately inside and opposite that door. No one gets past them without a check.'

'It sounds more like a Russian courtroom,' said Josef mischievously.

'The I.R.A. have already had one go at the Old Bailey,' Zabotin reminded him, 'and the City of London police don't take any chances now. I tell you, I've gone into this extremely thoroughly: it's not going to be easy. That's why I asked Moscow for help and why you two were selected. If Sydenham requests maximum security, that's precisely what he'll get and you will have to contend with. All the surrounding streets will be cordoned off. All cars will be banned from parking in the entire area. There will be snap searches of all passers-by. The police have got helicopters and might decide to use them. And they're certain to call in bomb disposal experts to search the place top to bottom every day.'

'Do they allow workmen inside, for heating repairs, or cleaning, anything like that?' Andrei asked him.

'No way,' said the colonel, tersely. 'A man known as The Keeper—they have old-fashioned titles, it's a historic place—is responsible for things like heating, lighting and cleaning of the court building. There are 114 men and women on his staff, they've all been screened, and every one is known to the police and to each other by sight and name. You wouldn't get your hand on a light switch, or a broom handle, without being arrested.'

'Are there any cells there?' Josef asked him. 'I dealt with a political prisoner once in Argentina, they had half the Army inside the court-room: but I walked into his cell dressed as a warder, and used a silencer. Simple job. They all assumed he was safe in a cell.'

'You won't get near an Old Bailey cell,' Zabotin promised him, 'unless you've been arrested first! I have made extensive inquiries into that possibility, believe me. Let me give you some facts and figures, my friend. They have seventy cells in all, situated about twenty-five feet below ground level. They came under the control of the governor of Brixton prison, not the Old Bailey authorities, and they are guarded by prison warders, like your Argentine ones and like the cells in any jail. As far as I can find out, a prisoner on a manslaughter charge, like this man Stevens, is what is called a "Category A" prisoner, which means that he has to be watched by two prison officers at all times.

'That's one point. Then again, no one spends the night in the Old Bailey cells, if that's what you were thinking of.

'Men on trial who are already in custody are brought in police vans from the Brixton and Holloway prisons each morning. They are taken down to the cells, led up a stairway leading into the courtroom to have their cases heard by a judge, and they are taken under escort back to the outside prisons each night. No one has ever escaped from an Old Bailey cell, by the way, that's a matter of record. Our position is complicated here because Mr Stevens—who has friends in high places—is on bail awaiting his trial. I asked our legal attache about this, and it's interesting. He says that if I am right, and the trial is heard in maximum security conditions, Stevens would be fed in those cells like all the other prisoners at lunchtime, but would be taken back to the "safe house" at night under escort. That means that unless you find some way to attack the convoy on its way in and out of the court each day, the closest you will get to Mr and Mrs Stevens will be in a seat in the public gallery.'

Andrei took him up at once.

'Can you tell us about the arrangements for feeding these prisoners?' he asked. 'Are they allowed to have meals sent in from outside by anyone?'

'Some are,' said the colonel. 'I have gone into that possibility in some detail, too. The position is this: anyone on trial but not yet found guilty can have food sent in by relatives or friends. It's the reverse of our own legal system here, everyone is innocent until proved guilty—can you imagine? But all the food has to be handed to prison officers inside the building for examination, and delivery to the prisoner. I shouldn't think it tastes all that good when it finally arrives. It gets poked, and prodded, sniffed *and* tasted before it goes into each cell.

'I'm telling you, they're experts these men! The criminals they have to guard are as cunning as monkeys. Even if you were allowed to buy food for Stevens, and I should think Sydenham might have something to say about that!, and put a bomb into his pie, it could not reach him undetected. That's out.'

'With great respect, comrade-colonel,' said Andrei, 'we are not thinking of bombs at this stage. Josef and I have to examine every way of piercing a complex security screen, and this is one of them. It presents a possibility, nothing more.'

Zabotin nodded. Of course, the man was right.

'There is a way,' he said, 'of reaching a prisoner *physically*. All prisoners are permitted to hold legal conferences in the cell, and they are privileged, in the sense that prison officers may not be present. I am told a relative may be allowed in on this basis. My criminal friends have even told me how a secret message can be passed between the relative, and the prisoner—by writing it on the cuff of his sleeve, for instance. I don't know if any of this helps you. But it's a way in.'

'If we could impersonate both lawyer and friend . . .' said Josef pensively, and looked at Andrei.

'Such men are sure to be known to the prison staff.'

'None the less it is a second way of piercing the screen. The evening has not been wasted.'

'Did you imagine it would be?' asked Zabotin coldly.

'Of course not, comrade-colonel. I merely meant that the background work which you have done for us has been exceedingly thorough,' said Andrei hastily.

The colonel left at midnight.

'Fancies himself, the colonel, doesn't he?'

'Careful, Josef. He carries a lot of weight at home. And I think he's talking sense, you know that? If these are two of ours and worth winning back, he's right to try for a peaceful contact first, and use us only as a last resort. A little friendly persuasion to bring folk back into the fold is always worth a try. If he fails, well, he's got us for stronger measures. This Zabotin is no bull in a china shop. He's smart.'

'I suppose you're right.' Josef yawned. 'Another drink?'

'Yes. Don't ruin it with water this time.'

'I'm thinking,' said Josef, 'about that Old Bailey building. Seems to me there's an awful lot of security there.'

'I agree with you, my friend.'

'I like the ambush idea myself. Little back streets. And an unarmed police force.'

'Let me give you some advice.' Andrei emptied his glass and looked at his companion. 'You haven't worked against the Brits before, have you? Well I have, in the Middle East, and you can forget all those ideas about them being a soft touch. They're hard bastards when they want to be, Josef, I *know*. They'd put us through the mincer as soon as look at us if they got suspicious of our intentions in those back streets. We're not protected by any diplomatic status like the Zabotin boy, we're not even transfer material like normal agents—we're expendable, you and me. I tell you the British are mean buggers and they'd give us a very hard time if we got caught. We'll do it like the colonel says and play it cool. It's not going to be easy to make a hit if we get such an order. Don't you ever think otherwise.'

'What's the matter: getting cold feet, Andrei?'

'Shut your mouth, little man. Don't ever say that to me. I'm careful, very, very careful. That's why I'm alive at the age of forty-two.'

Andrei walked across and poured himself another drink.

'You've got another ten years to go before you can say the same.'

5

THE APPLICATION

Until recently, sheer respect for the law was sufficient guarantee in Britain against any demonstration, or threat of violence, within the courts. A handful of bobbies at any Assize was enough to signal 'hands off' and no judge or jury would consider themselves in any danger as they went about their business of crime and punishment.

The I.R.A. changed all that when they bombed the Old Bailey, and revealed in one shocking day the vulnerability of the courts and all who work in them. Of the many measures introduced at the Old Bailey to tighten security, the most obvious shows in the vigilance of the police who stand guard behind a revolving door, next to the judges' entrance. These men know the system, the routine of the legal ants' nest that teems into life as each working day begins: they know counsel, clerks, messengers, library staff, cooks, cleaners, and resident press and will admit them all without an apparent second glance. But they have had first-hand experience, now, of what one moment's carelessness can cost, and no one prowls unchallenged through those long corridors where there is any shadow of doubt over identity.

Even allowing for this police zeal, the case of *Rex v. Stevens* brought unprecedented checks and precautions in its wake. Sydenham was a thorough man, and with the aid of the police, made doubly certain that nothing was overlooked by way of security this day. What he had to ensure was that no one, particularly in the press corps, connected Stevens' trial with the doubling of security measures, and he laid his plans with typical cunning. He had friends in the City police—the Force responsible for law and order within the square mile, including Old Bailey—and from

Snow Hill police station there emanated a report, unconfirmed but not denied, that a threat had been received on an unnamed judge's life. It was skilfully leaked to the right people, and by the morning of the trial the ancient building throbbed with rumour. Squads of extra police were on duty for all to see, and in their first editions the London *Evening News* and the *Evening Standard* carried bold headlines proclaiming a state of near siege around Newgate.

'POLICE CORDON OFF OLD BAILEY,' roared the *Standard*. 'Fears for judge's life.'

'THREAT TO JUDGE,' shouted the *News*. 'Police seal off the Bailey.'

Now, City policemen are all big men. Today, their helmets bobbed everywhere, in groups of three and four, below the steps of the Bailey, in front of 'The Magpie and Stump'—where seats were once sold at black market prices to witness the public executions—in ceaseless patrol down to St Paul's, and round to Ludgate Circus, as whole platoons of big men in blue hob-nobbed along Newgate Street and in High Holborn. From time to time these men spoke into pocket radio sets, calling up control in Snow Hill, they forbade any car to park within 800 yards of the court, they saluted plain clothed officers, and from time to time they questioned members of the public queueing for London's finest free show, a day in the public galleries of the Old Bailey. Sydenham had two of his own men posing as cameramen, with orders to photograph every man and woman in that queue: including, as it happened, Josef and Andrei, both of whom were also searched and who sent up private thanks for Colonel Zabotin's thoroughness in his eve-of-trial briefing. They stood well apart in the queue, and made no attempt to contact each other. Nor did they try to evade the photographers, for both were in London with a clean bill of health from the authorities.

Sydenham had also called on the Commissioner at New Scotland Yard for help, and it was generously given. Four squad cars patrolled the route to court taken by the Stevens, from Richmond over Kew Bridge into the City, maintaining radio and visual watch on their charges until they handed over to the City police at

Ludgate circus, a move that brought a miles-long traffic jam in its wake, and put most of London's citizenry in a snarling temper for the rest of the morning. Sydenham himself travelled with the Stevens. He and his driver were both armed. He personally selected the route over the last half-mile, a snap decision that took the convoy behind the back of the black Daily Express building, right by the Press Club in Shoe Lane, back into a line of traffic heading for Blackfriars bridge and then left, through Sea Coal Lane up to the very gates of the Central Criminal court yard. The two police forces promised him no delay, and were ruthless in blocking off traffic to let him through: John Stevens was down in the cells, his wife sipping coffee with a woman C.I.D. officer and Sydenham himself out on the streets again, inspecting his troops, within minutes of arrival.

The name Old Bailey has a majestic ring, like the chime of a bell. The Central Criminal Court sounds quite different, modern, more clinical, and to the new offender in some way perhaps more comforting, for it bears no instant reminder of rope, and hangman, or three weeks of eternity in some nearby condemned cell. But the names are the same: the building stands on the site of Newgate Gaol, and for the sensation seeker there is still the whiff of jail fever to be scented, a faint ghostly clank of chains to be heard, from its grey stones, and the public galleries are always packed as a result. Traffic on this morning of May 11 was exceptionally heavy. The newspaper stories drew shoals of casual sightseers. Blue police vans drove into the yard, bringing their wretched cargo of remand prisoners from Brixton and Holloway. The long line of people seeking admission to the galleries—the morbid and the curious, the sick who take their medicine from evidence in the sex trials, the idlers with a day to spare, relatives of the accused, chattering groups from grammar schools and their teachers—grew steadily, with umbrellas opening down the line as the rain splashed down in a grey cascade. Sydenham moved everywhere among them, fat and round-bellied, gleaming wet like an enormous toad, as he studied every face in the controlled confusion.

John Stevens had a distinguished covey of counsel to argue his fate. Sir Evelyn Hughes, Q.C., the Solicitor-General, led for the Crown with Mr Humphrey ('Nell') Gwynne, Treasury counsel barrister, as his junior. Another knight led the defence: Sir Gordon Rowe, Q.C., a household name among the public, dubbed 'Sir Gordon Quicksilver' long ago by the press, a lawyer who could charm a witness right on to the point of his blade and then leave him there, wriggling, for the jury to despise and discredit. His own junior was a barrister of bright promise, Mr Evan Reece, a young man already earning upwards of £15,000 a year.

Their presence presented a problem to Sydenham. They were there because of the importance of the case, yet ironically, by their eminence, made it certain that the press would swarm into their court like wasps at a jampot. He gambled on his attack-on-the-judge rumour to hold them off until counsel had won a ruling that the Stevens case would be heard *in camera*: then their hands would be tied. Meantime he busied himself with the work in hand and hoped for the best.

The two Q.C.'s were old adversaries, but personal friends in and out of court. They had discussed *Rex v. Stevens* informally, and each relied on the other to shoot straight in the duel about to take place. Sir Evelyn had been in conference with the Attorney-General, and was fully aware of the responsibility he bore. Sir Gordon had been dined by Sydenham, and also knew the course he must steer: his relief when he learned that his client was to appear before the Honourable Mr Justice Fisher had been profound. Now each of the lawyers knew what was required of him, and each was satisfied that justice could be done with honour to both sides. It mattered not at all in terms of prestige whether the accused be found not guilty, and allowed to walk out a free man, or guilty and given a suspended sentence, still to walk out free: they felt the nature of his offence was so finely balanced in law the jury could decide either way.

It was nearly ten o'clock, and they had missed each other in the robing room. Their title, Queen's Counsel, was originally given to a specially chosen few barristers as a mark of favour by the sovereign, in the sixteenth century, so they dressed as dandies, in a long silken gown with a flap collar to set them apart from their lesser brethren, who wore a shorter, stuff gown. It was this that earned them the name of 'Silks'. Now the two silks stood together in a corridor, away from the throng, talking animatedly. They wore silk gowns, black tail coats, and waistcoats with flaps to their pockets to announce themselves as Q.C's, but they were far from being court dandies.

Sir Gordon looked like some old turkey. His eyes were tiny, and bird-bright. His nose was like a beak, long and pointed: his thin cheeks were rosy red, inflamed by the unseasonal cold and rain, while a dewlap hung down from his chin, shaking and wobbling as he spoke. He stood in typical courtroom stance, hands on hips, elbows raised, so that his gown flared out behind him like a fan of dark shining feathers. A shabby wig lay forward on his brow, and his glasses were perched on the very end of his nose. He had long, skinny legs and his head bobbed up and down in a pecking motion as he complained to his colleague, in evident distress.

'Have you heard, Evelyn?' he screeched. 'Fisher's got the 'flu, damn and blast his soul, and we've drawn Morston Richards!'

'I know.' The Solicitor-General ignored the NO SMOKING sign and lit up. 'My clerk's just told me.' He was a head shorter than the defence counsel, and craned his neck to stare up. 'Of all the infernal luck!'

Sir Gordon bent closer. 'Did you see that small army of police outside? Did you, eh? Well, they're not there because any damned judge has been threatened, they're there to protect the life of my client. It's absolutely vital that your application shall succeed, I mean that, Evelyn. This is a matter of life and death.'

'I know,' said the Solicitor-General. 'I know just what you mean, my dear fellow. But we have to persuade Tyrannosaurus Rex now: my clerk says he's here and in a devil of a temper about something. I don't like the sound of it, Gordon.'

His own wig and gown had seen much service and were as shabby as his eminent colleague's.

'By God,' spluttered Gordon Rowe, 'if he throws it out ...' He thought for a moment and then asked, 'If he does turn it down, will you speak to the Lord Chief or shall I?'

No matter how opposing counsel may regard the advisability

of having a case heard *in camera*, under English law only the Crown—the prosecution—may make the application. Thus it now fell on Sir Evelyn to send a message to the judge's clerk, asking that they be granted audience in the judge's room. Such a request is a formality, and is always granted: but the ruling on the application may go either way. While no higher authority has power to reverse the decision of the trial judge, the Lord Chief Justice—if asked—may intervene. Even he can only request a reversal: he cannot order it. But he would be open to an approach from either side.

Only four people are present when such an application is made, the trial judge, his clerk and the two leading counsel. No notes are taken, and no record is kept. The atmosphere is somewhat less formal than in the court itself, where all will meet again to act on the application in a half-hour or so. Counsel address the judge simply as 'judge' and not 'my Lord' as they are obliged to do in court. The judge in his turn calls the Solicitor-General 'Mister Solicitor' and so on. While counsel appear in wig and gown, the judge remains bareheaded, demonstrating that the court is not yet in session. He hears out the Crown, asks defence counsel if he opposes the application for any reason, and gives his ruling right away.

'Let's see how it goes,' said the Solicitor-General cautiously. 'We may have no need to take it further.'

Sydenham approached them, wet as a seal.

'Good morning, Sydenham,' said defence counsel miserably. 'We've got bad news for you, my friend. Fisher can't take the case. He has influenza. And we have drawn Morston Richards in his stead. You've heard of him, I take it?'

Sydenham had been up all night. He had delivered his two charges safely to court. He was wet, and cold, and inexpressibly weary, and he had proposed to adjourn to Court number ten—the 'Magpie and Stump'—as soon as proceedings were under way inside a closed court. Now he stared at the lawyers, aghast.

'But surely—' he said. Sir Gordon cut him short.

'Morston Richards is a very different man to Fisher,' he told him. 'We have to accept that we may not have the application granted. If he says no, then it means trial in open court: in which case, I shall need urgent new instructions. You'd better put your thinking cap on while we're in there, with the judge.'

Sydenham's heart sank into his boots.

'Christ,' he said. 'I'd better speak to my director. How long have I got?'

'About half an hour,' Sir Gordon replied. 'Evelyn here will press as hard as he can. It might succeed, but I feel you should be prepared for the worst.'

'If we have to reveal Stevens' true identity,' said Sydenham deliberately, 'in open court, then he's as good as dead. I'm not exaggerating. Can't the judge understand that?'

Sir Gordon shrugged his shoulders.

'He might,' he conceded. 'But the man's an anachronism. He's got this thing about crimes of violence. And the thought of our client answering for his in such a way might appeal to his eye-for-an-eye philosophy. We'll soon know, one way or the other. You've got half an hour, at the most.'

It was 10.30. The two Q.C's left abruptly and made their way to the lift.

They knocked and entered the judge's room. It was sombre and spacious, panelled in redwood cedar, and dominated by a full length portrait of Sir Harry in the scarlet robes of office. The artist had caught him beautifully, a figure of vengeance: arms akimbo, resolution and harshness etched in every line of his face, with the single eye glaring down on a criminal world. It was a face without pity. And it was matched exactly by the old man who sat beneath it, waiting and watching as the two advocates were ushered into his presence by the clerk. Morston Richards had known they would come, and he knew why, and had given much thought to this audience. He sat behind his desk. His clerk was to his right, and the two counsel side by side directly in front of him. Two comfortable armchairs stood empty in the corners of the room: for this meeting the lawyers sat on wooden, hard-backed chairs.

Volume upon volume of legal tomes lined the bookshelves.

There were no flowers, such as some judges have in salute to Spring, even one as wet and cold as this. There were no ashtrays, for Sir Harry abhorred smoking. The green leather top of his desk was bare of documents, save for a few sheets of paper and a pen.

He murmured a civil greeting and painted a smile on his face as he waved the two men to their chairs. Sir Evelyn gazed at the judge, and thought he looked old and drawn, curiously frail without the wig. He knew his man, and proceeded very cautiously.

'Good of you to see us so promptly,' he said, 'since you cannot have had much warning that Sir Rodney had been taken ill.'

Morston Richards pooh-poohed the trifling inconvenience, and Sir Evelyn went straight into the attack.

'Now, judge, we thought we had better see you first, for we wish to talk to you privately about this case. I intend to apply to you to have it heard *in camera* as soon as the court sits, on grounds of high security. I don't want to say very much in open court for obvious reasons, but the facts are as follows.'

The judge's hands were thin and delicate as fine porcelain: his fingers began to stroke the table top as he listened to the application.

'The accused appears before the court as plain John Stevens, to all intents and purposes an ordinary English householder. In fact he is a Russian who defected to this country less than two years ago, and a scientist of such importance that ever since, he has walked in fear of assassination. I think it may be important to stress that he is not a traitor to his own country and one who came here for gain or treachery. He is married: his wife is here with him, and it was to save her from likely imprisonment that he himself agreed to come.

'She is a writer, a poet mainly, but also a writer of books. It was her books that brought her into confrontation with the Soviet authorities. Her first book was construed—perhaps rightly, I do not profess to know—as critical of the regime and she was given a blunt warning to refrain from such criticism. The book itself was withdrawn from counters inside Russia but a number of copies were smuggled out, translated, and given some publicity in the West. Her husband's eminence helped her to overcome the embarrassment and anger that followed: he was at the time President-elect of the Soviet Academy of Science, an enormously important figure who was known to, and trusted by, members of the Praesidium, and his sworn word that she could have known nothing of the act of smuggling was grudgingly accepted.

'It would seem that she was unrepentant as to its content, however, and she wrote a second book. Permission to publish was out of the question and when it fell into the hands of the Russian authorities she was arrested, interrogated and generally insulted. Her husband managed to get her set free but he was told that if she persisted in such works, she would be publicly disgraced and almost certainly jailed. Now, here was a loyal Russian citizen and a good communist—as well as a devoted husband—and apparently he pleaded with her to understand the actions and re-actions of the regime, and to submit to their wishes. We are talking about two intelligent, adult people, judge, and there is some conflict of evidence on what transpired as a result of that: anyway, what happened was that the manuscript of this unpublished book also found its way to the West, and this time it received considerable attention, wide notice and acclaim—particularly here in London—such publicity, in fact, that it could not be swept under some Russian carpet and ignored by the authorities.'

The judge interrupted him.

'Are you saying, Mister Solicitor, that she had in fact smuggled out the book unknown to her husband, or were there others involved?'

'I understand both may be true. She became involved with foreign intelligence agents and they arranged to have the work published abroad. It was certainly done without her husband's knowledge.'

'I see. Thank you.'

'The important thing was that this act of publication abroad, this open defiance of the regime, now forced everyone's hand. His wife was carted off for further questioning, and it took all her husband's influence, plus ministerial intervention, to get her released this time. She had had a frightening and unpleasant time of it and begged her husband to help her get away before she was sentenced, as she felt she must be, to labour camp or worse. After a great deal of heart-searching—for he was a patriot—he put love of his wife before love of his country and fell in with her wishes. Contact was made with British agents and a long term plan was hatched to get them over here. He was a scientist of international repute, as I said, and there was no doubt as to the value of his contributions to research in this country.

'On advice, the wife pretended to be properly penitent, and gave a solemn undertaking to write no more "subversive" books. She also agreed to put her name to a series of articles praising the actions of the regime, in Czechoslovakia and elsewhere. These appeared in newspapers and magazines, and were widely reviewed on Russian radio and television. And after a suitable trial period, she was allowed to accompany her husband again to certain conferences, in the way that one gives a bone to an obedient dog. This was the chance that the British intelligence men had waited and planned for. Husband and wife were spirited away and flown into hiding. The operation was regarded, I am told, as one of the greatest coups of modern times by any intelligence service.'

'I have no doubt it was,' said the judge, and made some notes.

'But even after these fugitives arrived here—unannounced, of course—they were both considered to be in very real danger of assassination: she for her treachery, he for the unique knowledge he possessed of Russian scientific advances. Indeed they still are, I can't stress that too highly, judge. They were given an intensive course in our language and customs, their appearance was changed, and they were kept in hiding for a very long time until their transition was judged complete. They had suffered considerable stress for long enough now, as you will appreciate: they pressed for a home of their own, a chance to live a normal life away from guards of any kind. A house was eventually found for them in a secluded area, known as Saddlers Hill, I have no doubt you know it, judge. Alas, they discovered there are serpents, even in Paradise. Before long that house was broken into and burgled by a man who dressed in a most frightening way. They surprised him in the act. They were utterly terrified—one must bear in mind their over-riding fear of assassination—and when they failed to get any response from a telephone especially set aside for their emergency use, the husband did what most of us would have done in like circumstances, he lost his head completely.'

'That I can well understand,' said Morston Richards, a little more warmly.

The Solicitor-General hesitated a little as he moved on to the thin ice below his application.

'Yes. Quite so, judge. Well, their emergency call had gone unanswered, and they firmly believed that they had an assassin within their walls. The husband ordered his wife to lock herself in the bedroom while he made his way downstairs to confront the intruder. Unfortunately, in his state of mind he assumed quite wrongly that he might be murdered at any moment and reacted accordingly. In the struggle, he shot and killed the burglar. He was arrested by the local police, and charged with manslaughter: the magistrates committed him to appear before you here today on trial.

'I intend to ask you that the trial may be held *in camera* judge, without giving any of that background detail to the court, on two counts: high security, and the man's own safety. As to the second count, I have already outlined the man's real fear of assassination should his compatriots discover his new identity and establish his whereabouts. But regard for the national security transcends even that, albeit that the two are completely and inextricably interwoven. The Russians have never learned where this man is. They have no notion of which country it is that harbours him. To tell them that, is to tell them also how far this country will have progressed in its research in the particular field on which this man was working. To disclose publicly that we are engaged at all on such research is not considered to be in the public interest at this stage. That is why I ask you, judge, to grant this application when I put it to you in the court below.'

One eye regarded the Solicitor-General.

'I see.' The judge's voice was non-committal. 'And do you oppose this application, Mister Rowe?'

'No, judge. I would expect it to be heard *in camera*, and such is my own desire.'

Morston Richards traced his fingers over the table-top and read through his notes.

'There are one or two questions I would like to ask of you before I give my ruling, Mister Solicitor.'

'I trust I have overlooked nothing pertinent, judge.'

'So do I,' said the old man drily. He lifted the black patch and rubbed at his dead eye.

'This state of mind of the accused, this morbid fear of assassination that led to the killing of the burglar—all this was a kind of slow-burning fuse, was it not, first set alight by the deliberate action of the British intelligence agents who smuggled that manuscript out of Russia and ensured its much-publicised appearance in the West?'

'It would seem likely, yes, judge.'

While the judge has the last word in such an application, the Solicitor-General has all the weight of the Crown behind him—he *is* the Crown—and may not be taken lightly: his view was that more than enough had been said to persuade any reasonable person of the desirability of granting what he asked, and his tone of voice was perhaps a trifle impatient.

'Yes,' said the judge, 'it seems very probable to me. And is it at the request of these same authorities that your application is now before me?'

'If the assumption is correct.'

'Very well, Mister Solicitor. We now come to a point that concerns me greatly. You have gone into great detail to illustrate the state of mind of the accused when he confronted that burglar. This I readily appreciate: he shot him, is that not right?'

'Yes, judge.'

'Did he grapple with this burglar, and disarm him? Is that how it happened, that the burglar was armed, and the accused took the gun from him and shot him with it in the struggle that followed?'

Sir Evelyn shifted uncomfortably in his chair. He would cheerfully have given his first day's retainer, a considerable sum, for a cigarette at that moment.

'Well no, judge. It was Stevens' own gun.'

'Ah. But the burglar was armed?'

'No. None the less I feel that would have counted for very little with any man in dire fear of assassination.'

'That may well be. Where did the gun come from?'

'It was given to the accused for his personal protection, because of the very real fear of assassination.'

'Yes. But by whom?'

'By the intelligence men responsible for his safety.'

Counsel may leave certain things unsaid in the hope of winning a point by default: but it is accepted that his word is his bond. He may not lie, nor would he, in answer to any question. Sir Evelyn looked at the judge and hoped that the next question might never come.

'This gun, this weapon handed to a man who walked in fear of his life and was prone to panic: it was properly assigned to the accused, and licensed with the appropriate authorities?'

The judge's voice lingered on the one word, *appropriate*.

'I have no instructions on that point, judge.'

A single eye fastened on the unhappy Solicitor-General, stayed for a moment, and then the judge nodded before passing on to his next question. To an outsider it might have seemed that counsel himself were in the dock.

'I see. The magistrates released this man on bail, did they not, after the remand hearing? Was he held in custody at any time after the shooting?'

'He was taken to the police station and detained in the cells. Shortly afterwards he appeared before a special court, and was then released on bail.'

'Bail was unopposed?'

'Unopposed, yes, judge.'

'And was the accused represented at that hearing?'

'Apparently not.'

'Had the intelligence authorities been advised of his arrest? Were any of them present at this first hearing?'

'I understand one such officer was in court, judge.'

'I see.'

The judge had the picture clear in his mind, now. Without knowing his name, he could visualise Sydenham at work, busy on the telephone in the early hours, pulling strings, careful to stay within the law but none the less controlling the course of events by subtle pressure and influence. He himself had seen the steam-roller at work in his years as advocate, and it never failed to anger him. Now he was 85 years old, a High Court judge: *his* word was law and his own position inviolate. There and then he made up his mind, and bestowed a bleak smile on the two counsel.

'Well now, gentlemen, the arguments in support of this application have been most ably put to me, and clearly it is made with the wholehearted support of defence as well as prosecution. The picture I have been given of life in communist Russia, where the state will tolerate no criticism and which at all times will act as a law unto itself, sounds horrifyingly real to my ears and indeed, it is borne out by the despatches which one reads every day in the free press. One can readily understand how any spirited man or woman, persons of honour and integrity, might be forced into treachery to strive for a place in freedom, here.'

Sir Evelyn was pleasantly surprised by those words, and brightened a little.

'However, as both of you are aware, I am deeply disturbed—every judge must be greatly concerned—by the growing incidence of violent crime in this country. Here we have a man accused of manslaughter, charged with shooting another to death, and whatever the circumstances surrounding that incident—which will not be argued or discussed here, but below, in my court—it is both right and inevitable that the person who fired that gun stand trial by jury. So he will be. This application is to have that trial heard in closed court, with the general public excluded, on two specific grounds, high security, and the safety of the accused. That is a matter for me to decide, and no other.

'In giving my ruling I have to consider many things. I can see at once the strength of an argument which says this was a hunted man, given a false identity and disguise because he walks in fear of his life: therefore, to have him reveal his true identity in open court would undo most, if not all, that has been done so far to protect his life. That is an argument which I shall weigh very carefully in my mind before giving a ruling. At the same time, the Crown has put forward a second argument, namely, that the security of this country may be endangered by any public admission that the accused is in Britain, and presumably working for Britain, on an unspecified secret project. He also says that it would not be in the public interest to have any reference made to this work at this time.

'The last argument is one which is bandied about very freely in government quarters these days, and often applied to almost any subject which ministers may not want to have revealed, for a variety of reasons. I am not entirely sure what the definition of the public interest may be in this instance. I can certainly see at once where selfish interests might be imperilled by such a disclosure: if, for instance, the British government—through this man's defection—had come into possession of secret information which it was unwilling to share with its partners in the NATO alliance, or its partners in the European community. Should that be the case, I can well see how any reference to the nature of this secret work could be a grave embarrassment to this country, and its rulers.

'On balance, I am inclined to think that may be the case, and therefore I cannot accept this particular argument. I am left, therefore, with the first two points made by you, Mister Solicitor, namely, high security, and the possible harm that the accused may suffer by having his case argued—and his identity made known—in open court. We need not concern ourselves if one is more important than the other, nor will I make any attempt so to do.

'Not that it matters overmuch insofar as this application is concerned. One could argue that they amount to the same thing in the end, since the assassination of the accused—should it come about—would have a vital bearing on state security, if his work is of the paramount importance it is claimed to be.

'As I see it, we must look at this application in its entirety.

There are certain matters arising from the application which I do not greatly like, and they arise not so much from what has been said as what has been left unsaid. I have already referred to the grim picture of life inside communist Russia, where blind servants of the regime lay down their own standards of behaviour, where the police state alone decides what is fit to print or proper to suppress, because no individual may challenge any act committed in the sacred name of the state.

'With that example in mind, and we have to bear it in mind because counsel has raised it, I feel we are entitled here to look at the role of our own intelligence services. Theirs is a difficult and dangerous task, but we must remember they do it of their own free will. Here are men and women whose names are unknown to the public and who cannot be called upon publicly, at least not in the normal run of things, to answer for any action they take in the name of the state. Recently there have been allegations, admittedly from doubtful sources, that these services have joined forces with criminals, and encouraged them to commit criminal acts in the interests of the state.

'True or false? We are not allowed to know. What are the interests of the state? We may not judge. They are what these men, and only these men, believe them to be in such circumstances. Consider the story of the accused, and go back to the beginning of all his troubles, the theft of his wife's manuscript that led to a split between him, and the state *he* served. Does anyone here seriously doubt that was the work of our own intelligence service? Of course they regard such actions as legitimate, and themselves as honourable men, and are all regarded by the man in the street as such. What they did here was to take a calculated gamble, and in this case, it paid off. But supposing it had not, supposing she had lost her family and her liberty in the process, who is to say the gamble was worthwhile in those circumstances? The probability is we would never have heard of it, for I do not doubt the details would have been suppressed by all concerned. You may be thinking, how does that concern this application? And I will answer you, in this way.

'We are examining here a request for a change in the normal

procedure of the law made on grounds that arise directly from that gamble. The hand of the intelligence services runs through this whole drama, like a thread in a quilt, and we cannot overlook it no matter if we approve or disapprove. I accept it is a service that acts always for what it believes to be a right and honourable cause. But, *they* smuggle these two from Russia, *they* hide them from the outside world for two long years, *they* put them into a private house after first arming the man, *they* surface again when he has shot someone dead, whereupon the magistrates grant bail at a hastily convened court with, one imagines, very few members of the public present. I have no doubt it can be argued that all of this was made neccessary by the wickedness of the Soviet regime. But I ask you, is our own behaviour here so very different to theirs, are these not two sets of similar, faceless people who think they can flout the law in the all-embracing interests of the state?

'And of course, this has a direct bearing on the application now before me, since it is their wish that the trial be held *in camera*. Is it really to protect the accused and nothing more, to safeguard the interests of the state and nothing more, or is it perhaps in part to hide from the public gaze some of their own blunders and mistakes and questionable methods?

'I read in the newspapers often enough that I am a very old man. That is true. I also like to think I am still a *useful* old man. I will tell you this much, I am an old-fashioned old man, and a very stubborn old man, who truly believes that the Common Law is what it pretends to be, and was meant to be, namely, the same law for us all, unprivileged as well as privileged. I will grant no favours in my court!'

His single eye shone defiantly.

'Counsel may argue in law as they see fit before me, and I shall always listen with undivided attention to such argument, and then advise the jury as I think right. Should I be seen to fail in that duty, if any decision of mine is found contrary to the spirit and letter of the law, why then, counsel have the right—and the duty—to appeal.

'But we are not debating any matter of law, in this room. We are considering an application for a man charged with a serious offence, one of the most serious in the calendar, with the public excluded from all but his arraignment and sentence, if any.

'I will have none of it.

'It was quite by chance that I was called upon to hear this application, following the illness of a brother judge. We do not know and need not concern ourselves with what his decision might have been. I have already said I reject the argument that to have it heard in open court is against the public interest, or the security of the state. As to the other argument, namely, the safety of the accused, I have given that full weight but my answer is that I reject that, too.

'Those responsible for his safety should in my opinion have seen to it that he was given protection from harm by people duly authorised by the law to carry arms. This is commonly done in all civilised countries where, alas, the threat of violence is known to exist.

'Had that been done, this man could not have been charged in this fashion, and no question of revealing his identity need have arisen. I am in effect being asked to close the stable door after the horse has already bolted.

'In my opinion it was wrong, irresponsible even, to hand a dangerous weapon to the accused, someone who had to be unaccustomed to the handling of firearms, and more than that, a person clearly liable to panic in an emergency, real or imagined. It was this decision as much as any act of his own that has landed him in court before me. Is it seriously argued by the Crown that whatever offence this man may commit, or be alleged to have committed, at any future date shall also and always be dealt with in closed court, in case an order should go out for his assassination?

'There are no special laws for such people: only one, the Common Law.

'If anonymity is his one sure shield against harm, then it was either an act of gross negligence, or another calculated gamble, that permitted him to live in a private house without adequate protection and safeguard. I am not going to be a party to any attempt to conceal that. Whatever the answer may be in law, violence has been done, and a man lies dead as a result. There is a charge to be answered, and my ruling is that it shall be answered in open court.

'Mister Solicitor, should you make such an application in the court, asking that this case be heard *in camera* on the grounds you have outlined here, then I must tell you it will be refused by me.

'I sincerely trust that what I have said in reply to the arguments put forward this morning will in no way be construed as a criticism of the application itself, which to my mind was properly made on the instructions given to counsel, and indeed, most ably put by him. I also wish it to be clearly understood that, in reaching my decision, I bore in mind that the application was supported by the defence. No doubt, as a result of my ruling, both you gentlemen may now feel it incumbent upon you to seek further instructions before taking your places in court.'

The judge gave them a wintry smile, and looked at his watch. Both counsel rose, and their faces were a sight to behold.

'It is almost eleven now, gentlemen. I will be in court at 11.15. I hope that gives you sufficient time to prepare yourselves. Thank you.'

Five minutes later, the telephone rang in his room, and Morston Richards spoke to the Lord Chief Justice. His reply to the request was succinct.

'It's my court,' he said stubbornly, 'and I'm making the legal decisions. I have already heard the application in great detail and refused to grant it. I regret that I have nothing more to add.'

He banged down the 'phone and beamed, with genuine delight.

Sydenham and Sir Gordon held a hurried conference as they waited for the judge to take his place.

'I still think,' said counsel earnestly, 'that we have an excellent case in law. We still intend to plead that there was no unlawful intent to kill, and that this was a misconceived case of self-defence. So much depends on the jury, of course. If they don't acquit, I wouldn't give much for his chances of leniency. Morston Richards is a man who bears a pathological hatred for anyone found guilty of violent crime. Now that the rope has been removed from his reach, I believe he sees it as a sacred duty to hand out as tough a deterrent as he can by way of severe sentence on every possible occasion. You and I have no way of proving that to be true: and a great many people in Britain seem to agree with him, if the newspapers these days are anything to go by. If our client is found guilty, Sydenham, his prospects of receiving a mild sentence from this judge—never mind a suspended sentence!—are nil. I must see that he gets acquitted, with no ifs or buts about it. I want him to be portrayed not merely as a man living under the shadow of assassination, but a man so broken by the stresses and strains to which he was subjected—you know what I'm talking about—that he went to pieces when he met that burglar and did what he did in the mistaken but wholly understandable belief that it was self-defence. To do that, I need to bring out *everything*. It will mean considerable embarrassment to you personally, and might appear to reflect discredit upon your department. Are you willing to have me do that?'

'All I care about,' said Sydenham, 'is that he walks out of here a free man.'

'Then this is the way to do it,' the Q.C. told him. 'I'll have to play Strip-Jack-Naked if you want him back.'

'He's pretty sick about standing trial at all,' Sydenham commented. 'He is already exhibiting grave doubts about the benefits of life in a free society. One more push, like a stretch in prison, and he would scream his head off to be allowed to go back to Russia. I'm not prepared to allow that to happen.'

'You've got to give me carte blanche,' said Sir Gordon. 'All the skeletons will have to be dragged out of your secret cupboards. I want that jury to end up blaming *you* for what happened, not John Stevens: are you game?'

'The Director isn't too enamoured at the prospect,' complained Sydenham, 'and Mrs Stevens might not like too many personal disclosures in an open court.'

'Tell them both from me,' said the Q.C., 'it's either an open court with no holds barred, or closed cell doors for a great many years to come. See what they say to that.'

'All right,' Sydenham told him. 'It's a deal. You get him off, and I'll see to it the Russians don't get him back.'

Sir Gordon corrected him.

'It's not a deal,' he said slowly. 'It's still a gamble, but with the dice loaded a little more our way. You've only got the K.G.B. to worry about. I've Morston Richards to fight!'

6

THE TRIAL: DAY ONE

Sir Gordon was prepared to be as chary in his acceptance of jurors as a bank manager considering an overdraft on a new account: there was an element of risk involved here, and his first duty was to exercise prudence. Jurors are called from a panel compiled from the electoral register, a kind of lucky dip, with the result that even the most carefully worded summing-up by a judge can bring a verdict that will leave the court speechless with amazement. No more than seven jurors may be challenged without cause—a process known as peremptory challenge: used with the skill born of experience, and a great deal of luck, it can sometimes help the defence considerably.

Persons exempt from jury service include peers of the realm, members of Parliament, clergymen, practising barristers and solicitors, registered medical practitioners and certain old lags, which still leave an enormously wide selection: by no means all of those available to serve suited Sir Gordon's book in these especial, current circumstances.

His client was a Russian and a devout communist, both of which points he intended to bring out early in the trial. Therefore he wanted no one who, on the face of things, seemed to fall into the upper middle class category, those who had about them the smell of boards of directors, big business or high executive status. He was also going to call Mrs Stevens, and pluck the heartstrings of the said jury, so he was inclined to have a small percentage of women jurors, and the more sensitive and impressionable they appeared, the better. He was also going to hammer home fear of the midnight intruder in these lawless times: so on balance he preferred the middle-aged and elderly to the young because the former would presumably have more to lose themselves, and therefore more to fear. If his decision to challenge had to be swift, and his selection based on rule of thumb rather than divine guidance, so be it: he was an old hand at this game, and his judgment of character both shrewd and sound.

'John Stevens,' called the clerk. All eyes went to the figure in the dock as the indictment was read aloud.

Sydenham personally had acted as his valet that morning, and turned him out with infinite care for his first day in court. Stevens was a big man, charged with a violent crime: he was taller than the prison officers at his side, but Sydenham had foreseen that and striven for clothes and bearing that would emphasise decency, cleanliness, and respectability. His long dark hair was carefully brushed, and it shone under the hanging lights, showing a hint of grey at the temples. His forehead was lofty and wide, quite smooth and unlined, and combined dutifully with his mane of hair to suggest dignity with strength of character, maturity with intelligence. He was slim enough, and held himself very straight—a brave stance that somehow sent out a silent message of uprightness and honesty dismayed to find itself in such a plight as this, on trial, in the dock, arraigned before judge and jury. His suit was clerical grey, his tie restrained, his shirt as white and pure as innocence itself. He looked a little nervous, which was understandable enough. His jaw was square, and clean-cut. His nose was large, but straight, and finely shaped: there were no pouches under his clear brown eyes, no crow's feet treading the corners, while his cheeks—like his noble forehead—were similarly smooth and unwrinkled. His ears were set close to his head.

It was a good, strong face, one that fitted a man of obvious position and responsibility. In every outward way he impressed as decent and respectable, everyone's picture of Mr Clean. It was difficult to put an exact age on such a man: forty, perhaps, not a day more, yet he carried himself with the assurance of a senior citizen, someone accustomed to wielding authority. Sir Gordon nodded approval as he watched his client. Morston Richards looked him over, too, and was not displeased with what he saw: somehow he had expected to find a different person to this tall, and imposing, figure.

The clerk finished reading the indictment, and asked: 'How say you, are you guilty, or not guilty?'

The law demands that the accused shall answer this question personally. In a clear voice, Stevens replied: 'Not Guilty.'

The clerk then called twelve jurors from those in waiting, and said to the man in the dock:

'Prisoner at the bar, the names you are about to hear called are the names of the jurors who are about to try you. If therefore you wish to object to them, or any of them, you must do so as they come to the Book to be sworn, and before they are sworn, and your objection will be heard.'

Sir Gordon scanned the faces that appeared, made his assessment on their character and possible outlook on life, put the calculations through his mental computer and made his decisions. He took as long as he dared, without upsetting the chosen twelve. In the end he had nine men, and three women, and the die was cast. Court and public gallery were only half-full at this stage: among the spectators were Andrei and Josef, and their eyes never left the man in the dock. One of Sydenham's lieutenants sat behind them, and alongside them, not knowing who they were. Down below the doors of the court opened noiselessly to admit the latecomers who had business there. The judge let it be known with a wave of his hand that the accused could be seated. Only then did Sir Evelyn begin his opening speech. It was brief and to the point. He told the jury about the house, the storm on the night of the shooting, in what circumstances the burglary was committed and when the shooting occurred, and how The Country Boy was found dead by the police on arrival at number 28.

'Members of the jury,' he continued, 'it is not denied what the accused said when those policemen reached the scene. They will tell you that one of them asked him "How did it happen?" and that he replied "He came at me, I thought he was going to kill me", and that shortly after that he admitted "Yes, that's my gun and I shot him with it".'

Sir Evelyn made a play of shuffling his papers and then, as he gazed at the jury, repeated the words, slowly.

'"I thought he was going to kill me. That is my gun. I shot him with it." Ladies and gentlemen, it was clear beyond peradventure that this man was going in fear of his life—for whatever reason—and that night he took the law into his own hands and deliberately shot another dead. Killed him by firing his gun—he admits that it was his own gun—several times, and at close range.'

He cleared his throat, and swung round to the court.

'I now call Police Sergeant Evans.'

'Sergeant Evans, tell the jury in your own words what happened after you had answered the 999 call and reached the house'—'Well sir, Mrs Stevens opened the door to us. She looked as if she had just got out of bed, standing there in her nightdress as it poured down with rain. I asked her what had happened, but she was too dazed to tell me. I judged her to be in shock and told my colleague to look after her while I went round the house. I saw the accused bent over on the sofa, with his head in his hands. There was a body on the floor, and the whole place reeked of gunpowder. I said to him "I'm a police officer, answering your wife's 999 call, do you want to tell me about it?" He didn't make any answer, he just stood up and handed me a gun.'

'Is this the same gun?'—'Yes, sir, that's it.'

Morston Richards called for the revolver, and looked at it long and hard before he ordered that it should be passed around among the jury. Then it was handed to a messenger and duly entered as an exhibit. Sir Evelyn waited until all was done, and turned back to the sergeant.

'Will you tell the court what happened next?'—'I examined the body on the floor. It had been shot a fair number of times, I could tell that, and there was blood all over the carpet. The dead man was dressed in an odd way, all in black. There was a torch beside him, and an open holdall, stuffed with silver and suchlike. I kept asking the accused to tell me what had happened, but he seemed not to hear me properly. Finally he said "He came at me. I thought he was going to kill me." I asked him why but he wouldn't answer. So I put it to him "Is this your own gun?" and he said it was. I said "Did you shoot him with it?" and he answered "Yes." While we were talking the Superintendent arrived with the Murder Squad, so I handed over, sir.'

Sir Gordon rose to cross-examine.

'Sergeant, you told the jury that the dead man was dressed all in black. It was a bit more than that, was it not: did he not look quite terrifying?'—'He wore a black jacket and trousers, black gloves and boots, and he had a black silk stocking drawn over his face.'

'Think of the effect a man dressed like that would have on a man in fear of his life, breaking into his house in the dead of night—would it not be utterly terrifying?'—'Well, sir, put like that I suppose it would.'

'At any rate, did it not have that effect on the defendant?'—'I don't know, sir.'

'Really! Have you not told the court that he seemed dazed, that he was unable to answer questions clearly, a man in a state of shock?'—'Yes, but—'

'He made no attempt to hide the gun, in fact the very first thing he did was to hand it to you?'—'Yes.'

'And then admitted it was his, and told you he had fired it?'—'Yes.'

'In fact he was utterly co-operative, within the bounds of shock?'—'Yes, I suppose he was.'

'Too shocked, too dazed to think about anything really except the need to assist the police?'—'Well, yes, in one way.'

'Was he or wasn't he, Sergeant Evans?'—'He was.'

'During your evidence you said you had asked him if the intruder had any weapon on him. Think about that torch you found, was it not a foot long?'—'Yes.'

'If a terrifying unknown man dressed from head to foot in unrelieved black came at you in the middle of the night holding something like that in one hand, might you not be forgiven for thinking it could be a weapon of some kind, a cosh or an iron bar perhaps, rather than a torch?'—'Yes, I suppose you might.'

'Depending how terrified you were?'—'Yes.'

'I ask you once more, did you not form the opinion that this man was dazed from shock and fright?'—'Yes.'

'Thank you, sergeant, you can step down now.'

The pathologist was a Dr Arthur Fawson. He gave his evidence in a dry, unemotional tone. When he rose to cross-examine, Sir Gordon pursued the same line of inquiry.

'Doctor Fawson, you have examined the victims of many shootings?'—'Oh yes.'

'With such a gun as was used here, at such close range: in the hands of an expert, or even a competent man, one shot would have been quite enough?'—'Indeed it would, at that range.'

'But here you had four shots, or was it five?'—'Four.'

'All hitting a vital part of the body?'—'In the sense that it was enough to disable him, yes.'

'At a range that even a poor shot would necessarily strike the target?'—'Yes.'

'Did you consider this to be wild shooting, such as a man overwhelmed by fear might attempt?'—'Absolutely.'

'Thank you, Dr Fawson, I have nothing more to ask you.'

After the lunch adjournment, Sir Evelyn called his final witness, Detective Superintendent Edward Wilson, the man who had charged Stevens with manslaughter. He was asked a great many questions about his arrival at the house, and then the Solicitor-General turned to the dead man.

'I think you recognised him right away?'—'Yes, sir. A man called Antony Williams. I first charged him many years ago, when I was detective-sergeant.'

'He was an old customer?'—'He was.'

'Did he have a nickname in the Force?'—'Yes, sir. We knew him as The Country Boy. He had a record as long as my arm, and at one time specialised in breaking into country houses, mansions, I mean.'

'A cat burglar?'—'Yes.'

'One who always dressed in this peculiar fashion?'—'That's

how I recognised him, even before I lifted the stocking mask.'

'Do you know why he dressed like that?'—'It was a kind of working dress. He was a simple character and believed that if he couldn't be recognised, he couldn't be charged.'

The superintendent joined in the general laughter that followed his remark.

'Was he mentally backward, is that what you mean?'—'He had no mental history. But he was retarded, in my opinion.'

'Modus operandi, that plays a big part in routine police investigation?'—'It does with every Force, sir.'

'And this retarded man, The Country Boy, what was his modus operandi?'—'He always chose the big, lonely mansions at first. Even when he came down in the scale, so to speak, he always liked the houses with a biggish garden, and always chose that way to make his approach and getaway. It was like a trade mark. And, as I said, he always dressed top to toe in black. He was a joke in the Force.'

'A joke, superintendent? It's been suggested in this court that he was a terrifying person?'—'I certainly wouldn't have regarded him as terrifying.'

'Not even dressed like that?'—'You'd normally be lucky to see him. He always ran at the first sign of trouble.'

'I see. Did he have any record of violence?'—'None at all.'

'Never attacked anyone in the course of a burglary?'—'Never, so far as I know.'

'And never resisted arrest?'—'Not once.'

'Never carried an offensive weapon of any kind?'—'Never, as far as I am aware.'

'What did you say when you had examined his body?'—'I asked the accused to tell me how it happened, but he made no reply.'

'Did you question Mrs Stevens?'—'Yes, but with the same result. She seemed completely shocked. We made them both a cup of tea in the house before taking them to the station. I ordered the accused to be taken to an interrogation room, and sent Mrs Stevens off with a policewoman until she calmed down.'

'Would he say anything to you in the station?'—'Not a word.'

'And Mrs Stevens, what about her?'—'She kept asking if she could make a telephone call. I said "You mean, to a solicitor?" and she said "No, to a friend who can tell you all about us." I asked her to write the number down, and dialled it. There was no reply.'

'At what time was this?'—'Half past four, quarter to five in the morning.'

'What did you do then?'—'After consulting other officers, I decided to charge the man Stevens with manslaughter. I cautioned him first, and then charged him. That was at about five o'clock. He made no answer, and was taken back to the cells, pending further investigation.'

'Did Mrs Stevens eventually succeed in making that telephone call, and speak to someone?'—'Yes.'

'Superintendent, I don't intend to ask you any questions about that telephone call at this stage. Did the accused appear before the magistrates that same morning?'—'Yes, sir. He was remanded to appear again within fourteen days for a full lower court hearing.'

'He was granted bail?'—'He was.'

'Was that unusual in the circumstances?'—'No, sir. I was satisfied that he was otherwise known to be a man of good character and so the application was not opposed.'

The judge spared the superintendent no more than a quizzical glance, and wrote steadily on the pad that lay open before him.

Sir Gordon watched him carefully. Then he said he had no questions, and the superintendent stood down.

That was the case for the Crown: simplicity itself. It stood four-square on the evidence of its expert witnesses, it included identification of the gun and the man who fired it, it had established that the dead man was a non-violent person who from his record lasting more than thirty years had never been known to carry weapons or use violence of any kind, and it showed beyond any doubt that Stevens had fired the gun to kill the intruder.

'Members of the jury, the case for the prosecution rests.'

Sir Evelyn had done all that was required of him in law, and no more. He made no mention of his application to have the case heard *in camera*, he had studiously avoided all mention of the background that he had previously given the judge, and he had said nothing in court to excite more than a paragraph at most in any national newspaper. Up in the public gallery, those spectators who remained shuffled their feet in boredom. Andrei had long since gone. Josef stayed on, keeping his eyes on the man called Stevens, but was unable to place him. Mrs Stevens had not appeared in court, nor was Sydenham anywhere to be seen.

Sir Gordon rose to his feet, looking pointedly at the court-room clock. It showed that the time was now twenty minutes to four, and he knew that, at eighty-five, Morston Richards was quick to tire these days.

'My Lord,' he said, drawing his gown about him, 'although it is our intention to call but a few witnesses for the defence, their evidence may take some considerable time to be heard. In view of the hour, I do not know if your Lordship proposes to adjourn?'

'Thank you, Sir Gordon,' said the judge, taking his cue. 'I feel this may well be a convenient moment to break off. Court is adjourned until 10.30 tomorrow morning.'

As he strode out everyone rose, and the usher began to shout: 'All persons who have anything further to do before my Lords the Queen's Justices ... and give their attendance here again tomorrow at 10.30 in the forenoon. God save the Queen, and my Lords the Queen's Justices.'

The court emptied of people as swiftly as water flowing out of a bowl. Briefs were re-tied in pink ribbon and dropped into leather despatch cases, the two Q.C.'s nodded gloomily to each other, a bewildered John Stevens was whisked down to the cells below the dock, the reporters filed out, and Josef left the gallery between a group of High School girls and Sydenham's men. As soon as the court was clear, the bomb disposal experts brought in by Sydenham checked the benches for anything suspicious left behind among the debris of the day.

'All clear, sir.'

'Right. See you tomorrow, first thing.'

* * *

The Honourable Mr Justice Morston Richards was photographed by waiting cameramen as he walked out of the court: he always walked home, and smiled at the photographers, knowing their pictures would show him against a background of newspaper placards which read 'THREAT TO KILL OLD BAILEY JUDGE.' He bought copies of the evening papers, and saw that the scare story had been relegated to their inside pages: but he realised it had to be brought to life again for the newspapers next morning. Sydenham assembled his convoy for new routes back to Richmond. Josef met Andrei in a café at Holborn where they admitted to each other that they were unable to identify the man called Stevens as anyone else. Inside the Russian embassy Colonel Zabotin studied the newspaper reports for the umpteenth time and sighed, wondering if he might not have been wrong after all. There was a ring of truth about that bomb scare and yet: the security precautions were so very convenient.

He decided to order Josef and Andrei to keep watch again next day—as an insurance policy, he reminded himself.

7

THE TRIAL: DAY TWO MORNING

Sir Gordon made no opening speech for the defence.

'I call John Stevens,' he said in a loud voice, and leaned forward to watch with his hands on his hips, and his gown flaring out behind, as his client walked from the dock to take his new place in the witness stand.

Security men seemed to outnumber staff and spectators today. They lined the court, they sat in the gallery, they lurked in every corridor, while two more with field glasses kept watch from behind the windows of 'The Magpie and Stump', a task greatly envied by their colleagues. Sydenham was reacting sharply to the continued exposure of John Stevens to public view, and possible danger. This morning he had ordered two separate convoys, and two different routes to court for his charges: half of London still groaned under the effect of unending traffic jams, and Mrs Stevens herself had only just reached the Old Bailey, twenty minutes behind schedule. Sydenham was edgy, he smelled trouble though none was apparent and until the hearing resumed he had moved restlessly among the grey wigs and black gowns, nervous as a game bird awaiting the opening shots of the season. Josef was back in the gallery. He was under a precautionary surveillance because Sydenham's men had recognised him from photographs of the gallery queue taken on the previous day: although not under direct suspicion, his movements at court would be closely watched from now until the trial ended.

Something of Sydenham's own tension had been passed on to John Stevens earlier on. He had been stubbornly difficult in the car that morning over the question of oath taking.

'I shall refuse to take that ridiculous oath,' he said, when Sydenham began to brief him for the day. 'Everything about me is a lie, starting with my English name. Anyway I do not believe in your stupid Christian religion. I regard the Bible as nothing more than a story book for ignorant children.'

The British agent sighed, for he had troubles enough.

'You may well be right,' he said patiently, 'but the important thing for you to remember is, not to upset the jury. They're used to dealing with non-Christians in our courts, don't worry. All they want is a promise to tell the truth in answer to counsel's questions.'

Stevens laughed angrily at that, and Sydenham sought quickly for some remark to lighten the gloom.

'Be thankful you're not a Chinese,' he told him. 'If you think swearing on a Bible ridiculous, listen to this. At the Bailey a Chinese is given a saucer and has to throw it down and break it, while an interpreter says to him "You shall tell the truth, the whole truth and nothing but the truth—and if you do *not* tell the truth, your body will be cracked, like this saucer." Don't concern yourself with trifles. Judges don't always imagine that the taking of an oath automatically means they have to believe everything they hear: it's a kind of sedative for the jury, that's all.'

Stevens flared up at that.

'I should never have been made to appear in court like a common criminal! You should have stepped in and used your powers at the beginning: the police should be pleased by the elimination of a burglar.'

Sydenham was quick to warn counsel that his man was exhibiting signs of nerves, and now Sir Gordon eyed his client carefully as he took the oath of affirmation rather than swear on the Bible.

'I, John Stevens'—he took a long time over saying the name—'do solemnly, sincerely and truly declare and affirm ... that the evidence I shall give shall be the truth, the whole truth, and nothing but the truth.'

It was a poor start. Stevens looked about him warily, as if he had suddenly woken up in a strange room. His eyes dwelt first on the judge and weighed the gaunt face, the good eye and the black patch, and the rat-trap mouth, but found no comfort there. He looked at the strange robes, picking out every detail. Morston Richards wore a black tippet, or scarf, over his scarlet robe, firmly secured under a broad black sash. A broad tapering band of scarlet ran from his right shoulder across to the left side of his body: he wondered what it could mean. It is known as the 'gun case' but there were few in court that day who could have told him why, so obscure is its origin (it lays over the stole, some say, to denote that a judge is of temporal dignity only). And since this was the Easter sitting, the judge's robe carried slate coloured silk trimmings, rather than the ermine that denotes Michaelmas and Hilary, or autumn and winter, sittings. The Black Cap, the square of black cloth that used to be placed on the judge's wig as he passed sentence of death, lay to one side, with his gloves. His short 'working' wig had no side curls, only a vertical curl at the back and two short ones, like tiny pigtails, hanging down behind. He wore a starched and snowy wing-collar with two plain bands dangling in front—a relic of the days when this style of dress passed from the Church into the legal profession. Stevens thought it all part of a weird mumbo-jumbo, but none the less he was impressed: he recognised that he was looking at the product of history, a symbolic garb that had emerged over the centuries.

He realised with a start that his counsel was addressing him.

'Your name is John Stevens, and you live at Saddlers Hill, is that right?'—'No!'

His reply was clear, and deliberate. The jury sat up with a start, and the courtroom fell quite silent. Sir Gordon smiled.

'Then I will re-phrase the question. What is your name?'—'Alexandrei Petrovitch Geria.'

The jury looked suitably baffled. Up in the public gallery, Josef's face brightened with sudden recognition, as if he had found the missing section of a jigsaw puzzle.

There was a murmur of surprise from the court, instantly quelled by the usher. Morston Richards gazed on the witness and nodded his head, as if satisfied by some inner thought. Sir Gordon himself was in no hurry. He watched the reporters scribble away, he gazed round at the jury, he looked back at his client, and sorted through his papers for a long time, before he resumed.

'I want the jury to be in no confusion. Your real name is Alexandrei Petrovitch Geria—I hope I have that right—but you appear before this court charged with manslaughter under another name, that of John Stevens?'—'Yes. That is right.'

'There is no case of mistaken identity, you are one and the same person?'—'Yes.'

'Will you please tell the court, tell my Lord and the members of the jury, how that came about? Just a simple explanation at this time will suffice.'—'Certainly. I am a Russian citizen, and I was born in the Soviet Union. I lived there most of my life and under my own name. Some time ago, however, I decided to approach the British authorities, and asked for asylum in this country. As soon as it was granted, I took this assumed name and have been known since as John Stevens.'

All eyes were on the tall figure in the witness box, and once again, Sydenham had seen to it they were not disappointed in what they saw. Gone, now, was the hesitation and reluctance to speak that had been evident when he first took the oath. The expression of caution, of wariness, had given way to one of determination and new confidence.

The witness grasped the handrail in front of him and stood upright.

The change in him was quite perceptible. He looked much more assured, someone bent only on telling the truth. Today he was dressed in blue, dark blue suit, the palest of blue shirts, a sober tie: a man who bespoke dignity and calm. As always, he positively shone with cleanliness. And now, to match the careful valeting, his whole bearing seemed to be one of relief at being allowed, at last, to appear in his true colours.

As the realisation of what his name meant sunk in round the court, so the first murmurs of surprise grew into a roar. A handful of reporters hurried from the press benches to telephone the shock news to their agencies and newspapers. Up in the gallery, Josef was by no means alone in craning forward to study every detail of the witness's appearance.

'Silence! Silence in court!'

The usher's voice rang through the room, and the babble died down. Morston Richards looked about him, and spoke to the men and women in the public gallery.

His face was like a scroll of parchment, lined and wrinkled, jaundiced by age. His good eye gleamed with anger, while the black patch alongside showed up against the ivory yellow of his skin like a blob of tar on old stonework. He waited for silence, and made it clear from his expression he was not prepared to wait overlong. When he finally spoke, his voice was stern, and carried with it all the ageless authority of the bench.

'Unless the public remains properly behaved,' he said, 'I shall have the courtroom cleared. No noise or demonstration of any kind will be tolerated here. There will be no further warning.'

Sir Gordon turned once more to the witness.

'Now,' he said, 'you have told us your real name and your nationality. I put it to you that you are the same person, the same Alexandrei Geria—holder of the Lenin Prize, and an internationally acclaimed scientist—whose disappearance from a conference room two years ago gave rise to an international storm?'

The man in the witness box gave a little bow, one of pride.

'Yes,' he said. 'I am that same man.'

The Q.C. let the jury have a good long look at him before he resumed his questioning.

'In fact you have been in this country all the time?'—'Yes.'

'In hiding?'—'Yes.'

'Using the name of John Stevens for security reasons?'—'Yes.'

'But never able to adopt it legally, since that would entail publicity and defeat the whole purpose of the change?'—'That is so.'

'And until recently, living under this assumed name at the address which appears on the charge sheet?'—'Yes.'

'The knowledge that you had been charged under this name lay behind your reluctance to take an oath—any oath—which bound you from the outset to tell the truth, the whole truth, and nothing but the truth about yourself to this court?'—'That is absolutely right, I felt I was taking part in a lie from the very beginning.'

'I am sure that my Lord and all members of the jury will understand that.'—'Thank you.'

Sir Gordon hitched his gown about his shoulders and swung round to face the judge.

'My Lord,' he said, 'we find ourselves in a unique and difficult situation here, and seek your Lordship's understanding in the examination of our client. What this man has said is not in dispute. It is the very cornerstone of our case that by his defection, by the circumstances surrounding his arrival in Britain, his life has been in real and constant danger from the moment that he changed sides.

'It was the intention of the Crown, fully supported by the defence, as your Lordship is aware, to make application to have this trial heard in closed court, for reasons which some may think have now become obvious. That no longer applies, but inevitably the defence is bound in examination to have to touch upon certain matters which, it can be argued, might best be left unsaid in open court. I put it to your Lordship that in such a situation, I have to conduct my case almost as a man in chains, certainly under formidable restraint, and with that in mind I seek the court's indulgence should I seem on occasion to lead rather than to follow.'

'The charge against the accused,' Morston Richards reminded him drily, 'is that he is alleged to have committed an act of manslaughter, under whatever name, and it remains the firm view of this court that any such charge should be heard in open court, so that justice can manifestly be seen to be done. Are you saying, Sir Gordon, that because the charge is to be so heard, that your client's expectation of obtaining justice is in any way lessened?'

'Indeed, no, my Lord,' said counsel hastily. 'Merely that there are certain facts in this case which in my view, and also, it would seem, in the view of the Crown, should not be made public, and that in consequence, my client should have the right to be guided as to what, or what not, he may refer to in his defence.'

'You will put such questions to your client as you see fit,' the judge told him. 'And so, no doubt, will the learned Solicitor-General. I will rule on what should, or should not, be said in this court, if and when I am asked. But neither of you will be permitted to lead the witness.'

Sir Gordon was well pleased. He had paved the way for the course he had plotted earlier with Sydenham.

'As your Lordship pleases,' he said with a bow. 'But I fear I may have to tread on very thin ice, none the less, on matters of security.'

'Your skills as counsel are widely acclaimed at the Bar,' the judge replied. 'And I have no doubt you will successfully overcome the danger of falling in. You may proceed.'

'Very good, m'Lud.'

He turned to the witness, who had understood none of the byplay.

'You have heard his Lordship. You must put out of your mind any attempt to withhold any of those facts which you may have had reason to think were better left unsaid. I am going to start by dealing with this question of your identity, and the work on which you were engaged. You will answer my questions fully and frankly, but at the same time, you will try to confine yourself to answering the questions *and no more*: do you understand?'

The witness nodded his head. As far as he could see, the lawyer was now contradicting the briefing he had earlier been given by Sydenham, and he could not think why.

'Yes. I think so.'

'How old are you and where were you born?'—'I am forty-one years old, and was born in a village near Brest-Litovsk.'

'Tell the court about your early family life.'—'My father was a farm worker and my mother helped him when she could. There were five children, and I was the youngest. Our village was over-run early in the fighting of World War II, and my parents, my brothers and my sister, were all killed.'

'What happened to you?'—'My uncle worked on the railway.

He and a group of his fellow workers rescued many families, and the orphaned children, and we were taken eventually to Moscow. I don't remember a great deal about any of it, except the overcrowding and the hunger.'

'Of course. Time is a great healer. How old were you when the war ended?'—'I was eleven, nearly twelve.'

'And even at that age, a very remarkable scholar?'—'I don't know how to answer that. The war years were very difficult, and standards at all schools suffered from the shortage of teachers. But I did very well in the circumstances, yes.'

'I just wanted to establish your background. You spent the whole of those formative years in one state school or another?'—'Yes. Also in camps, away from the fighting zone.'

'I will pass over the intervening years, for they need not concern us now. But is it true that you became the youngest student ever to enrol at university in the history of communist Russia?'—'That is quite true. I entered MV Lomonosov at the age of fifteen. The Rector admitted me personally and congratulated me. It was the greatest day of my life, or so I thought at the time.'

'I'm not sure my Lord and the jury can follow that. Did you say MV Lomonosov? What and where is that?'—'Forgive me, it is more widely known to you as Moscow university. The name comes from Mikhail Vladimir Lomonosov, founder of the Russian Academy of Science.'

'Precisely. A university devoted almost entirely to science and scientific research, a truly enormous centre, a kind of battery-production line for scientists?'—'I can't agree with your last remark. It is certainly the biggest university in the communist world. There are more than 2,500 teachers and 20,000 students: but to call it a battery-line unit is to denigrate a very great seat of learning.'

'I apologise, it was not my intention: what is one taught there?'—'The vast majority are science students attending faculties or branches of physics, chemistry, geology, that sort of thing.'

'You spent a long time there?'—'Seven years.'

'And is it not a matter of official record that no student,

before or since, has won higher honours in any Russian university?'—'I am told that is so.'

'Will you outline for us a résumé of your career from the time you left?'—'I went first to the research centre at Novosibirsk. We were working on the application of nuclear power to industry, engine propulsion, mainly.'

Sir Gordon was quick to steer him away from the joys of engine propulsion.

'After four years there—four quite outstanding years—you were awarded a large sum of money by the authorities for an invention that brought you considerable fame and prestige?'—'With two other colleagues I helped build an atom-powered, low-cost marine engine which is still in production for the Soviet navy. For my part in the invention I was awarded 200,000 roubles, about £18,000 in your money at the then rate of exchange.'

'Who made that huge payment to you?'—'The State Committee for Inventions and Innovation. Of course, such an award is worth more than mere money. As a result, I was encouraged to write several papers, which in turn brought my name and my work to the notice of far more eminent scientists, at the Academy. In that sense it brought me prestige: not prestige, you understand, in the sense of national fame. The personality cult was discouraged.'

'Yes. I believe you were still only twenty-six years of age?'—'I was twenty-five.'

'A young Russian with a star-bright future?'—'Scientifically speaking, yes.'

'What happened then?'—'I was transferred to another atomic research centre, at a place called Dubno. The Americans christened it "Atomgrad", surely you must know of it?'

'None of us are too technically minded, I'm afraid. What kind of research centre is it?'—'It houses the Joint Nuclear Research Institute, which is the world's foremost pioneer centre in all atomic research. It is the scientist's dream. We had a 50 thousand million electron volt protonsynchroton at Dubno, a plant that laymen would call an "atom smasher". There was nothing like it anywhere else in the world at that time, and it is still unrivalled except by America. It was a whole city in the middle of nowhere, a great complex of concrete towers and bright steel domes and vast laboratories: a place where Man could truly begin to explore the unknown.'

The witness was relaxed and confident now, and the jury spellbound. But enough was enough, and Sir Gordon sought to lead him away from the undoubted glories of Russian Dubno.

'I am sure it is all you claim, a wondrous place. It also proved a vehicle for advancing your career still further, did it not?'—'Yes. There was new scientific thinking in the air, and work was begun on a completely new project: research into a new form of energy, something so revolutionary that once harnessed would make nuclear energy seem as out-dated as the steam engine.'

'And you were playing a leading role in all this?'—'My principals considered that I had helped to make certain significant advances, and I was rewarded with another grant of 200,000 roubles by the state committee.'

'Were you not promoted also?'—'I was honoured. Following the award, I was invited to become a member of the Academy of Science, and I moved to Moscow again.'

'Professor—I shall address you as that from now on, because that is what you are, a learned professor—am I right in saying that such an invitation is the highest honour that can befall any scientist in Russia, this invitation to become a Member of the Academy?'—'Absolutely! There are only 200 or so full members in all.'

'And such membership would automatically bring you into contact with the rulers of your country?'—'That is true. Foreigners do not appreciate the very close liaison that exists between leading politicians and scientists in Russia. The Academy is perhaps the third most influential body in the whole of Soviet Russia, below the Praesidium and the Council of Ministers. A full Academician is a very high ranking person.'

'As a loyal Russian citizen, and good communist, you were very conscious of this honour?'—'Oh yes.'

'I am informed that prior to your defection you had been

chosen as President-elect of the Academy?'—'That is so.'

'The highest of high honours was within your grasp?'—'Yes.'

'You had also been awarded the Lenin Prize on top of those two huge cash awards?'—'Yes.'

'I shall come back to this later. Now let us turn to your domestic circumstances. You were married by this time?'—'I had been married for some years.'

'With one child, a son?'—'Yes.'

'The child is with you here in Britain?'—'No.'

'Where is he?'—'I don't know, for sure.'

The witness spoke very quietly now, and his anguish was very marked.

'You do not know if he is dead or alive, even?'—'Every moment of our waking lives my wife and I think of our son, and hope that he is alive and well. But we have no means of knowing.'

'And no way of finding out?'—'None. We may not say who we are or where we are. We are not able to make contact with our families or our old friends. People here have tried to get news for us, but with no result. Not so far.'

'This is part of the terrible price you are having to pay for your act of defection?'—'Yes, part of it, the worst and most cruel part. No words of mine can describe our agony of mind.'

He was very close to tears. His head hung down, and he bit his lip to keep them back as the questions continued. His answers came automatically, and the figures about him in the court seemed to become blurred: in his mind he travelled back to Russia, to the time and place where he met the woman he would marry, and whose talents and intrigue were to bring about his own downfall and exile....

It was the morning of November 7, the anniversary of the Revolution, and all Moscow was agog with pride and excitement and patriotic fervour as the long parade of troops and hardware, civilians and slogans, trundled or marched through Red Square. Red banners of gigantic size tugged and flapped in a wind that came from the steppes, rumpling the pictures of the leaders they bore into grotesque shapes. Occasionally showers of light snow huffed and puffed over the parade, forewarning of the long winter to come. Not that the spectators minded the cold: this was the greatest show on earth, for all of them. Monster lorries rolled past, hauling rockets, inter-continental ballistic missiles as big as whole trees in the timeless forests of the Virgin Lands. They heard the rumble of half-tracks and tanks, and the stomp of goose-stepping military boots. It was a display of might and power without equal in the world, and every Communist heart rejoiced, loud Red voices shouted in salute, like the Romans of old welcoming Caesar home from the wars.

The young star from Dubno, Alexandrei Petrovitch Geria, sat in an honoured place close to the Mausoleum among a select group of fellow stars, young intellectuals and officers who would be the new leaders of Russia within a decade or so, men and women drawn from every walk of life that mattered if the Soviet dream was to become reality. There were scientists like himself, astronauts, men of letters and medicine, up-and-coming regional Party organisers, young Communists, writers, soldiers, sailors and airmen from the military academies, architects, technicians, physicists and engineers, all incredibly young, all passionate and dedicated believers who held the future of Mother Russia in their heads and their hands.

Geria had brought a magnificent fur coat and cap for the visit to Moscow this year, as befitted the place of honour he was to occupy at the parade: he pulled the ear-flaps down, rammed his hands deep into his pockets, stamped his feet and hummed each tune in time with the music from the loudspeakers, proud as any peacock as the picture of national might and progress unfolded before his eyes.

'Is there much more of this, do you know?'

Geria turned in surprise to the speaker. She was huddled in furs, as he was, and she was very young. Her eyes were watering from the cold, and her nose was as red as a cherry. There was something in her tone that mocked the great parade and reduced it without a word of comment to the circus ring.

'What's the matter?' he asked the girl. 'Aren't you proud to be here on a day like this?'

'It's not that, comrade,' she retorted, and laughed at him. 'It's just that I'm dying to go to the lavatory! If this doesn't end very soon, I shall have to disgrace the memory of Lenin.'

Geria was shocked. He looked about them, but no one seemed to have heard.

'Shhh,' he admonished her. 'Please don't talk like that.'

'Well it's true, just the same,' she said, still laughing. 'I can't help it, I want to go. Sorry if the idea offends you.'

She was not pretty. A stray wisp of hair told him she was dark, like a Georgian: her eyes—running, watery eyes—were indigo, her cheeks red and chapped with cold, her lips full and sensual. It was the nose that made her plain. It was short, wide at the nostrils, quite flat, and it was raw from wind and sleet. She looked very tiny, he thought, as she fidgeted from among her furs.

'You didn't offend *me*, it's just that there are a lot of people here who might expect you to show a little more respect at a time like this. After all, it's November 7.'

She giggled.

'Even good communists have to go when nature calls. There's nothing disrespectful in that.'

He found himself smiling with her.

'Well, it won't be too long now, they're nearing the end. Here come the pen-pushers.'

Columns of poets and writers marched by, out of step, shivering with the cold, each group identified by a banner naming one of the republics, but all bearing the identical message.

'CITIZEN WORKERS IN LITERATURE AND THE ARTS ALWAYS SERVE THE TRUE IDEOLOGY! DOWN WITH BOURGEOIS REACTIVISM! SERVE THE NATION BY TELLING THE TRUTH!'

Geria watched the girl rise to her feet, cheering and clapping.

'That's what I am,' she said. 'A writer. Don't you sneer at us as pen-pushers, my friend, we are the people who can really show this country the way ahead. That's the true Russia there, marching along right in front of your nose, don't you ever forget that.'

'I was wondering what you did,' he answered. 'You look so young.' And he added quickly, 'No offence meant by that, either. I was just curious about you.'

The marchers had passed their stand, and it was her turn now to examine him. The fur cap was crammed down low on his head, brown muffs hid his ears, the collar was pulled up around his neck: he looks like a great big mole, she thought, and laughed to herself at the idea. His eyes were the nicest part about him, nut-brown, clear, the standard-bearers of good health. His nose was big, but not really ugly, almost a Roman nose: where on earth did he get that from? He turned his head for a moment, and she saw his chin. It receded, weakening the profile, spoiling an otherwise strong face. She measured his height, over six feet tall: he dwarfed her. Now that he had unbent a little, she liked him, approved of his shy and gentle manner.

'What about you?' she asked him. 'What do you do?'

'I'm a scientist,' he answered proudly. 'I'm here from Dubno.'

'Oho,' she said, suitably impressed. 'I've often wondered what it's like. It's the Science City, that's what they call it, isn't it?'

'It's a frontier town in a way,' he told her. 'But I don't mean that in a backward sense: more like living on the frontier of knowledge, you know what I mean? Everything is new. Everything is so big. Enormous workshops and laboratories, all reaching for the sky, manned by scientists peering into the unknown. I don't know how to explain it to you properly. I can't do it justice in words, that's for writers, like yourself. But it's how I like to think of Russia today, young and fearless and challenging somehow.'

It was the longest speech he had made since arriving in Moscow, and he marvelled at the way in which she had brought him out. The girl gazed at him with shining eyes.

'You make it sound dramatic and mysterious,' she said. 'But also, a bit like a damned great factory, if you don't mind my saying so. What do people do at nights? Don't you have theatres, and the ballet? None of the marvellous restaurants we have here, like the Baku and the Aragvi and the Uzbekistan? Don't you have places where you can eat and drink and be romantic, as well as laboratories looking up at the stars?'

'I expect so,' he answered slowly, 'not that I ever go out very much. I usually eat at the Science Institute, the food's quite good there: well, not to compare with Moscow, naturally, but good enough for a hungry man. I'm afraid I've never been to the ballet, not once, in all my life. I expect you writers would think that a pretty boring life, eh?'

'How long have you got in Moscow?' she asked him suddenly.

'Another week,' he said. 'I have to present myself at the Academy tomorrow to discuss a new project. Nothing that would interest you, scientific stuff, but the talks will last a few days, they warned me. I'll be here till next Monday or Tuesday at least.'

'Good,' she replied. 'In that case I can show you the inside of a theatre, I'll pull strings to get you tickets for the Bolshoi, what about that? In turn you can buy me a nice dinner or two. I'll pick the eating places. It will make a change from the Science Institute, I can promise you that.'

'Thank you very much,' he said awkwardly. 'I'd like that.'

Neither of them had eyes for the Red parade now.

'Are you from Georgia?' he asked.

'No. What made you think that?'

'I don't really know. Your hair, your colouring, maybe. One of my friends comes from the Kura valley. He's very dark, like you. I just wondered.'

'Not me! Moscow born and bred. I can't help it if I look like a gypsy.'

'I didn't mean that. Truly, I didn't.'

The celebrations had ended, the parade dismissed, and they had not even known. The huge army of war widows in their baggy shapeless suits had taken its place in Red Square and had begun to sweep it clean. Grey clouds scudded over the Kremlin towers, waiting with fresh supplies of snow and sleet. Geria and the girl walked slowly to Okhotny Ryad into Sverdlov square, and stopped outside the Metropole hotel.

'This is where I'm staying,' he told her. He was desperately anxious that she should not go. 'They've taken the whole floor for the science delegates. Of course, you live in Moscow, you don't need any hotel room.'

'Not in the city any more,' she said. 'At Peredelkino, and that's a long journey, fifteen miles. I'd like to come into your hotel if I may and use one very important facility, if you don't mind.'

'I'd completely forgotten why you first spoke to me,' he said, and laughed with her. 'Of course, come in, please do. We can eat one of those meals afterwards, too, if you like.'

'I do like. Very much.'

He hesitated for just one moment more.

'Do you know, we don't even know each other's names? I'm Alexandrei.'

'Katerina.'

He gazed on her tousled hair, the darkest of blue eyes, and full red lips and could not believe he had dared to think her plain. She was beautiful!

He discovered he was in love, for the very first time in his life, later that night as they danced to the old-style band in the hotel, their bodies warm and close, and both of them unaware of the crowd that milled around them.

Alexandrei Geria suddenly became aware that a man in a black gown and grey wig was speaking to him in a loud voice. With a tremendous effort, he left the Metropole in Moscow and came back to reality, and the witness box of the Old Bailey courtroom in London. He was surprised to find that an usher was handing him a glass of water.

'Are you feeling quite well?'—'Yes. I'm all right, thank you.'

'I will leave that distressing subject for the moment: let us return to the period immediately preceding your defection?'—'Very well.'

'I want to ask you something about where you were living and the work you were doing at that time. You had moved to Moscow, I think?'—'Well, I was travelling between Dubno and Moscow a great deal. We had an apartment in Moscow as well as the dacha at Peredelkino. There was also a small flat at my disposal in Dubno.'

'By now you were married, and President-elect of the Academy of Science?'—'Yes.'

'Rewards for your work on a special project?'—'That is so.'

'Can you tell the jury in layman's language what kind of project it was?'—'We were attempting to harness a new form of energy. I actually headed a team of thirty or more research workers.'

'This was secret work?'—'Very much so.'

'I don't intend to probe too deeply into the subject, and I doubt if his Lordship would allow it, in any case. But may we know something about it, in the most general terms?'—'Well, I—'

Before Geria could answer, the Solicitor-General jumped to his feet, and Sir Gordon gave way.

'My Lord,' said Sir Evelyn, 'my instructions are quite clear on this matter. I submit most earnestly that to disclose any details of the work the defendant was engaged on at that time, or to make any reference to it now, would not be in the public interest. I therefore ask your Lordship to rule that a simple description, of "top secret work", will suffice.'

The judge shook his head.

'As I understand the question, the defence sought nothing more than a vague and non-scientific description of the work that the accused was doing—for a foreign Power—more than two years ago. I regret that I cannot uphold any objection to that.'

'With respect, m'Lud, my instructions are that no reference in any form whatever as to the nature of his research is either desirable or in the public interest: further, in our view, such matters cannot possibly be relevant to the charge before us.'

Morston Richards bridled at that.

'The defence has subjected this court,' he said icily, 'to a long and hitherto uninterrupted account of the defendant's early life in Russia. At times the jury might have wondered what *that* had to do with the charge that lies before us. Should there be any doubt, I will attempt to remove it. Surely it was given to underline his value to the Russians, and thereby the danger in which he has been placed by changing sides? Whether the jury accepts it or not, is not for me to say: but how can they attempt to weigh the danger, or its possible effect on the behaviour of the accused, if they are now to be forbidden to hear anything at all, even a vague and unscientific account, of the work that he did?'

The Solicitor-General stood his ground.

'As your Lordship is aware,' he replied stubbornly, 'it was not our wish to have this case heard in open court. Before today the Russians did not know where this man could be found. Therefore they had no means of assessing what he might, or might not, have given to the country which offered him asylum. With great respect, m'Lud, I submit that any discussion of his work, past or present, is neither in this country's interests nor that of the public at large.'

Little patches of purple began to show in the judge's cheeks.

'I regret, Sir Evelyn,' he said, 'that whatever your instructions may be, and whatever views may be held on my decision to hear this case in open court, this court will abide by such rulings as I may choose to give. I now order that the last question be repeated to the witness, and an answer be given to the jury. Please proceed, Sir Gordon.'

Sir Gordon was delighted at his eminent colleague's discomfiture.

'You have heard his Lordship. Will you please tell the jury in general terms something about this work that you did for so long, and for such high rewards?'—'Very well. We were trying to isolate and harness an entirely new form of energy, something far, far in advance of nuclear power.'

'Can you be a little more specific?'—'It's not easy, with laymen. We refer to it simply as "scattering matrix".'

'I'm afraid none of us is any the wiser for that, professor. Bear with me. What was it you sought, in layman's terms?'—'Basically I suppose you could describe it as growth energy: the secret of nature's own production line, the unknown process that turns an acorn into a tree one hundred feet tall, a tiny egg into a 500-pound turtle, a crawling infant into an adult capable of running a mile in four minutes. The amount of energy produced—and consumed—by every living creature and plant in its lifetime is colossal. We know it is fed by an intake of food and drink, protein and vitamin, sunlight and chlorophyll: but as yet no one on earth can say how, and why. I was trying to identify and control that process of energy production.'

Sir Gordon looked baffled.

'Forgive me for saying so, but that doesn't sound very secret or lethal?'—'I have been compelled to describe it in the most elementary terms. Once you find the secret of the scattering matrix you would have it in your power to control the prolongation of human life—better still, specially selected human lives—to produce an abundance of super-crops in climatically suitable parts of the world, and so on.'

'I see. You could abolish famine?'—'That nation that first discovers this secret might do that. On the other hand it might choose to act selfishly, within its own frontiers.'

'You sought the secret of eternal life, did you not, the elixir that has always eluded mankind?'—'Yes, we did. Man already knows how to transplant the heart and other vital organs. And once the scientist is able to control the rate of growth—and conversely, decay—then he has the full secret of the elixir. It would be entirely possible to keep a political leader, or a mathematical genius, or brilliant soldier alive as long as one wished. This would be wholly admirable if such knowledge was shared. But the nation to find the secret would without question use it entirely selfishly.'

'Could anything else be done with this knowledge?'—'Yes, and this is the crux of the whole matter. Energy means power. To harness the scattering matrix would be to tap the source of *unlimited* power. Thus, it would be a simple process to produce a bomb, a bomb many thousands of times more powerful than the hydrogen bomb, a bomb just as powerful as the inventor wishes to make it.'

'The first nation to achieve this breakthrough would automatically become master of the world?'—'If such knowledge was wrongly used.'

'Able to bomb any other nation it chose out of existence?'—'Easily.'

'Yet at the same time, be capable of sustaining life in its chosen leaders for as long as it wished?'—'Oh yes.'

'It would be dependent on no outside source of supply for grain or rice or foodstuffs of any kind?'—'Completely independent.'

'All powerful?'—'Exactly.'

'You were the head of such a research project?'—'I was.'

'Had you made significant advances?'—'I don't know if I should answer that.'

'I'll put it to you another way: your former masters believed you knew more about it than anyone else?'—'In the Eastern bloc, yes, certainly.'

'How much did the team know, and how much was your knowledge alone?'—'No single assistant was allowed to work with me in Dubno for more than a limited period. And none of them were allowed to work together elsewhere, at least, not prior to my defection. I alone kept the master notes. It would take a very long time, perhaps several years, for anyone to pick up the thread where I left off, and start a new project.'

'Did that mean you were within an ace of becoming the most potentially significant man in the world of science?'—'It would be quite presumptuous to think that. We had no knowledge of how far any other nation, or foreign scientist, might have progressed in the same field. We believed we were ahead. But even we were still in the field of pure research.'

'None the less, your defection would count as an enormous blow to the Russians?'—'I imagine it would. A disastrous setback.'

'Because of your unique overall knowledge?'—'Yes.'

'You were the one man they could not afford to lose, and you believed they would do anything to prevent your knowledge from falling into the wrong hands?'—'I still do.'

'Precisely! Hence your overwhelming fear of assassination?'—'Yes.'

'A fear that was always with you, day and night?'—'Very much so.'

Teams of reporters were moving swiftly in and out of the court room, relieving each other in half-hour breaks so that every word of Geria's evidence could be filed to their newspaper offices, and from them, all round the world. Already in Britain, the contents bills were announcing their most sensational wares for many a day.

RUNAWAY RED ON TRIAL—ASSASSINATION FEARS
RED DEFECTOR SHOT BURGLAR/Feared it was assassin
OLD BAILEY SENSATION: RUNAWAY RED REVEALS ALL
FAMOUS DEFECTOR IN OLD BAILEY DRAMA

Now Sir Gordon kept on at his man relentlessly. He had this real fear of assassination firmly planted in the mind of the jury and he harped on it, like a wife making the most of her husband's infidelity.

'Who in the Russian hierarchy would have known the true importance of your research work?'—'Only a limited number.'

'Come now, those at the very top would have to know about matters of such high state security?'—'Well of course, this was our most secret project. The First Secretary of the Party knew, naturally. The chairman of the Council of Ministers—I imagine—would have to know, he is the equivalent of the British Prime Minister. Then the chairman of the Committee for State Security would be told something. Likewise the head of the K.G.B.'

'Exactly: and all men in a position to order your death if they so wished?'—'Undoubtedly.'

'By the act of defection you became Public Enemy Number One?'—'Something like that.'

'And as a result, you have had to look over your shoulder every moment since your arrival here in Britain, have you not?'—'That is an understatement. I began to regard each new day as a bonus.'

'And what effect did this begin to have on you?'—'There were times when I thought I would go out of my mind. I don't know if I am a greater coward than most other men. But the realisation that at any moment of any day or night I was a target for murder unnerved me completely.'

Up in the public gallery, Josef decided to sit it out until the lunch adjournment and seek positive instructions. He accepted that from this moment on security would be redoubled, and the task of striking at Geria—if that was the order—would become harder and harder to carry out.

'On top of all this there was the nagging doubt about your child's well being?'—'Yes, I think we talked about him every single day since we came over.'

'How did this affect relations between your wife and yourself?' —'We began to quarrel.'

'You blamed her for your misfortunes?'—'Yes, I'm ashamed to say I did.'

'Both for the loss of your child, and this constant fear of assassination?'—'Yes.'

'The two of you were in a special place, and under guard day and night, all this time?'—'Yes.'

'A nightmare time for both of you?'—'Unbelievable.'

'Quarrelling and fighting between yourselves?'—'Yes, yes, yes!'

'There is no need to be ashamed of your distress, Professor. I think most of us would have given way under such a strain. But I have to ask you to tell the court about this difficult period because we are trying to show your state of mind in the months leading up to the manslaughter charge, you understand?'—'I suppose so.'

'What was the outcome of this bickering?'—'I became impotent. I still am.'

'I didn't mean that. It led you to make some request to those who were guarding you?'—'Ah. Yes. I begged them to let us move into a private house, on our own, away from the guards—anywhere out of the goldfish bowl.'

'And was that request granted?'—'After a long time, and after many conditions were laid down.'

'By the authorities?'—'Mostly.'

'I won't ask what they were, they are no concern of this court. There were a number of conditions laid down by you?'—'Well, I asked for a gun of my own.'

'A loaded revolver, at your disposal in the house at all times?'—'That's right.'

'But you had never fired a gun in your life?'—'I was given basic lessons.'

'Weren't you afraid of guns?'—'I was a lot more frightened of assassination.'

'Where did you keep it'—'At first I used to carry it around in my pocket. After a while, we put it in the bedroom, in the drawer at my bedside.'

'You were ready to fire at shadows?'—'Not quite. But I was terribly apprehensive.'

'Did your guardians not suggest you should keep a dog?'—'Yes, many times. But my wife is absolutely terrified of dogs, we've never had one.'

Morston Richards interrupted the questioning at this point.

'There are one or two questions I wish to put to the witness,' he said ominously, 'on this matter of guns.' One eye regarded the professor.

'Are you telling the court that those men whose responsibility it was to safeguard you and your wife tried to dissuade you from having a gun?'

'Yes, my Lord. They said it would be safer if we had a dog.'

'But you had your way in this matter? On this desperate and dangerous decision?'

'You see, my Lord, I wanted above all else to save our marriage, and it seemed to me we had to begin again in a place of our own. But a house is no good to dead people, and I was convinced that one day they would come to kill us if they could: there was no question of my wife agreeing to a fierce dog, but equally, it was my duty to look after her, and I thought a gun was the answer. For our personal protection. In the end I said unless we were given a house of our own, and a weapon for personal protection—at very least—I would never work for this country.'

The judge seemed satisfied with the rambling answer, and put another question.

'Who gave you this weapon?'

'One of the men who looked after us.'

'Obviously, but which one?'

Geria looked at him, across to counsel, and back to the bench, and finally said: 'I ... I'm not sure, there were so many people ...'

'Very well,' said Morston Richards, and turned to counsel.

'Sir Gordon, the court will require to hear sworn evidence from the person who handed this gun to the accused, the circumstances in which it was handed over, and to see the licensed firearms certificate if such a document exists.'

'As your Lordship pleases.'

The Q.C. bowed, and quickly turned to catch Sydenham's eye. He signalled defeat to the fat man by the slightest shrug of the shoulders, and shuffled his papers prior to questioning his client once more.

Like the judge, like millions of people everywhere, Geria had a peculiar detestation of firearms. In his own case, the loathing dated back to the day when the skies were loud with the roar of dive-bombers, and hordes of German troops stormed in below their protective umbrella to raze his village and murder his family. He hated the sight of blood, he was appalled by the thought of armed violence, and it passed his comprehension that the authorities should fail to grasp the sacrifice to principle he had made in demanding a gun to protect his wife—all the family he now had. Why was the judge, that hideous old man on the bench given the ridiculous bourgeois title of 'Lord', so anxious to pinpoint responsibility for possession of the gun? The worms of doubt began to crawl in his mind, vague suspicions began to form, his own fearful reluctance to defect for whatever reason began to reassert itself: he began to realise, only too clearly, that he was as much a prisoner of the democratic system as he had ever been in communist Russia.

He shut his mind off from the court, and turned back through the years, recalling vividly the sense of peace and security that marriage to Katerina had given him in their early years together....

It was one August, and they were on holiday at the dacha,

strolling hand-in-hand through woods that were silent and green and drowsy with the wild-flower scents of high summer. He carried a rucksack on his back and hummed a tune of pure content as they walked along, close to the lake. From time to time he stole a glance at his bride: she was tanned, and full of life, brimming over with happiness, as slim and graceful as the fawns that ran ahead, startled by the closeness of the humans who had intruded into their silent world. Suddenly, Alexandrei and Katerina came to the water's edge. It was deep and clear, curtained off from all other eyes by a ring of fir trees that climbed straight and tall into the cloudless sky.

There was no wind: the surface of the lake shimmered and sparkled in the sun like hammered brass. Dragonflies hovered over the reeds: kingfishers darted low over the water, seeking food, beckoning the two humans to come on in. It was still, and warm, and the prospect inviting. Alexandrei threw off his rucksack, and lay back against a grassy mound. Katerina touched his eyelids shut with her fingertips, and knelt down to kiss him on the lips. Moscow was a million miles away.

'Alex.'

'Mmmmmm?'

'Let's go for a swim.'

'I'd love to. But I didn't bring the costumes.'

'Fiddlesticks, there's no one to see us but the birds, and the deer! Come on.'

She undressed quickly, and ran down to the lake. Her skin was very brown, and her whole body seemed to ripple as she darted, naked, from the shadow of the trees into bright sunlight. He watched her as she stood there, with her hands raised above her head, and thought how beautiful she was. She dived in and vanished beneath the clear green water, showing only a trail of bubbles as her sturdy legs thrashed, taking her down, deeper and deeper. Alexandrei flung off his own clothes and ran after her, calling her name.

'Hey, Katerina! Katerina, wait for me!'

They swam for no more than five minutes. The water was still bitterly cold, as if the ice had melted only three hours rather than three months, earlier. They came racing back into the shallows and climbed out, gasping with shock, laughing with the sheer joy of being alive on a beautiful day.

Alexandrei handed her his thick shirt.

'Here, dry yourself with this. I can hang it out on the branches while we have lunch.'

She took it and stood there, rubbing her body deliberately, smiling at him from dark blue eyes, teasing him. He picked up his pants and began to dry his own body. He looked at her and grinned.

'Shameless hussy! Get some clothes on.'

The blue eyes mocked him.

'Katerina, get yourself dressed. What if someone should come along?'

She poked her tongue out at him.

'Nothing for you to eat, husband, until you show me that you love me.'

Shamelessly, she lay down on the grass and held out her arms. He knelt down and kissed her. Her arms went round his body, and she drew him to her, kissing him back, darting her tongue between his lips, stroking his cold back with caressing fingers.

'Quickly,' she said, and her voice became hoarse. 'Alex, quickly, quickly, oh Alex, I love you so.'

He slipped his great hands under her buttocks and crushed her to him, murmuring her name over and over again. She cried out in joy as he entered her and arched her back in ecstasy as they made love.

That was the moment that their son, Mikhail, was conceived.

Both of them wanted a child and the boy's birth brought a period of great happiness to their marriage: but it was not to last. Mikhail was only one year old when the first summons came from the ministry in Moscow ordering Geria to report at once for 'urgent consultation'.

He had absolutely no idea what lay in store for him when he arrived at the vast, greystone building. He was still in his thirties but already had begun to look far older than his years. The mounting strain of work at Dubno, of meeting the challenge and setbacks of such important research with the Kremlin looking impatiently over his shoulder, the continual travel to and from Moscow by plane to report on progress—all this was beginning to take a toll and to show in his appearance.

His hair, always thin and lank, had all but vanished. The big nose had become decidedly beaky. Deep furrows creased his forehead, while sharp lines and grooves plunged from nose to mouth, and from mouth to chin. He was beginning to put on weight: folds of flesh had started to gather at his throat and a noticeable pot trespassed on a once-athletic waistline. Bags and dark pouches sagged below his eyes. He had never been a man to dress smartly, and because of the urgency of the summons, it was a shabby, puzzled, old-young man who finally presented himself to the minister. He would never forget his feelings of shock and bewilderment—pain, almost—as he listened to the first of several accusations of his wife's 'dangerous tendencies' and her 'counter-revolutionary thoughts'.

It was a long time before he realised that he was too valuable to be harmed, and that this fact alone saved her from public disgrace (and, later, from the labour camps). He thought the State was being merciful and was actually grateful. He was also too much in love, and too naive, not to accept that she might in turn be withholding much of the truth from him. As a result, her attitude both baffled and hurt him and he failed to appreciate what it was that made her so ominously defiant, and unrepentant.

'I don't intend to discuss the rights and wrongs of my book with you, Alexandrei,' she had said. 'You haven't read it. You don't know the first thing about what it is supposed to say and mean. You took that man's word for it that it was somehow critical of the regime without demanding to see it for yourself so that you could form an adult opinion both as a husband and scientist. Well, let *me* tell you something: only a very wicked, or very frightened, regime could consider it necessary to have my book burned.'

'Katerina, don't talk like that,' he said, nervously.

'I'll talk as I like—to you!'

'Of course you may, but I don't mean that. All I'm trying to say is that you must be careful what you say to others. You know what will happen if you go around talking like that. I don't want you to get hurt. I couldn't live without you.'

He turned a deaf ear to her protests when her friends were rounded up and jailed as the State, in its blindness, decided *someone* had to suffer for the sins of smuggling her work to the western world. She, in turn, began to avoid him. She began to sleep alone, and she would weep hysterically if Mikhail vanished from her sight even for a moment. He plunged back into his work, seeking to let the crisis right itself in time. But it was a long time: they were like strangers to each other for months, husband and wife in name only, two people who observed the conventions for the sake of their son and those relatives who came to stay with them, but no more.

If he suffered at home, his career prospered as never before. Honour upon honour was given him by the State. He was awarded the Lenin Prize, with all that that means to a Russian citizen. He became President-elect of the Academy of Science. He was moved from the outer regions of Dubno and installed in magnificently-equipped, new laboratories on the outskirts of Moscow. The Gerias were given a skyscraper, luxury flat in the heart of the city, as well as the continued use of their dacha at Peredelkino—riches, indeed, in a nation where at that time, three and even four families counted themselves lucky to be able to share two rooms for all purposes, bar the communal bathroom and kitchen. He was twice called upon to lead scientific delegations abroad, one to Bucharest, the other to Warsaw. And he had become a wealthy man, by any standards.

He remembered how Katerina suddenly changed in her attitude towards him: when he arrived home one night she returned to his bed, without explanation but also without passion, like a wife who has taken a lover and submits only to allay suspicion. Geria never queried her. He had no idea that she might have spent those months secretly writing another book. Instead his world turned upside down one Spring evening when he arrived home to find the K.G.B. in his flat. There were three of them, stripping the apartment leisurely and systematically. There was no sign of his wife or child.

'What the devil's going on? Who are you men?' Geria was important enough by now not to stand on ceremony with mere policemen.

'Are you comrade-Professor Alexandrei Geria?' A hard-faced man in long leather coat looked him up and down.

'I am. And I demand to know what the hell you are doing in my flat.'

'Colonel Yerov, state police. I regret that I have orders to search this apartment. Your wife has been taken to our headquarters for questioning. Your son is being looked after by your neighbours.'

It was then that he learned about the second book, and how his wife had personally taken it to the offices of *Izvestia*—almost as if she were inviting arrest. His first reaction was that she must have had a nervous breakdown. He rang the ministry, he rang the President of the Academy and two members of the Praesidium until he finally secured Katerina's release in the early hours of the morning. When she got home she told him of the terrors of interrogation in Lubyanka and for the first time he began to fear for her freedom.

'Katerina, I can only help you if you tell me the truth. Did you have any part in smuggling that first book out of the country, any knowledge that it was happening?'

'No.'

'Then why didn't you let well alone? Why write a second book that you know can only hurt us all?'

'It was never intended for publication, I swear it, it was written as a kind of personal protest, a penance, don't you see? Just writing the words down was like putting salve on a wound, it helped me to accept what they have done to my friends and my own family. But after I spoke to my father yesterday, I don't know, Alexandrei, something snapped in my mind. I walked into that newspaper office, they all know me there, and I shouted at them, "Here, read this, it's all about justice in this marvellous country of ours." They sent me home but of course, they had to hand the book to the police.'

She began to sob.

'They were horrible to me, Alexandrei, *horrible*.'

She showed him the bruises on her head.

'Katerina, are there any other copies of this new book?'

'One other.'

'Have you given it to anyone?'

'No. Not to keep. I showed it to some friends.'

'Did they give it back to you?'

'Yes. I hid it in the dacha. That's why the police haven't found it.'

'I'll collect it first thing in the morning and take it to the authorities myself. Don't worry, I'll use it to help you, you've got to trust me, Katerina. I won't let anyone hurt you, I promise.'

He remembered how she trembled as she clung to him, and what she said as she wept.

'Darling, let's leave this dreadful country: it isn't Russia any more, it's like some gigantic prison, I'll kill myself rather than let them lock me up again....'

The thought of escape from Russia burned in his mind all that night, repelling him, frightening him yet tormenting him with the dreadful suspicion that maybe the only sure way to save his wife now was to help her to flee before it was too late. It stayed with him as he went to the minister and pleaded for compassion and mercy for Katerina as he handed the second copy in.

'Thank you, comrade-Professor, I'll see that your prompt and typical action is brought to the attention of the authorities. They may be inclined to treat her leniently if what you say is right: is she mentally ill, do you mean?'

'Well, I'm no doctor, but no—I don't think my wife is unbalanced in the sense of insanity: more of a nervous breakdown, I'd say. It seems to have been brought about by a curious guilt complex about some friends of hers who were taken away for questioning last year. Apparently she thinks they are still in prison. I told her what you yourself said, that our country isn't run by savages, but she wouldn't listen to me.'

'I believe some of them did prove, ah, unco-operative,' said the minister and wrote something on a piece of paper. 'I'll look into it. Now tell me, is your wife willing to enter hospital voluntarily for treatment?'

'Of course. She's a loyal citizen who has fallen ill, nothing more.'

'Your wife has brought all this on her own head.'

'I fully agree. Imagine walking into *Izvestia* with the manuscript, well, I mean, it must surely point to a nervous breakdown, one doesn't need to be medically qualified to diagnose *that*. We need your help, minister, both of us. How can I possibly get on with my work when my wife is arrested, her family and friends carted off to jail, my own apartment searched by the police? I was absolutely horrified to see them there, I can tell you: I could so easily have had notes of my research there and what would you have thought of me if any details of that became known prematurely?'

'I'll see what can be done, comrade-Professor. Your action in bringing this second copy of the book to me speaks for itself. We'll get her into hospital as soon as possible.'

'I don't know how to thank you, comrade-minister.'

'Just work hard for the nation, that's all anyone has to do.'

Geria could hardly believe his luck as he left the ministry. After that, there was no turning back. There were secret messages and clandestine meetings, ending with that night in Vienna when the stranger stood waiting inside their hotel room....

Geria shook his head and forced himself to listen to what was being said in the courtroom. Sir Gordon was addressing the judge.

'M'lud,' he said, 'I have dealt at length with my client's life and work in Russia. For security reasons, we don't propose to ask him any questions at all concerning the details of his actual defection. However, I intend to question him on all that has transpired since his arrival in this country, since in our respectful submission all of that matter is relevant to his subsequent actions on the night of the burglary. In view of the hour, may I ask if your Lordship wishes me to begin that questioning now, or after the adjournment?'

'Thank you, Sir Gordon, I myself think this afternoon might be a better time to begin. Court is adjourned until 2.30 p.m.'

8

THE TRIAL: DAY TWO AFTERNOON

The courtroom was filled to capacity after the adjournment. The public gallery was full, but neither Josef nor Andrei were there. Every seat was at a premium after the disclosures of the morning. The press were admitted only on a ticket basis, as they are for all major trials: one to each reporter representing a daily newspaper, evening paper, agency and so on. Since photographs inside the court were forbidden, at least one Sunday paper had sent an artist to sketch the dramatic scene. The chatter died away abruptly, the rustling and fidgeting ceased as the judge stalked in to take his place.

Sir Gordon resumed his questioning at once.

'Professor, you heard me tell his Lordship there would be no questions put to you about the circumstances of the defection?' —'Yes.'

'We will start with your arrival here. It was made in conditions of greatest secrecy?'—'The entire first class section of our plane was booked for the flight. My wife and I disembarked on the runway, and were put in a car with darkened windows.'

'Did you share a feeling of elation at your safe arrival?'— 'On the contrary. We were very tired and bewildered, and of course, desperately worried about our son. It was possibly the most desolate moment of our lives.'

'But your wife had finally escaped the threat of persecution?' —'That was true. But the fate of the boy was uppermost in our minds.'

'None the less, you came here voluntarily?'—'That's not the same thing as coming *willingly*. I took no pride in what I had done. I was ashamed, as a father, to leave my young son behind and alone. I was ashamed as a patriot, to have defected from my homeland, and this was the greater shame.'

'I am quite sure that an English jury will understand those feelings of remorse. Tell us what happened after you left the aircraft?'—'We were asked to sign a paper, asking for political asylum, which we did. Then we were driven very fast to a house some miles away. It was dark, for we had landed in the early hours of the morning. We were met there by a doctor, who gave us both an injection, to make us sleep.'

'I don't want you to say where the house was. But can you describe it to us?'—'Yes. I got to know every inch of it, like my own face in the mirror.'

Geria stopped halfway through the sentence and put a hand to his face. Then he added: 'Not that it's my face any more, it's been altered quite considerably.'

The jury sat up at that, and every eye in the room focussed on the witness's smooth, unwrinkled features. Sir Gordon, however, let it pass by.

'I'll deal with that in a moment. Will you just tell us about the house?'—'It was an old building, tall and narrow, very solidly built. There was a small back garden, which was totally enclosed by a high wall. The house was divided into apartments. We had the middle one, with security guards living above and below us.'

'How big was your apartment, the middle one?'—'Living room, dining room, bedroom, bathroom at the end of a landing, and a small kitchen. The main rooms were of a reasonable size.'

'Was it well furnished?'—'Well enough. We had television, radio, lots of books, newspapers delivered every day, fresh flowers, plenty to eat and drink. The furniture was old but comfortable.'

'No telephone, of course, or means of communication with the outside world?'—'None.'

'Was there anything that struck you as odd about the apartment?'—'Well, it had no windows.'

'None at all?'—'One in the bathroom, high up on the wall, but even if you stood on the side of the bath, it was still too high to see out.'

'Why was that?'—'We were told windows could be dangerous.'

'Did that worry you?'—'We didn't say anything at first, in case we should appear ungrateful. But after a time the effect was claustrophobic.'

'How long did you live in that windowless, claustrophobic apartment?'—'Four or five months altogether, I suppose: it seemed a lot longer at the time.'

'You were allowed out, surely'—'We could go into the garden ten minutes after making the request. That gave them time to make sure the road outside the house was clear, and so on. It was winter time, of course, and it always seemed to be wet and muddy in the garden. We didn't ask to go out much in the end. Sometimes we were taken for drives in the car, to look at the fields, and to see the outside of shops, things like that.'

'Always with an escort?'—'Yes.'

'Even in that little wet and muddy garden?'—'Always.'

'But you were moved eventually, to a bigger house?'—'Yes. We became very restless and unhappy after a time. My wife was ill, fretting about Mikhail partly, but mainly because she found it hard to sleep in a room without windows. Finally we insisted on a move. It was hard for everyone there, guards included, but we were the goldfish in the bowl, not them. We felt we were being watched in our most intimate moments—I doubt if we were, of course, but the thought was there, and it began to get us both down.'

'You were happier after the move?'—'In some ways, very happy. We went to a lovely house, with a big garden and many trees: but there were always guards. And we were forbidden to converse in our own language, which we found an intolerable burden at times. But it was the never-ending lessons which got me down the most.'

'What lessons were those, professor?'—'Intensive crash-course lessons in the English language and way of life. We both had a good basic knowledge: English is a compulsory subject in all Russian schools, as you may know. But we had to achieve perfection. There were microphones everywhere, not to spy on us, we believed them there, but to correct *all* mistakes in conversation.

The most intimate things were played back to us on tape, all the time. It was humiliating. They said our lives might one day depend on it, and we accepted that. But we were both old enough to find it terribly wearying to talk and think all day, every day, in a foreign language. The lessons had begun back in the first apartment, and they never ceased. I began to dread the start of each new day. We were being fashioned into different people. Already we looked different, now our whole minds were being changed.'

'But did you resent this, knowing it to be for your own protection?'—'Very much so. I felt after a time as if I was tied hand and foot, unable to move anywhere of my own free will, incapable of any original thought. Although they said this was a perfectly natural reaction, I began to despair. Slowly, that big house in the country turned into another kind of prison, one where I was a prisoner of the mind as well as body: trapped in a world where I had to speak in a foreign tongue, think and act in foreign ways, listen only to foreign broadcasts and television shows, and to go only where I could be seen, by foreign guards.'

'You became impotent, I think you said earlier?'—'That was the cruellest part of all. As the walls closed in on us, my wife turned to me more and more for love and affection but I could give her none. It took us both a long time to accept *that*. There were times when she would scream at me, or breakdown and weep uncontrollably. Deep down she knew I loved her and this made it all the harder to bear.'

'The plastic surgery was done before you left the first apartment was it not?'—'Yes. We were told it would help us take our place in the outside world without fear of recognition—and possible assassination—and so I agreed to have it done.'

'I think you should make it quite clear to the jury, this was not compulsory treatment?'—'No, we gave our consent. But Sydenham, I mean the guards, pointed out the many advantages of having such treatment, especially from the woman's point of view. I think it's correct to say we were persuaded rather than compelled.'

'You look very well on it: you're not complaining about the

end result?'—'It depends on how you look at things. You see, I'm not *me* any more. I was born Alexandrei Petrovitch Geria, for better or for worse, now I'm John Stevens, I look different, I stand differently, I talk differently, I behave differently, I'm a different person mentally as well as physically. I'm not nearly as happy as I used to be. I don't recognise myself in the mirror, some mornings. I've got hair on my head now, something I lost years ago, but I'm not sure I want it: this hair isn't mine, it's stitched on, it's set into permanent waves like a woman's, and it's nothing like the colour nature gave me. I'm no longer me, I'm an impostor, a walking, talking cheat. Don't ask me if I have any complaint, ask yourself this—do you think my own son will know me if he is ever allowed to see me again, eh?'

It was Sydenham who first raised the subject of plastic surgery. They had grown to trust him, this Humpty Dumpty figure who appeared each day rather like a personal Genie, ever patient and courteous, seemingly able to anticipate their every problem. He would appear out of nowhere, suddenly materialise, and it was quite uncanny how he always picked a good moment psychologically to make his entry, as if he had been listening in to their private thoughts. He rarely came empty handed: there would be some small gift for Katerina, a box of chocolates or some flowers, or the copy of a recent scientific report for Geria to study. They had been in the apartment for some weeks and time was beginning to drag. Today he waddled in and handed Katerina a glossy fashion magazine. His blue eyes were devoid of guile, his face bland and smiling.

'Good morning. I brought you this, my dear: high time we began to get you a decent wardrobe together.'

She began to flick through the pages. Sydenham ran an eye round the small, windowless room.

'I've been making inquiries about the possibility of a move from here,' he said to them, in a non-committal voice.

Geria nodded politely, but made no reply: it seemed to take them not much further. Katerina sensed there was more to come, and continued to look through the magazine.

'How about a nice cup of coffee,' Sydenham suggested to her, 'before we go into serious discussion on important matters like your wardrobe?'

'Of course,' she said. 'It won't take long.'

As soon as she had gone into the kitchen Sydenham returned to the subject of moving house. He chose his words carefully and left his audience in no doubt as to what was required of him.

'Wherever we go from here,' he said to Geria, 'it will have to be to another closely guarded house. You're not ready yet to take a chance in the outside world, not on your own.'

'But,' the scientist protested, 'that's precisely what we do want. And as soon as possible.'

'I know,' said the fat man, 'and believe me, I'd like to help you. However, there are problems. Your command of the language isn't right yet, by a long chalk. There's also the question of physical appearance. There is still a tremendous outcry in Russia over your disappearance. I don't think there is any doubt that their execution squad will be hunting for you in every major country in the west. If you walked out looking like that you'd be dead in a week.'

'You want to disguise us?'

'In a way. We think it's safer to give you a permanent new look. Plastic surgery, as a matter of fact: how does that strike you?'

Geria had begun to look quite old. Worry and sleepless nights had accentuated the dark pouches under his eyes. He was putting on weight again, through lack of proper exercise. He was as bald on top as Sydenham. Deep creases lined his forehead, and ran down by the sides of his mouth.

'You mean an operation?' He sounded distinctly unhappy.

'The surgeons can do wonders nowadays, good Lord, you wouldn't feel a thing! Think of all the film stars who have cosmetic treatment, my dear fellow: I imagine your wife might even welcome it, and I mean no disrespect by that, she's a very handsome woman. What they would do is make her look even younger. What woman wouldn't jump at the chance?'

'I hadn't thought about that.' Geria was a little less apprehensive. 'I'll speak to her about it.'

'Excellent. It's for her safety—and yours. If they find either one of you, they can strike at the partner, too. Can't be too careful. I was rather hoping you would lead the way, and prove to her there's nothing to it, you know what I mean?'

'I see.'

'I didn't say too much when I first came in, didn't want to worry her unnecessarily: but the fact is, a sizeable Russian delegation has just flown into London. You can be certain some of the delegates aren't all that they are made out to be. One or two might be casting their net for news of you.'

'We're safe enough here.'

'Nowhere safer! But you want to move, not that I blame you for that. And there will always be someone out there looking for you. This is one of the difficulties I face when I raise the question with my superiors.'

'I suppose it is.'

'If only I had some kind of lever to use to help make them look at things from your point of view. Have you thought any more about the possibility of working for us?'

'You know my views on that.'

'Yes, and I respect them. However, if you should change your mind, I'm sure I could get far more co-operation from my own people in meeting your requirements!'

'I see what you mean.'

'Make up your mind anyway on the proposal for plastic surgery. It has to be your own decision, no one can compel you to do anything you don't want to.'

'I'll let you know as soon as I've spoken to Katerina.'

'Correction, she's not Katerina any more, she's Katherine Stevens.'

'Sorry. I keep forgetting.'

'That's all right. It will come in time. Everything will come in time, you see.'

It was dark when they reached the private clinic. Geria's face was muffled in a scarf, he wore plain-lens spectacles, and a wide-brimmed fedora hid his bald pate.

'You may look like a music hall character,' Sydenham joked, 'but not even your own mother would know you like that! Come on.'

Two big men stood casually in the shadows, along the street. Sydenham nodded to them, just as casually, and quickly led the way into the building. They went along a corridor, past a uniformed attendant at a reception desk who seemed to be expecting them, into a lift that squeaked its way to the fifth floor, down another corridor, through a deserted waiting room, and into a bright, warm and inviting office-cum-consulting room. Geria looked swiftly about him, not knowing quite what to expect after such a cloak-and-dagger entry.

There was no name on the door of the consulting room. A life-sized photograph of a naked woman, an ageless beauty with firm, high breasts, an exquisitely shaped nose and skin as smooth and white as alabaster, hung on one wall. Beneath her feet, row upon row of books slept on beds of polished, redwood shelves. A thick carpet of Burgundy hue clothed the entire floor, soothing and soft as a lullaby. On every side concealed lighting shone softly down in perfect harmony. Velvet curtains tumbled from ceiling to carpet in an elegant waterfall, and a false fire flickered and spun in the hearth. It was a lesson in the art of window dressing, rich with the promise of beautiful things to come.

A dusky, smiling man looked up from a pile of letters—here was someone whose services were clearly much in demand—and sprang up to greet his callers warmly.

'Come in, come in, gentlemen, my word! what punctuality. Now that's one thing every busy professional man greatly appreciates, good time-keeping. How are you?'

He shook hands with them, Sydenham first, pressing his thumb hard on fat fingers as if in some secret signal: and as he welcomed Geria, his eyes roved lovingly over the scientist's haggard features. He was Sydenham's Mister Fixit, artist and sorcerer, a magician who could correct the whims and vagaries of nature with rare skill, and infinite subtlety.

His eyes were very observant, and dark as sloes. They noted the sagging pouches, measured the creases and worry lines, counted each crow's foot and pucker, they lingered joyfully on the receding chin with the anticipation of a mountaineer spying some fresh peak to conquer, and they lit up as they homed in on Geria's large, misshapen, Roman nose.

'My name is Gulam, Dr Ram Gulam,' he said as he pirouetted round the big man to examine him in profile.

His own face was shining and plump, a round Bengali moon that needed no artifice to render it so flawlessly smooth and unlined. His teeth sparkled white in his face as snow on a mound of coal. A diamond as big as a pea flashed from the fingers of his right hand. He smelled ever so faintly of expensive after-shave perfume.

'Please be seated,' he told them, and waved them to waiting chairs. 'I understand there are certain special security measures I have to discuss first with Mr Sydenham.'

He smiled at Geria.

'Rest assured nothing will be done without your own consent and full permission. It is not the first time he and I have had to work together for the common cause. We shall not keep you long.'

Geria remained in the armchair as the two of them vanished into an adjoining room. He began to study the books by his side: one of them caught his eye and he read its title, surely the longest and most forbidding ever to appear in print.

'Nasenplastik und sonstige Gesichtplastik nebst einem anhang über Mammplastik, und einige weitere operationen aus dem Gebeite der ausseren Körperplastik.'

He knew sufficient German to translate that.

'Plastic surgery of the nose and other parts of the face, with a supplement on mammaplasty, together with certain other procedures in plastic surgery of the body surface.'

Geria was like many another otherwise intelligent man, and

for no good reason he feared the very name surgeon with a rare and quite groundless dread. The very thought of an operation, of the scalpel at work, made him sick. He was the kind of coward who would endure weeks of toothache rather than face, for five minutes or less, the muted whine of the dentist's drill, a legacy from boyhood memories of pioneer dental treatment in Russia. He had conveyed something of his fears and doubts to Sydenham already, and now, as he sat alone among the textbooks, his hands crept slowly over the skin of his face, they traced the familiar, bony ridge of his nose and sent out peculiar alarm signals. He got up and prowled uneasily round the room. There were books whereever he turned, and he picked some at random as if hypnotised, unable to say no to his questing fingers and frightened eyes. He forced himself to read words that struck terror into his heart, words like bayonet-saw, skin flap, Humby knife and skin hook. With a horror born of vivid imagination he saw himself pinned on the operating table with the surgeon bent over him, peering from eyes made huge by a magnifying lens, and then cutting, stitching, slicing and probing at his face, and taking the hook to raise his very skin from raw tissues. Beads of sweat gathered at his brow, they trickled down from his armpits, the palms of his own hands felt wet and clammy. It took an enormous effort of will to bring himself under control, to convince himself he was doing this more for Katerina than himself.

In the next room Sydenham and Dr Gulam looked at the photographs on the desk in front of them like two generals studying a battlefield before the assault.

A dusky finger pointed to Geria's nose.

'Rhinoplasty,' said the surgeon. 'We'll need to do something drastic about that. I'll get rid of the hump, reduce the whole nose in size, straighten it, shorten it: intranasal surgery, no scar visible anywhere afterwards. Like this!'

He sketched a new nose, straighter, smaller and far more handsome, on a sheet of paper.

'I'll get rid of those bags under his eyes, too. I expect you know how they're caused, Sydenham, rupture of the periorbital fat due to weakness of the orbicularis muscles. Very ageing. Very disfiguring—and in his case, dangerously noticeable.'

'Is that difficult?' Sydenham asked him.

'Good Lord, no. Calls for fine judgment, of course, take away too much and the lower eyelid may get dragged down: too little, and the bags remain. Suturing is tremendously important to post-operational success. One has to make minute stitches, and have the edges fitting perfectly—but once they're out, the scars will disappear rapidly and your patient looks years younger. See what I mean, here.'

He drew two eyes on the sheet of paper, above the new, handsome nose and devoid of any hint of bag or wrinkle.

'Fine, fine,' said Sydenham. He peered down at the photographs again. 'I'd like you to pin those ears back while you're at it. Christ, look how they stick out.'

'Simple.'

Two new ears were added to the sketch, sitting close to Geria's skull.

'Like that?'

'Marvellous! Will you give him a complete face-lift while you're operating, like you did with the Pole?'

'A *forehead* lift.' There was a hint of rebuke in the correction. 'Yes. I just make an incision *there*, prise the skin loose right over the forehead, and pull it up tight till the creases vanish.'

'You make it sound so easy,' Sydenham commented admiringly. 'Like a girl pulling her stocking up. No wrinkles allowed.'

'There's a little more to it than that, my friend. Fail to pull it tight enough and the creases will remain. Pull it too tight and you'll give the poor devil a mask, something unreal. But when it's done right, by an expert, the effect is to raise the hairline and eyebrows a little. This gives a much more youthful look to the patient.'

He pencilled in new, raised eyebrows on the paper face.

'I'll have to give him hair. Plenty of hair. I have to hide the marks of the forehead lift inside the hairline, do you follow me? Now, what sort of hair would you like him to have? Something like this, perhaps? Look at that, now, we've taken ten years and more off his present appearance.'

They looked down on the new face with pride.

'He's overweight.' Sydenham was remorseless. 'Can't you cut away the abdominal fat? He can afford to lose a stone, easily.'

The surgeon gazed at Sydenham's enormous frame without comment. After a pause, he said: 'That would need weeks in bed afterwards. I personally always advocate exercise and strict diet wherever possible. The patient will feel better and look better for it.'

'Exercise is a bit of a problem with this patient,' Sydenham grumbled. 'Think about it, anyway.'

'You've missed the most important feature,' the surgeon reminded him. 'The chin! I'll square it up, so. Nose and chin have to marry, that's absolutely essential. I'll talk it over with him, make a series of plaster casts and draw a number of sketches, until we get it exactly right.'

'He's a wee bit nervous, I told you that over the 'phone,' said Sydenham. 'He only agreed to come here at all when I persuaded him it would make his wife feel better about having a face-lift herself. In fact, she can't wait, but don't let him know that. How many operations will he need?'

'At least two. Eyes and ears and forehead lift in one session, nose and chin in another. There may have to be dentistry, too.'

'For God's sake, don't tell him that! Mention teeth and he'll run a mile. Some bloody moujik gave him a bad time when he was a kid, and he's never forgotten it.'

'Even with the most expert treatment one can find problems of alignment afterwards.'

'As long as you don't mention it in advance. Just let him see how good he will look when it's all over. I want him out and about and happy to work for us as soon as possible.'

'Then that's roughly what I have in mind.'

He held up the new face of John Stevens.

'Magnificent. I don't know how to thank you.'

'No need for thanks. If your man can walk without fear for the rest of his life, that will be all the thanks I need.'

They walked back into the consulting room.

Geria looked pale, and wan. It was clearly a time for all good men to come to the aid of the patient, and Dr Gulam gave him a dazzling smile.

'This is not the normal doctor-and-patient consultation,' he said, 'but a meeting rather, of three intelligent men who have an unusual problem to solve. In my professional opinion it calls for an unusual prescription before we get down to business. How about a drink?'

'Splendid idea,' Sydenham replied. 'We've all had a long and trying day. I'd love a Scotch.'

'And you, Mr, ah, Stevens?'

'Thank you, I would like a drink very much indeed.'

Three bumper measures were quickly dispensed.

Then the surgeon said: 'Mr Sydenham has told me you do not entirely welcome the thought of plastic surgery, Mr Stevens. Well, the decision is yours, and yours alone. But there is no need to feel afraid. Most of my patients are ladies and many of them come to me more than once. Who was it said they were the weaker sex, eh?'

'My wife also needs treatment,' Geria answered. 'She's as nervous as I am. I thought it would help us both if I came along first.'

'Then you're not a coward at all. That's the action of a brave and very devoted husband.'

'Unfortunately I don't feel very brave. Will it hurt?'

'No, it won't.'

'Does it take long?'

'The patient is anaesthetised and feels nothing. In your case you would attend this clinic for two separate operations, if you agree to the facial re-structure I have in mind. You will be delighted with the results, I promise you that.'

'What do you intend to do to me?'

'I was hoping you wouldn't say that, Mr Stevens. My patients come to me for a variety of reasons: after an accident, maybe to correct the indignities of nature, or just because they want to look younger. Sometimes Mr Sydenham will introduce a friend to me, someone whose life is in danger and who needs help. None of them say to me "What are you going to do to me?" as if I'm some kind of ogre, they ask "Can you please help me?" and that's how I would like you to look upon my services. I can help you, if you so desire. I wouldn't lay a finger on you if I thought you were unwilling to go through with it for any reason. It's up to you.'

'I'm sorry. I do need help. So does my wife.'

'She will have to tell me herself what she wants. As for you, I have now seen you in the flesh, I have looked at the photographs so kindly provided by Mr Sydenham, and I have made a few rough sketches to show you what I suggest can be done. Here.'

Geria looked at the sheet of paper in astonishment.

'As you see, I propose to remove all lines from the face, and to take away those pouches beneath the eyes. That is straightforward cosmetic work, widely done by many eminent surgeons. The effect is to beautify, to rejuvenate.'

'I see.'

'Nothing whatever to fear there.'

'I suppose not.'

'Also, the nose and jawline are recognisable features. I suggest we straighten the one, and strengthen the other. I will be happy to show you some before-and-after photographs of other patients.'

'Please, I don't doubt your skills, doctor.'

'And as you see I propose to give you a head of hair. This is commonly done and doesn't require the services of a surgeon like myself. However Mr Sydenham feels that the fewer people who know about your transformation, the better. You surely do not have any worries about the fitting of a toupee?'

'Not about that, no.'

'Plastic surgery has been practised in many lands over hundreds of years, in one form or another. In recent years there have been some astounding advances in every technique. I am a graduate of the Mount Sinai hospital in New York: I believe my work is not unknown. If you so wish, my services are unreservedly at your disposal.'

'That is very kind of you.'

'Then I will take the case.' This was to Sydenham, a contract signed and sealed. 'How soon can the patient attend?'

'The sooner the better. Mr Stevens is anxious to leave his present quarters, and it is essential that he should not be recognised by certain people.'

'Very well then.' Strong dark fingers flicked through the pages of an appointments book. 'Consultation next Monday, here, at the same time. We'll book Mr Stevens in for his first operation on the following Thursday.'

'That will be first class.'

It was Sydenham who answered. Geria held out his glass for another drink.

At first, everything went well. Wrinkles and crow's feet vanished, the dark bags fled from under Geria's eyes, to leave him rejuvenated as the doctor had promised. He suffered some discomfort for a few days but very little pain. The bandages came off, he wore dark glasses to hide the bruising for a while, and that was all.

The rhinoplasty, or remodelling of his nose, was also an unqualified success. When the wads of paraffin gauze had been taken out, the internal stitches removed, and the Plaster of Paris bandage taken away, the patient was astounded by what he saw in the mirror. The ugly hump had gone, the beak had disappeared. Here was a nose to be proud of, long and straight and slender, a classical nose—a little large, maybe, but still a nose that would have graced any marble bust in the British Museum.

The trouble lay with his jaw. It hurt. It did not fit. The teeth were minutely out of alignment. Sydenham was with him in the room, as always, and Geria looked at him in alarm.

'My jaw hurts me,' he said. He was speaking thickly, like a smoker with a pipe in his mouth.

'I expect it's bound to feel strange for a day or two,' Sydenham replied soothingly. 'Don't worry, it will be fine.'

But it was far from fine. It remained an obstinately ill-fitting and uncomfortable jaw. What had happened was that the lower jaw was set fractionally too far forward, so that the bite of the teeth was affected. The surgeon performed a corrective operation during which more bone was taken from the lower jaw to reduce it in size. Then it had to be set back to match the upper jaw, and wired into position, an unpleasant and exasperating business. Geria fretted and brooded, and then had to undergo intricate dental surgery. He spent several weeks in the clinic in all. He hated the dentist as he had never hated anyone before in his life. He grew to loathe the doctor and to detest Sydenham. He could not wait to be released.

He looked exceptionally well, a different man. His ears were pinned back. He had a remarkable new head of hair, brown and luxuriant, hair that tumbled in a love-lock over his wide, unlined brow: the only tufts that were his showed in some grey at the temples, a not unbecoming mixture. Everyone who saw him marvelled at his nose. Since he had refused point-blank to undergo surgery for the removal of stomach fat, he had been put on a series of exercises to reduce even further a figure greatly slimmed by dieting, and the wiring of his jaws. He had walked in looking like a man in his fifties and had shed ten years in half that number of weeks.

'Where's my wife?' he demanded of Sydenham one afternoon.

'Just two doors down the corridor,' he was told. 'She sends you her love.'

'I want to see her.'

'As soon as the bandages come off. Be patient, she asks after you every day.'

At first he failed to recognise the woman who walked into his room a few days later. Her visit was unannounced: she was young, and beautiful, and for a long while stood in the doorway, gazing at him without a word. Her hair was blonde. It had been allowed to grow to shoulder length, and had been set by loving hands. It waved, and curled, and shone like a cap of gold. Her face was oval, and she had a tiny, tip-tilted, perfect nose. Her skin was utterly smooth, not a crease or a line to be seen, and her eyes were darkest blue. She wore a dress of jersey wool that clung to her body and showed off a slim girlish figure, with long legs and shapely breasts. She stepped into the room and turned sharply, so that her skirt flared out.

'Don't you know me? Have I changed so much?'

'Katerina!' He ran across and took her into his arms, crushing her.

'Hey, be careful,' she warned him, and gently pushed him away. 'They said you wanted to see me, so I came as soon as I could. But my poor body is all stitches, so don't squeeze me like that.'

'What have they done to you?'

'I don't really know: miracles, I think. Do you like the new me?'

He held her at arms' length.

'I ... I'm not sure. You're a different person, your face, your hair. I didn't know you when you came through that door.'

He found it strangely difficult to analyse his feelings as he looked at her. The girl he had courted and married had been a sturdier one than this delicate creature, dark-haired and vivacious, with a gamin face, a cheeky smile and unspoilt manner. Here was someone else, elegant, polished and chic: she wore strange looking shoes, a short revealing dress, and she looked like a model from one of the glossy magazines that Sydenham used to bring to the apartment. She smelled of perfume and hair-spray. She was paler, and slimmer and somehow taller than he remembered. All at once he realised, with a real pang of regret, that she no longer looked *Russian*. She was fragile and manufactured, like so many other western women, not earthy and real like the girl he first met in the snow, in Red Square.

'You look very beautiful,' he managed to say.

He still slurred his words slightly. The knowledge made him feel curiously ill at ease in the company of this lovely creature who faced him so confidently.

'And I think you're handsome, too.'

She had seen him often enough since the operation and her compliment was mechanical, forced.

She sat down, very carefully.

'We'll be going home soon.'

'Home?' He could not remember home any more.

'Out of here, I mean. Mr Sydenham told me today, it won't be long.'

'Yes.'

She leaned across and kissed him on the nose, and felt him flinch. 'Does it still hurt?'

'No, not at all. It's just that I can't get used to it. I keep on thinking, it isn't mine! A form of mental rejection, I suppose.'

'Well, you shouldn't, it's a lovely nose. Does your poor mouth still hurt you?'

'It doesn't hurt, it's just damned uncomfortable with this clamp. I'm sick and tired of feeding through a tube. And I can't talk properly.'

'You've lost so much weight. You look so much taller, and years younger.'

'So do you. Although I liked you just as you were.'

'Wait till you see the rest of me.' She smiled a secret smile and whispered in his ear. 'The doctor's given me a new bust, raised them up, made them firm, just like they were before I had Mikhail. It makes me *feel* so young! I had that done just for you, darling.'

Geria was delivered home a few days before they were due to leave the apartment. It was a curiously subdued reunion from the beginning, for all that Sydenham left them alone and the guards stayed tactfully out of sight.

They kissed and stood apart almost at once, shyly, gazing in awe at the new face that confronted each partner, finding embarrassment mixed with surprise, and—to their mutual dismay—feeling a barrier, a wall of self-consciousness, between them. Neither could explain this instant reaction, but both felt it at once, and sharply. As they spoke, they found themselves stealing sly glances at each other, and not knowing whether to laugh or to cry. Each experienced a sensation that the change in the other was mental as well as physical. Somehow, Geria felt he did not want this blonde stranger, he wanted to hug and kiss the woman he had grown to love, someone he remembered with Georgian-dark features and a lazy laugh, a girl who teased him and joked about his receding hair—not this pale, well-dressed newcomer who preferred his wig because it made him look younger, and who kept staring at the square jaw that had caused him so much discomfort and distress. If she approved of the changes, he resented them, but he could not explain why, except that he knew they filled him with a strange sense of loss. They found it difficult to talk, and even harder to talk easily over a drink. After a time she made him a meal, but while he ate he was aware that she watched him as he chewed on each mouthful, and he was desperately conscious of his new teeth that fitted so perfectly in shining, white rows.

She went to bed first, and called him in. She stood naked by a single bedside lamp, and held out her arms to him, whispering his name. True, she called him Alexandrei, the name he had been given at birth, but she said it dutifully in the English way and instead of responding, he stayed where he was and stared at her, he examined her, as if he had found a stranger inside the room instead of his wife.

'Look,' she said proudly, and held her arms high above her blonde head, showing him her body. To his eyes, it looked like a reproduction of the picture hanging on the wall in Dr Gulam's office. Try as he might, he found it was John Stevens who looked at her, not himself. He felt a sense of shock, he would have turned and run from the room if there had been anywhere to hide. He did not know what to say. He began to undress quickly. All the while she stood there, swaying in the lamp light, painting her smooth-skinned body with light and shadow, smiling at him.

'Hey, I asked you, do you like me, the new me?'

He heard himself say 'You look beautiful' but he avoided meeting her eyes, the stranger's eyes. He was careful not to touch her as he put out the light and climbed into bed. He found no ally in darkness. She snuggled close, and kissed him, and began to fondle him, but his own body refused to respond.

'Darling,' she said. 'Tell me, what's wrong?'

'I don't know,' he answered. He sought for words that would not wound. 'I just don't know what's happened to me. I've been waiting for this moment all the time we've been apart, I love you, you know that, I love you more than anything in the world. But I've nothing to give you, I can't help you, I'm all empty inside. I can't get this stupid notion out of my head that we're two different people, that I don't *know* you any more ...'

She began to weep.

'There's only the two of us now,' she wailed, 'you and me, I'm frightened, and so lonely, I need you more than ever. I saw how you looked at me when you came home today, what am I going to do?'

He put his arms round her. 'Of course I love you, you know that.'

'Then show me. Prove you love me.'

'It's no use, Katerina, I can't.'

After a long time, her tears ceased. All the while he held her close, but it was as a father comforting a child: he tried to find the right words to say, but none would come, he felt the warmth of her, but could not respond. Both pillows were wet with tears before they fell asleep.

It was the same the next night, and the next and it stayed the same even after they moved to the house in the country. At first they became closer, they tried to comfort each other with kindness and understanding. Finally they began to quarrel, and it was Geria who broke under the strain. He tried to hide his humiliation by blaming her for all that had happened, for bringing about his defection, for causing the loss of their son, for all his unhappiness. Now he was a prisoner of the body, as well as of the mind. He found the constant lessons, the sense of confinement, the guards and the microphones, above all his inability to make love, an intolerable burden.

In the end he took his troubles to Sydenham.

'You know there's trouble between us?' he asked.

'Yes,' said his guardian, who had listened to many an unhappy recording of the scenes between Geria and his wife, and had refused to intervene.

'I'm impotent. Forty years old, and impotent.'

Sydenham said nothing to that.

'It's driving us both mad. If I had the chance, I'd go back to Russia tomorrow.'

'You know that's impossible.'

'Then I might as well be dead. You've got to help us.'

'If I can, I will. You know that. I have nothing but sympathy for both of you.'

'Is there any news of our son?'

Sydenham hesitated.

'We feel certain he's alive and well. Our agents are seeking ceaselessly for some news of the boy, but no, we've nothing yet.'

'Well, we can't go on like this. I want you to let the two of us move into a house on our own away from you watchdogs, a house without microphones, a place where we can be ourselves, with no restrictions.'

Sydenham puffed at a cigarette. 'How would that help you overcome the worry about your son?'

'Nothing will ever do that. But I honestly think it would bring my wife and I together again, it would help us make a new start.'

'It would be taking an awful chance. I don't think you realise even now how badly your old comrades want to find you. Especially your wife.'

'How would they begin to find us, two people living in an ordinary house in the middle of an English town?'

'You're an amateur. You'd be up against real professionals.'

'Look at me, Sydenham, I'm going out of my mind.' Geria began to cry. 'I beg of you to find a way to help me.'

Sydenham was used to tears: years in Intelligence had made him damp-proof. This was the opportunity he had waited months to grasp, and he decided to apply a little pressure, to make the tears run a little faster.

'I'm afraid you've been damned unco-operative in your behaviour recently. You've refused our help, refused to take part in the lessons, treated us all with open hostility for months now. Listen, if you walked out of this garden right now and tried to pass yourself off as an Englishman, the local bobby—never mind a trained investigator—would have you taped inside five minutes. You haven't made it easy for yourself or for us.'

'I'm sorry. I told you and I mean it, I feel as if I'm going slowly mad. I don't know what I'm saying half the time.'

'There might be a way to help you.' Sydenham watched him closely as he put out the bait.

'Help me then. Please.'

'You appreciate, of course, any final decision on where you live, and in what circumstances you are allowed to live, doesn't rest with me? I can only recommend.'

'I realise that.'

'Do I have to spell it out for you? You could start to work for our side, take up the research where you left off in Moscow. Now just hold on a minute.'

Sydenham held up a hand.

'I know what you said when I first raised this with you, and I know you've repeated it since—you came here only to save your wife, but you won't betray your own country by giving its secrets to a foreign power. We in turn have been pretty generous and patient with you, I think you'll admit that?'

'Certainly.'

'Yet it was you who came to us for asylum, we didn't approach you, don't forget that. It was you who made secret contact with our embassy in Moscow and begged them to find a way to help your wife, was it not? We took you both in, without conditions, without reservations of any kind. It was hard and dangerous work to smuggle you out of Vienna, we had to kill two men before you and your wife could go free. We've spent a great deal of time and money since to keep you both alive, how long has it been, one year, more? Yes, more than a year, my friend. Suddenly, because things haven't turned out the way you hoped, you want to turn the clock right back, go back to Russia or failing that, move the two of you into one more house in this country so you can mend a broken marriage. Where's the house going to come from, have you thought about that? Who's going to pay for it? I want you to think about it, because it matters. Don't you think you might owe us something in return?'

'I have already offered my services in the field of general science.'

'It might take you a very long time to buy a house that way.'

'I told you, I might be weak and foolish, but I'm no traitor.'

'Who's talking about being a traitor? I'm talking about repaying a debt to us, a debt of honour.'

Geria made no reply to that.

'You must see, it would be impossible for you to go back to Russia. Until they know where you are, the boy's safe, you're the ace up our sleeve. If you go back he becomes a pawn, a lever to force your wife to crawl back and take what's coming to her.'

'They wouldn't dare.'

'Believe me, they would *insist*. They might think we were holding on to her as a guarantee your research work would never be completed.'

If you think we'd ever allow you to go back, you've got another think coming, my friend, said Sydenham to himself. Aloud, he said:

'One way and another, they will blame her for everything that has happened. They had a lot of money and pride invested in you, a real scientific breakthrough within their grasp. You really think they wouldn't demand their full pound of flesh once they had you back again?'

'I suppose you're right.'

'You know it. Look what they did to her friends, and her family.'

Again, Geria had no answer.

'I don't like talking to you like this. You and I, we've been good friends through a very difficult year, haven't we?'

'Yes.'

'I want to help you. You've got to give something in return.'

Silence.

'Look, I'll exceed my authority, I'll *guarantee* you that house on your own, no guards, no restrictions, a new start—if you will allow me to go to my government and say you will work for us. Take up where you left off. Don't think of it as treachery, true research has no frontiers.'

'I don't know what to say. I'm at my wits' end.'

'Just think about it. Take all the time you want.'

* * *

Sir Gordon beamed at his witness. He was doing extremely well in arousing sympathy from the jury. Now he had to steer him back on course again, and deal with this difficult question of the gun.

'You may not question counsel,' he told him. 'We are not in a position to say if your own son would be able to recognise you now. However, I am sure you have the unbounded sympathy of the court.'

He moved on very quickly as the judge looked up.

'What you are saying is that plastic surgery had a twofold effect, that it altered your appearance—as the surgeons intended—yet worsened the position between yourself and your wife?'—'Yes.'

'It rendered you impotent, and caused you to quarrel with her incessantly?'—'I don't know if any single thing caused my impotence, or a combination of many, but that was the outcome, yes.'

'Finally you had your way and moved into another house?'—'Yes.'

'The same house where the burglar was shot dead?'—'Yes.'

'You have explained that your wife has a fear of dogs. But did you have no safeguard of any kind in this house where you now lived on your own?'—'Oh yes. We were visited from time to time by the security people. We had to ask them not to come so often, as a matter of fact, it was getting more and more like the old days. And we were given a telephone number to ring in emergency, day or night.'

'With a selected man on duty and available each night?'—'Yes.'

'Was there no burglar alarm?'—'Yes. It was fitted into the main part of the house and operated on a room temperature system. But it went wrong because of the fuel shortage and the frequent long power cuts, I believe.'

'Why then did you insist on a gun?'—'It may seem hard to understand, but you must remember we had been under close guard ever since the defection. I was never a particularly strong or brave person and the constant fear of assassination brought home by the sight of those guards had a peculiar effect on me. Although I wanted them to leave us alone, I felt afraid, almost naked, without them. I slept badly for a long time. Sometimes I used to imagine sounds, and I would get up, four and five times in one night, to search through the house. The logical answer seemed to me to have a gun of my own.'

'And you obtained one without difficulty?'—'Certainly not. They wanted their own man to sleep in the house.'

'But you refused?'—'I did. I was quite adamant, no more policemen in my house, ever.'

'Why? Most of us would have felt far safer in your shoes if we had a guard on the premises.'—'I was desperately trying to make our marriage work again. Both my wife and I believed that the presence of guards, and all that they reminded us of, were the basic causes of my impotence.'

'Did the gun help?'—'I don't know the answer to that. It helped set my worst fears at rest. It was a promise that I would look after my wife—and myself—from then on. At least, that's what it was supposed to mean.'

'Did it help you sexually?'—'No. I remained impotent. And I still am.'

'Did not the move into this private house help you in any way?'—'Once again, it turned out to be a palliative, not a cure. We felt a lot better at first. We became very close again, and the quarrelling ceased. But no more.'

'Why did you not consult a doctor?'—'I did. I was taken to a psychiatrist.'

'What did he tell you?'—'He told me what I already knew, he said that I was a victim of all my pressures and misfortunes. He seemed to know all about me. He said that the quickest way for me to get well again was to plunge myself into work.'

'I see. Did you follow that advice?'—'Faithfully.'

'With what effect?'—'None at all. Then I realised that Sydenham, I mean the authorities, I'm sorry, had put him up to it.'

'Why did you think that?'—'Because he picked the psychiatrist!'

'In fact, you remained in a highly strung and nervous condition throughout your time in this private house?'—'Yes. At times I thought seriously about committing suicide. Oddly enough, I did feel some relief while I was at work. But as soon as I returned home, a sense of failure and humiliation would always return, it was like living a nightmare. I began to imagine things.'

'What kind of things?'—'My wife and I began taking walks in the evenings, after I got home. I became convinced we were being followed.'

'Did you actually see anyone?'—'Yes, lots of times.'

'But you had no means of knowing if they were innocent people or not, is that what you mean?'—'That's right. I saw every one as a potential assassin.'

'Is that when you began to carry the gun on your person?'—'Yes. But I quickly put it away in my drawer upstairs, and I never took it out again until that night—'

'Just answer my questions, professor. What happened to make you put the gun away, when you were obsessed with this thought of being followed by an assassin?'—'I nearly shot a youth one day. He came from behind and spoke to me, my hand was on the gun and I almost fired it but came to my senses in time. He only wanted to know the time. After that I put the gun away, right away.'

'Professor, you are not by nature a violent or aggressive man, are you?'—'Absolutely not, no, no.'

'Nor a quarrelsome one?'—'Never. Not in my normal state of mind.'

'You had never had a gun before?'—'I hate them.'

'Why did you not hand this one back?'—'I wanted to, but I couldn't bring myself to part with it. I knew if I did that, they would insist on the guards coming back into the house.'

'You have heard what the police said about the night of the burglary?'—'Yes.'

'Do you deny shooting the intruder with your own gun, this gun that had been given to you for self-protection?'—'No. I shot him.'

'Why did you do that?'—'I thought he was going to kill me.'

'But he wasn't armed?'—'I didn't know that until the policeman told me. I never even stopped to think about that, I just thought he was there for one reason only, to kill me and my wife.'

'I ask you again, why?'—'It was the only thought in my mind. The way he was dressed was very frightening. It never occurred to me he was a burglar, such a thing could not happen in Russia.'

'Are you saying you don't have burglars in Russia?'—'I am quite sure they do. But *my* house was never broken into. We had a large circle of friends, and none of them was ever burgled. It's not a subject of public discussion in the Soviet Union, the newspapers never publish stories about burglaries, as they do here.'

'Did you say anything to this man before you shot him?'—'Yes, I spoke to him in Russian, that will show you I'm telling the truth, that I believed he was a Russian come to kill me.'

'You didn't tell the police this?'—'I didn't tell them anything, I had to wait for Sydenham. But it's true.'

'Did he answer you?'—'He didn't answer me in English.'

'What language did he speak in?'—'A kind of bastard German.'

'How did you react to that?'—'It upset me, I didn't know what to do. I started to point the gun at the floor, away from him anyway, and the next thing that happened was, he jumped for me.'

'You thought he was going to kill you?'—'I suppose so. I didn't stop to think, it was just a split second of time. I—the next thing I knew, the gun was firing, and I could hear my wife screaming, upstairs, so I kept on firing.'

'Your only intention was to defend yourself, and protect your wife from harm?'—'From assassination. That was all I could think, he's here to kill us both.'

'Before you came downstairs to confront this unknown man, had you tried to call for help? From this day-and-night emergency number?'—'Yes. But no one answered.'

'You made a number of calls?'—'Yes. I don't know how many.'

Sir Gordon looked at the jury. He thought he could see sympathy and understanding in every face, and was well satisfied.

'Thank you, professor, I have no further questions to ask you.'

The Solicitor-General crossed-examined him only briefly.

'You have told us in great detail about the pressures you were living under, and no one can doubt them. However, I want to clear up one or two points for the jury about this gun. You said that you insisted on having one?'—'Yes.'

'Even against the advice of those who were guarding you, all professional men who knew the risk it would entail?'—'Yes, I made it clear that they were very unhappy about it.'

'I know you did. But you insisted, none the less?'—'Yes.'

'Fully intending to use it if the occasion should arise?'—'It was more of a symbol. I was telling my wife, and maybe myself, too, I don't know, that I was going to look after her from now on, that we would have no more guards living in our house.'

'Answer my question. Was it your intention to use the gun if you had to?'—'I never thought about it that way.'

'Very well, I will leave that for the jury to decide. You don't deny you held the gun in your hand as you walked downstairs?'—'No.'

'And pointed it at this unarmed man the moment you entered that living room?'—'If I did, I did so automatically.'

'You fired four or five shots at point blank range?'—'Yes, so I was told.'

'Did the burglar not cry out for mercy as the very first shot struck him?'—'I'm not sure.'

'Think again. Well?'—'Yes, I suppose he did.'

'But you kept on firing?'—'Clearly I did.'

'You were determined to kill him?'—'I wasn't thinking clearly about anything.'

'I put it to you once more, you insisted on having a gun of your own though you were offered adequate protection and you were quite determined to use it if you had to? I'm not saying you were a mad-dog killer, but someone who demanded a gun and was determined to use it if the occasion arose?'—'It wasn't like that at all.'

'Determined to use it on anyone who might come after you to avenge your defection?'—'No.'

'Did you regret killing this man?'—'Of course I did.'

'Did you say as much to anyone at the time?'—'I don't think so. I really don't know.'

'Well, let me ask you this, and I remind you that you are on oath: did you not say at a later stage that Britain should consider itself well rid of such a criminal, or words to that effect?'—'Yes, but I didn't mean it that way. What I meant was that I shouldn't be charged with a crime, I was just an innocent man defending himself.'

'Thank you, no further questions. You may stand down.'

Geria looked shaken and angry, and Sir Gordon rose quickly, to cut off any outburst.

'That's all, professor. You must leave the witness box now, and return to the dock.'

To the judge, he said: 'My Lord, the defence has only two more witnesses to call, but again their evidence may take some time. In view of the hour, I do not know if your Lordship would prefer to adjourn at this stage, and hear them tomorrow?'

'Do these witnesses include someone who will tell this court, once and for all, on what authority the accused was issued with a revolver?' Morston Richards asked him bluntly.

'Yes, my Lord. I shall call the officer who was in charge of all security arrangements; he will be my third, and last witness.'

'Very good,' said the judge. 'Court is adjourned until tomorrow morning. Shall we say ten o'clock, so that we may make an early start?'

Both counsel bowed, and the court-room quickly emptied.

9

THE WAY THROUGH THE SCREEN

Colonel Zabotin drove to the trade delegation complex in Hampstead before the court rose, and was sitting in the sound-proofed apartment when Andrei and Josef returned. Copies of the two London evening newspapers lay open before him, and he was cock-a-hoop with what he read.

'You see,' he boasted, smacking the papers with the back of his hand, 'I was right! My judgment has been one hundred per cent sound! And Geria, of all people: they must have been mad to put him up in open court!'

'Congratulations, comrade-colonel,' said Andrei drily. 'But being right doesn't make it any easier for us. That's a fortress they've got him in there, that Old Bailey. We don't get as much as a peep at them, coming in or going out. The British are using dummy cars and heavy escorts. Every approach to the building is thick with police, and all have radios, Josef was questioned a long time today, and searched twice, before they let him inside. If you want us to kill Geria there, it's going to turn out a kamikaze mission rather than an assassination.'

Josef nodded his agreement. Their job was to kill, not be killed. He, too, had been very impressed by the show of strength.

'No need for a bloodbath of any kind, I'm glad to say,' the colonel told them. 'I've had Moscow on, and the orders are quite clear. They don't want us to touch these two, at least not yet awhile. We have to send them a message reminding them they have a son at home, a helpless child whose future lies in his father's hands. We want these two back. Moscow is prepared to offer a straight deal, the boy's life in exchange for their return.

And they have instructed me to put a time limit on their acceptance.'

Andrei brightened visibly.

'That makes sense,' he said. 'Except the British might not like it. And they hold the whip hand, they've got Geria.'

'Think about it, though,' said Zabotin. 'I'm not even sure now that Geria will get off without some form of punishment, perhaps a prison sentence. You see what these papers are implying, they say the lawyers wanted the trial held in secret, but the judge refused: and they make it clear he's a very tough judge. I'm beginning to think British justice really is incorruptible, and this trial isn't rigged. Now, if Geria goes to prison, he's ours. We can contact him, blackmail him *and* get him out. We've done it before in an English prison: remember Blake?'

'That's true enough.' Andrei smiled with genuine warmth at the memory of double agent George Blake's remarkable escape from prison. 'Our people actually told him how and when to make the break, by setting up a two-way radio link into his cell. A fantastic operation.'

'I like the idea of friend Geria doing a little stretch in an English prison,' said the colonel slowly. 'I like it very much indeed. We would know exactly where he was, we would certainly be able to contact him one way or another—especially with the help of my gangster friends. A few months in the cells would hardly endear him to his British protectors. He'd come running to us, like a dog.'

He looked at Josef.

'Let's have a drink to help lubricate our thoughts.'

He raised his glass.

'Here's to a long prison sentence for comrade Geria,' he said. He rubbed his chin. 'On the other hand, we have to plan for every contingency. If they set him free, we lose him again. So: we have to find a way of getting a message to him before the trial is over. I need ideas. You two haven't wasted your time today—I hope. Let's hear what you have to say.'

'Josef was the one in court today,' Andrei reminded him. 'I kept an eye on what happened outside the building. Very rewarding it was, too. Sydenham sends the escort cars into a place called Snow Hill police station, just round the corner from Old Bailey: they're parked in the yard there. I followed one this morning. It came out at 11.45, two men inside, and drove at snail's pace to a cul-de-sac in the Knightsbridge district. Both the men got out and went into a building called The Outdoors Club. That was at 12.15 or so. They came out again at 12.40 carrying two trays of food, like a couple of waiters, everything in silver dishes. They drove back with it to the court. Those meals can only have been for Geria and his wife. Can you find out from your contacts, comrade-colonel, the procedure for sending meals to people in the cells at the Old Bailey?'

'I can,' said Zabotin.

'We might be able to use the information,' said Andrei. 'Josef and I could arrange to meet those two police waiters tomorrow lunchtime, and deliver the meal for them. When comrade Geria eats his sturgeon, he will find your message wrapped around one of the bones saying Moscow wants him back.'

Zabotin considered the suggestion.

'It could work,' he conceded. 'But a lot of things would have to fall into place for you. They're no ordinary waiters you're dealing with, for one thing: they're Sydenham's men. And even if you overpower them, the police at the Old Bailey won't know you. They might ask some very awkward questions! But if you get away with all that and send the meal in, there are still two bodies and an official car to dispose of, and quickly. Sydenham will be on to you the moment his men are reported missing. He will know that the food has been doctored, and he'll know why.'

Andrei shrugged his shoulders.

'I don't care how good those men are, Josef and I can take care of them, don't you worry. We can also make sure it will be a long time before anyone traces the car or the bodies. Of course, you're right, the police at the Old Bailey won't know us, but does it matter? Who can they know for certain in the huge intelligence crowd swarming round the court, except the fat man, Sydenham? And he won't be there, checking dinners, he'll have quite enough on his own plate.'

Andrei grinned at his little joke.

'He'll find out soon enough what's happened. But Geria will have had your message. What he chooses to tell Sydenham about it is up to him, we can't control that in any case. My own guess is he will lie through his teeth if he thinks the boy wants him back badly enough.'

'Well,' said the colonel, 'it might work.'

He turned to Josef. 'Any other ideas?'

'We've got the fancy dress,' said Josef. 'Wigs and gowns, I mean. I think there's a chance of bluffing our way in as lawyers, maybe. But there's an even greater risk involved. The only time we could see him in the cells would be at the meal breaks, and Sydenham or the real lawyers are sure to be around. If we got trapped in there we would never get out again. It would be worth the risk if we had to kill Geria. But not to give him a message, comrade-colonel. I like Andrei's way. It's simple and direct, and that kind of plan always stands the best chance.'

'None the less, Sydenham will get to know about the message.'

'Yes,' Josef admitted. 'But we get to Geria first, as Andrei said. We maintain the initiative, one step ahead all the time.'

Zabotin made up his mind.

'All right,' he said. 'Do it your way, Andrei. But if anything goes wrong, you two are on your own. Stay away from the embassy, admit nothing. If you get caught, we disown you. Now then, let's think about the message.'

'Before we do that,' said Josef deliberately, 'I think I can reassure you on one thing, comrade-colonel. You won't have any cause to worry about us running to you for help. Every member of the squad knows perfectly well that he can't expect any help from our diplomats.'

There was the faintest of sneers in the word 'diplomats' and Zabotin picked him up instantly.

'Just so that we all know where we stand.'

He hauled himself out of his chair and began to pace up and down. 'Moscow has sent orders for you both to stay on indefinitely. Geria will have a time limit in which to answer my note. If he refuses to co-operate, you don't leave until you've made quite sure he never works for anyone else. If he goes home quietly, he goes with you.'

'What about the woman?' asked Andrei.

'The amnesty applies to her too,' said the colonel. 'At least, that's what I'm told. So mind your tongue when dealing with her. We want the husband back, that's priority number one, and if she can be persuaded to travel with him, that makes your task easier. What really happens to her once they're home is no concern of yours or mine.'

'I agree,' said Andrei. Josef remained silent.

'We're agreed, then,' the colonel told them, 'about tomorrow. You intercept the food and deliver it to the Old Bailey. I've got to go back to my own office and make one or two arrangements: I'll be back here before midnight. This is what we'll do.'

He ran through the outline of his plan.

'Make your way back here after getting rid of the car and the bodies,' he said, at the finish. 'And lie low till we know what is going to happen to Geria. Either way I will get you back to Moscow after that. Any questions? Right, I'll see you at midnight.'

10

THE TRIAL: DAY THREE MORNING

Morston Richards took his place on the bench, old and wrinkled as Father Time. His clerk sat on one side, a duty under-Sheriff on the other. The judge carried a posy of flowers, like a priest who holds the Cross to ward off evil; a custom that dated back more than two hundred years. In the eighteenth century prisoners brought in from the stinking Newgate Gaol carried the jail fever, typhus, in their hair and clothes and more than sixty people, including two trial judges, had died. The 'remedy' then, still observed, was to disguise the stench by using flowers and herbs. Sweet-smelling posies covered the bench, and the ledge of the dock itself. It was the same today, for the custom is solemnly observed on two days of each month from May till September.

The bouquet was quite noticeable. It reminded Geria of forgotten early summers in Peredelkino. The judge, and the ageing Q.C.'s, paid it scant heed. Sir Gordon had only two more witnesses to call, and he was impatient to be done.

'I call Katerina Geria.'

She looked demure and composed as she affirmed: like her husband, she was a good communist, not a Christian. A hairdresser had called at the 'safe house' and on Sydenham's instructions had made her as near angelic as any sinner can look. Blonde tresses gleamed and sparkled in the bright lights of the courtroom, like corn in the early morning sun. A black band on the crown of her head served as hat: she wore a two-piece black suit and white blouse, while a single red rose lay pinned to her lapel. Apart from a wedding ring she wore no other jewellery.

The women jurors looked at her closely but they searched in vain for the marks of plastic surgery they knew she had undergone. Her skin was without a blemish, pale and smooth and translucent as a lake on a wind-less day. Her nose was small, perfect, curving ever so slightly into a tilt, above full red lips that exactly matched the rose at her throat. She was very lovely. Every reporter looked at her with wise old eyes and jotted down suitable praise in the notebook at his side. The court was utterly silent.

'You are Katerina Geria, wife of the defendant?'—'Yes, sir.'

'And, like him, a Russian?'—'Yes. I was born in Moscow.'

'In that country you won a reputation as a poet of great distinction, and you were also a writer of books?'—'I wrote a great deal of verse at one time. I had eight volumes of poetry published in Russia and neighbouring Communist countries. It is true that I wrote two novels, but they were banned. In the Eastern bloc, anyway.'

'Before you fell foul of the regime over those books, were you not a highly privileged and high-ranking Party member?'—'Well, I was certainly privileged, but not at any time a Party official, and of course, there is a big difference. I was an enthusiastic Communist from the first moment I could think for myself—I think you could call it my first love affair, in a way. I wrote a book of verse called *Patriotic Thoughts* when I was still a schoolgirl. It was published, and copies were distributed to every school in the Soviet Union. As I see it now, it was a rather naive work by a patriotic child, but it was considered a remarkable achievement by one of my age. It was this publication that led to the privileges you have mentioned. A royalties system operates in Russia, just as it does here and *Patriotic Thoughts* brought in a lot of money. My parents used that money to better the whole family. Subsequent books brought bigger rewards and long before I was married I was able to live very well. I was known to some members of the Praesidium. I had a dacha at Peredelkino, a car, a telephone—in those days a private telephone was a considerable privilege! I was a member of the Communist party, but I did not hold Party rank.'

'You served in one of the ministries?'—'I worked for the ministry of Culture for a while. I was one of a group of young writers turning out what we called "instant jingle", straightforward propaganda, pure and simple. I hated it. At the end of my first year in the ministry, I dried up, words refused to come from my pen. I asked to be allowed to return to what I could do best, creative poetry. Eventually, they agreed.'

'You were already developing into something of a rebel?'—'I couldn't stomach the thought of being a paid hack. If that is being a rebel, maybe I was. I was certainly unaware of it at the time.'

'Did you—do any writers in Russia—enjoy real freedom of expression?'—'Communist Russia has produced some of the greatest writers to be found anywhere in the world. It's not communism that presents a barrier to free expression, it is the little men who try to interpret it.'

'At any rate, how did these little men come to figure in your own life?'—'I wrote a novel that was interpreted, wrongly in my opinion then and now, as disloyal. After that, my whole life began to change. I was no longer invited to official functions. People I had looked upon as friends began to avoid me. I found it increasingly difficult to have contributions accepted by newspapers and magazines.'

'Were you publicly reprimanded, or harmed in any way?'—'No. My husband intervened and smoothed things over. But the book was destroyed.'

'Even so, a copy appeared later in western Europe?'—'Yes.'

'With what result?'—'I was called before a disgusting man who threatened me.'

'Threatened you with what?'—'Blackmail. The first weapon dictators always use.'

'To blackmail you with what?'—'Saying that I had had affairs with other men.'

'Was there any truth in that?'—'I had known several men before I married Alexandrei.'

'How could that information harm you?'—'He had photographs of me with some of these men, taken after my marriage.

It was quite true that I had seen them, but nothing more. Unfortunately I hadn't told my husband about it—I didn't want to cause any jealousy—and this man chose to interpret that in his own way.'

'Did anything happen to these men, the ones in the photographs?'—'Yes. They were rounded up and imprisoned.'

'They were all writers?'—'Yes. They were made to take the blame for whatever had offended the regime in my book, I suppose. They were accused of being dissidents and reactionaries.'

'Was it true?'—'They had independent minds. That is a very dangerous thing, in Russia today.'

'What did you do about it?'—'I had a husband and a young son to consider. I begged this man not to say anything to my husband, and I signed a confession of guilt. He said it would be kept by the authorities as a guarantee of my future good behaviour. By that I presumed he meant political behaviour, but the wording of the "confession" was deliberately obscure.'

'How old were you at this time?'—'In my early thirties.'

'And a passionate young woman?'—'Physical love has always meant a great deal to me, more than most, perhaps.'

'You wrote a second book, in secret?'—'My husband was spending a great deal of time in Dubno and elsewhere away from Moscow. I had plenty of opportunity.'

'Did you ever intend it to be published?'—'Not at the time. I knew it could never be published in Russia, of course. I wrote it as a personal protest against injustice, to me and my friends.'

'But you took it into the office of a newspaper and demanded that the editor should read it?'—'I did. I had heard that some more of my family and friends had been carted off for interrogation. This was typically blind, and spiteful: they daren't strike direct at me, because of my husband, so they persecuted a great many innocent people. I was determined to do something about that if I could.'

'There was more to it than that, though, wasn't there?'—'Yes.'

'I'll come back to that in just a moment. Your husband interceded once again to save you from punishment?'—'He let it be known his work was bound to suffer if I was ill-treated. He also used that as a lever to get some of my friends released.'

'You also produced a copy manuscript?'—'Yes, one they hadn't found.'

'There were others?'—'Yes. I was of course in touch with an underground group. My husband knew nothing about this, in fact this is the first time I have admitted it in his presence. Through the group I was in contact with foreign intelligence agents, and they arranged to have copies of this new book smuggled out for publication.'

'Still keeping this secret from your own husband?'—'I had to. I don't say that with any pride. Among other things, I didn't want to hurt him.'

Geria stared at her from the dock as if unable to credit his own ears. Katerina avoided his eyes, and steadily faced the Q.C. They had gone over this ground before the hearing was resumed, and she knew exactly what was required of her.

'Some of what you will have to answer,' Sir Gordon had told her, 'may hurt your husband's feelings, but don't worry about that: he'll survive. Our only concern is to get him off. Just answer the questions, and trust me.'

He addressed her again.

'Were you not taking a grave risk in walking into that Russian newspaper office with such a manuscript?'—'I knew precisely what I was doing. I had made up my mind to escape from Russia, and to persuade my husband to come with me. It was necessary to suffer a little before I could hope to do that.'

'It was part of a carefully laid plan?'—'Yes.'

'What did you hope to gain by this?'—'I had already been told the book would be published in Britain. If they thought I was responsible for that, nothing could have saved me. I had to get rid of my copies now, publicly, and deny any further involvement under questioning by the K.G.B. There are dissident groups in Russia, everyone knows that: but if they couldn't prove my connection with any of them—if I could stand up to the interrogation—then I would have to be given the benefit of the doubt, if only because of my husband's value to the state.'

'That was a fearful gamble to take?'—'It was a calculated risk, taken on advice.'

'You were taken to Lubyanka by the K.G.B.?'—'Yes. But it worked out as I had hoped. My husband stepped in and I was released fairly quickly.'

'And after the book appeared in Britain, with a great deal of publicity?'—'I made a public statement saying it was a forgery, a capitalist plot to discredit my husband, through me.'

'You even appeared on Russian television, and defended the right of the authorities to censor all works of art, books, plays, and the like?'—'I did.'

'You met western correspondents and repeated the claim that the book was a forgery?'—'Yes.'

'Under questioning by them, you admitted you had made errors of judgment in the past?'—'I did. But I denied the book was mine. My husband knew otherwise, of course, and he accepted that I was doing this to save myself from imprisonment.'

'You succeeded in persuading the authorities that once again you were innocent of the act of smuggling?'—'As long as they were unable to prove any connection, it suited them to give me the benefit of the doubt. Later events proved that I did succeed in convincing them I had undergone a change of heart.'

'They struck a bargain with you?'—'Yes. I appeared before a ministerial committee, asked official forgiveness for writing the two books, and gave a sworn undertaking there would be no repetition. I strongly denied any connection with dissident groups.'

'You then began writing for publication once more?'—'Yes, a number of articles and poems in praise of the regime.'

'I believe you referred to the former invasion of Czechoslovakia and called it an honourable and necessary act of statesmanship?'—'To my eternal shame, yes, I did.'

'Had you undergone such a change of heart?'—'Never!'

'You were not doing all this, as many believed, just to save your own skin?'—'No, it was all part of a carefully laid plan.'

'Whose plan?'—'I was acting at all times on the orders of British intelligence agents.'

* * *

Swiftly, the reporters began to slip out of court to file their copy. Red runaway's wife tells all—it was heady, sensational stuff. Sir Gordon spoke to Katerina again.

'You are saying that British agents ordered you to do all this, even at risk of dire punishment?'—'I had already sought their help to leave the country. What they wanted was to set in motion a chain of events that would persuade my husband to join me. We accepted that there was considerable risk involved, but we relied on my husband's very considerable influence to protect me, certainly as long as they were unable to prove any connection between me and the act of smuggling the book out. And that's how it proved. Such an illicit traffic certainly exists, and to my knowledge the writer need not have any personal involvement.'

'What did you hope to gain from all this?'—'The freedom to write as I wanted, what I wanted. I regard that as the most important thing in life. I certainly put it above self, and family.'

'You deliberately deceived your own husband to achieve this end?'—'There are many interpretations of what I did. He thought he was working for Russia, I felt he was being used by evil men who wanted only to dominate the world. We have been talking about my books as if they were wicked and treacherous. They were nothing of the kind, neither an attack on communist Russia nor on communism itself. The second one was an exposure of the evil men who wield power in Russia today, a very different affair. I wanted to escape. I wanted my husband to work in a society that would not abuse his skill and knowledge for selfish ends. And I never intended that our son should be left behind, so helpless and defenceless.'

'Mrs Geria, you were either very brave, or very foolhardy?'—'To this day I can't find the answer to that. Nothing, but nothing, has turned out as I hoped.'

Katerina remembered very clearly the night that the plot was hatched. She had already made the first clandestine approach: now a spy from England came to follow up, and he arrived at the dacha without warning, at a time when her husband Alexandrei was away in Warsaw with a scientific delegation.

He had come to Moscow ostensibly as an exhibitor at the Trade Fair: it amused him to think of it as a kind of tit-for-tat response to the misuse of Russian trade delegation quarters back in London. She was about to go to bed when she heard a knock at the door. A stranger who spoke in fluent Russian said that his car had broken down, and did she have a telephone in the house he could use to call his friends?

Before she could answer, the stranger took a piece of paper from his pocket and handed it to her to read. As soon as she realised who he was, she said aloud:

'I'm sorry, but the 'phone here is out of order. If you walk down the road, only two or three hundred metres, you'll see another house, that's Guschov, the musician, you know? He has a telephone. I think he'll be able to help you, comrade. I'll show you the way.'

She closed the door behind her, leaving Mikhail asleep, and walked with the stranger into the garden. It was a moonlit night, with a breeze whispering through the larch trees overhead.

'I can't stay long,' said the man quickly. 'We've got the new book. It will be published this Christmas. We'll see to it that it gets plenty of publicity.'

'Can you get me and my son out of the country before that happens? I'm terribly afraid of what they will do to me.'

'I'll try. I can't promise you anything. It's not easy.'

She began to shake violently.

'This time they'll put me in prison. For sure.'

He came to the point right away.

'Before I can promise you anything, I have to tell you this. My government insists that your husband must come with you.'

'The first man I saw asked me about that. I told him, Alexandrei would never agree, he's too loyal and patriotic.'

'If you want our help, that's the price we are asking.'

'He would never do it.'

'Then you've got to make him. Force his hand. Convince him

it's the only way to save you from a lifetime in the labour camps.'

'It could still mean that.'

'I don't think so. Now this is what we want you to do,' he told her, and outlined the plot. 'It will call for a lot of courage on your part. Will you go through with it?'

'Yes.' This time she did not hesitate.

'Good. Make quite certain your husband can't back out at the last minute. Get *him* involved, persuade *him* to make the final contact with us. Make him ring that number we gave you. Just the code word, nothing more. We'll do the rest.'

'I'll try.'

'I want you to understand this, there's no deal without him. Much as I would like to help you personally, it's beyond my power.'

'I understand.'

'Remember, patience and courage. You will need plenty of both *but have faith in us*. We'll get you away, don't worry.'

She was terrified when the K.G.B. called at the skyscraper flat to take her away for questioning although she had tried to steel herself for it. The colonel put his boots up on her polished table top and helped himself to her husband's drink and cigarettes while she took Mikhail to her neighbour's flat.

One of his men went with her and waited outside the apartment as she put the child to bed.

'Mummy won't be long, darling,' she said. Her voice choked. 'She has to go with that man to sign some papers, that's all. But Daddy will be right here when you wake up.'

Mikhail looked up at her with knowing eyes.

'Will you be here too?' he asked. She busied herself with tucking him in, and said nothing.

'I don't like that man,' said Mikhail. 'I don't want you to go with him,' and he began to cry.

'Ssshh,' she told him, 'Mummy will be all right, silly. But if I'm late coming home, you be a good boy with Daddy, won't you?'

In a little while he was fast asleep. Katerina kissed him goodbye, and walked quickly out of the room. She whispered a few words to her neighbour: they all loathed the K.G.B.

'Don't do anything foolish,' she said. 'Just watch over the boy until my husband gets home. He'll get me back, you wait and see.'

She had done exactly as the spy had told her: now her courage was about to be put to the test. Her legs felt strangely weak as she went back into her own flat. The colonel watched in silence as she put on a coat and gloves. All the while his men were opening drawers and nosing through the contents, like ferrets in a rabbit warren.

As she stood there trembling, he said, 'You brought all this on yourself, you know that?'

She said nothing, but looked down at him.

'Stupid bitch.'

He called to the man nearest to him, 'Hey, you! Take this woman to Lubyanka. You'll find the reception committee all waiting.'

The K.G.B. man drove her into the courtyard of the dreaded building, carefully locked the door of his car—even here, in the safest parking lot in all Moscow—and led her without a word through the iron doors that opened into the administrative block. Side by side, and still in complete silence, they climbed up two flights of stone stairs. He escorted her along a corridor, lit by a line of bare bulbs, as their footsteps clanged and echoed into the loneliness that seemed to hang in the air.

He came to a halt, and hammered knuckles as big and red as a pig's trotters on a steel door.

'Come.'

He took Katerina's arm and pushed her inside, pausing first to doff his cap.

She looked around her with eyes that were wide with terror. The room was small, and cold. Metal filing cabinets that were scratched and scarred lined the wall to her right. A single bright light burned over the desk in front of her, a naked bulb, like the others in the corridor. The floor was covered in green linoleum, the air rank with the stink of cheap tobacco. There was one window, a square of about twenty inches, heavily barred in case someone under duress might be tempted to squeeze through and drop thirty feet to the concrete yard below.

Katerina shivered, and not only from the cold.

She knew the man behind the desk. He was dark, and squat, crouching forward in his chair, like a toad about to hop on her. His eyes were small, and sly. Like the K.G.B. colonel who had come to search her flat, like the brute who had brought her to the Lubyanka, he wore a topcoat of gleaming leather that reached down to his ankles.

The smile he bestowed on her was as false as an undertaker's grief at the sight of death. He looked her up and down, and his eyes undressed her, gloating over what they saw. The manuscript she had taken into *Izvestia* that afternoon lay on the top of his desk, and his fingers drummed a tattoo on the white pages. He seemed to be in no hurry. He was the same man who had interrogated her over the first book, the one who held the photographs of Katerina with her lovers, and the one who held her signed confession of guilt.

'You can get out,' he said to her escort. 'Don't hang around. She's going to be here for some time yet.'

The door slammed shut. There was nowhere for Katerina to sit down, and her legs ached. She shifted wretchedly from one foot to the other, waiting for the questioning to begin. The man at the desk lit another cigarette: the match scraped so loudly that the sound made her jump. He nodded his head up and down, revelling in her nervousness.

'You surpassed yourself today,' he told her, still smiling.

She tried to remember what the English spy had told her: patience, and courage.

'Feeling proud of yourself, are you?'

She made no reply.

'I asked you a question. Are you proud of yourself?'

'No.'

'That's better. There isn't very much to be proud of here.' A stubby finger slowly turned the pages of the manuscript. 'Over there in my files, I have a piece of paper signed by you, a promise not to write any more subversive filth, do you remember putting your name to that document?'

'Yes.'

'You must have taken a long time to write this. Did your husband know anything about it?'

'No.'

'I'll have to ask him about that. You must have spent months writing this scandalous muck. It's hard to believe he knew nothing of what was going on.'

'I wrote that while he was away, at Dubno. He had no idea.'

'Well, I suppose it's possible. After all, he knew nothing about your boy friends, did he?'

She had no answer to that. Her questioner came from behind his desk and stood very close, so that their bodies touched. She was almost as tall as he was. One of his hands came up and he stroked her behind. She could smell his tobacco breath as he spoke to her.

'I think I can recognise one of the characters in this new book of yours, Katerina. It's me, isn't it?'

She felt sick.

'You don't make him sound a very nice person, not in the book. But I've been nice to you, haven't I? I haven't shown your husband any of those pictures, I haven't branded you for the little tart we know you to be, now, have I? Answer me.'

'No.'

His hand was still stroking her.

'Say that I've been nice to you. Tell me.'

'You've been nice to me.'

'Get down on your knees and thank me.'

She was shaking so violently that she was forced to hold him as she knelt down. He pawed her, all the way.

'Now say it.'

'Thank you for being nice to me.'

Suddenly he swung his arm and caught her a tremendous blow with his open hand, not on her face where it would bruise, but on the side of her head, behind the ear.

She skidded across the linoleum, like a puck on a skating rink, and thumped into a filing cabinet. Her head hurt, her teeth ached, and she heard strange, guttural noises. It was the sound of her own voice, pleading with the toad not to hit her again, begging for mercy. Now he began to shout at her.

'And this is how you repay me for being nice to you, insulting me in your filthy book! Get on your feet, you cow, or I'll start playing football with you, to teach you some manners!'

Katerina struggled up. She was gasping for breath, wheezing with sheer terror. The interrogator reached out and grabbed her by her hair, and dragged her to the front of the desk. He held her for some minutes, glaring into her frightened eyes, tugging at the roots of her hair, shaking her head from side to side until the tears poured down her face.

'That's better.' His hand came away. She wondered if her hair had been torn out: the pain was unbearable. 'I think we know where we stand now, you and me. You will answer my questions promptly, respectfully, and truthfully, you understand?'

'Yes. Yes.'

'*Yes, gaspadeen* Vorov. Show a little respect.'

'Yes, gaspadeen Vorov. I'm sorry.'

'Better and better.'

He lit another cigarette and walked casually back to his chair. Katerina remembered what the English spy had said: 'You've got to crawl to these people make them think you're beaten, play for time until your husband understands the danger you're in and comes with you to freedom.' She looked at the toad's back with hatred. She summoned up every ounce of her courage as he began speaking again.

'Now. You can begin by giving me the names of this group you work with.'

'There is no group, gaspadeen, I swear it.'

'Don't lie to me. You'll go inside for thirty years if you lie to me.'

'Jail me, kill me if you want, I can't stop you! But there isn't any group of dissidents. I don't even *know* any.'

She knew now that he had no information, only suspicion, and it was enough to sustain her.

'For the last time, tell me the names, or I'll beat them out of your hide.'

'I'm telling you the truth, I swear I don't know any names.'

'We'll see about that. Why did you write this filth?' He slammed a hand down on her book.

'I don't know, I don't know.' She rocked her body backwards and forwards in anguish. 'I must have been mad, I knew it could never be printed ... it was just that my friends were in prison for something they had not done, I felt so helpless.'

'Have you shown this to anyone else?'

'No. No, gaspadeen. No one else saw it until today.'

'You're not only a whore, you're a lying whore. That's what you said the last time.'

'It was the truth. You held an inquiry, you know someone else got hold of a copy and smuggled it out of the country.'

Vorov was inclined, still, to think that was true. There was no doubting in official minds that a disease had begun to manifest itself after Czechoslovakia, a germ of revolt that spread quickly and dangerously among certain intellectuals: writers in particular. Any one of a score of dissidents might have intercepted that first book. That was the only thing that had saved her from labour camp—that, and the influence her husband had. Vorov had tapped her husband's several telephones ever since the first incident, in Moscow, Dubno and in every hotel he had stayed in, and he was quite certain that Geria himself was in no way involved. Even so, his nose told him this woman was not all that she seemed. What it was she was hiding from him, he could not be sure: but there was *something* there to be dug out. He decided to throw her into the cells for the night and question her again tomorrow, when he'd had time to read through this manuscript more thoroughly. If that didn't work, he would try to get an order to have the boy removed to an institution. Perhaps that would loosen her tongue.

'I know you are lying, little Katerina. Perhaps you'd like a little time to think things over.'

He picked up the telephone on his desk, and gave his orders. A few minutes later, there was a knock on his door and two women guards entered. They were big women, with police faces.

'Take this dirty cow out of my office and find her a bed for the night. I want you to wash her mouth out for her, she's an awful liar, this one. I'll let you know when I want to see her again.'

They took her down to the prison section. There they stripped her, put her under an icy shower, forced her to gargle with mouthwash, gave her a rough linen smock to wear, and marched her to the cells. Katerina was numb with cold, her head throbbed with pain, and she longed for sleep. The cell was really a cage, iron bars set into a concrete base, with no heating of any kind. An open latrine bucket stood in the corner. This she would have to share with seven other frightened creatures who lay on their bunks without a word as she was pushed in to join them. She was thrown a single, thin blanket and a horsehair pillow. Her bunk was at the top of a row of four, and directly beneath a powerful light that stayed on, all night.

Even so, she slept.

At one in the morning, the door crashed open.

'Get down here.'

She climbed down on to the cold floor. She was almost ready to break.

'Get dressed and follow me.'

Her own clothes were flung down in a heap. Katerina felt her head would burst open with the pain from that earlier blow. Her underclothes felt cold as shrouds to her skin, and at the thought of what her questioner would do next, she began to cry.

'Stop that snivelling. You're going home, woman, you don't know how lucky you are.'

Half an hour later, she was back in the apartment with her husband....

Sir Gordon was watching her closely.

'These orders you were following from British intelligence, did they work out according to plan?'—'Yes. After a long time.'

'You and your husband came to a secret agreement to defect together?'—'I told him how I had been treated. I don't think he was in any doubt that I was in danger. I explained to him that I would pretend to co-operate with the authorities, while planning our escape. It took almost another year to accomplish that.'

'He played an active part in making the arrangements?'—'Yes, he was never really under any supervision himself and found it easy to make the necessary contact.'

'You had to work very hard to win the opportunity to defect, and convince the authorities of your change of heart?'—'Yes. I told you some of the things I did. I also wrote a letter to *The Times* in London, denouncing the book as a fraud. The letter was actually drafted for me, but I signed it, and it was published.'

'Was there any reaction?'—'Yes, a very clever one. The publishers replied through the same columns, saying that they had acted in good faith: but they duly apologised and withdrew the book. I suppose British intelligence advised them to do this, but it aroused considerable comment in England at the time, and had a very favourable effect in Moscow. There was always room for genuine doubt—outside K.G.B. circles, of course—that I had ever been involved in the smuggling of that book to the west. This seemed to settle it, once and for all.'

'And after a decent interval, you were invited once more to official functions?'—'Wherever my husband appeared in public. The idea was to refute western propaganda by showing us together, and back in official favour.'

'You began to travel with him?'—'Not very far at first. I went to Kiev and Leningrad. The British told us to be very patient. We were very careful as to what we said in private, and it began to pay dividends.'

'None the less, it was remarkably trusting of them to allow you to join him for the trip to Vienna?'—'Not as trusting as you might think. I was taken aside and warned that Mikhail would be regarded as hostage against our safe return.'

'Did you withhold all knowledge of that warning from your husband?'—'I said nothing until we reached Vienna and were contacted by the British agents. I didn't know if I could bear to leave without my son, never mind him. We had very little time to make the decision, in the end. They wouldn't take me without Alexandrei, so I persuaded him, to defect, finally. It was a hideously difficult time for both of us.'

'Were any promises held out to you concerning your son?'—'We were told that "every effort" would be made to bring him to us later.'

'But the Russians won't release him?'—'Well, of course, they didn't know where *we* were until this trial was held. I hope now that common humanity will now prevail, and they will let him come to join us.'

Morston Richards peered down at the lawyer.

'Sir Gordon, this court has followed you patiently through thc steppes of Russia for nearly two days now. We have allowed you the greatest latitude in your questioning of witnesses, but once again I feel I should remind you the charge before us is one of manslaughter. I think it would be more to the point if you brought the lady nearer home, to the house on Saddlers Hill.'

The Q.C. smiled, and bowed. He had squeezed every conceivable ounce of sympathy from the jury for his client and was content.

'As your Lordship pleases.'

'Mrs Geria, I will turn now to your arrival in this country. Your husband has told us of his revulsion at being cooped up in a windowless, claustrophobic apartment for so long: were you as unhappy there as he was?'—'I was a lot more composed, certainly at first. But they were very hard on him and the more he became discontented, so this began to have an effect on me, too. I was better equipped to take it because I realised what they were up to.'

'What about the crash-course in language and customs, that sort of thing?'—'My husband refused to take up the research work he had been doing in Russia, and many pressures were put upon him to persuade him to alter his mind. The unhappier he became, the harder they drove him, in the hope he would agree to *anything* just to gain some respite. If I complained, I was taken out for a drive in the country. When he complained, they found fault and increased the pressure.'

'He was on the rack, and they were turning the screws?'—

'That's how I looked at it, certainly.'

'What was your attitude to treatment by plastic surgery?'—'I jumped at the chance, what plain woman wouldn't? Alexandrei dreaded it. I gave a promise not to let him know my true feelings.'

'You had a face-lift?'—'Among other things! I had a new nose, every line and wrinkle removed from my face. They also gave me a mammaplasty, raising of the breasts, you know? I came out looking and feeling like a young girl again. I was so happy, I could have cried.'

'But your husband's treatment produced a quite opposite effect, did it not?'—'I warned them to be careful. He had this pathological dread of surgeons and dentists, particularly dentists. I can't tell you how bad he felt when they had to re-set his jaw, and wire it up in a clamp. He felt very mixed up, too, about his new face. He used to stare in the mirror for hours, calling himself a fraud and impostor.'

'It also had a disastrous effect on his feelings for you?'—'No one could have foreseen *that*, of course. It was awful! From the beginning he avoided me, physically. He said he didn't know me any more. He used to wake up and bend over me, staring: then he would say that he wanted to find the real me next to him one morning, the girl he had married, a girl with dark wavy hair and a flat little nose, things like that. I know it sounds amusing but it was nothing of the kind, it was pathetic to hear. He couldn't bear to touch me. I needed his love now that we were in a strange country, without our son, but somehow both his mind and body seemed to reject me. We became worse than strangers to each other: I mean, you could love a stranger, physically that is, if the need was desperate enough, but my husband and I became enemies for a while. Every sentence turned into a blazing quarrel. We said terrible things to each other. The apartment, and then the country house, turned into the worst kind of prisons for both of us, and not only because of the presence of guards and the sense of confinement, though that was bad enough for two active and intelligent people. We were compelled to live together every minute of the day, to eat together, to dress and undress side by side, to lie down in bed within touching distance and yet all the time we were wholly unable to make love to each other. It was a nightmare situation.'

'He was impotent?'—'Completely. And if that meant I spent my nights in a torture chamber, he spent his in a kind of strait jacket: I think perhaps his was the greater torment.'

'How did you resolve the situation?'—'In the only way two adults can, by patience, self-discipline and a lot of compassion. We made a pact to try not to quarrel. That was a beginning. Then one day he said he felt he could get better if only we could be allowed to live on our own, completely alone, and from that moment on I did all I could to persuade—to persuade the authorities to let him have his way.'

'And they agreed?'—'Yes, but they put a price on it. A life on our own in return for his research work. It was what they always sought, I realised that. None of them cared what happened to me or my son from the very beginning, it was Alexandrei and his secrets they were after.'

'Did things get better after you moved into this paradise?'—'In some ways, not in others. He was far less quarrelsome. But no matter how he tried, he remained impotent. He began to get very depressed and jumpy. He started to imagine all sorts of things.'

'Why was your husband so vehemently opposed to the presence of a bodyguard in this house?'—'I told you, he found their presence inhibiting, he blamed that as the last straw that made him impotent.'

'And did not jealousy play some part in his attitude, too?'—'It may have done.'

'He was acutely aware of his failure to love you, and did not want any other men around?'—'Perhaps.'

'Did he have reason to feel jealous?'—'There were times when I was taken out alone for a drive by the guards. It was no more than a break in routine, but if I came back and said I'd had a good time, he would get very depressed. If I said nothing, he became suspicious and started to ask a lot of foolish questions.'

'Did you yourself want a bodyguard in the house?'—'I would have much preferred that to my husband having a gun, certainly.'

'Did you not suggest one guard in particular might stay with you in number 28?'—'I may have done, I don't really remember.'

'Come now, Mrs Geria, you are on oath. Well?'—'Yes.'

'Why was that?'—'Because he was very kind and understanding.'

'In what way?'—'Just sympathetic, that's all.'

'Did your husband suspect you were lovers?'—'He may have suspected it, but it was not true.'

'I am not suggesting that it was, Mrs Geria, I am talking about your husband and his state of mind. He knew you were a very passionate woman while he was impotent, for whatever reason?'—'I couldn't help that. All they wanted was that my husband should work for them.'

'I put it to you that this man was suggested as a bodyguard as part of a plan to make quite sure your husband started work again, and soon?'—'That was never discussed with me.'

'And that he agreed to every condition but this, and took the gun as the only way of making sure you and he could live alone together?'—'That is not true.'

'But it all went wrong, and a burglar broke into the house to wreck all these carefully laid plans?'—'That is a terrible thing to suggest.'

'Did you really believe your husband could protect you, if an emergency came about?'—'I keep telling you, it didn't matter *what* I thought. My husband was absolutely determined we should be in a house on our own. The security people wanted to make sure we were adequately protected, but at the same time, their principal concern was to get him back to work. I could understand their point of view. They were doing this for their country.'

'Are you telling us that jealousy played no part in his insistence on having a gun in his possession?'—'You are twisting these things round! I don't want anyone to have the wrong impression about my husband. Until my troubles began in Russia, he was the sweetest, gentlest person imaginable. He abhorred any kind of violence, and I doubt if he'd ever held a gun in his hand in his whole life. But now it was different. We both believed, very sincerely, that the K.G.B. would send someone to kill us if they could find us. This was our opinion, and our own guards lost no opportunity to impress that fact upon us, day after day. There was no need to play any tricks to convince us that we had to have protection of some kind. I doubt very much if my husband could really think straight about anything at that time, or he might have said yes to a bodyguard. But once he fastened on this idea of having a gun, nothing would dissuade him. What really lay at the back of his mind, all of it, I mean, only my husband can tell you, but one thing is absolutely certain: fear of assassination, real and constant fear, was most certainly part of it, and the greatest part.'

Sir Gordon was well pleased.

'Thank you, Mrs Geria, I have no further questions.'

The Solicitor-General was mercifully brief.

'I just want to ask you a question or two about that gun. When he asked for it, did he also ask for lessons on how to fire it?'—'I really don't know.'

'Did he or didn't he?'—'I tell you, I don't know.'

'As you please, we will leave it to the jury to decide. He was certainly given some lessons?'—'Oh yes.'

'How many?'—'Two, I think.'

'Did he say anything to you afterwards?'—'Yes, that it was easy to fire, or words to that effect.'

'Did he not also say "The first K.G.B. man to show his face in here will be dead before he knows what's happened to him?", or something like that?'—'They were only words. He was trying to reassure me, nothing more. It was like any husband saying to his wife, don't worry, I will look after you whatever happens.'

'Thank you, madam, I have no further questions.'

It was just after twelve noon when the black Jaguar drove into the mews behind the Outdoors Club, that culinary mecca for British sporting men that lies just off Knightsbridge. Sydenham was one of its 1,100 members (fees, 120 guineas per year): not that he cared so much for recreational shooting as for the game birds that graced its dining tables from August 12 onwards throughout the winter. It was here that he sent a driver, with an escort, each morning of the trial to pick up the meals especially prepared for Alexandrei Geria and his wife. Today's selection was porterhouse steak, medium rare.

Unless they are actually serving a prison sentence already for some previous offence, in which case they will get plain prison fare, all persons standing trial at the Old Bailey are allowed to have meals sent in to their cells below the court during the lunch adjournment. It is a considerable concession, extended to all who are presumed innocent in law until the jury decides otherwise: but in no way does it follow that the prison officers responsible for security in the cells look upon the Good Samaritans who bring such meals with smiling eyes, or without suspicion.

On the contrary, they remain obstinately watchful and suspicious. The most stringent precautions are taken to ensure that no cake, pudding, or pie, trifle or tart hides a gun, a file, a flick-knife, or hidden message. Every item of food is examined with the thoroughness to be expected of men long accustomed to the infinite cunning of the criminal classes, and others.

Most meals destined for Old Bailey defendants come from either the 'Rex' café, opposite, or from 'Lieto's', another Italian-owned café along the street, close to the 'Rumboe' public house. At both these establishments, orders for delivery in the lunch break are taken before eleven a.m. Relatives and friends then call back to pick up the food at the appropriate time and carry it back, personally, to court: there can be few sadder table services anywhere in the world. There is only one way to take the food in, through a single revolving door leading from the street. It is not always easy to carry a tray loaded with say, sausage and chips, fruit pie and custard and a drink, through such a door in the busy lunch break without mishap.

No sooner are the 'waiters' through that revolving door than they are seen, stopped and checked by duty policemen. Then they set off again down four steps, turn right, past the lifts area on the lower ground floor, and on through a door marked 'BARRISTERS AND SOLICITORS ENTRANCE TO PRISON DEPARTMENT'. On again, past another door—a genuine and priceless prison antique, this one, the same solid oak main door that once led into Newgate Gaol—until the food, a little colder now, reaches the main prison area entrance. It grows colder still as a bell is rung, and the carrier waits until a warder opens up to accept the food. Even now it may not go straight through. The name of the prisoner waiting to eat it has to be printed on an accompanying card. This in turn is checked against a written list: then the food is examined to make sure it contains nothing unlawful, and Borgia's food tasters in ancient Rome were never more thorough than these men. Only after all that has been done does the meal proceed, in the hands of prison officers, to the hungry men and women in the cells.

Even Sydenham had no power to alter this procedure. However, he was a close personal friend of the prison governor, and these cells are the domain of the governor of Brixton Prison. Thus he had done enough to guarantee that the meals for Alexandrei Geria would be hotter, and better, than most delivered via normal channels. The food from his club was prepared and cooked by a man rated by connoisseurs as one of the finest chefs in London. One day he had sent salmon steaks from the Thurso river, in Caithness. On the second day it had been a classic, if simple, Coq au vin. Today, porterhouse steaks. Napkins of shining white linen accompanied the meals, while the utensils were silver, and not plastic. The rolls were warm, the pats of butter cold. The wine that went with the food was carefully chosen by a thoughtful steward, even though restricted as to quantity—no more than half a pint per prisoner—by prison regulations.

While Mrs Geria's decision to eat with her husband was voluntary and required official permission, it was welcomed on grounds of security. She was entitled to enter her husband's cell—as is any relative—for what is known as the legal conference, with a member of the defence team. All legal conferences are privileged, and prison officers are obliged to remain outside, in the cell corridor. The young lawyer who took Mrs Geria to her husband's cell held only the briefest of 'conferences', to conform with regulations: whereupon he stood out in the corridor for the remainder of the recess with the officers. Sydenham was not being as selfishly indulgent as it may have seemed. With the Gerias locked in a cell, twenty-five feet below ground, guarded at all times by two hefty prison officers standing a few feet away, they were safe from attack—while his own hard-pressed men could relax briefly, and eat themselves. From time to time one of the warders looked through the spyhole, a square opening set in each of the seventy cell doors below the Old Bailey and measuring six inches by four, to make certain all was well: for the rest, Geria and his wife were left in peace. The system had worked perfectly during the first days of the trial. Today, as Sydenham himself was waiting to give evidence, he had left it to the police to send out one of his car crews when it was time to collect the food from his club.

'You want anyone in particular to go, sir?' asked the sergeant.

'No,' Sydenham told him. 'Ring through to Snow Hill at the appropriate time and tell them to send one of my cars to the club. Anyone handy will do.'

The black Jaguar left the City police compound in plenty of time, purred along the Embankment, doubled back into the Mall and pulled up in the mews cul-de-sac behind the club at 12.04 exactly. His men were not due back with the food until 1.15. This left time for a breather, and a smoke. The mews was deserted when they arrived. The score of houses in it were among the most expensive and desirable cottages in the capital, valued at more than £100,000 each: charming but still pokey dwellings that, like all mews buildings, started life as nothing more grand than lofts for a nobleman's falcons in long-gone Tudor times.

Few modern bluebloods could afford to live in such splendour today, far less keep hawks there: now they were owned by the nouveau riche, actors who demanded (and received) more than a million dollars per film, financiers who could make the price of a house in one afternoon on a single shares transaction, and their ilk. Each mews house was thoughtfully screened off from such tiresome distractions as a parked car by elegant curtains: and this was not the type of neighbourhood that expected nosey faces at any window at any time. No one noticed the Jaguar pull in. The driver switched off, yawned, and looked at his wristwatch. He and his companions got out, taking their time, and thoroughly approved of the silence, and emptiness, that greeted them. They had just lighted their cigarettes when a green van backed in, partly blocking the entry.

A powerfully-built man with fluffy white hair opened a door, swung his legs out from the driver's compartment, nodded affably to the two security men as he caught their eye, and slowly walked back to open the rear doors of his van. There were two enormous wicker baskets inside. He dragged one back along the floor of the van, lifted it on to his back with a grunt, and carried it to the door of a house just behind the Jaguar. The basket seemed to be heavy, and he had to struggle. He set it down gently, undid a leather strap that held the top section in place, and came back past Sydenham's men.

'Laundry,' he said by way of explanation, though none had been asked. 'Bleedin' 'eavy, an' all.'

The escort gazed at him as if he were a worm that had crawled out of the soil. He jerked a thumb at the van.

'I'll give you exactly thirty seconds,' he said in a voice that proclaimed officialdom, 'to move your heap out of here. You're blocking the exit.'

His hand slid gently into his pocket. You never knew.

He and his driver had their backs turned to the wickerwork basket that had been dumped in the courtyard. As they faced the fluffy-haired man, the lid of the basket began to open noiselessly. Josef's black mop of hair showed first, then up popped his pale face, like a Jack-in-the-Box. He held a gun in his hand, a pistol with a long barrel, and the fat drum of a silencer screwed into its mouth. Josef aimed first at the man with his hand in his pocket. At that range, he was as fast and deadly as a rattlesnake.

'Pop!' went the gun, with a sound like a cork being drawn from a bottle. 'Pop!' it went, maybe a half-second later. Andrei caught both men as they fell, with hands as sure as grappling irons. He draped the escort over the floor of the van, face down, picked up the driver and flung his body inside. Exerting all his strength he then took the 170 pounds deadweight of the escort, and heaved it in beside the driver, like a porter throwing a carcase of beef into a cold store. Ten seconds, and all was done.

Josef climbed in after the bodies and started to ferret among their clothing.

Andrei breathed hard as he walked back to the driving seat. He backed the van to the far end of the mews, waited until Josef was finished, and locked the doors. He put the keys in his pocket, and slipped a card under the windscreen wiper. On it he had written, 'ACME LAUNDRY. BACK FOR COLLECTION, 2 O'CLOCK.'

He looked at his wristwatch. It was 12.20 p.m.

'Got the passes?'

'Here,' said Josef and held two wallets aloft.

'Those bodies, will they bleed?'

'Not to notice,' said Josef. 'I covered the heads with a plastic bag. They'll do till we get back.'

Each of them pulled on a wig. Josef did something to the wallets: then, when he pronounced himself ready, they strolled round the corner and climbed the stairs leading to the Outdoors Club. A white painted door with an elegant brass knocker stood open for business. The reception desk lay halfway down a hallway that was lined with pictures of old hunting scenes. The steward looked up from his register as the two strangers approached. His wise old eyes appraised their clothing, counted the cost and the cut, and searched their faces: he knew at once they had no more than passing business here.

'Good morning, gentlemen,' he said politely enough. 'And what can I do for you?'

Andrei pulled out his dead man's wallet, and produced the identity card. His bore the name WALTER COOK, but his own face now stared up from beneath a plastic cover. The steward ran his finger through a list of names pinned on the reception desk, and nodded.

'Thank you, sir,' he said. He made no attempt to examine the pass that waited for inspection in Josef's hand. 'If you'll just sit over there'—he pointed to two chairs in the bay—'your trays will be ready in a moment.'

He went through to an inner office, and carefully closed the door behind him. He was a bright old man, with silver hair and a

Regency-stripe waistcoat, and he had dealt with Mr Sydenham for a great many years. He hummed a tune under his breath as he dialled a number that connected him to a special switchboard, manned by police officers at Snow Hill.

'Outdoors Club here,' he said to the operator. 'Name of Walter Cook here for the special delivery. Is that all right?'

'Quite right,' the policeman answered. 'I'll warn the Old Bailey lads the food is on its way. Thanks, Dad.'

The old steward went out to the kitchens and took one tray, first making sure that the silver lids were firmly in place. He felt them to double-check they were also piping hot. He folded a napkin, motioned the chef to do likewise with the second tray, and led the way back to his desk.

He beamed at Andrei. 'Here you are, Mr Cook,' he said. 'All ready.'

Andrei thanked him, and signed a chit: 'Walter Cook, pp Mr Sydenham, two meals.' He and Josef took up the trays and went out to the waiting car. They set the trays down on the floor in the back, clipped on their safety belts and joined the flow of traffic heading back for the Mall.

'I'll stay inside the car,' he told Josef. 'That's how they did it yesterday. You take the food in. If there's any trouble, shoot and run for it. I'll have the engine running.'

'Right.'

They dawdled along, clock-watching, and well ahead of schedule. Cars began to hoot impatiently behind them. Andrei took a chance and stopped on the Embankment as long as he dared, keeping an eye open for uniformed police. It was exactly 1.12 p.m. when he came to the road block, showed his pass to a City policeman, and was waved through to the revolving door of the Old Bailey. A few photographers hung about. Men and women were pouring out of the building. Two more policemen converged into the Jaguar: one was talking into his blue pocket radio. Andrei gave them a casual wave of his hand and stayed at the wheel. Josef took the first tray out and carried it through the revolving door. His heart was pounding, his eyes everywhere. He put the tray down on the police counter and said, 'Steak number one.'

He looked quickly round the hall, but there was no sign of Sydenham. So far, so good. 'I'll get the other tray right away.'

He winked at Andrei as he leaned in for the second tray, but said nothing. He had to struggle through the revolving door this time. The police stared silently at him as he approached.

'There, that's the lot.'

As he turned to leave, a sharp voice called him back. 'Hey, you forget something, mate?'

Josef swung round. He had no idea what he should have remembered. The worms of doubt began to crawl in his belly. What could he have overlooked? He dropped his hand to his side, ready to shoot and run if need be, when he felt his fingers touch the wallet. He took it out, showing the photograph inside the flap. The policeman took the wallet from him, and studied is carefully. He read the name on Josef's pass, RONALD KING. He looked at the photograph under the name, and compared it with the pale face before him. Josef had pasted it in less than an hour before and had no worries on that score: even so, the policeman was slow and scrupulous and Josef was frantic with worry lest Sydenham should come along.

With an enormous effort of will, he produced a grin, like a conjurer pulling a rabbit from the hat.

'Get a move on, chum,' he said. 'It's my drinking time you're wasting. And the guv'nor won't like it if that food gets cold.'

To save time at the prison area entrance, Sydenham had arranged that a uniformed policeman would carry each tray on the next part of its long journey to the cells.

The duty man looked at him and returned the smile.

'You gave me a bit of a turn there for a minute,' he said. 'I thought for a moment you were reaching for a gun instead of your wallet. Okay, I'll see to the rest. Enjoy your pint, you lucky bugger.'

As Josef walked away on legs as weak as tissue paper, a pencil held in a hamlike fist ticked off the name: RONALD KING on a printed list and entered the time, 1.16 p.m., and the date, Friday, May 13.

Sydenham reached the desk less than a minute after the Jaguar had pulled away. He saw the trays and looked round for the driver.

'Just gone, sir,' said the policeman. He pushed the written list across for Sydenham to look at. The fat man saw the entry, and nodded.

'All right. See that it gets down as quickly as possible.'

Mrs Geria and the solicitor had already joined Alexandrei in his cell when the food arrived. Two prison officers carried it in, and raised the lid of each dish for a final look at the contents. They knew it had been supplied by and paid for by Sydenham, and had little doubt that it was what he guaranteed it would be, food and nothing else. A delicious aroma of steak, and meat juices, and steaming fresh vegetables, filled the cell.

With his meal, Geria was served with a plastic beaker of wine. The wine was a Chambertin, carefully selected by the wine waiter at Sydenham's club. Zabotin had discovered that wine is permitted in the cells, and had toyed with the idea of sending in a message to the Gerias via the label on a bottle. But his informants warned him this could not succeed. Prison regulations say that a half-pint may be served, and no more: but they lay down that the bottle itself may not be handed to the prisoner. It has to be uncorked, and tasted, by the prison officers, who then measure a half-pint exactly into a marked plastic beaker. The remainder of the drink is then kept for use next day, assuming the trial has not ended beforehand. It is not greed that causes the prison officers to taste all the drink that goes into the cells below the Old Bailey, it is caution. Many a relative in the past has sent in an innocent-seeming glass of orange juice to those same cells, knowing that the recipient will shortly be locked up for a great many years: and to cheer him on his way, the 'orange juice' has been laced with a half-pint of neat gin, or vodka.

Mrs Geria had opted for water. She and her husband sipped their beverage politely and looked at their solicitor, who rose to his feet.

'Is everything in order, officer?' he asked.

'Yes, sir,' said the senior warder. Porterhouse steak and Chambertin, by Christ! It was getting more like the bloody Savoy every day in here. All he said aloud was: 'We'll be back about thirty minutes for the trays.'

Alexandrei and Katerina began their meal without enthusiasm. He put a fork into a potato and chewed, very slowly, as she watched. Her evidence this morning had opened his eyes to many things he had long suspected but, out of loyalty, had steadfastly refused to believe. She gave him a peck on the cheek.

'Don't be sad,' she told him. 'I said what I had to say. They're all afraid of that terrible old judge, and we all have to try to take as much of the blame for what happened on ourselves, don't you see that? Mr Sydenham is going to have to give evidence himself this afternoon. He said he expects to have an awful time, but he doesn't mind. He told me, the only thing that matters is to get you off.'

Alexandrei nodded glumly, and put down his fork, leaving the rest of the meal untouched.

At that very moment, he felt he would cheerfully have given ten years of his life to be back in Russia again, driving from the Lenin Hills down Bolshaya Kaluzhskaya street for a sight of the Donskoi monastery, or perhaps to walk by the lake at Pederelkino and watch it awake to spring, to smell the dark cold of the forest and hear the voice of his son, calling excitedly as he ran ahead along muddied paths. He yearned to see the Spasskaya Tower on the Kremlin once more, the Kremlyovsky Palace, the Dom Soyuzov and its Hall of Columns, and Pushkin square. He longed to be home again in his native land, with a rare and fierce longing, for he hated this grim English building with its judges and lawyers who bowed and scraped in their wigs and gowns. He had come to detest the very sound of Your Lordship, m'Lud, may it please you my Lord, and the rest of the mumbo-jumbo in which the English took such a curious pride, and even respect for the system it upheld.

But most of all, he loathed this cell. He felt he could not breathe properly inside its brick walls, so oppressive did he find it. A single window stood at the back, made of frosted glass, and heavily barred. No British chancellor spends a farthing more of his Budget than he can help on the prison population at any time, and the furniture provided for him and his wife—and legal adviser—was Spartan indeed. It consisted of a small wooden table, one chair, and a wooden bench, all bolted tight to the floor so that nothing could be smashed, and used as a weapon. The spyhole through which he was watched, like some dangerous animal, was made of unbreakable glass and looked down on him menacingly from the top of his heavy cell door. Every time he saw it, it reminded him of the one-eyed judge who waited upstairs to punish him. He felt trapped, shut in, unable to breathe. The whole cell seemed to him impregnated with the reek of fear and confinement.

The walls of every Old Bailey cell have to be regularly whitened to hide the graffiti left behind by men who have no prospect before them except privation and loneliness. The one he was in now cried out in shame for a coat of whitewash. Those who had sat where he was now sitting must have been maniacs with only one thought in their heads, and he was appalled by the words and crude sketches his wife could not help but see as she ate with him.

The solicitor felt the tension between them, and rose to his feet.

'I think we can call our conference over,' he said gently. 'You might like to be alone for a while. I'll be outside in the corridor with the officers if you want me.'

This was the great concession they enjoyed each day, thanks to Sydenham: twenty minutes alone, to seek comfort in each other.

'Thank you,' said Katerina. They watched him go out and the door clang shut. A face peered through the spyhole, and vanished.

'Eat your food, Alexandrei,' she told him. 'It will do you good.'

She took a small piece of meat for herself and passed the dish. They began to eat in silence. As he pressed on the handle of his knife, cutting the meat, Geria felt it move, quite distinctly. He paid no attention, and chewed on. As he cut again, the handle came right away from the blade. He swore with annoyance.

'What's the matter?' Katerina asked him.

'My damned knife,' he said in astonishment. 'It's come apart.'

He wiped the blade with his napkin and tried to push the ends together. He tried a second time, and now something caught his eye. In the hollow of the handle, where it grips the spike end of the blade, he saw something long and white, the length of a needle. His heart missed a beat, for he knew at once what it must be. He nudged Katerina, and jerked his head as a reminder of the nearness of the spyhole.

'Keep eating as if nothing's happened,' he hissed.

Then he rolled the napkin to deaden any sound and began to tap the silver handle against the table top. After a while, a stick of rice paper fell out. He unpicked it with fingers that trembled, flattened it and read what was written inside in minute, spidery lettering.

> 'Mikhail is ill. If you wish to return without harm and see him once more, ring this number when you can. Tell no one. Wear something red in court to signify assent.'

A telephone number in the London area was printed above and below the message. Geria bent down and took off his shoe and sock, put the piece of paper between his toes and dressed again quickly. He bent close to his wife and repeated what the message said.

She said nothing, but began to eat, mechanically.

'Whichever one of us gets the chance must ring that number,' he said in a low voice. 'The boy's ill. We should never have left him. I'm going back to my son, Katerina, and nothing is going to stop me.'

She was as white as the paper he had just read.

'It's a trick,' she answered. 'You must know what would happen if we went back to Moscow.'

He shook his head. He was wild with excitement.

'No,' he said. 'It is we who were tricked, the British tricked me into coming here, and they tricked you into making me come. You said so yourself in the court this morning! You said, all they wanted was to get me here, what happened to you was no concern of theirs. They made us both betray our country, don't you see?'

Her own hands began to shake now, and she pushed her food aside.

'But I went to them first! I'll be locked up for the rest of my days if ever I set foot in Russia again. It's a trick,

I tell you, how do we know Mikhail is really ill?'

'Katerina, they've handled this food, they could have killed the two of us with poison as easily as they sent that message if they wanted. They must mean what they say, they won't hurt us if only we go back.'

'You go,' she said, 'if that's what you want. We don't have much of a life together these days, you and me. But I'm not going. Once they get their hands on me ...' and she shuddered.

He took her wrist and pressed it, hard.

'That child needs us,' he told her once more. 'Never mind if he's ill or not, what kind of a life is he going to have if you and I turn our backs on him a second time? It might take time: I might even go to prison, but you—you've got to ring that number, for Mikhail's sake.'

'No. You must be mad to ask me.'

'Listen to me, Katerina. I saved you from harm once before and I can do it again. My work makes me important, they'll listen to me, they will have to. I wouldn't go back if I thought they would hurt you, not even for the boy, you know that. But at least 'phone these people. See what they have to say. Do that much, at least, for your own child.'

She stared down at her plate, wrestling with her conscience.

'Please, Katerina, I beg of you.'

'All right,' she heard herself say. 'For Mikhail. I just hope you realise what you're asking.' She took a red chiffon scarf from her handbag and tied it round her throat. Geria felt like shouting with joy as he climbed back into the dock later that afternoon. He was going home, no matter how long it took, he was going home. Now that he had come to a decision, he could face the rest of the trial—even the possibility of imprisonment—with indifference. As he took his place in the dock, he allowed the judge's face to fade into the background, he made no attempt to listen to what counsel had to say, he gave no more than a casual glance as Sydenham took his place in the witness box.

The lawyers could ask him whatever they liked. Sydenham could tell all the lies he wanted.

He was going home!

11

THE TRIAL: DAY THREE AFTERNOON AND EVENING

Andrei and Josef wasted no time after delivering the food with its hidden message.

They drove back to the mews, and while Josef changed the number plates of the Jaguar with a set placed ready in the van, Andrei wrapped the bodies in dust sheets from the second basket and crammed them in the boot of the car. They worked silently and efficiently and unnoticed. At five past two they pulled out of the cul-de-sac, and started on the road to London airport.

Josef waited on the apron outside Number Two airport while Andrei took the Jaguar in for long-term parking. He had a suitcase in his hand, a mackintosh over his arm, and a trilby hat to cover his white hair as he handed over the ignition keys: the key to the boot stayed in his pocket.

'Look after the car for me,' he said to a young attendant, and gently pressed two pound notes in his willing palm.

He smiled and added, 'Make sure it's there when I get back!'

'How long will you be gone?' he was asked.

'About three weeks,' he replied. 'Perhaps a little longer, it depends on business.'

'Going somewhere nice, sir?' asked the attendant, wistfully. He spent all his working days battered by the dinosaur shrieks of the jet fleet, the very air he breathed was filled by their kerosene stench, but he had never known the magic of flying: he had yet to see the world above the clouds.

'Oh, New York, Chicago, Los Angeles,' said Andrei glibly, lying through his teeth to set a false trail. 'Just depends on how the old sales talk goes, you know? Must rush, look after the old bus for me while I'm gone' and he walked swiftly away from the car, and the bodies of Sydenham's men. Two minutes later he was back in the van with Josef.

'Let's dump this somewhere round Earl's Court,' he said. 'No point in taking more chances than we need with a stolen vehicle. Then split up and make our way separately to Hampstead, after dark, eh?'

Josef nodded happily. He knew now exactly what the British meant by that strange expression, a 'piece of cake'.

Sydenham was briefed quickly by Sir Gordon outside Number One court, the sombre oak-panelled room which has seen so many offenders, poisoners, stranglers, spies and traitors stand in its dock in the past. Their names made legal history: Crippen, George Joseph Smith of Brides-in-the-Bath notoriety, Lord Haw Haw, Thompson and Bywaters, mass murderer Christie, and 'Lonsdale'—the Russian spy who ran the Portland naval espionage ring with the Krogers, Houghton and Gee. Their own conversation was gloomy enough.

'I'm going to have to put you through the hoop,' said the Q.C. 'I want that jury to spend their weekend positively weeping for Mr Geria.'

Sydenham smiled: only lawyers find the processes of the law majestic in all respects. 'I can take it. Just hand him back to me a free man.'

'I want to draw the judge away from our client: I want him to vent his wrath on someone else as we approach close of play, so to speak. I'll set the pattern by throwing some awkward questions at you myself. Morston Richards is bound to get very hot under the collar about the gun. You must dig it under the bombardment and simply plead danger of assassination as justification for all your actions. Use your head. I shall couch my own examination in words that may sound critical, even hostile but for God's sake, don't get rattled, it's all in a good cause. I want the jury to go to bed tonight thinking that wicked devil Sydenham, and that poor man Geria.'

'Fire away,' said Sydenham. 'They can't hang me.'

'I know his Lordship a lot better than you do,' the lawyer warned him again. 'Sounds contrite at all times. Don't challenge him. He really is another Jeffreys, that man. I suppose you realise,' he added gloomily, 'that the first one, the Bloody Assize character, actually learned his trade in this very courtroom? He was Common Serjeant in 1671 and later became Lord Chief: he really made everyone quake in their shoes, the witnesses who stood in his way as well as the poor devils in the dock. I'm going to put you in a position where you will be forced by your answers to create sympathy for Geria. Just remember that.'

Sydenham cast an eye on the inscription above their heads, set over the entrance to the courtroom. 'Poise the Cause in Justice Equal Scales,' it read.

'If that means what it says,' he answered, 'we won't have too much to worry about. My conscience is clear. Lead on, MacDuff.'

As soon as Sydenham had taken the oath, Sir Gordon turned to the judge.

'My Lord,' he said, 'this witness you are about to hear is the last to be called by the defence. Your Lordship has made it plain that the court requires an explanation as to how and why the defendant came to be given a gun. The defence will welcome such an explanation and it is a matter on which this witness will be questioned. There are, however many other matters relevant to our case I must put to him, and since he is a member of the security forces, m'Lud, I ask that he may be allowed to write down his name and address on a slip of paper which will be handed to the bench.'

'Very well, Sir Gordon. The witness will be referred to simply as Mr S.'

One eye contemplated the figure lolling in the witness box, and clearly did not like overmuch what it saw. At no time did Sydenham cut a fine figure of a man: today he looked preposterous. Gross body and big head merged into one swollen outline, like a gigantic pear-drop. He was hairless. His girth was stupendous, vast, a circumference of incredible size, and an affront to anyone as spare and figure-conscious as the judge.

Sydenham was normally a fastidious dresser, but by now the strain of his many duties, and demands on his time, were beginning to show. His suit was creased, his shoes grubby, collar and shirt cuffs feeling the effect of London rain and London grime—not dirty, but soiled, and spoiled. His face was puckered and weary. He slumped in the box because his feet ached from the seventeen-stone burden they had supported since five o'clock that morning. Ever since the trial began he had lived on too many cigarettes and insufficient food: now he coughed incessantly, not loudly, but irritatingly, in a wheezy, chesty, gravelly grumble. The smile that normally lived in his mouth had gone. Now the corners turned down, drooping with fatigue like the rest of him. He even managed to look somewhat vague and detached, as if his mind might be on more important things: it was in fact ticking through the things he had done, and not done, to ensure the security of everyone about him. If the judge did not greatly care for what he saw in Sydenham, it was likewise true that Sydenham resented the extra trouble and work that Morston Richards had caused him by his stubborn refusal to have the case heard *in camera*. His eyes showed something of his feelings. They were bright blue, and cold, and they met the judge's one without faltering or flinching.

'Mr S.—I shall call you that, as his Lordship has directed—you are a senior member of the security forces of this country, is that right?'—'I am a member, yes, sir.'

Sir Gordon held up a daily newspaper.

'This is one of many reports arising from the proceedings in this court, describing the arrival of the defendant in this country as a triumph for the intelligence services. Is that your own view?'—'Without any doubt. It represents the greatest coup for many years.'

'Within the bounds of security, will you tell us, Mr S., what was your own part in that?'—'It is very difficult for me to answer that in open court. I was involved in some of the original planning and preparation.'

'And since the defendant set foot on British soil, can you tell us in general terms what your role has been?'—'I have been responsible for his safety. And that of his wife.'

'A supremely difficult and exacting task?'—'Yes, very much so.'

'With much that can never be told?'—'I am bound by the Official Secrets Act.'

'Quite so. However there are certain matters on which I have to question you, matters that have already been raised in evidence. I want to deal first with the building, the "safe house" as it has become known, where the defendant and his wife stayed immediately after their secret arrival here. It has been described by the defendant as windowless and claustrophobic. Do you agree with that?'—'Yes. It is the very nature of such a building. Our concern was their physical safety. There was—and still is, in my opinion—a very real risk of assassination.'

'At any event, the defendant complained about it?'—'Not unnaturally. It was not an ideal choice for a prolonged stay. Unfortunately we did not have overlong to prepare for his arrival.'

'Oh? I thought this had been planned for some time?'—'The actual opportunity to defect came quicker than we had anticipated.'

'These cramped quarters had a depressing effect on the defendant?'—'Yes.'

'He said they were like a prison?'—'I expect they did seem like that at times. It was no one's fault.'

'You drove him pretty hard, though, did you not?'—'I'm afraid I don't understand. We always treated Mr and Mrs Geria with the greatest kindness and understanding.'

'He had left his son behind in Moscow?'—'The Russians saw to that.'

'His wife has told the court that firm promises were given to her that some way would be found to bring the child here, to join his parents. Is that true?'—'I wouldn't know about that. My duties lie here, in this country. I was not party to any conversation in Moscow.'

'Both the defendant and his wife constantly implored you to see that promise was honoured?'—'They discussed all their problems with me. I assured them that everything that could be done to help them, would be done. To my certain knowledge very many attempts were made to trace the boy. I can't say any more than that, I'm afraid.'

'Very well, I'll leave that for the moment. Let's go back to this "safe house". You instituted a series of lessons for these two, lessons in our language and customs?'—'Yes.'

'A crash course?'—'An advanced course, certainly.'

'Requiring hours of study every day?'—'Yes.'

'How many hours?'—'It varied. There was no set amount.'

'Three, four hours? More?'—'Sometimes.'

'Mr S., is there a name for this course, an unofficial one but none the less very apt?'—'There are no set courses or even plans in such cases, because all circumstances vary so greatly.'

'I'm talking about an unofficial name, a slang expression, if you like. Do you call it the Chameleon Course?'—'Some people do.'

'A course of treatment designed to alter a man in every way, mentally I mean?'—'Yes.'

'It's just another kind of brainwashing, is it not?'—'Nothing like that at all! It is purely protective, specially thought out to help any defector live his new life without fear of recognition and possible assassination.'

'I don't want you to misunderstand me, Mr S. No one in his right mind would blame you for the harshness of the course, or deny its necessity. I fully accept your only concern was to protect the defendant, for the threat of assassination was very real in his case, was it not?'—'Yes. It was. And I now consider it greater than ever.'

'Any man of forty might find such a course tough going, don't you agree?'—'Yes.'

'In fact, the harder you drove him, the greater his protection would ultimately be?'—'Certainly.'

'None the less, being human, he might come to resent it?'—'Yes.'

'He certainly showed signs of great stress, from the beginning, is that not right?'—'He was very good at first. After a while, the strain began to show, yes, that's true enough. But we always tried to show the greatest kindness and courtesy to both of them, as I said.'

'I accept that. I am merely concerned with my client's state of mind. He was overwrought?'—'Yes.'

'He asked you if another house could be provided, somewhere where the pressure would be less intense?'—'Somewhere that provided more physical freedom.'

'It was about this time that the suggestion of plastic surgery was made?'—'Possibly.'

'Did you know that he was mortally afraid of doctors and dentists?'—'He told me that he had always been afraid of dentists. He had had very crude treatment as a boy in Russia.'

'None the less, you persuaded him to go ahead with such treatment?'—'You make me sound like an ogre. It wasn't like that at all.'

In spite of the caution, Sydenham was too edgy: he ran a finger round his collar and glared at Sir Gordon.

'What I am trying to show is that time was against you, that deadly enemies were assumed to be hunting for the defendant, and thus you had to use every means at your disposal to safeguard him?'—'Well, I agree with that, yes.'

'On what did you base that assumption?'—'Every defection from whatever country it may be is followed by a phase known as damage assessment. Then comes the critical period, called "A.C.A." or appropriate counter-action. Because of this man's unique scientific knowledge we had to accept that it would be swift and merciless, once they traced him.'

'Precisely. So you yourself raised the desirability of plastic surgery?'—'For that reason only, yes I did.'

'For both the defendant and his wife?'—'They were both prime targets for assassination. Yet they both wanted to be moved into quarters that were less closely guarded, less inhibiting. We were faced with the unhappy fact that both were so easily identifiable, physically speaking.'

'He was not very happy about it, though, was he?'—'He gave the surgeon written permission to operate.'

'Reluctantly?'—'He didn't like dentists, no one does. He didn't like the thought of an operation, even a simple one: few people do. But he appreciated the dire necessity and he voluntarily signed a paper asking that plastic surgery be carried out.'

'And that's exactly what I'm trying to elicit, Mr S., his state of mind?'—'Very well. Of course he was unhappy.'

'He had what is commonly known as a face lift?'—'Yes.'

'He had his ears pinned back?'—'Yes.'

'His nose reduced in size and altered in shape?'—'Yes.'

'He was given an implant, and had the shape of his jaw changed?'—'I don't know how it's done. But he had a very distinctive feature, a receding jaw, and this was changed.'

'None of which could have been very pleasant for a man who was depressed and overwrought and unreasonably afraid of doctors and dentists?'—'I don't suppose it was. But it was infinitely preferable to the risk of death.'

'The re-shaping of the jaw did not go quite the way it was planned?'—'He developed problems with the bite of his teeth, and required further treatment.'

'His jaw had to be wired?'—'Yes.'

'And he was given advanced dentistry?'—'He received the finest and most skilled surgery available. It was unfortunate that he needed a lot of dental treatment.'

'When it was over, he had difficulty in recognising his own wife, did he not?'—'Yes, I'm pleased to say.'

'Pleased? In what way?'—'Well, if he didn't know her, she was safe from her enemies.'

'And after all was done, they were moved to new quarters, somewhere in the country?'—'To a very beautiful country house.'

'Did he begin to show any improvement in his mental state?'—'No, much to our surprise and regret.'

'Why was that, do you think?'—'He and his wife began to quarrel.'

'What about?'—'Personal things, matters between husband and wife.'

'His wife has told us he became impotent?'—'Unfortunately,

yes. But how great a part in that was played by the effect of plastic surgery, is impossible to say. That's not my opinion, it's a medical one.'

'At all events, you knew about it?'—'Yes. We lived close to each other, all of us. We couldn't help but know when there was trouble between them. Also, we had a system for er, monitoring all conversation in certain rooms, not to eavesdrop you understand, but to enable us to have a regular playback of tape recordings so that we could keep watch on their progress in English.'

'Yes, of course. Did the defendant know about these hidden devices?'—'Obviously he did. We went through the recordings together.'

'Did he know *where* they were?'—'No, that would have defeated the whole object of the exercise.'

'I see. And was the Chameleon Course still going full blast?'—'I really must protest, sir. We were all of us working round the clock to try to help these two people. Tuition in language and customs was a vital part of the training they had to have in order to lead a natural kind of life once more.'

'I accept that completely. But the crash course went on?'—'Yes.'

'With the defendant growing more and more unhappy?'—'Yes. But not necessarily because of the course.'

'He came and discussed his sexual predicament with you, by that I mean he told you of his impotency?'—'Yes he did.'

'What was your answer to that?'—'I told him we would get him medical help.'

'You chose the doctor yourself?'—'It was essential to have a doctor who was utterly trustworthy, because in order to help his patient, he would have to know all the facts that might have produced this condition.'

'Do you know what he prescribed?'—'I wasn't privy to their talks. I know he suggested a return to work as one answer to mental stress.'

'But the defendant had already offered to work, had he not?'—'He wanted to do general scientific work. We told him that was not possible at the time.'

'Why?'—'For a variety of reasons. It meant we had to vet a whole new range of people, for one thing. A man of his knowledge and advanced technical background would have been sure to cause comment and inquiry. He was tense and edgy and liable to fly off the handle. I discussed his request with my superiors, and it was turned down.'

'His wife has told this court it was no more than a delaying tactic, designed to force him to take up his previous research or do nothing at all?'—'I am astonished to hear that. It is quite untrue. The only pressures he felt were those in his own mind.'

'At any event, you came to an understanding with the defendant?'—'Yes.'

'A satisfactory one from your point of view?'—'In some ways. Not in others.'

'I'd like you to explain that remark, if you will?'—'Certainly. He came to me and offered to take up work, well, work that was in the view of my superiors an acceptable risk from the security point of view. He laid down one condition, namely, that he and his wife should be allowed to live in a house on their own, as ordinary private citizens. That was not as simple as it sounds.'

'Security-wise, do you mean?'—'Yes. It was always our intention that one day he and she would be able to do this. But he wasn't ready for it, in my view. I urged very strongly that he should have one of my men living in, or a guard dog, at very least.'

'But he refused?'—'He was quite adamant. If he was to work at all, it had to be on his conditions. They wanted to be left alone.'

'And you agreed?'—'Very reluctantly.'

'You were sorry for him?'—'I was immensely sorry for both of them.'

'These conditions he laid down, did they include the right to have a gun for self-protection?'—'Yes. It was a paradoxical situation, he wanted to be on his own, to live a life without bodyguards, yet he was terrified of the thought of assassination. He got it into his head that a gun was the only answer, and nothing I could say would dissuade him.'

'But you tried?'—'I spent hours trying to tell him that a gun in the hands of an amateur can bring nothing but grief. I very much regret that I ever gave in to him.'

'I am quite sure the defendant does, too. None the less, you gave him a gun. Was it your own decision, to arm him?'—'Yes. My decision and therefore, my responsibility. My former chief, who is now dead, gave his verbal approval but that was after I had issued the weapon.'

'Why did you give it to him?'—'Because he insisted on it, and I was unable to dissuade him.'

'Did you honestly think it gave him any real protection?'—'It put him in with a chance, even against a professional assassin.'

'Do you arm people as normal procedure?'—'Of course not. But this wasn't a normal situation. He badly needed protection.'

Sydenham was tempted to add 'And, after this case, he's going to need protection more than ever', but he bit off the words in time.

Sir Gordon held a revolver high over his head. 'Is this the gun you gave him?'—'It looks like it. I cannot be sure from here.'

The judge watched closely as the exhibit was handed to Sydenham.

'Now, is that the same gun?'—'Yes. A Smith & Wesson .38 hammerless revolver. With the small 3½" barrel. That's the one!'

'An exceedingly deadly and powerful weapon?'—'I'm afraid they all are. This particular type is very accurate, which is why I chose it.'

'Did you give instructions in its use?'—'He was shown how to use it in emergency, which is not quite the same thing, sir. I told him to watch out for the "kick" when he pulled the trigger, if the need ever arose. I told him never to contemplate use of the gun unless he was certain his life depended on it: in fact I told him the best thing he could do was stick it in a drawer and forget all about it.'

'What other precautions did you arrange for his protection?'—'We called at the house at frequent intervals. It had a sophisticated burglar alarm system, linked to central control. I also gave him an emergency telephone number to call, day and night.'

Morston Richards stared down at Sydenham, and interrupted. 'Sir Gordon, there are certain questions I wish to put to this witness myself.'

'As your Lordship pleases.'

The judge looked as old as Methuselah, thought Sydenham, as he waited in the box. He coughed nervously, and slipped a lozenge into his mouth. He would have given anything for a drink, he thought.

'You told counsel that you had issued this deadly and powerful weapon to the accused on your own initiative, is that right?'

'Yes, my Lord,' said Sydenham, and sucked his lozenge stolidly.

'Tell me, have you authority to do that? Can you go round issuing dangerous weapons to anyone you think fit?'

'We ourselves are not normally armed, my Lord,' said the intelligence man equably. 'But should an occasion arise when it is felt that lives are at risk, we have access to weapons. They are not issued lightly, and all persons to be so armed would be properly licensed. If the situation demands it in my opinion, then I do have the right to order an issue of weapons, yes.'

'I'm not talking about that,' snapped the judge. 'Of course there are times when security needs can only be met by extreme measures. I ask you for the last time, do you have any authority to give a loaded gun to someone like the accused, anyone who feels his life may be in danger?'

'No, my Lord, I do not.'

'Then you were acting outside the law in this instance, were you not?'

'Well, my Lord.' Sydenham floundered for a moment. 'These were exceptional circumstances. There was no doubt in my mind that a real threat of assassination existed. I had to weigh many factors, and I came to the conclusion, rightly or wrongly, that foremost among them was a duty to give protection to this man in the best way I saw fit.'

'But in doing so you broke the law,' the judge retorted. His voice was icy. 'Can it be, perhaps, that men in your position feel that they may be above the law?'

'We do not.' Sydenham's tone was resentful.

Morston Richards crouched forward, the better to view this recalcitrant witness. It might have been Jeffreys speaking, three hundred years before.

'That is as well.' A bony hand clutched his eyepatch, and his voice sounded like a rasp. 'The law of the land applies to us all.'

Sydenham thought of his huge responsibilities, his hours of ceaseless vigil, the one-sided battle he was compelled to fight against a host of enemies whose sole aim was to cripple the country he served, and all for a wage less than that earned by a competent bricklayer: and he did what he had been told he must never do with this judge, he lost his temper.

'Unfortunately, I'm not playing a game of cricket,' he said, goaded beyond endurance. 'I have to deal with enemies of the State, my Lord, and there is no set book of rules which governs their conduct. Many of the duties assigned to me are repugnant. There are times when fire must be met with fire.'

'You are impertinent. In the opinion of this court, you committed a wrongful act when you gave this weapon to the defendant. I hereby direct that your conduct be brought to the attention of the minister responsible so that an inquiry may be held, and a report made. I further direct that a copy of that report shall be made available to this court as soon as possible, whereupon you will be called before me again. I shall then decide what further action may be necessary. That is all.'

Sydenham fumed, but held his tongue. Sir Gordon was delighted. He hoped that Sydenham would get off with no worse than a reprimand, and privately felt it no bad thing: meantime, his smokescreen had worked beautifully. The judge wrote steadily for some minutes as the court waited in silence. At last he looked up at counsel.

'You may now continue with the questioning of this witness.'

'Very good, m'Lud.'

'Did you say there was a burglar alarm installed?'—'Yes. A system that reacts to differences in room temperature such as would be caused by the presence of an intruder. There was a national fuel crisis at the time of the break-in and the alarm became inoperative.'

'Would you describe it as an efficient system?'—'It's a first class alarm system. In the event of a power cut, or series of cuts lasting up to forty-eight hours, it goes on to a battery-operated fail-safe supply. Through an oversight this had expired unnoticed.'

'Your oversight?'—'My responsibility.'

'A very costly omission?'—'As it turned out.'

'Everything seemed to go wrong for you that night?'—'It's an illustration of the old saying, it never rains but it pours, I'm afraid. I had given my own number for emergency call that week, for we were under considerable pressure. However long it might take me to get to him personally, I had made arrangements to have men with him very quickly—in a matter of minutes—while I myself was on the way to the house, should an emergency arise. But there was a violent storm that night, accompanied by gale force winds. As it happened I had called on the defendant and his wife earlier to make sure that all was well. In view of the blackouts I offered to stay with them, but they refused. On my way home, a tree was blown down: it fell on my car and wrecked it. I lay unconscious for some time, and had to walk some miles before I could get fresh transport. I knew nothing about the shooting until the early hours, next morning.'

'So the position was this: here was an overwrought man, one who lived in constant fear of assassination, who awoke during the night to find an intruder in his house and all his front-line defences gone, no lights, no burglar alarm working, no answer coming from his emergency number?'—'That's exactly how it was, yes.'

'Any normal person would have called the police right away?'—'He had positive instructions not to do that if he could help it. We didn't want to advertise his whereabouts unnecessarily, and he had been imagining all sorts of things lately.'

'Yes. So it comes down to this, does it not, the only line of defence he had to fall back on was the last resort, the gun?'—'That's why I gave it to him. As a last resort.'

'You saw how the intruder was dressed. Did you think it terrifying?'—'In my opinion, he asked for what he got.'

'Thank you, Mr S., I have no further questions.'

Sir Evelyn did not cross-examine. Nor did he address the jury again, but made it clear the case for the prosecution rested firmly on the evidence of his professional witnesses. Sir Gordon was back on his feet within minutes, and used all his eloquence in his closing speech.

'Members of the jury, I doubt if any twelve persons called upon to weigh the guilt or innocence of any defendant in this historic courtroom can have been faced with a more difficult task. There is no precedent for any case as tragic as the one to which you have listened for the past three days. These have been days of great drama, and they have been reported in great detail by the newspapers, although of course you will put those reports firmly from your minds and concentrate solely on the evidence you yourselves have heard. That you will have feelings of pity for the defendant, I do not doubt for one moment. Who could fail to find pity in his heart for such a man as this, who has suffered and is still suffering, so much stress and strain and private torment?

'However, it is my bounden duty to remind you all, as his Lordship most surely will, that pity can and must play no part whatever in shaping your verdict at the end of the day. That must stand on the law, and the law alone. Our defence here is clear and straightforward. We say, and on the evidence we have presented ask you to accept without hesitation, that there was no unlawful intent on the part of the defendant to kill the burglar Williams: we ask you to find that here, beyond peradventure, was a misconceived act of self-defence. If you do accept that legal argument, then it is your duty to acquit my client.

'Think about him for a moment, and reflect on the unique circumstances in which he found himself on the night of the burglary. From the little we have been able to learn about his work in Russia, it is obvious—indeed unarguable—that it was of the highest importance, and work which, if successfully carried through, could have a decisive effect on the whole balance of world power. Putting aside for the moment all the intrigue, deception and power-politics that were used to influence his final decision to abandon his son and his country and defect to Britain, you are still left with the knowledge, the absolute certainty, that from the moment of defection his life was in grave danger from the assassin's bullet. You heard Mr S., the last witness: who among you can doubt he meant it when he gave it as his professional opinion that from the second he stepped out of that plane from Vienna, the defendant was nothing more than a prime target for assassination?

'By its very nature, few of us can be privy to the details of the ceaseless underground war which is waged every day, silently and tenaciously, between the opposing security forces of all the nations of the world. But from the little we have heard here, none of us can doubt that it is a vicious battle, played for the highest stakes men can put on the table of chance, their lives. From time to time the pages of certain secret campaign histories may be opened to us by world events, and we are permitted to gaze briefly inside and see what has been done in this country or that, by one secret service or another. Whenever you read of some fresh revolution or bloody terrorist campaign anywhere in the world, so you will hear allegations of sinister, shadowy figures in the background, C.I.A., or K.G.B. or some other intelligence organisation. And you have to be blind and deaf not to know that our own intelligence services stand accused of similar involvement on occasion—Ireland and the I.R.A. campaign, to quote but one example.

'Whether such organisations are served by wicked men, or by men of honour, patriots all, each doing what he considers to be honourable and essential if repugnant at times, is not something that need concern us here. What concerns us is the defendant's state of mind over a period of nearly two years, leading up to the night when a masked intruder broke into his home. It has been said, not once but many times during this trial, that the threat of assassination which hung over the defendant was real and terrible, it was a monstrous, ever-present possibility that dogged him wherever he went, like a shadow. Can any of you doubt its reality? I think not. You heard the evidence, did you doubt that every moment of his waking life he went in fear of sudden death by the bullet, bomb, knife or poison—the list is endless. He would not have been human had it not preyed on his mind, and begun to affect him, in the several ways that it did.

'He loved his wife very dearly, enough to abandon his own son and come with her into hiding here when she was in trouble with the authorities, being persecuted and threatened with imprisonment in a Russian labour camp. Such was his over-riding fear of assassination thereafter that he voluntarily agreed to undergo surgery as a means of disguise, and we know both his early fears and after effects of the operations. We also know that both this couple were given the "Chameleon Course", the personality changer, the crash course in indoctrination: brain washing was how I described it, although this was denied. We have heard how the drudgery and sheer slog of that course affected the defendant, and in the end, perhaps not surprisingly, from all the attendant terrors and pressures he became impotent. Do you remember how he described his feelings then, members of the jury? How he found himself in some kind of monstrous prison-without-bars that shackled him in both mind and body? Do you wonder, could anyone wonder, that he sought so desperately for a way out of the nightmare, and in the end came up with the understandable but wholly illogical conclusion that the solution for all his troubles was to be left completely alone. And when he was told, "It's not safe to let you live alone" he demanded a gun.

'His Lordship has had much to say about the gun in this case, and I do not intend to rake over the ashes again, as to how and why such a weapon ever came into the hands of the defendant. The important point for you to accept, members of the jury, is that he had a gun, an accurate and deadly weapon, inside the house at Saddlers Hill with him: a gun that was given to him, rightfully or wrongfully, for self-protection in an emergency.

'The case for the Crown, so succinctly put by my learned colleague, the Solicitor-General, is that my client took the gun in his hand on the night of the shooting *with intent*: that he intended from the beginning to use it on the assassin he fully believed was waiting down there for him. But we say, members of the jury, that now that all else had failed: now that his burglar alarm was out of action, and his house in utter darkness, now that he could get no answer to his call for emergency help, and now that he knew for sure that an intruder was in his house in the dead of night—an intruder my client must be forgiven for thinking was a K.G.B. agent come to kill him—we say that he very bravely went down those stairs to save his wife from harm and intending only to use that gun in his hand as a weapon of self defence. We say he did not walk down those stairs intending to kill anyone! You have heard for yourselves evidence of character, evidence that has not been challenged, showing him to be a man of quiet temperament and gentle ways. There are other guides to his character, which I think we can fairly use here. He is not only a Russian, a Russian by birth and thought and life-long training, he is—and I believe the whole world acclaims him as such—a great Russian intellectual. That he chose to come here and make the supreme sacrifice of abandoning his native land for the love of a woman, makes no difference to the essence of his chemistry, his real character. In this context I will quote to you a famous reference, Baedeker's *Guide to Russia* which was published in 1914 and which many hold is as true to type today as it was when first published in pre-Revolution days:

'"Their character (that of the great Russians) has been influenced not only by a long history of feudal despotism, but also by the gloomy forests, the unresponsive soil, the rigorous climate, and especially, the enforced inactivity of the long winters. Even the educated Russian gives comparatively little response to the actual demands of life: He is more or less the victim of fancy and temperament, which sometimes leads him to a despondent slackness, sometimes to emotional outbursts."

'Despondent slackness and emotional outbursts? Normally gentle ways, and quiet temperament? It is our very case, ladies and gentlemen, that this man, an intellectual and scientist of world renown, a gentle and loving husband and father, was so pushed to the limit of endurance by stress and strain, so consumed by the fearful knowledge that assassination could await him at any turn, that once he knew there was an intruder in the house, any act by the man he surprised that night—even an attempt by an unarmed man to knock the gun from his hand—was therefore and immediately construed by him as an act that was a prelude to a death by violence.

'Do you remember the other side to his nature, which he showed on the occasion when he thought he was being followed by an enemy, and had already taken to carrying a gun on his person? The moment he came to his senses and realised that he might have shot an innocent person in mistake for an assassin, he reverted to type, took the gun back to his house, shut it away in a drawer and never once attempted to take it out thereafter, until the night when he was awoken by his wife and told that there was an intruder in their home.

'From all that you have heard, do you wonder that he fired the gun? Is that an act one could reasonably expect an ordinary man to commit even here, in an English suburb? I say to you, yes, in those circumstances he did fire that gun, and kept on firing it: but in a misconceived act of self-defence. There never was in his mind any unlawful intent to kill. He thought only to defend himself, and his helpless wife, from what he construed as the first move of the assassin who had tracked him down after two long years. He had been told by experts, conditioned if you will, to expect such an attack.

'He himself told you something that indicates the gap between East and West thinking in the twentieth century, members of the jury, and it must have rung true in your ears, that in Russia—where the media is State-controlled, and crime is not news—that it never occurred to him he might be the victim of a simple burglary. He thought, and who can blame him, here was the assassin: and what he did then was done in a misguided but none the less sincere act of self-defence. We therefore say you must acquit him on the charge of manslaughter.'

It was now almost five o'clock, and it remained only for the judge to give his summing-up and send the jury out to consider their verdict. Morston Richards decided otherwise. Whether he saw through the defence smokescreen, and felt that the jury should have more time to form a calmer, more reasoned verdict: if he felt that the defence witness who had so angered him merited a weekend in which to dwell on his impertinence and to spend it in one more tense forty-eight-hour round-the-clock watchdog session, or whether—at eighty-five—he was simply tired, no one could know for sure.

All he said was:

'Members of the jury, the hour is already late. You have sat in this courtroom for three full days, and I know you are anxious to return to your families as soon as possible. However, there is a great deal for you to consider in this case, and I feel it would be best if I gave my summing-up on Monday, and then asked you to retire to consider your verdict, rather than burden you with what could prove to be a very long sitting tonight. May I remind you, once again, not to discuss the case now before you with any person whatsoever once you leave these precincts. The court is adjourned until Monday at ten a.m.'

When the judge had gone, Sir Gordon lit a cigarette and turned to his junior, Evan Reece, in utter exasperation.

'All this talk of assassination is beginning to have its effect on *me*,' he murmured. 'I find that the most alarming thoughts persist in running through my mind each time I gaze on the departing back of Tyrannosaurus Rex!'

The crew of the Jaguar were not due to report back to the police compound until 3.30 p.m. and the duty sergeant decided to give them a few minutes grace before listing them as overdue. Finally, he went personally to the Old Bailey—a walk of only a few minutes—as his radio operators tried to call up the missing car. He was told that Sydenham was in the witness box, and having a stormy passage. He then told the facts as he knew them to Sydenham's deputy, and asked for instructions.

Immediately a note was sent in to Sydenham, via the defence lawyers, warning him what had happened, and telling him that 'appropriate action' was being taken. At the same time every police car in London, both in the City and Metropolitan areas, was warned to keep a lookout for the Jaguar. A check was made with the Snow Hill control desk, who confirmed that two men using the correct identity cards had collected the food from the Outdoors Club and delivered it to the Old Bailey. Four foot patrol P.C.'s gave independent corroboration of its departure, in the direction of St Paul's, a few minutes later, with its two-man crew on board. When Sydenham came bursting out of the court once his evidence was completed, a massive search was under way for the car crew throughout London.

'They've been nobbled,' he said at once. 'No doubt about it. But why?' He looked at his deputy. 'Did you get a description of the two men carrying these I.D. cards? Right, get on to it now.'

Three minutes later, he knew for sure that his two men had never reached the Outdoors Club steward's desk.

'That's it!' he barked, smacking one fist into the other, 'they've got at the food. Get the top man round here from Bart's Hospital at the double, I want Geria and his missus checked over for possible food poisoning.'

'Court's rising now, sir,' said his deputy. 'Mrs Geria is waiting inside. I must say, she looks right enough.'

'So did her husband,' Sydenham told him, 'when I saw him last. But it's as well to be on the safe side, move it, now.'

He marched down to the prison section, and rang the bell. Within minutes he was inside the cell, with the scientist and his guard of two prison officers. He told them briefly what had happened.

The senior warder took him outside, into the cell corridor, while Geria waited for the doctor.

'I don't think you've anything to worry about, sir,' he offered. 'Those two didn't eat enough today to keep a sparrow alive—never mind make him ill ... left nearly all their grub. My mate and I remarked on it at the time.' A thought suddenly occurred to him. 'We both tasted the food ourselves, as we always do. I'm all right. Joe's all right. And come to think of it, your prisoner looks as fit as a flea himself.'

'He does, doesn't he?' said Sydenham thoughtfully. An awful suspicion was forming in his mind. 'Where are the trays, have they gone back to the police desk yet?'

'Yes,' he was told. 'Remains of the meal are in the swill bin with a few score others.'

Sydenham said, 'Right. Geria stays here until the doctor has examined him. I'll get the trays into a laboratory for forensic tests. Keep a good eye on the prisoner.'

He ran back and located the trays. Deliberately, he touched nothing and failed to notice one knife with a loose fitting handle. The food had been scraped off each plate but tiny pieces of meat, vegetables and gravy could still be seen.

'Get those up to the Yard for immediate examination,' he said to his deputy. 'And stay with the bloody things till you get some kind of sensible answer. Ring Snow Hill with any news.'

Then he went back to the courtroom and found Mrs Geria. She was sitting down with a woman police officer. Her face was expressionless as she watched him approach. As he got near she stood up and gave him a weary smile.

'Are we ready to leave, Mr Sydenham?'

'Not quite,' he replied. His eyes searched her face. 'Are you feeling quite well, Mrs Geria?'

'I'm tired,' she said, 'but no more. Why do you ask?'

He waved the policewoman away, out of earshot.

'Mrs Geria,' he said slowly, watching her eyes, 'the men I sent to collect lunch for you and your husband this morning have vanished. I have reason to believe they were intercepted, and killed for all I know, by two other men who took their place and delivered the food to this building. Can you think of any reason why they should want to do that?'

'No,' she answered quickly. Her fingers toyed with the red scarf round her neck.

'I can think of a number of possible explanations,' he told her. 'To poison the food, for one.' There was no sign of fear in her face: but something else, relief, perhaps? 'Or to send in some kind of message with the food, maybe.'

She made no attempt to reply.

'Do you feel all right?'

'Yes. Perfectly well.'

'Was any message sent in with the food?'

'No.' He sensed that she was lying. 'None that I saw.'

'You were with your husband the whole time. Did he say anything, or behave oddly while you were eating the meal?'

'He was quite normal. As normal as any man can be, sitting with his wife in a prison cell.'

'You're quite sure of that?'

'Of course.' Her tone was defiant.

'In that case, we'd better have a doctor take a look at you. As a precaution, you understand. There's one on the way to your husband now.'

'I don't think it's necessary.'

'I'm going to insist. I can't afford to take any chances. But there's no need to tell you that, though, is there? I want you to wait upstairs in the Matron's room, until the doctor comes.'

'Of course. I'll go at once.'

No one who believed she might be in the slightest danger could be as calm as that: Sydenham felt he knew all that he needed to know, by now. He was willing to bet he could sit down and write out the message, word for word. As he left the court, an aide reported to him.

'Doctor's here, sir. And an ambulance on the way.'

'Good.'

'Do you want him to see Mrs Geria first?'

'No. Send him down to the husband, make sure he turns the bugger inside out while he's at it.'

The aide looked dumbfounded.

'Mr Geria hates doctors. Perhaps the sight of a stomach pump will stir his memory up a bit. He's no more poisoned than you are! But we've got two men missing, and that bastard knows more than he's telling us. Give him a bloody rough time while you're down there. The works.'

The convoy, heavily reinforced by cars carrying armed police, took the Gerias at last back to the safe house by an emergency route. Sydenham was not with them. Instead, he telephoned instructions to the guards in the house.

'I want every room bugged, landing, kitchen, the lot. When I get there tonight I want to hear every word they've said to each other. Make sure there's no paper lying around, I don't want them writing notes to each other if it can be avoided. You follow me?'

'Right, sir.'

'I'll be along as soon as I get finished here. I want you to maintain maximum security precautions at all times, got that?'

'Yes, sir.'

'If you want me in a hurry, ring the Magpie.' Sydenham gave him the telephone number, and lit another cigarette, his sixtieth of the day. Lights burned right through the huge building as an army of men and women went to work, cleaning and polishing at the close of another week of crime and punishment. Judges and Silks had all gone. All those prisoners not on bail had stepped into Black Marias and been driven back to their cells in Brixton or Holloway jails. Wigs and gowns had been put away, the public audience had vanished into city streets, the solicitors had left, the barristers were back in chambers in the Temple, the whole machinery of the law had been switched off for another weekend. Soon it would be deserted, save for the police, and the ghosts who haunt the Old Bailey. Sydenham himself was desperately weary. First he spoke to the police and told them where he could be found that night. Snow Hill, and Scotland Yard, both reported in turn there was no sign yet of the missing Jaguar or crew. Then he called his Director and assured him he would keep in touch throughout the night. Lastly, he did what everyone in authority does when they need help in a matter of urgency: he sought out the Press. He knew exactly where to find them at this hour.

Sydenham pushed open the door of the 'Magpie and Stump' and went in. His Humpty-Dumpty figure was unmistakable. Three of the Old Bailey reporters spotted him at once: one of them added a large Scotch to his round, and silently placed the glass in Sydenham's hand. All of them had listened to his roasting that day from Morston Richards and all had reported it in their stories, as impartial observers. He accepted that. None of them could quote him on the trial at this stage of proceedings. All they sought now was background information to use after the verdict, on Monday night. The police had so far released no news of the missing Jaguar.

'By God,' said Sydenham as he drained his glass, 'I needed that.'

They waited, knowing he had not come in to seek sympathy.

'Got a bit of news that will interest you,' he said after a decent interval.

He looked into his glass. 'No one else knows about it yet. I thought you fellows deserved the first break, since it's your story.'

They were all ears. The Magpie had seen a thousand such scenes, as every big trial draws to its close.

'One of my escort cars has disappeared,' he said, 'and two of my men with it. It was the car I sent to get food at lunchtime today for Alexandrei Geria and his wife. We are very concerned about the fate of my two men. Nothing has been heard of them since they left Snow Hill police station yard at 12.15 this afternoon.'

He gave them the names and full description of his men, and the number and colour of the car. He was careful to give them the name and location of his club as well: the more eyes and ears he had prowling round there, the better he liked it.

'Any idea what might have happened to them?' asked one reporter. 'Any speculation?'

'Plenty of ideas,' said Sydenham deliberately. 'But I won't elaborate on them now, if you don't mind. I sent that car out at 12.15, as I told you. But two unknown men turned up at the club to collect the meals and then delivered them to the Old Bailey. I didn't know my own men were missing until the court rose tonight.'

'Do you have a description of these two men?'

'Yes,' Sydenham replied, accepting another glass of Black Label, 'not that I put much reliance on it, because I imagine some kind of disguise might have been used. I don't know, I'm only surmising. Both my men were armed, by the way, and they had to be overcome. We don't know where they were intercepted, but knowing them, I'd say they wouldn't have gone quietly.'

Questions came at him thick and fast. First editions were not far away: they had to squeeze information out of him like juice from an orange and rush to telephones.

'You can't quote me,' Sydenham warned. 'I'm still Mr S., someone you don't know. This is background stuff for you to dress up. You'll get quotes from the police to harden up your stories. I'm giving you the gen, and you can use it any way you want. But no mention of me, okay? Well, now, why would anyone want to hijack a Ministry of Defence car? Answer, I don't know. If you want to speculate, I can tell you that we called a doctor to examine Mr and Mrs Geria, but they were both found to be in good health. If it was an attempt to harm them in any way, and I can't say that it was, so be bloody careful in your speculation, it seems to have failed.'

His glass was empty. Seconds later, a refill was given to him without a word.

'Thanks. Now, what else? Ah yes, who do we have in mind for the job? Answer, we don't know, and we have a completely open mind. Again, be careful how you speculate there. There are so many terrorist groups around at this time, and anyone could be hoping to cash in on the trial publicity. If I hear anything, I'll see that a statement is put out through the Press Association, fair enough? The main thing right now is, I want that car found, and my men found. And I haven't worded that the wrong way round: I am convinced that the car will lead us to the missing men. Well, that's it.'

At one moment he was the centre of a throng, a king among his courtiers, the next he was alone. The three reporters he had spoken to were on their way to the Press Room in the Old Bailey, and their telephones. He decided to wait on, in case any more showed up.

Within an hour, he reaped the first catch from his net. One of the pressmen came back into the bar, and this time it was Sydenham who paid.

'Here,' said the reporter, and handed him an envelope. 'Take a dekko at that.'

He opened it and took out a photograph. It showed the Jaguar car outside the revolving door, and Josef, full face, carrying a tray in his hand. Sydenham studied it closely but said nothing. Inside the car, but blurred by the rain on the windows, he could just make out the outline of a second face.

'Is that the car?' the reporter asked him.

'That's the one,' said Sydenham. This was the break he had hoped for. 'Look, I want this picture. Badly.'

'It's yours,' he was told. 'We're blowing up a bigger print, trying to get a closer look at that second face inside the car.'

'Do something for me,' Sydenham asked him. 'As soon as you have it, rush the print round to Snow Hill fast, will you? They'll be waiting for you. Now I must be off, cheers.'

For so huge a man, he could move with tremendous speed. The door opened, and he was gone.

Copies of the enlargement were run off in hundreds and circulated at once to all police stations. It was issued—by permission of the newspaper that owned the copyright—to all other newspapers and to the television stations, and was shown on screens throughout Britain on the late night news bulletin.

The wives of the missing men saw it, but they had already been warned. Alexandrei and Katerina saw it on their set in the safe house, while men with earphones listened to their comments. Colonel Zabotin saw it. So did Andrei and Josef, who were with him in the flat at Hampstead.

Like the two wives, like Alexandrei and Katerina, they were in no way surprised.

'Well,' said Zabotin, 'Mr Sydenham has wasted no time. That's a clear shot of you, Josef, we'll need to change your appearance here and there. Andrei, if that's all they have of you, you don't need to worry over much, although the physical descriptions are pretty fair. Both of you lie low here until we hear from the Gerias.'

He did his conjuring trick with the cigarette lighter and smoked away thoughtfully.

'I regret the deaths of those two men,' he said, 'but I accept you had no option. As it turned out, your scheme worked beautifully. Geria got the message, and his wife signalled acceptance of our offer in court this afternoon. All we have to do now is sit back and wait for our phone call: it could take weeks, Sydenham will be watching her like a hawk. We'll know better once they decide what to do with comrade Geria, to stick him in prison or whatever. Meantime, I think this is as good a time as any to lay a few red herrings.'

He picked up the telephone and called the Press Association in Fleet Street. Without giving a name, he asked to be put through to the news desk. As soon as he was answered, he gave the codeword which is used to identify genuine I.R.A. claims for an outrage. Then he said, in a voice which had a slight but noticeable Irish accent:

'You can stop guessing who is responsible for abducting the car from the Old Bailey today. We did it, and we shall hold the two men until our two women political prisoners are transferred from Holloway Jail to a prison on Irish soil.'

He rang off at once. From the time he had first spoken to the operator until the line was cleared, his call had lasted eighteen seconds, and there was no chance of tracing the number from which it had come.

'That will be reported to the police,' he announced, 'and although Sydenham won't want to believe it, there has to be an element of doubt for a time. At least it will be in all the papers tomorrow morning.'

Andrei brought a bottle to the table unasked, and poured three drinks.

'Here's to a safe journey home,' he said. He sounded happy, like a tourist at the end of a good holiday. 'May I ask, comrade-colonel, how you intend to get the four of us out of this country unnoticed?'

'Certainly,' said Zabotin. He spoke for several minutes, outlining his plan. 'How do you like that?'

'Excellent,' said Josef. 'Straightforward and simple. The fat man might try to stop us, of course.'

'I want everything done from now on without bloodshed if at all possible,' said the colonel. 'Two dead is enough. It evens the score in Vienna. Try to keep it that way.'

'Set your mind at rest,' Andrei told him. 'We don't put anyone into a wooden box unless we have to. With respect, you diplomats have the wrong notion of our duties. I've never known a single case of unnecessary killing by any member of the squad in all my years, did you realise that? We're not terrorists,' and he made the statement with some pride.

12

THE VERDICT

In a joint operation, the City police and Scotland Yard began the mammoth task of checking every car park, parking zone, and bomb site in the capital that Friday evening, and had not completed the search by the time that the trial was resumed on Monday morning. The city and metropolitan districts of Greater London lie inside an urban wheel housing more than eight million people, and to the harassed officers on duty throughout the weekend it seemed most of them owned a car of some kind. There were simply not enough men to check the movement of traffic, and each possible hiding place. London airport was not even on the list, at that time.

Sydenham spent hours in conference with his Director. Both were certain the telephone call to the Press Association was a red herring, but were powerless to authorise any statement to that effect.

'Use of the codeword sounds impressive,' said Sydenham, 'but when you think about it the claim doesn't stand up. If there was a terrorist group wanting to seize two hostages—and nothing more—they would never run the double risk of delivering that food to the court. I agree it bought time to hide the bodies and the Jaguar. But the risk outweighed the possible advantages.'

It was the forensic reports that turned suspicion into near certainty. While the food showed no trace of poisoning, or the wine of adulteration, a loose handle on one knife bore marks to indicate it had been prised away: and dust particles in the hollow contained what appeared to be specks of rice, or rice paper. The handful of Cypriots who washed dishes at the Outdoors Club were not overpaid for their services, and it was conceivable that one might have been afraid to admit he had damaged a knife, or even tried to hide the damage with crude running repairs: conceivable, but not likely.

'It's a K.G.B. job,' Sydenham insisted. 'Cook and King were murdered before they reached that club. We haven't found anyone who heard anything or saw anything, but those two men would have to be killed before they would quit on a job. There are a million permutations of the methods that could have been used, but they were done in, no doubt about it.'

'I quite agree,' said the Director. 'But if we challenge the telephone call and say we think they're dead, we are going to look even bigger bloody fools than we do now if they should be produced alive at some later date.'

'That knife handle,' went on Sydenham doggedly, 'held some kind of bait for the Gerias, and they swallowed it—literally, for all we know. In my opinion the opposition is using their boy as blackmail, against a free pardon if they go back. We'd do precisely the same thing, in their position. But both husband and wife have clammed up completely: nothing worth a damn on the tapes since they got back. And I daren't use any pressure on comrade Geria, he's quite liable to stand up in court on Monday and start spouting the odds.'

'To tell you the truth,' the Director said, 'I won't lose any sleep if the judge gives him ten years: at least we'll know where he is.'

'The lawyers still think they'll get an acquittal,' Sydenham replied. 'In that case I'd like to move Geria and his wife to another hideout, and wait for them to make contact with their Russian friends. I want my pound of flesh for Cook and King, sir. Zabotin will be behind this, somewhere. Let's make it easy for him and have his men walk right into our parlour. I'll allow the Gerias to think we've been fooled by the phoney I.R.A. message. Then I'll put a telephone their way, suitably tapped, of course. And not making it too easy, either: keep them on tenterhooks for a week or two, so that they get desperate enough to take chances.'

'I like the sound of that, Sydenham.' The Director could see distinct signs of strain in the fat man's face, and opened a cabinet. 'Care to join me in a drink?'

'That's very good of you, sir. I feel a bit jaded.'

'I've spoken to the minister. He'll set up an inquiry to keep the judge happy. It won't report for a month, at least. You will be completely cleared by the findings, of course.'

Sydenham swallowed his whisky gratefully.

'I was against giving him a gun, I told you that when you first raised the matter. But what could we do? The politicians were riding on our backs the whole time, they couldn't wait to have comrade Geria back at work on his research. The whole operation had cost us a fortune, and they were screaming for dividends.'

'Just so long as you don't make the same mistake again.'

'I won't, believe me,' Sydenham told him. 'I'll have a man sleeping in, and if he rogers Katerina on the sly, too bad. It's all gone sour on us, I know that better than anyone. The work he's done so far isn't worth a damn. It's going to be quite a problem all the time we've got him, sir, you can drive a horse into the water but you can't make him drink the stuff.'

'It's up to you to find a way, Sydenham.'

'Our trouble is, we're too soft. If we used K.G.B. tactics we'd make him work, fast enough. But we can't. You saw what the papers did with those references to brain-washing. I came out of that box sounding like a character from the Spanish Inquisition, and all I ever did was try and keep the stupid bastard alive. The surgeon did a marvellous job with that plastic surgery, it was no one's fault his jaw wouldn't fit first time, dammit. And I only suggested that tit-lift to keep her happy. Who could have possibly foreseen that while it made her want to dive into bed, it would make him impotent?'

'I doubt if it did him any harm with the jury.'

'That's true enough. But I think it might mean we've lost him as a result. I don't trust him an inch now she's given her evidence. We are going to have problems with that laddie for a long, long time to come.'

'He mustn't be allowed to go back.'

'I'll see that he doesn't. Personally. I intend to give him just enough rope to hang the others, and no more. An eye for an eye, we owe them that. Then he goes back to work or I'll know the reason why.'

'We must also make every effort to try to get that boy of theirs over here. Drum up some publicity on Russian inhumanity in holding on to him. We'll get the minister to sound off about it.'

'It might help, but I doubt it. We'll have to work on Mrs Geria. I doubt if she feels too happy at the prospect of a return to Moscow. Especially after the evidence she gave in court on Friday.'

'Yes,' said the Director. 'That was first class thinking on your part to get counsel to make her admit all that in open court. I should have thought she must have burned her boats completely there.'

'I was banking on that. We don't know what was in the message, of course.'

'True. Anyway keep at it, and let me know the moment you hear any news of those two missing men.'

Morston Richards gave a long and detailed summing up, and there were many in court who felt it could only result in a verdict of guilty. Towards the end, he said, 'So much for the background to this case. Both counsel made it clear during the trial that, had the choice been theirs, they would have preferred to plead in closed court: no doubt they felt that security requirements should supersede all other considerations.'

He sniffed, loudly.

'I made it abundantly clear that I disagreed. I reminded counsel, and I remind you all now, that the accused is being tried on a charge of manslaughter, and whatever the tragic circumstances that may have led him to the dock, it is the events of the night of the shooting that you must most closely examine when considering your verdict. I have practised law in this country for a great many years, and I have never been one for justice done behind closed doors. A man has undeniably been shot dead. An act of violence has undeniably been committed. At a time such as this, when the whole country rings with the sound of violence and every day one hears of the use of firearms, I cannot think it right that such a case as this should be heard *in camera*. In my view, nothing that has been said here could be construed as harmful to the security of the state. If, on the other hand, some of what has been given in evidence has been harmful to the reputation either of an individual, or a state department, then that is quite another matter. This court is not one whit concerned with reputations, it is concerned with justice, administered under the common law, and administered in the open so that all may see for themselves that justice is done.

'Cast your minds back, then, members of the jury, to the house that was entered and all those who were in it, on the night of the shooting. This was the nub of the case for the Crown, admirably put to you—you may think—by the Solicitor-General, and he brought out a number of arguments in law that you may consider significant. The intruder, Tony Williams alias The Country Boy, as he was known to the police, was unarmed. It is not enough to say that no weapon was found, although that is true. Williams had a long record of crime, and evidence was given by police officers who had previously arrested him for housebreaking offences. The superintendent who conducted this investigation knew him of old, and stated categorically that he had never known him to offer violence when apprehended. On the other hand the defendant said in his evidence, "he jumped for me, I thought he was going to attack me and so I shot him". You must now ask yourselves if you believe that, if it balances with the professional knowledge of a police officer who apprehended this same man on previous occasions, and who told you —on oath—he had never known him offer any act of violence during or after a crime. Do you think it is reasonable to accept that on this one occasion, and only this one, the change in his character was such that he did become aggressive and violent? Or do you reject that'—pause—'as an excuse, a cover up, by the accused to account for his own act that night, an act that resulted in the death of another? That is an issue which you must now decide for yourselves, and yourselves alone.

'Then there is the matter of the gun. I have had something to say about the gun to the last witness for the defence, but do not concern yourselves with that now. The unhappy fact that you must consider is that the accused had possession of a gun, a Smith & Wesson .38 hammerless revolver that had been selected for its efficiency and accuracy. And what you have to decide, ladies and gentlemen, quite simply is this: did he fire it in a misguided act of self-defence, as his counsel claims, or did he descend the stairs holding the gun ready loaded and having formed a deliberate and unlawful intent to kill whoever he found there? You heard his wife describe him as a gentle man, normally incapable of causing the slightest harm to anyone. Of course'—pause—'a wife's view of her husband might tend to exaggerate his virtues: that again is for you to decide. And against that view you have unchallenged evidence, including evidence from his own lips, that he insisted he be given a gun, against all the advice of his guards. Again, it is for you to decide if that is consistent with the view that he was a gentle person incapable of harming another.

'The accused received lessons on how to fire the gun. It was never made clear if he asked for those lessons, or if they were thrown in as some kind of bonus with the illegal issue of the weapon itself, but you may feel it worth noting that it was the accused who insisted on a gun at all. Without that insistence there would never have been any need for such lessons. You may also feel it important in this context to recall that the accused did not deny he said "The country should think itself well rid of such a criminal". His explanation of that—here in court—was that he did not mean what he said, but was merely putting himself forward as someone who should not have been charged since he was only defending himself at the time. You must ask yourselves, did he go down those stairs with an unlawful intent to kill, thinking the intruder to be an assassin in waiting, and then—on discovering he had made a mistake—say to the police later in effect, "I don't know why you're bothering to charge me, you should be grateful to have a burglar put down for you"? Or was his command of our language so poor, even after that long and much-resented Chameleon Course, that he meant something quite contrary to what he actually said?

'The defence in this case has been built on the claim that the accused walked under the constant shadow of assassination from the moment of defection, and it was this growing pressure that led him to think any intruder found in his house at dead of night might be an assassin. Now, I find that a reasonable claim, and a fair picture of the accused's state of mind. That would be a fearsome pressure for any man to live under. But none the less you must still weigh in your minds what effect this might have on him, whether he was bent on killing anyone of whom he became suspicious, or if he pulled the trigger honestly believing that it was kill or be killed, in other words, an act of misguided self-defence? When those telephone calls for help brought no response, did he go down stairs determined to kill whomsoever he found there, *had he already formed the intent to kill*, or did he not make any attempt to fire the gun—as he now claims—until the burglar first sprang at him?

'The only other person who could have given an answer to that is dead. There is no one else now to say whether or not he acted in a provocative and aggressive manner to the accused. The prisoner says he did, but that senior police officer who knew Williams very well indeed said in his evidence, he had never known him act in such a fashion hitherto. Again, it is for you to say where the truth lies.'

Morston Richards had spoken for two hours. The bailiff cried:

'I swear by Almighty God that I will well and truly keep this jury in some convenient and private place, with such accommodation as the court shall direct ... I will not suffer any person to speak to them, neither will I speak to them myself touching the trial had here this day without leave of the court, unless it be to ask them if they are agreed on their verdict.'

The jury retired. The prison officers took Geria by the arm and led him to his cell below the court to await their verdict, the longest hours of a prisoner's life. Katerina was not in court today: in spite of her protests Sydenham ordered her to stay in the house at Richmond.

'I'll 'phone you with the news,' he said. 'I don't want you to show yourself in public again until after this is over and forgotten. We are fairly sure the hijacking of our car last Friday was the work of an outside terrorist organisation, so a double chance of danger for you both now exists. Plan a nice meal for the three of us: we can celebrate his acquittal together.'

'What will happen to us now, Mr Sydenham?' she asked. 'Even if he gets off we won't be able to go back to our own house, Alexandrei, John—I don't know what to call him now!—won't be happy at Richmond, and quite frankly, neither will I.'

'As soon as he is free,' Sydenham told her, 'I'm going to take the two of you away for a long holiday. This has been a terrible time for both of you. Let's see what good food and sea air can do! I will promise you both a minimum of fuss, and security, you'll be left alone as far as possible until you feel ready to pick up the threads again. Now, how does that sound to you?'

'But what if they send him to prison?' she asked. 'Could it be for a long time?'

'I honestly don't know,' he said. 'But I really don't think it will happen. We'll just have to wait and see, I'm afraid: try to be patient.'

He remembered what he had told her, with such confidence, as he walked across the court to speak to Sir Gordon.

'I didn't like that summing up one little bit,' he said.

'It was more or less what I expected,' the Q.C. answered. 'I thought I detected certain signs of restlessness among the jury as his Lordship rambled on, you know. I've spent a lot of time over the years, Sydenham, watching the jury during a summing-up. And unless I'm beginning to lose my touch, then this one made up its mind to acquit last Friday, and nothing has changed its mind. Don't abandon hope, my friend.'

'It sounded bloody one-sided to me, all the same.'

'We'll see.'

The Solicitor-General joined them.

'Any news of the missing men, Sydenham?'

'Nothing. The search is still going on, as you know. Unless that Jaguar is hidden in some private garage, which I doubt, then we shall find it sooner or later. When we find the car we'll know what happened to my men.'

'I sincerely hope so.'

'But I don't think we'll see them alive again.' Sydenham was still very angry. 'That bloody judge and his open court!'

Then he added more quietly, 'I'm going across to the Magpie, gentlemen. The press boys will be out in force today. I intend to give them a little bit of colour in exchange for yet another appeal in their papers for news of my missing car crew. Someone has to know where that damned Jaguar is.'

'You are a veritable Daniel among the lions,' said Sir Gordon in gentle mockery. 'I imagined you'd never want to speak to them again after their references to your brutal security measures the other day.'

'Sticks and stones,' Sydenham commented. 'I don't mind. It was my idea it should all come up in court, anyway. You told me your client needed all the sympathy he could get. If he got it, at my expense, too bad.'

It was 12.45. He left the two lawyers to their own devices and went down to the revolving door to give personal supervision to the delivery of today's meal for Geria. Four men were in the car this time, all armed. Sydenham identified them himself, and waved them through: he was secretly hoping there might be another message accompanying the food, although he doubted it very much. A hidden camera would record Geria's every movement inside the cell this time, and Sydenham had given strict instructions that he was to be left alone for as long as possible without arousing suspicion. Then he walked across the road into the lions' den.

The jury came back at 3.30. The fact that they had taken as long as this to arrive at a verdict gave the defence team some uneasy qualms, and Sir Gordon eyed them closely as they filed into court. Geria alone seemed unconcerned. Sydenham had seen to it that his man looked at his best, whatever his fate. His wife had taken a red carnation from one of the flower vases at Richmond and pinned it in her husband's lapel as he left that morning, for good luck. Sydenham saw him bend his head to smell the bouquet, as the judge drummed his fingers silently on the bench and waited for the foreman to speak.

Sir Gordon could read nothing from the jurors' faces. He wondered what Morston Richards might say if they told him they could not agree on any verdict. It would mean a retrial, a fresh chance of acquittal for his client, and he was amazed to discover how passionately he wanted his man acquitted. A plaque outside No. 1 court, set in the great marble hall of the Old Bailey, records the failure of an earlier judge to browbeat his jury into returning a verdict of guilty. He threatened them, reviled them, locked them up for the night without any food or drink, fire or tobacco, with the threat: 'We shall have a verdict, by the help of God, or you shall starve for it!' Sir Gordon personally felt convinced that if this judge could find a way to put the clock back, he too would threaten to starve this jury until it returned the verdict he sought.

Whatever the truth in that, his fears proved groundless. In reply to the age-old question after their return to court, the foreman of the jury told the judge they found Geria not guilty. It was the verdict of them all, he said.

One or two spectators in the public gallery began to clap and cheer, but they were quickly silenced. As the court settled, Sydenham was beaming. Sir Gordon wagged his head in pleasure, and experienced the same genuine surge of delight that had come with his first acquittal many years before. The Solicitor-General felt that honour was satisfied. Geria himself seemed unmoved. He stood very straight in the dock, fingered the red carnation in his lapel, and gazed round the court with no expression showing on his smooth, unlined face.

Morston Richards looked frail and old as he sat hunched in his scarlet robe, but he was not quite done with the accused.

'Prisoner at the bar,' he growled, 'the jury has seen fit to acquit you on the charge of manslaughter.' His eye gleamed as it studied the scientist: he reminded Sir Gordon in that moment of an old tiger that sees a tethered goat removed to safety, while powerless to show itself and spring. 'You will therefore leave this court a free man. There are a number of things I wish to say to you first. It is to be hoped that all who have listened to, or read, the evidence given in this case, and above all you yourself, the central figure in this trial, will now pause to reflect on the awful dangers that attend possession of firearms by members of the public. I address this warning to you now because, if what your counsel has said here be true, you will now return to that shadowy world where the threat of assassination lurks in wait for you at all times: so I say to you, beware, lest you succumb to pressure once again and in consequence find yourself before another court of law, with another verdict brought in. You should understand that, had the verdict gone against you today, I would have had no hesitation in sending you to jail for a long time. Of course, it is not for me to comment on the finding of the jury who tried you, nor do I. What I am doing is to warn you of the dangers you may run in the foreseeable future.

'There is something else I want to say to you. You are a foreigner who sought sanctuary in this country of ours. You might do well to remember *that* as you walk out of this courtroom without let or hindrance of any kind. The country whence you came is not blessed, as this one is, with a long tradition of equal justice before the law of all who live within its frontiers, native and foreigner alike. Here your plea was heard by free men and women, sitting in open court and now you have been set free—not by me, the judge, not through some sly intervention by the State—but by the verdict they reached without interference, pressure or influence of any kind. Not only do I urge you to remember that, I hope others will bear it in mind—all those who might seek, for whatever reason, to tamper with the processes of the law. For them as for you, it is an object lesson in democracy. We in this court have heard something of the terrible circumstances which drove you to seek asylum here, yet we have listened, too, to the growing unhappiness you have felt since your arrival among us. Perhaps what has happened in this court today will cause you to modify that view. I hope so. In spite of all that has befallen you, you have much to be thankful for, in my opinion.'

The old man in scarlet glared at the scientist, Cyclops outraged.

'You are undoubtedly a man of intellect, a sensitive man, an *educated* man. Your counsel used the words of a world-famous guide-book on Russia to describe something he felt was inherent in your character. He spoke of "Little response even by an educated Russian" to the demands of life, and spoke of a temperament "which sometimes leads to a despondent slackness and sometimes to emotional outbursts". If that indeed be true, and should you ever again fall victim to a similar outburst of high emotion, you would do well to think first of this: while a court can set any man free, it can bring none to life.

'Alexandrei Petrovich Geria, brought before this court under the name of John Stevens, you have been found not guilty of manslaughter, and are hereby discharged.'

13

THE EXECUTION

Sydenham dined with the Gerias that night in the house at Richmond, and saw to it that the drinks flowed very freely in celebration of the verdict.

No one mentioned the two men still missing, fate unknown, during the meal. It was much later, over the brandy, that the agent raised the subject, when they began to discuss future plans.

'Your wife raised the next question with me this morning,' he told the scientist. 'Where do we go from here? Obviously, you don't want to stay here a day longer than necessary, you want to get away somewhere and try to forget what has happened. I agree wholeheartedly. Tell me, would a holiday somewhere down in the west country appeal to you? I guarantee you peace and quiet, and a minimum of security, until you feel ready in your own mind to start work again.'

Geria avoided Sydenham's eyes. He held his brandy balloon in both hands, rolling the spirit round and round, watching it cling to the sides of the glass, wondering how to answer, hoping to allay suspicion.

'Right now,' he said, after a pause, 'I feel as if I'm wandering in a huge wood, and utterly lost. I can't find my way back to my starting point and I don't know how to get out. I feel desperately tired and I couldn't even begin to think about work just yet. What did you have in mind, exactly?'

'A long holiday,' Sydenham answered promptly. 'To get you right away somewhere where you can relax, and unwind, in safety. We can't put our heads in the sand and simply pretend that business of the missing car never happened. It seems to have been nothing more than a terrorist demonstration. If that is so, then there is a new element of risk involved now for you and your wife, from an unknown terror group as well as the K.G.B. You have had a pretty gruelling time of it lately but even so, we've got to face facts: there is danger for you on all sides now if you go back too soon to another private house. Your description is widely known, for one thing. On the other hand our first priority is to get you well, physically and mentally and that means a holiday with the minimum of security precautions. I think a long break in some remote part of the country would be the ideal solution. I know a place in Cornwall that might fit the bill.'

'I'd like to get away, certainly,' said Geria. 'If your guards would leave us alone as much as possible, I think it might suit me very well.'

'A friend of mine has an old farmhouse,' Sydenham told him casually. 'Miles from anywhere. If the weather improves, it would be a marvellous hideout for you: not too many visitors at this time of year, you and your wife could stroll along deserted beaches, visit the occasional country pub, a spot of fishing maybe. What about that?'

Alexandrei exchanged a qufick glance with Katerina but Sydenham was occupied with his cigar clipper.

'That sounds perfect,' said the scientist. 'Let's do that. As soon as you can arrange it.'

'It will take me a day or two to set things up. We could leave here perhaps on Thursday, by the weekend anyway. How about you, Mrs Geria, do you like the idea of a quiet country holiday?'

'John' and 'Katherine' and 'Stevens' had been discarded by unspoken mutual agreement, although they still spoke in English.

'If that's what Alexandrei wants,' she replied. 'Mr Sydenham, is there any news of our son?'

'No,' he said. 'I've never lied to you about your boy, and I don't intend to build up any false hopes now. All our efforts to trace him so far have met with failure.'

'In that case,' she answered, 'the sooner my husband and I get out of this house and away on our own, the better. The longer we sit here and brood, the worse he feels.'

She yawned, and stood up. 'Excuse me. The wine has made me sleepy. I'm going to bed.'

Sydenham and Geria stayed to finish their cigars.

'There was a lot of sense in what that judge said to you,' Sydenham pointed out to the Russian. 'About the danger of having a gun in the house, I mean, and how lucky you were to go before a British jury.'

'I think we should understand each other, once and for all,' said Geria. 'I've learned a great deal during this trial. About myself, I mean. In future I shall do what I have to do, without any fuss or argument. You don't have to worry, I shall not ask you or anyone else for a gun again. In return, I want you to respect my wishes: keep those guards of yours out of my way. Give me a chance to find myself once more. No more surgeons, no more brain washing. That judge set me free this afternoon. Don't put me back into another kind of prison.'

'Your life is still at risk,' Sydenham pointed out. 'I have a duty to see that no harm comes to you, or your wife. Surely you understand that?'

'I have no illusions now,' said Geria with a wistful smile, 'not any more, after hearing you and my wife give your evidence. Your government wants only one thing from me, to take up my research work again. Why should we pretend otherwise, my friend? Well then, I give you my word, I *will* start work again—when I am ready. At the moment I need time to re-adjust. Let's take that holiday you spoke about, and talk things over again say, in a month, two months, time.'

'Of course. That's what I had in mind. Another drink?'

'Thank you, no. I shall go to bed.'

Geria walked unsteadily to his bedroom. Katerina was wide awake. He closed the door clumsily, but once inside he moved soberly enough, and bent over her, holding a finger to her lips: they had learned to live with hidden microphones. He switched on a lamp by the side of his bed, took a piece of paper from a drawer, and wrote on it. This he passed to his wife.

It said: 'We are going on Friday. Phone the number then.'

She nodded in silent agreement. There was no point in telling him yet that while she would help him to escape, she had no intention of returning to Moscow herself.

He set a match to the slip of paper and held it as it burned into ash, unaware that Sydenham and one of his men watched him through a one-way mirror on the wall.

They moved out of the safe house before first light on the Friday morning. Two cars escorted them to Northolt. It was a beautiful morning, with a bright yellow sun lighting the field as they climbed into two separate helicopters: Sydenham and Geria in the first, Katerina and Sydenham's second-in-command in the other. They strapped themselves in as the green and brown Army whirlybirds shuddered and shook as their rotor blades began to turn, scything through the air. Then they took off, streaking across country, at 3,000 feet, free from traffic and prying eyes. The fields below sent up smoke-signals of mist as the sun warmed the wet grass. The two planes flew line astern, one hundred yards apart, chuttering through the bluest of English spring skies at exactly the same speed and height as if pulled by a single invisible string. Surrey and Hampshire, Wiltshire and Devon were swept from under their feet: they roared over the mighty wilderness of Dartmoor and watched its trout streams sparkle in the sun. They began to close up after they passed the Tamar bridge and dropped simultaneously on to the landing strip chosen for Sydenham outside Bodmin.

Three cars were drawn up in a meadow. Sydenham led the way, as they ducked under the whirling blades of the helicopters. A police inspector saluted Sydenham, and handed him the keys of one of the cars.

'We'll take you to here,' he said, pointing to a map, 'and then peel off. The house has been cleared and prepared for your friends, as you instructed.' One eyelid closed briefly as he looked at Sydenham. 'Everything's ready.'

When the luggage had been packed in the boot, Sydenham held the door open for the Gerias. 'Nearly there now,' he said pleasantly. 'It will take us about an hour from here. Not feeling sick after the trip, Mrs G., are you?'

Katerina was very pale.

'No,' she said. 'I'm all right.'

An hour later, the three of them were on their own. They climbed a steep hill by the sea, and then swung inland again, moving slowly through narrow leafy lanes ablaze with wild flowers, scattering a great host of nesting birds, hedge-sparrows, blackbirds, goldfinches and wrens. They passed a crossroads, drove past a farm and climbed steadily for another mile. Through a gap in the crumbling stone hedgerow they saw the sea, a glimpse of bright blue come and gone in an instant as the lane swung and turned: then it dipped sharply, and curved for the last time, to reveal the farmhouse.

It was hundreds of years old, built of stone and dressed in ivy, tucked in behind the shoulder of a great green hill. Men had lived here since the Bronze Age, and from the beginning they had learned respect for the wind, always seeking shelter from the hill. When the first house had been built, from stone and rock hauled up in tiny carts, it had been sited here, and when this house had been rebuilt from the same stones in the seventeenth century, its walls had been made a yard thick as further protection. Even now, on this gorgeous May day, the wind blew cold enough. The chimney that served its open fires leaned over at an angle and had been clamped to the stonework by thick iron bars. The trees that surrounded it were gnarled and bent, all trained by the wind to point one way and tell without any need of a compass which was south-west. The roof was newly done, in grey Cornish slate. The house stood among a cluster of barns and outhouses, all empty and fallen into decay, for it was many years since this had been a working farm. Now it was a retreat, for Sydenham's unknown friend. The garden was wild and unkempt, a rough mixture of grass and weeds and hardy flowers growing across the slope of the hillside, as if the owner had tired of the struggle and made a secret deal with Nature to let the bees, and the wind-blown seeds, have their way. What had once been a farmyard for geese, and strutting cocks and heaps of steaming dung, was a mudpatch now, used in the season as a convenient park for tourist cars. Sydenham's was the only one there today. Behind the car, a hundred yards distant, stood a single cottage. The Gerias could see sheep and cattle, grazing on distant slopes: herring gulls wheeled and soared overhead, crying for food, using the eddies of the wind to aid their constant search.

The lane that had brought them here moved on past the farmhouse, stayed inside the shelter of the hill, and then dropped away to the right, down and round to a rocky cove that lay hundreds of feet below the farmhouse, and out of sight. From the farmyard they could hear the sea, and smell its salty freshness, but that was all. The nearest village lay two miles away: a shop, a pub, a thousand-year-old church, and a dozen cottages. Sydenham had chosen their holiday home with great care. He opened the door, and led the way into the farmhouse.

'This is where you will stay,' he told them, 'and I think you'll like it. There will be no one else in the house to worry you. Don't let that sunshine fool you, it gets cold and windy here at nights: you'll need the heating. Bedrooms and bathroom upstairs. All the food you can eat in the kitchen. Drinks in the cupboard, over there,' and he swung open a door to show them.

'There's no telephone,' he laughed, 'but that won't worry you two! I shall be sleeping in that cottage across the farmyard: I've got two more men on the way to join me and that will be your total security force. I've arranged with the local police to keep an eye open for strangers. I know you both love the countryside, well, you won't find anything to beat this anywhere in the world. I want you both to relax and forget what's happened as quickly as you can. If you need anything, ask me, I'm at your disposal.'

'Can we go out?' asked Geria, wondering.

'But of course.' Sydenham saw no point in telling him the road that led down to the sea ended there, full stop. If they walked the other way, into the village—where there was a telephone—they would have to pass under the windows of his cottage.

'I think you ought to let me know,' he said mildly, 'if you intend going beyond that village: then I'll have to keep tabs on your movements, orders, I'm afraid. I will be very happy to take you out at any time in my car—any time that you wish. Otherwise there are no restrictions, and that applies to the length of your stay here as well as your personal movements. Don't attract any attention to yourselves when you meet the locals, you're here as ordinary holidaymakers. No one knows you: forget about the shooting, forget about the trial—just relax and get well.'

He lit a cigarette and smiled at them winningly. His ablest technician had wired the farmhouse for sound and assured him the Gerias could search for a month without finding any trace of hidden microphone or sonic bug.

'It's a splendid choice,' said Alexandrei, who could not believe his luck. He spoke to Katerina, who was quiet and thoughtful. 'Don't you think so, my dear?'

'It's nice and quiet,' she agreed in a small voice.

Sydenham carried their bags upstairs, puffing with the effort. 'There you are. Now if you don't mind, I have to leave you to it. I've got to call London and report our safe arrival. You know where I shall be if you want anything. By the way'—he paused at the door—'you'll see a button on the wall of your bedroom. It's for emergency use: if you need me during the night, I can be across in a matter of seconds.'

He checked that the doors of his car were locked and went into the cottage. Before he rang the Director, he went to the kitchen and turned what appeared to be a dial on the electric cooker. At once he could hear Alexandrei's voice.

'... to be careful,' he was saying. 'Do you know where we are, Katerina, any idea what this place is called?'

'I saw some signposts as we drove in,' she answered, 'but I can't remember any of them. The names are very different to the ones we used to see in London, almost another language.'

Sydenham turned the sound down to eavesdrop level, and rang his headquarters.

'All settled in nicely,' he told the Director. 'I'll call you when the others arrive. When they move in here, I'll go to the village and look over the security arrangements there. All we have to do now is sit tight and wait. I don't think it will be long before someone starts the ball rolling in our direction.'

'It's already started,' said the Director. 'The Russian ambassador called at the Foreign Office this morning to deliver an official protest about what he called the "kidnapping" of comrade Geria. He is demanding to be allowed to see him personally, in company with a Red Cross representative to investigate charges of brain-washing and torture, and to ask Geria if he wants to go back to Moscow.'

'I don't like the sound of that,' Sydenham commented. 'It looks as if Geria might have told them he's willing to play. We know they got a message to him. But I'm damned if I can see how he could have sent one back.'

'We've rejected the Note out of hand,' said the Director, 'of course. But it shows things are moving. This was just the first, official move in the grand strategy to try to snatch him back. You'd better be right about this move, Sydenham: I don't want any slip-up.'

'Any news of the missing car crew, sir?' Sydenham changed the subject, diplomatically.

'None. The police are going to stage a reconstruction of the journey from the Old Bailey to the club and back. We're hoping the T.V. and newspapers will give it full coverage: it might do some good.'

'Yes. I'll keep in touch, sir.'

Sydenham sighed and rang off. It irked him to stay in Cornwall while the hunt continued for his missing colleagues, but it irked him even more to accept that he might have lost the first round to the Russians—if indeed they had heard from Geria. As soon as his reinforcements arrived at 3 o'clock he drove at once to the village to organise his final security arrangements. A yellow G.P.O. van stood inside a barn some way behind the single public phone booth. Two big men in gumboots and overalls came up to meet him as he climbed out of his car.

'All set?' asked Sydenham, without preamble.

'All set, sir,' one of the men in overalls told him. 'There are six private telephones in the village, plus the one in the public booth over there. As from yesterday morning, no calls can be made in or out without our knowledge and interception. The recording apparatus is in the van. It's been manned on a 24-hour basis by operators working out of Plymouth.'

'First class. Boat crew's standing by?'

'Yes. You can have a launch off that Point within the hour, day or night.'

'Choppers?'

'Same two, on standby. I've billeted the crews in a local pub. They're hoping the emergency lasts for a month.'

Sydenham climbed back into his car and drove back past Bodmin to call on the police inspector who had laid on the reception committee for his helicopters.

'I've got another favour to ask of you,' he said as they shook hands. 'More work for your boys, I'm afraid. Do you mind?'

'Fire away,' said the Cornishman.

'I think this pub might be used as a contact point,' Sydenham told him. He marked it on the survey map and showed the inspector. 'I've arranged a tap on all incoming and outgoing 'phone calls, so I might be able to give you more definite information later. Meantime I'd like to be informed if any tourists book in to local guest houses in the area. Men tourists, especially.'

He handed over several copies of the photograph showing Josef entering the Old Bailey.

'That's one of the bastards who nobbled my car crew,' he said. 'I doubt if he still looks like that, but it's a help. The man with him was never photographed. All we have on him that's useful, is that he's big, six-footer or thereabouts, powerfully built and somewhere in his forties. The pair of them have a perfect command of English, incidentally. If you hear of anyone who might fit their size and build, even remotely, let me know at once. For God's sake don't let your men go near them, these two are dangerous. Information only, please: I can take care of the rest.'

'Fine.' As Sydenham rose to leave, the inspector added a note of caution. 'That's real smuggler's country round your farmhouse, did you know that? There is a network of old footpaths running right round the headland, every one of them leading down to the farm. That's the way I would pick if someone asked me how to get through your security screen, sir. You'll have your work cut out watching the coast line, especially if they use sea mist as cover.'

'I've been here before,' said Sydenham with a grin. 'I've had a word with the coastguards. I've got a launch, and two helicopters on call. My men are in the farm. I've got the local 'phones tapped. Your men are watching the surrounding roads. I don't care how these flies walk into my parlour, we'll get them.'

They found the Jaguar next morning.

The young man who had taken the keys from Andrei had not seen the T.V. programme, nor had he read any newspaper beyond the sports pages. However he had a girl friend he wanted to impress, and so he decided to borrow the car for one night only. First he took the keys from the office and went to clean the car thoroughly, inside and out, during his lunchbreak.

When he opened the boot, he was violently sick.

The Director rang Sydenham with the news.

'Both very dead,' he announced. 'Shot through the back of the head. Professional job. Single shot apiece, close range. Doubt if they knew much about it.'

'Any dabs on the car?' Sydenham asked him. 'That could be useful, if our friends show up here.'

'Not a one,' he was told. The car was being beautifully cleaned ready for a drive with girl friend. We might get something inside the boot, but I doubt it.'

'I suggest,' said Sydenham quickly, 'that no one mentions that for a while. Drop a hint that some fingerprints have been found. The more the papers play up the find, the quicker we're liable to get some action at this end.'

'Yes, I'll do that.'

'King was an old friend of mine,' Sydenham added, thoughtfully. 'If ever we find the two gentlemen who intercepted that car, I'd like to give them a present. Something to remember us by.'

'Well,' said the Director, 'as long as the details don't get back to a certain judge I know.'

'I will attend to it personally,' Sydenham promised. 'You see, sir, he's not the only one who holds strong views on the use of violence.'

He called at the farmhouse later and broke the news to the Gerias. Alexandrei's face remained expressionless.

'I'm sorry to hear it,' he said, without much conviction.

'So am I,' said Sydenham. 'Of course, we still don't know who was responsible. If it was the I.R.A. it's hard to see what they hoped to gain, since my two men are both dead. Now it becomes just one more senseless murder. Nothing left to bargain with! Well, it merely underlines what I've been telling you two all along, don't wander too far without alerting us first. Have you been out yet, by the way?'

'Just a stroll round the headland,' Geria answered. 'A wild and desolate spot, I must say. We saw no one at all. By the way, Katerina and I were wondering, where are we? Is this what they call Land's End?'

'No,' said Sydenham, and told him the name of the hamlet. 'You're a long way from Land's End. Tell you what, I'll get you an ordnance survey map tomorrow, so that you can see for yourselves where we are.'

He returned to the cottage, spoke briefly to London, and then settled down to wait. His men took it in turns to monitor talk in the farmhouse. It was casual, too careful. After ten o'clock they heard the sounds of a T.V. programme in the background. Then, silence. At 11.20 p.m. Sydenham's telephone rang.

'He made a call from the public phone box,' a voice told him. 'Very interesting, sir. Want to come up and listen or shall I read it back to you?'

'Nothing on for tonight, is there?' Sydenham asked him. 'No, I'll be up later. I'll just make sure he comes back, first.'

He checked that his revolver was loaded, and slipped it in to the shoulder holster. He dressed in dark raincoat and sou-wester cap, and turned the hall light out before he went into the farmyard.

Clouds scudded overhead, and through the breaks, a three-quarter moon picked out the farmhouse to his right. He stayed in the shadows, moving quietly towards the thick stone walls, waiting for the chance to cross the open space of the yard in complete darkness. His own stealth was matched by the score of wild creatures abroad, each stalking a different quarry and all making maximum use of the conditions. An owl flitted by, low and fast, using the wind to glide down the hill. A dog-fox picked up his man-scent seventy yards off and gave him a wide berth as it headed for the open fields, and the plump rooks that sat there, half-asleep. The rabbits heard the man and sensed the fox, and bolted for their burrows. Rats and mice hunted through the barns for scraps of food: they heard Sydenham, and smelled him, and stayed snug to the walls as he crept by. He took up position under a whispering elm, and waited: the wind carried the roar of the waves as they pounded on the rocks, far below.

Geria came down the lane, walking very quickly, keeping to the grass verge. It was five minutes to midnight. Sydenham saw him enter the farmhouse, and a few moments later saw a glow of light at the bedroom window. That meant Katerina was awake and had acquiesced in the telephone call. Then he headed for the village.

One of his men was waiting as he arrived. 'Worked like a dream, sir,' he told him. 'He fell for it hook, line and sinker.'

He led the way inside the barn, and handed Sydenham a pair of earphones. The number Geria had called was listed and identified. Sydenham gave a thumbs up sign, and the recorder was switched on.

'Hello,' said a man's voice, in English. 'Who's calling, please?'

'I'm ringing about my son. I got your note the other day: this is the first chance I've had to make contact.'

'I understand. Just a moment, please, and I'll find someone who can help you. Hold on.'

After a pause, a third voice came on the line, a strong and confident voice. Sydenham frowned in concentration as he tried to place it.

'I need to be quite sure you are who you claim to be. Let me ask you one question to establish beyond doubt your identity, my friend. That university you went to, what was the old name for its location.

'The old name was Vorobyove.'

'Excellent. Where are you calling from?'

'A public paybox.' Geria gave him the number.

'Can our conversation be overheard, is it possible?'

'No. I chose this booth quite by chance. It is more than two miles from the place where I am staying.'

'Ring off, please. I'll call you back.'

Tick, tick, tick went the recording machine for perhaps a minute. Then the voices began again.

'Where are you located, exactly?'

Geria repeated the name of the headland where the farmhouse stood several times.

'Wait, I have a map of the area in front of me. Ah yes, I see where that is. You are on the coast, that's good. First, are you willing to accept our offer?'

'Tell me what's wrong with my son, damn you.'

'The only details I have are that he was involved in an accident some weeks ago and sustained head injuries. He is being well cared for in hospital. The injuries were severe and necessitated an operation.'

'How do I know that's the truth?'

'You may be quite sure that it is. Our offer was made to you in good faith as soon as we knew where you were. Our ambassador has already repeated it to the British government. He is prepared to give a written undertaking to the International Red Cross that you and your wife will not be harmed in any way if you return. He has also said your decision to come back has to be a voluntary one. Have the authorities there told you nothing of this?'

'Not a word.'

'I have to say it, it doesn't surprise me. You have been the victim of lies and deceit for a long time, comrade. However, the ambassador's Note was official, you should be able to verify the contents from the English press. The *Morning Star* will almost certainly carry a full report.'

'I see. Thank you, I'll look for it.'

'Is it your wish to return?'

'Yes. I don't know about my wife.'

'Your son is particularly asking for her, you should try to persuade her for his sake. She is not going to be punished in any way for what happened more than two years ago. Point out to her that such an undertaking has already been given to the Red Cross.'

'I will.'

'The British authorities have made it quite clear they are not prepared to release you. So we are obliged to take other measures, to remove you from custody. Be ready to move at short notice. Do not attempt to ring this number again.'

'Very well.'

Tick, tick, tick went the recorder again. It was the end of the call.

'His call was timed at forty-three seconds, including the delays. Theirs back to him lasted more than twice as long. Do you want a replay?'

'No. Run off copies of the tape and send them to London.'

'Right, sir.'

'Don't relax your watch on the 'phones until I so order.'

'Very good, Mr Sydenham.'

Back at the cottage Sydenham called his Director, and reported on the recordings.

'Went precisely as planned, sir. I have copies of the tapes on their way to you now. I think I recognise that second voice you will hear: it's friend Zabotin. You can get a positive identification from the file recordings easily enough. Whoever it is, may I strongly recommend an application to the F.O. to have him slung out at once, on the evidence of that declared intention to take "other measures" to snatch Geria?'

'I'll put the wheels in motion as soon as I hear the tapes.'

'Fine. And I'd like to request hourly reports from now on

on all traffic moving out of the trade delegation quarters at Hampstead. If you can set up a police stop-and-search on some pretext, sir, prison break in London or hunt for bombers, anything would do.'

'I'll speak to the Commissioner now.'

'Thanks, sir.'

'Good luck, Sydenham.'

At the same time, Colonel Zabotin was giving his final instructions to Josef and Andrei.

'Start moving out at once,' he said. 'I rather think our friend was a little optimistic in thinking his telephone call could not be tapped by comrade Sydenham. I'll take you out of here in case of a police search. You have your documents, and you've got plenty of money. Don't attempt to book in anywhere in the area, don't go near the hotels or boarding houses, got that? You travel separately: Andrei, you take the car we're holding ready for you. Josef, you will go down by the first available train. Hire transport for your own needs when you get to Plymouth.'

'Right.'

'Josef, you will make contact with the Gerias and remove them from the farmhouse. Andrei will let me know where you can find him after that. The timetable will depend on how quickly Josef can deal with the opposition at his end. The longer it takes, the harder your final journey is going to be.'

'Yes, that's all right.'

'It's as plain as the new nose on comrade Geria's face what the fat man is up to. He did everything tonight but hand him a telephone. Make sure you don't get caught up in the trap.'

'No problem, comrade-colonel.'

'There won't be any difficulty with Geria, he's ready to come crawling back, you heard him just now. The wife might be different. Use all your powers of persuasion, Josef, but don't kill her. Leave her if you have to: we want the husband back as a willing worker.'

'Very well.'

'If you run into problems, Josef, Andrei will come for you.

Pass all messages through me: you know the number we use. Good luck to you both. See you in Moscow, one of these days.'

They shook hands and left in Zabotin's car. Josef was at Paddington station, Zabotin back in the embassy, and Andrei on the road west before the first police road-block was set up on the Highgate roads.

At four in the morning, Sydenham was roused with yet another negative report.

'No one moved out of the trade delegation quarters yet?' he said. 'Christ, I thought they would move quicker than this. Look, it has to start from there, they had to be sitting there, waiting, for the call to come. Yes, keep those road-blocks on until further notice. If I can have a description of our visitors in advance, we're halfway home.'

He padded round the cottage, unable to sleep. He had the uncomfortable feeling that the hare had started running while his hounds still waited in the traps, and he could not afford to take the slightest chance now. He roused his men and they spent the rest of the night watching the door of the farmhouse, in vain.

Andrei looked at the boats carefully, and finally chose the eighteen-footer as most suitable for his purpose. He would have liked a bigger boat, but he wanted to take her out alone, no questions asked: so he compromised, and settled on the bass boat. He paid cash, hiring for a week in advance, and added a sizeable deposit against possible damage.

'Sure you won't want me to come with you and your friends?' asked the old man. 'I know these waters. It can beat up mighty rough out there when the wind swings round.'

'No need,' said Andrei easily. He wore a dark blue reefer jersey and a blue woollen hat pulled down tight over his fluffy hair. 'I can handle a boat. But we won't move if there's a smell of bad weather, and we won't go far at any time, I promise you, Dad.'

The two of them stood on a sandy beach, in the lee of a stone harbour wall. There was a light south-westerly blowing in their faces, rippling the surface of the water. A dozen small boats chafed at their moorings, eager to be away on the making tide. Round lobster pots with weathered ribs were piled high against the wall, rusted chains swayed and groaned with the rhythm of the waves, and hungry gulls cried overhead, willing the little fleet to put to sea and start fishing.

The old man tapped out his pipe.

'As long as you know what you're doing,' he said. 'Lot of folks get drowned every year who don't.'

A thought suddenly occurred to him. 'Where are you staying if I need to find you?' he asked.

Andrei searched his mind for the name of a village he had driven through that day. He gave it, and added:

'We've rented a cottage there. Can't remember the name of it off hand. Tell you tomorrow,' and before the fisherman could ask any more questions he pointed to the boat.

'Let's take her out,' he said. 'See how she handles.'

Andrei took the helm and showed himself to be competent enough. He asked a great many intelligent questions, and he took note of the marks as the old man showed him the hidden dangers of submerged rocks, and tricky currents. Then he took her in, and tied up: they were both well satisfied, and shook hands on the deal.

'I'll meet you here on the harbour wall tomorrow morning,' he said. 'Make sure you lay on some fine weather for us,' and he drove off.

Josef parked his car in the farmyard at about the same time. His hair was fashionably long, and as blond as Katerina's: it blew about his shoulders as he gazed casually round. He wore a denim jacket and trousers, and his eyes were bright blue now: the contact lenses Zabotin had supplied changed his whole appearance, and combined with the wig to make him look very young. He reached into the boot and took out something that looked like a miniature vacuum cleaner: he had bought it in Plymouth that morning. He swung it on to his shoulder, and took the lane that led down to the sea, holding a spade in his free hand. He paid no attention to the cottage and gave only a passing glance at the farmhouse. Sydenham watched him through field glasses until he disappeared from sight. Then he walked across to Josef's car. It was unlocked, and he checked glove compartment, seats, the shelf on the rear window, but there was nothing that gave him any clue to the identity of the young driver. He found a torch, an old anorak, a bag with the remains of some sandwiches inside, and a newspaper, dated that morning, nothing that was in any way likely to arouse suspicion. He pulled the bonnet release and looked at the engine. He used a skeleton key to open the boot, and looked in there. Still he was doubtful. He walked to the cottage again and telephoned the inspector.

'Got our first customer,' he announced. 'Nothing suspicious, but I'd like a check on the licence plates, please.' He read out the number.

'Local registration,' said the inspector. 'I'll check and call you back. It won't take long.'

Next Sydenham summoned his two aides.

'Walker,' he said to one of them, 'I want you to stay in the farmhouse with the Gerias while I go down and speak to chummy.' To the other man he said, 'You stay by the 'phone here till the inspector calls you back with the registration check. Right, I'll see you.'

The path to the sea was steep and narrow. The hedgerows were ablaze with gold, lined with clusters of wild primroses and daffodils. A cloud of butterflies danced in welcome as the fat man hurried by. It took him less than five minutes to reach the cove, but he groaned at the prospect of the climb back. At first the beach seemed to be deserted. It was shaped like a crescent, and backed by cliffs that rose sharply to great clumps of gorse and bracken on the skyline. Sydenham noticed his man suddenly, sixty yards along the sand, bending over something behind a rock. He heard a whining noise and hurried to investigate.

The long-haired youth saw him coming, and welcomed him with a friendly wave of his hand. Then he disappeared from view again, behind the rocks. Sydenham heard the whining sound again and fairly ran over the last fifteen yards of sand and shingle. When he arrived at the spot, he saw that the mystery machine was no more than a coin detector, and its whine the sound of powerful batteries. He was breathing hard and felt a little foolish.

'Thought you were someone I knew,' he said, by way of explanation. 'Came running down to say hello.'

The long-haired youth spared him no more than a glance, and continued to dig in the fine gravelly sand. 'Don't know anyone round here,' he replied. 'Drove over from Plymouth for a spot of prospecting.'

'Looking for anything special?' Sydenham asked him. He felt in his pocket for a cigarette. His gun lay comfortably within reach.

'Friends of mine come here sometimes,' said the young man. 'They've found one or two valuable coins, right here. That farmhouse up at the top used to be an old Cornish Mint, did you know that?'

Sydenham shook his head. The visitor stood up, and cleaned his hands on his denim trousers. Sydenham measured his height, and found that it matched the height of an unknown man who had delivered a tray of food to the Old Bailey not so long ago. He was sensible enough to acknowledge it might be no more than coincidence, but he was wary. He looked at the young man's eyes, but they were as blue as his own: whereas those at the Bailey had been very dark, and luminous. Even so, he wanted to know more about the friendly young coin collector.

'On holiday?' he inquired.

'Day off,' the young man answered. He declined the cigarette that was offered him, with a shake of his head and a smile. Sydenham saw that the spade lay to one side, ten feet away, and judged it safe to bend his own head for one moment to shield the flame of his lighter. He was not the first to underrate Josef. At once, he took a vicious chopping blow to the back of the neck. He was too strong to go down, but he was shaken and hurt, and in the split-second that he failed to react, so Josef hit him again, this time coming up and under. A hand as flat and hard as a breadboard sliced into Sydenham's throat, crushing the Adam's apple: the fat man uttered dreadful sucking noises as he fought for breath, his legs buckled, and strange sounds buzzed and echoed in his ears. As he toppled forward Josef seized him by the shoulders of his linen jacket and helped him on his way, smashing Sydenham's head hard into a rock. He went down like a poleaxed steer and lay inert as blood ran from his ears and nose into the shingle.

Fingers groped inside his jacket and removed the gun. Josef took his spade and began to dig furiously. Then he rolled the body into the hastily dug grave, and shovelled enough sand on top to hide it from casual view. Surf was pounding the beach and would soon cover the spot. If Sydenham was not already dead, then he would suffocate or drown in the very near future. Spade and coin detector were flung into a small, natural cave. Ten minutes later, breathing hard, Josef opened the door of the cottage and tiptoed inside. He could hear the unsuspecting aide talking on the telephone.

'Thanks, inspector,' he was saying. 'I'll pass that on to Mr Sydenham when he gets back. Goodbye for now,' and as he put the receiver down, Josef hit him once with the butt of the fat man's revolver. He was careful only to stun: there was no point in killing this one, although his life was of no consequence.

Josef ripped the shirt from the Englishman's back, tore it into strips, and gagged him. A brief search in the kitchen produced a nylon clothes-line: he used it to bind his victim, looping it from neck to wrists and back to his feet, arching his body like a bow.

'Don't struggle too hard,' he said softly, 'or you're liable to find yourself short of breath, my friend.'

He had no idea how many other guards there might be. For a moment he toyed with the idea of extracting the information from the helpless man on the floor: then his eyes lit on the bell on the wall, above the telephone. He guessed what it must be, and gave it a tentative buzz. He watched through the curtains, gun in hand, as the farmhouse door opened and Walker began to stride briskly across. He had no chance to defend himself.

'Hello,' said Josef, as Walker came through the door. 'Take it easy and you won't get hurt. Turn round, and put your hands on the wall.' His gun pointed straight at Walker's head. The big man obeyed without a word. Josef clubbed him senseless, tied him up, and dragged both men into the big walk-in larder, locking the door behind them. He looked at his watch. It was still only 6.20 p.m. and a long time to darkness.

He sprinted through the yard, and hammered on the farmhouse door.

'Open up,' he shouted. Alexandrei let him in. The scientist was shaking with reaction now that he was about to be rescued.

'There isn't much time,' Josef said. 'You don't need to bring anything with you. Get into the car, quickly.'

Geria hesitated, turning to Katerina. 'What about you?' he asked.

'I'm not coming,' she said flatly. 'I've told you that all along, Alexandrei. If you go, then you go on your own.'

He began to argue with her, and Josef exploded.

'There's no time, I tell you! Get in the car, the pair of you!'

'I'm not coming,' she screamed, and tried to push past them to the door. Josef reached out a hand and seized her by the hair, dragging her back inside the hall. To Alexandrei he said again: 'Get in the car. *Now!*'

Still he hesitated. 'Let her go, please don't hurt her.'

'I'm not going to hurt her, I'm going to tie her up so she can't raise the alarm, that's all. Now, for the last time, get in that car.'

Josef let go of Katerina, and she retreated further into the hallway. He felt in his pocket, found Sydenham's gun and handed it to her husband.

'Look, no one's going to hurt her: here, you hold on to the gun, man, and go sit in the car. I'm going to tie her up, nothing more.'

Geria took one last look at his wife as he pocketed the gun. 'I shall tell Mikhail you chose to stay here,' he said bitterly, and ran out.

Katerina began to whimper, and Josef struck her across the lips.

'Diddums hurt her nice new mouth?' he laughed. 'Shame!' and hit her again. She fell on her knees, sobbing with pain. Josef's hand went inside his denim jacket and came out with another gun, one that had a silencer screwed into the barrel and had last been fired in a mews in Knightsbridge. She tried to scream, but no sound came from her mouth, The walls of the house were three feet thick, and Geria heard nothing from the car, not even a noise that sounded just like a cork being drawn from a bottle.

It began to rain as Josef's car rattled along the lane. He took the gun back from Alexandrei and put it in the glove compartment.

'Is she all right?' asked the scientist.

'She shed a few tears,' admitted Josef, 'but you couldn't expect much else in the circumstances. I just made sure she wouldn't give the alarm, that's all.'

He drove carefully through the village, alert for police cars, but saw no one.

'What happened to Sydenham?'

'I had to hit him,' said Josef. 'Left him on the beach. The two guards are tied up in the cottage. We have to dump this car where it won't be found, and hide up until it gets dark. I've got a friend who will come to collect us.'

They drove into a seaside town, and followed the signs that said, 'Public car-park. 300 vehicles.' A red-and-gold barrier rose to let them in while an automatic time-machine fed a ticket into Josef's outstretched hand. He parked the car on the top floor and locked it. Then the two men walked into a shopping precinct in the wet streets below. They came to two telephone booths, side by side.

'You go into that one,' Josef ordered, 'and pretend to be making a call. I'll use this one and let the embassy know where we are.'

He had a clear view of Alexandrei's back while he made his

own call. This was a number outside the embassy and used for more than a year by Zabotin to evade telephone-tapping. It was answered by a voice Josef did not recognise, and he identified himself by code.

'This is a Red Star call,' he said. 'I need to trace Andrew fairly quickly.'

'The man you were expecting,' he was told, 'had to leave the country today rather urgently for home. This is his deputy, and I know your problems. Do you have transport?'

'Not any more,' said Josef. 'I'm afraid it's no longer reliable or safe on the road.'

'No problem,' said the voice. 'I'll contact Andrew and tell him to pick you up. How many friends do you have with you?'

'Only one. The wife didn't wish to come, and we were a bit pushed for time. I had to leave her behind.'

'I see. Where are you, exactly?'

Josef told him.

'We'll see that Andrew picks you up. Any particular time in mind?'

'I think it best to wait until after dark, in view of all the difficulties. Half-past ten?'

'Half-past ten. He won't wait.'

'I understand. Goodbye.'

Josef tapped on the panes of the second booth and beckoned to Geria to come out.

'We'll be met here at 10.30 tonight. I think we'd better keep out of sight until then. Come on.'

Five minutes later they were sitting side by side in a cinema, trying desperately to concentrate on a film in which cartoon animals played the story of Robin Hood.

A tiny ledge of rock saved Sydenham from either suffocation or drowning. His battered head wedged against it as Josef rolled him into the shallow open grave, leaving a gap of about seven inches below: and the air lasted long enough for him to regain consciousness before the tide seeped in to drown him. He became aware of two things as he came to his senses: a terrible pain in his skull, and the coldness of the seawater that soused his legs. He could see nothing. Sand and gravel half-filled his mouth. He tried to move, but something seemed to be holding him down. Then he remembered, and wrenched himself free. He managed to struggle to a sitting position and stayed still for a blessed moment as air pumped back into his lungs. He felt his throat tenderly, and tried to swallow some spittle: after a minute, he finally succeeded. He put up his hand to his forehead. It was split open and raw, and it took him all his courage to wash it clean with seawater that stung and scalded before it ran down to mingle with tears of pain that he could not hold back. He raised his left arm, slowly, like a man whose joints have seized with arthritis, to look at his watch. It had been smashed by an unintended blow from Josef's spade, so that he had no means of knowing how long he had been there, part-buried and unconscious. Now the surf rushed in over his legs, and boiled round his waist, filling shoes and socks and trousers with icy water and fragments of stones and shells: as it retreated, he could feel the ground being sucked away beneath him. He was still too dazed to move. He tried to shout, but his feeble croak was blown away unheard, on the wind.

Summoning all his strength, Sydenham clawed at the rocks and finally managed to get to his feet. He could see the winding path that led up the hill to the farmhouse, away to his left, but there was no way now to reach it across the beach. He was cut off by the tide, and it was making, fast. The only way to get out and raise the alarm was to climb the rocks behind him. The cliff top was no more than sixty or seventy feet above his head, but its face was treacherous, slippery from spume and drizzle: even if he had been uninjured it would have proved a testing climb. Sydenham was an excellent swimmer, but he doubted his strength to make his way out into that pounding surf and back again to the safety of the far end of the cove. He had to go up. He dug his fingers into a crevice, got one knee on to a boulder, and heaved. His fingers slipped and he fell back to lie face down, sick and dizzy, as another wave burst over him. He began again, inch by inch, ledge by ledge, to climb the rockface. At last he was able to reach up and seize a prickly clump of gorse and haul himself on to the footpath. It had taken him half an hour and he could have wept at the thought of the lead Josef had gained. It took him another fifteen minutes, weaving and staggering like a drunk, to reach the farm buildings at the top of the hill.

He saw that Josef's car had gone from the yard. He wasted no time on the farmhouse but burst into the cottage, shouting for his men. There was a thumping noise from the kitchen to tell him they were alive, and he bent down to untie them.

'Look over the farmhouse,' he ordered, 'while I use the 'phone.'

He rang the inspector to tell him what had happened.

'They haven't got all that start,' Sydenham said. 'We might be bolting the stable door too late, but let's have a go: I want road-blocks set up on all routes leading out of Cornwall, in case they try to head for London. I'll get those choppers of mine up right away to help. Ask your motorised patrols to keep an eye out for the hired car. And there's one other thing—can we have a report on all cars stolen after, say, six o'clock this evening in a radius of fifty miles?'

The inspector said something to him and Sydenham answered: 'Yes, boats too, good idea.'

Next he called London and reported to his Director. It was now 7.30 in the evening. The Director alerted airports, flying clubs, seaports and docks to watch out for the fugitives.

'I'll have a word with the Navy,' he said. 'You've got a lot of coastline there to watch, though I can't see them getting far with a boat. Still, it's worth a try.'

Walker came into the cottage, carrying Katerina in his arms. Her face was ashen and her head lolled back. She had been shot, and Sydenham assumed her to be dead.

'Get a doctor, sir,' Walker told him. 'That little bastard didn't try to kill her. He just put a bullet through her leg to stop her running over here, and setting us free. She's passed out from loss of blood, but she'll live.'

The other security man brought in a bowl of hot water and bandages.

'When you've seen to her,' Sydenham asked him, 'clean up this head of mine, will you?'

He opened a cupboard and took down a bottle of Black Label whisky. He poured a little into a glass, and held Katerina's head in his arms as he let the spirit trickle between her swollen lips.

'We've got a doctor coming to see to that leg,' he told her. 'This is just a measure of the world's finest first aid.' A little colour began to creep back into her cheeks. Her eyes opened, and she looked up at his bruised and battered face, and his wet, torn clothing.

'You look as if you need it more than I do,' she said, and smiled. 'Don't waste your time here looking after me. I'll be all right till the doctor arrives.'

'No point in tearing off into the night,' he said, 'until we know which way to go. As soon as we get any news, Walker and I will have to leave. Wilson here will go with you to hospital, and keep an eye on you. That's one guard I think you'll be pleased to have,' he added quickly. 'Meantime I'll join you in the first aid room.'

He poured himself an enormous tot and drank it straight down.

'Don't worry,' he told her. 'They haven't got away yet. I can still stop him taking your husband out of the country.'

Josef and Geria left the cinema at twenty-five past ten. It was raining hard, and the wind had risen. It was pitch dark beyond the glow of the street lights, and they walked back to the deserted precinct following the beam of Josef's torch. A clock chimed half-past ten as they reached the phone booths. They had to wait more than twenty minutes before they heard the sound of footsteps.

Josef slipped a hand into his coat pocket as a tall figure dressed in dark sweater and coat, came out of the shadows. Geria remembered another man in black who had stepped out of the night into his life, and trembled.

'Got here as soon as I could,' said Andrei, and clapped a hand on Josef's shoulder. 'I was stopped twice by the police on the way down. You've really set things alight. Are you all right?' He ignored Alexandrei.

'Fine. Have we got far to go?'

Andrei told him where the boat was moored. 'Our friends will wait for us until daylight. If we can't get away tonight, same drill tomorrow.'

The scientist interrupted them. 'What's happening? Where are you taking me?'

'I suppose it's all right to tell you now,' said Andrei coldly. He could not bring himself to welcome the defector, coming home. 'There's a Russian trawler fleet heading for this coast tonight. One of the ships will wait for us just beyond the three-mile limit, and right opposite the headland where the fat man had you hidden. I've got a boat all ready to take you out. Let's go.'

Old Mr Pascoe stayed late in the pub to celebrate the hiring of his bass boat, and it was close to midnight when he walked home. He lived in a village where everyone's living came from the sea: if he was too old to go out with the crabbers these days he could still eke out a pension with gentle, round-the-bay mackerel trips in summer and a spot of bass trolling in the autumn. It had been a pleasant surprise, having the man from London arrive at short notice to book *Miranda* for a week's fishing, and nothing for him to do in return but sit in the pub and wait. For no other reason than the rum inside him, he decided to take a last stroll round the harbour, sniff the weather and generally make sure all was well.

He could see at a glance she was gone from her moorings. It was low tide, so there was no chance she could have broken away and left unaided: she should have been lying on her side there, on the wet sand, with all the others, like fish out of water. Someone had gone down there between the time he had entered the pub and left it again, to untie his boat and drag her out far enough to ride in the water. *Miranda* was ply-built, and weighed a good fifteen hundredweights: and that meant not some*one*, but two men at least, maybe three, and hard work at that. It was goodbye to his week's hire. It was a funny old night, with a sea mist creeping in now, more like November than May, truth to tell—and who in his right mind would want to steal a bass boat and put to sea in conditions like that?

Mr Pascoe stormed back into the pub and hammered on the door until he was re-admitted. No village of that size in Cornwall boasts a policeman, and—for once in his life—he needed to call one, quick.

'We'm 'ad *Miranda* took,' he roared, by way of explanation for his return, 'and I want they devils taught a lesson, by God!'

The Director called Sydenham with a warning about the trawlers.

'The Russians have a fleet of a hundred vessels in your area,' he told him. 'The Navy's been shadowing them for days, but of course, they've only just learned of our urgent interests in coastal shipping. As well as genuine fishing vessels they've got a handful of electronic intelligence-gathering trawlers gathering to monitor the sonar detection posts off Portland.

'If they maintain present course and speed, they will reach international limits off the Cornish coast before 2 a.m. However, the Navy reports one ship heading away from the main fleet. If you draw a line on the chart—as I have just done—it shows her steaming straight for that damned farmhouse you're sitting in. That's smart thinking on your part, Sydenham.'

He had been bristling at Sydenham's apparent reluctance to give chase after Josef's successful strike. Now he was properly contrite.

'Need any more help?' he prompted.

'Well, sir,' Sydenham answered cautiously, 'not just yet. We might have to take some, ah unorthodox measures tonight to stop comrade Geria making off, and I'm not altogether sure I want too many unbiased witnesses. If the Navy see to it that the Russian trawlers stay outside the three-mile limit, I think we can handle the rest from this end.'

'Mrs Geria was successfully operated on an hour ago. You can tell her husband when you find him.'

'I will,' promised Sydenham. 'But somehow I doubt if he'll be in the mood to listen.'

The second call he wanted came from the inspector almost at once. He told Sydenham about the stolen boat and pin-pointed the harbour it had sailed from.

'Two men at least involved, sir,' he said. 'That sounds like your party, sir. They could make the rendezvous by four in the morning, at latest. Weather's not so good. Finding the *Miranda* will be like looking for a needle in a haystack. Are you sure you don't want any help?'

'We'll manage,' Sydenham told him. 'Thanks all the same.'

'I hope you've got a searchlight. The *Miranda* is painted dark green, with a single white band running bow to stern. Good luck.'

To save time, Sydenham called up his boat's crew and arranged to drive to meet them in a harbour five miles down the coast. He went on board before one in the morning, but it was cutting things very fine, as the skipper told him. They looked at the chart in the cabin. Sydenham drew a line to show the course that the spy-ship was taking. He marked in the fishing village from which *Miranda* had been stolen, drew another line and a red circle where they met, not far from the headland he had just left.

'Somewhere inside there,' he said. 'That's where it has to be. The Russians who have pinched the *Miranda* are no more sailors than I am. There's only one way they can find that rendezvous by night. They will have to hug the coast all the way down till they reach the headland, and then steer due south till they find the lights of the trawler fleet.'

The *Sea Pink*, the launch he had chosen for the sea-hunt they now faced, was ideally built for the job. True, she was over forty years old, but she rode low and easy in the worst of weather, and she had seen wartime service as an auxiliary air-sea rescue craft. Her powerful diesels could still make fifteen knots. Her owner was one of Sydenham's former colleagues, now retired: he rented out the *Sea Pink* to teams of skin-divers who liked to spend their holidays exploring wrecks off the Cornish coast. She could sleep six, and towed a small dinghy. She had parachute flares on board, and a powerful spotlight mounted on the cabin roof. The skipper had a shotgun stowed under the chart locker tonight. He was in his sixties, but still a powerful man. His son, another six footer called Peter had come with him as crew. Sydenham stood with him at the wheel as they cast off.

'Good of you to come, Ben,' he said. 'Now it might get a bit warm later on. Tell your boy to keep his head down. These bastards are armed, and they're rough.'

'Cloud's clearing,' Ben replied. 'We'll get some help from the moon later on.' He took a cigarette from Sydenham and added in a low voice, 'Peter can take care of himself.'

While they had shown the greatest resolution in all they had accomplished, Andrei and Josef were still forced to base their getaway plans on terms dictated by Sydenham in his choice of hideout: by sea, and without adequate equipment. Andrei could handle a boat well enough, but he had had to take one without compass or emergency power: he had no charts, and, as a novice matelot, did exactly as Sydenham had predicted. He took the one sure way to find the rendezvous without wandering, lost, all over the ocean, by hugging the coast until he could identify the headland, and then strike out to locate the trawlers on deadline reckoning.

First, he had to be careful not to raise the alarm too soon. So he had to row them clear of the harbour, a longer and harder task than he dreamed it would be. Then, when he judged them to be safe, he ordered Josef to take the tiller while he tried to start the engine.

Most boats are prima donnas to strange hands, and *Miranda* was no exception. Andrei pumped and primed, cursed and swore, and swung the starting handle a score of times as he kneeled awkwardly, while the bass boat rolled and pitched in the lively swell. Twice he got her going, and twice she spluttered to a halt. Fumes from the reluctant diesel clung to her wooden ribs like body odours to an old crone, and they mingled with the unforgettable reek of mackerel, chopped days ago for lobster bait. The night wind was chill, clouds of spray burst over the rolling cockleshell craft, and her landlubberly three-man crew began to lose heart. Alexandrei was the first to succumb. He put his head over the gunwale and began to retch, loudly. The sounds made Josef decidedly uncomfortable, in his turn: he had had a long hard day with little to eat or drink. He found that his stomach rose with each lift of the boat but stayed sickeningly in mid-air as *Miranda* slid down into the trough of each successive wave. They lost way and came close to foundering before Andrei managed to start the engine. At last he made his way back to the tiller a very shaken man, pointed the bows parallel to the coastline that loomed out of the night, and chugged along, hoping for the best.

After a time the light began to improve, and the sea to abate. As the cloud cover began to disperse he could see shafts of moonlight shining through the gaps, falling like the beams of a searchlight across the dark sea. He knew that the hunt must be under way by this time, on land and afloat, and he kept *Miranda* away from the moon beams as far as he could. He could not form any estimate of their speed, for he had no way of gauging the pull of wind and tide. A few stars came out but he was unable to read them. He was chary of the rocks that he knew lay in wait, like footpads, all down this wrecker's coast, yet he was forced to stay close in to have any idea at all of his progress. It was a nightmare journey. Eventually he saw a blaze of lights ashore, to his right: then two more, close by, and he thought he knew what towns they might be. He opened the map he had bought that morning, struggled to keep it flat in the wind, shielded his torch and studied it carefully. Those *were* the towns, he knew where he must be. It was a considerable feat of amateur navigation.

'We're nearly there,' he called to Josef. 'Go forward and keep your eyes open. There's a great rock off the headland that should give us our mark.'

The rock he sought was a miniature island, known as 'The Scaffold', a granite platform that towered eighty feet above the highest tide, surrounded below by rows of coral spikes that had claimed many lives over the centuries. Behind 'The Scaffold' the bottom shelved steeply, forming a bay that was sheltered from wind and waves, and it was here that Sydenham waited to intercept the runaways. He had the cliffs behind him and was invisible to eyes watching from the sea. The *Sea Pink* had cut engines and used the dinghy as sea-anchor as watch was kept. Patches of mist glided across the surface of the water like ghostly sails in the moonlight. All at once they caught the beat of an oncoming engine. As the mist cleared *Miranda* rose a greentop, and was betrayed.

'I'll wait till they make the turn,' said Ben. 'Then we'll run 'em down.'

He loaded the shotgun and slid it on top of the wheelhouse locker. Sydenham and Walker checked their revolvers for the last time. Peter reached out a massive hand and made sure the boathook lay handy.

'Look over there, sir,' said Walker, clutching at Sydenham's arm.

They saw the lights now, two red and one green, bobbing at the masthead of a distant ship. Sydenham realised the spy-trawler must have found his launch on her radar screen, and decided to dash inside the three-mile limit, thinking her to be *Miranda*. Andrei saw the lights too and swung the bass-boat round to meet her.

'Head 'em off,' ordered Sydenham. The engines of the launch thundered into life and she surged forward, cutting through the water like a shark after scad. Alexandrei heard her at once, and shouted a warning to his companions.

Andrei kept his head.

'Start shooting if they get too close,' he told Josef. 'They won't fire back in case they hit our friend, here.'

He put *Miranda* into a bank of sea-fret and vanished into the enveloping mist. Ben saw him, and at once turned the *Sea Pink* into a raking curve, trying to stay between Andrei and the trawler. She was less than a mile off now and closing fast on the little boats. Sydenham was growling obscenities into the night: he had made as big a miscalculation of their chances of intercepting the bass boat as Colonel Zabotin had done in plotting its route. Another ten minutes of this hide-and-seek in the mist and moonlight and he would have lost Geria, for ever. As they roared into a patch of open sea, he switched on the spotlight and began to play it over the waves, trying to find Andrei, hoping the light would cause the spy-trawler to turn back. Josef opened fire at once. He had no chance of hitting them, but he caused the four men to duck—and stay down: he was buying time.

'Wait till they come alongside,' Andrei shouted to him. 'Keep firing at the crew. I'll put the light out!'

As the launch closed they could make out the dark figures of Sydenham, Walker, and Peter, getting ready to board. Andrei grabbed Geria, and pushed him down behind the wooden engine cover.

'Jump for it if you have to,' he screamed. 'Don't let them take you back!' He sat by the tiller again, biding his time: at twenty feet he fired, into the light. There was a crash of glass, and the sea between the two boats was plunged into darkness. Josef fired steadily at where he hoped the three figures might be. The *Sea Pink* bumped against *Miranda* and shot past, blind and momentarily helpless under fire. Andrei saw the lights of the trawler less than half a mile off and exulted: he could not know she was already beginning to turn, away from the firing.

Ben brought the launch round for another run.

'You all right?' he shouted to his son. Then, 'You okay, Mr Sydenham?'

No one had been hit, thank God.

'Give me those flares,' Sydenham ordered. 'I want you to ram her, Ben.' To the others he said, 'Get ready to fish them out of the drink, we're going to sink her.'

A parachute flare hung in the sky, turning the clouds pale green, lighting the water below.

'Leave Geria to me,' bawled Sydenham. He struggled to throw off his coat. Walker clung to the handrail, ready to jump. Peter crouched in the stern, boat-hook in hand. The bows of the launch ripped into *Miranda* with a splintering crash. Andrei still managed to get two shots off. The first caught Walker high in the shoulder. and he skidded along past Sydenham to fall back into the well of the boat. Andrei's second shot shattered the wheelhouse glass but Ben held on to cut *Miranda* in two. Then he switched off the engines, and fired a second flare.

It was like daybreak, with sea and sky aflame with red and green: a surrealist dawn. Sydenham saw Alexandrei and shouted to him, but the scientist dived over the side. He swept by the launch so close that the fat man clawed down to reach him, but missed with the rise and fall of the boat. Sydenham went in after him, gasping with shock as the water closed over his battered head. Peter saw Andrei tread water, apparently looking for Geria: he leaned out and cracked the metal tip of the boat-hook hard across his skull, using all his force. Then he, too, dived in to try to retrieve the body. Walker lay in the well-deck, groaning as the pitch and toss of the launch flung him from side to side. Ben fired another flare and kept watch for the third man, Josef.

Like so many fat people Sydenham was a fine, strong swimmer, for weight and size were no hindrance now, as they always were on land. He was desperate to reach Alexandrei before either of them should fall victim to cramp. He caught up with him when they were thirty yards from the *Sea Pink* and seized the long, brown hair he had ordered to be stitched on months before.

'Don't be a fool,' he gasped, 'you can't get away.'

Alexandrei turned like an eel and struck out.

'Let-me-go!' he spluttered. 'I'm going home,' and he hit Sydenham, this time with a hard blow on the face. Now they fought in earnest, with the slow, clumsy action of men in water but both physically strong and both good swimmers. Alexandrei broke away but, slowed down by the bout of seasickness, felt the fat man seize his hair a second time. They had drifted a long way from the launch and there was no hope of Ben finding them in the dark troughs. The Russian closed with Sydenham and clawed at his face. The agent was tiring fast, and knew what he must do. He trod water, summoned every reserve of strength took Geria by the throat, and squeezed. He dug his fingers into flesh, found the wind-pipe, fastened on like a limpet to a rock, and squeezed. He increased the pressure until his fingers went numb, and still he squeezed. Water burst over their heads, they drifted further and further into the darkness, but he would not let go. Alexandrei arched his body in agony, he threshed the water with his legs, he clawed and scrabbled at Sydenham's face, bubbling sounds came from his mouth, but Sydenham clung on, and squeezed. Suddenly Alexandrei's body ceased to jerk and struggle: Sydenham increased the pressure still further, until he was sure. At last he let go. The moon shone down, long enough and bright enough for him to see the scientist sink gently below the waves.

'You fool,' he said: there never was a more reluctant executioner. He struck out for the launch. In a little while he felt himself seized by the strong arms of Ben and his son. They dragged him aboard and for a moment he lay at their feet, vomiting and choking.

'Too late,' Sydenham gasped. 'He's gone. Kaput. Drowned. What about the others?'

'Only saw one,' Ben told him. 'Peter went after him but couldn't hold him. Reckon he must have drowned, too.'

'Good.' Sydenham was still gasping for breath. 'What about Walker?'

'Shoulder wound,' said Peter. 'He'll be all right.'

Away in the night they could see the lights of the spy-trawler as she headed for the open sea. Ben handed down a bottle of brandy, and Sydenham drank some, gratefully.

'One last look round,' he said. 'Then we'll head for home.'

As if on cue, they heard a faint cry. Ben started the engines, dead slow and the *Sea Pink* nosed forward towards Josef. He saw the launch and began to shout, louder this time.

'Help,' he called. 'Help me, help me, I'm drowning.'

'Let me get him,' said Sydenham.

He walked to the stern, and stood by the wounded Walker.

Josef reached up a hand, and grabbed a dangling rope fender. He was utterly spent. Sydenham shone a torch in his face. At first he did not know him: the blond wig had given way to a mop of wet black hair, the eyes were dark and luminous, with contact lenses discarded long ago, in the cinema.

'Ah,' said Sydenham, in evident satisfaction. 'The Old Bailey waiter, I believe.'

Josef clung on to the fender, but he would not beg.

Sydenham reached down for the boat-hook.

'Here you are,' he said. 'Something I owe you, for Cook and King,' and he rammed the boat-hook like a lance into Josef's mouth.

The Director thumbed through a sheaf of papers on his desk in the Board Room.

The first was headed TOP SECRET—EYES ONLY, and followed the recovery of three bodies off the coast of Cornwall, one of which had been identified as that of Alexandrei Petrovich Geria, the Russian scientist and defector. A number of documents were pinned to it.

'Sir,' it read,

> 'At the coroner's inquest three days ago on A. P. GERIA (see addendum), verdict of death by manual strangulation by person or persons unknown was recorded, and not death by drowning as previously claimed in press reports.
>
> 'Injuries were found on all three bodies, but in my opinion the circumstances do not warrant any official inquiry.
>
> 'Mrs Geria has submitted a voluntary statement (attached hereto) in which she describes how she was shot and wounded by two unknown assailants who abducted her husband. It is abundantly clear both from his own evidence in open court at the time of his trial for manslaughter, and now from his widow's statement, that he had no wish to leave this country for any reason.
>
> 'In my view, he must have tried to escape when the stolen fishing boat was successfully intercepted, and had managed to injure his kidnappers (a starting handle, or perhaps a boathook,

would be consistent with the injuries found on their bodies) before he himself was finally overpowered, strangled, and thrown into the sea.

'One man was seen to jump into the water during the chase, but a prolonged search at night failed to yield any trace of bodies, and all were presumed drowned (see statements by agents S and W).

'Geria's body was identified by his widow. No one has been found to claim the others. In view of the proximity of a Soviet trawler fleet at the time, senior diplomats from the Russian embassy were called in, but they were unable to identify these two bodies and officially disclaimed all knowledge of them.

'In view of events during the Old Bailey trial, it now seems likely that an outside terrorist group may after all have been responsible for this new kidnap attempt. One possible interpretation of the theft of the small fishing boat is that they might have been attempting to reach the Russian trawlers with a view to handing over the kidnapped man in exchange for money to buy arms. Since all three died in the attempt, it remains no more than conjecture.

'Although head injuries sustained by the two unidentified men are consistent with the explanation put forward in para 4 (see medical statement by our departmental pathologist), death in both cases was due to drowning.

'The untimely death of A. P. Geria is a serious loss to this country and is much regretted. In my professional opinion it was undoubtedly hastened by his exposure in open court. If there should be criticism of security arrangements following the trial, it must be borne in mind they were kept to an absolute minimum at his personal request and put into effect with the greatest reluctance because of his state of mind, and physical condition, both of which were referred to in court.

'In view of these facts, and because of the varied security aspects involved, I respectfully submit no further official action is necessary or desirable other than a brief ministerial statement at a suitable time to the House of Commons.'

Below these papers lay another, and shorter memorandum, also marked EYES ONLY.

'In view of her considerable services to the intelligence departments involved in arranging the defection of A. P. GERIA, and his subsequent murder by persons unknown, urgent recommendation is made herewith for suitable ex gratia payment from public funds to the widow MRS K. GERIA.'

The Director looked at the text for the day on his desk calendar. It was from The Second Epistle of Paul to Timothy, and read:

'Alexander the coppersmith did me much evil: the Lord reward him, according to his works.'

He smiled, and stamped the papers APPROVED.